PLANET FOLLY

by
Jamie Johnson

Published by JamesCafe.com

ISBN: 978-0-9899211-4-5
Print Edition

Cover design by David Namminga

"Only two things are infinite,
the universe and human stupidity,
and I'm not sure about the former."

—*Albert Einstein*

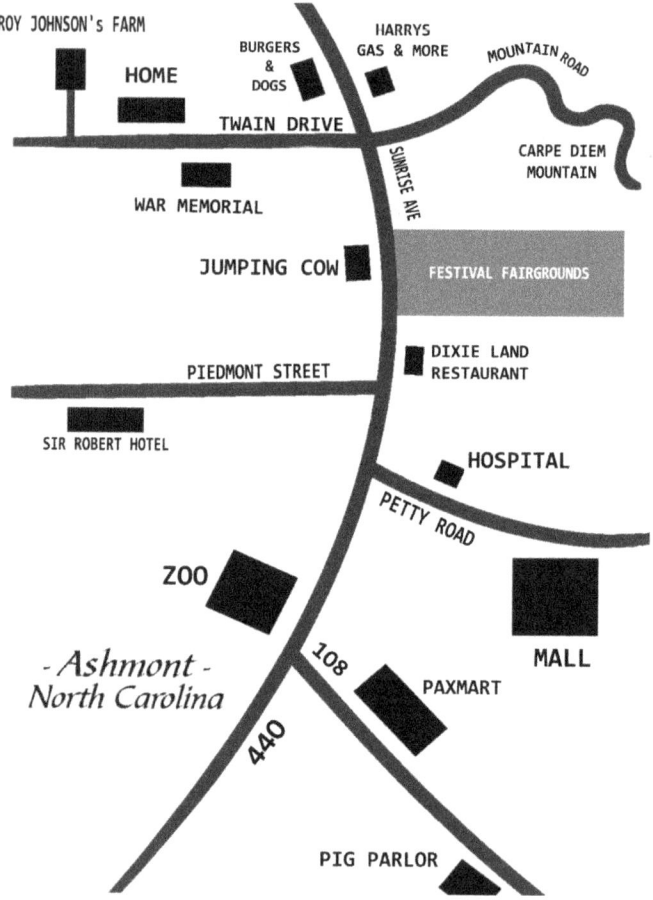

Chapter 1
TUCKER WISE

The stars burn bright,
Over time and space
Shining love and peace,
Upon every race
But fools will be fools,
With their foolish endeavors
The fools can be fooled,
Stars are forever

He must have read it a hundred times. It was just a simple verse inscribed on an old rock. No one knew who wrote it or when it was written, but it had been deemed important enough to be placed at the center of Novem's government complex. The chiseled inscription on the ancient tablet still remained legible, despite being weathered from the ages. No matter how many times Menza read it, it never seemed to make sense. Maybe one day.

"It's got you stumped, huh boy?"

He hadn't noticed the man standing beside him.

"Yeah, it sure does." He turned towards the man.

"Oh my, you're...you're," stammered Menza.

"Relax, son," said the old man, displaying the slightest of smiles. "Yes, I'm Tucker."

Menza couldn't believe it. Standing alongside him was TUKR-9999, the legendary founder of Novem's modern space program. Tucker, as he was universally known, was the first Novem to travel outside Hammerhead Galaxy. Not to mention the fact he was deep IOS—a founding member of the Intergalactic Open Society. He was sometimes referred to as the star czar.

"It'll be clear to you one day," said Tucker, nodding towards the tablet. "You just need to get some TSA's under your belt. I understand you're off on your first assignment next week, one year on planet MWG91177-3, or Earth as the locals call it. That's quite a journey."

Menza was shocked that Novem's number one authority on intergalactic travel was aware of his mission, researching an insignificant planet nearly a trillion time space arcs away—or TSA's, as they were commonly called.

"Yes sir, next Tuesday as a matter of fact. I'm honored to be given the opportunity to travel the stars. I guess I should thank you since you're the one that pioneered the program."

"I was just a little spark," said Tucker. "The flames of knowledge have a life of their own now, and you're part of it. Congratulations."

"Thank you, sir. It's a dream come true for me. I'm so pumped. I wish I could jump into the biocraft right now!"

"That's one reason you were chosen," said Tucker. "Your enthusiasm and zest for life made quite an impression on the IOS selection committee, not to mention Carma the office manager."

Menza blushed. "Oh no, you heard about her birthday flight?"

Tucker smiled. "Carma was my personal secretary for years, so we go way back. Yeah, she told me about you taking her for a champagne-induced midnight joyride in our experimental quantflow craft. She still adores you even though you scared the heck out of her, especially when you zipped between those two asteroids—missed 'em by inches according to Carma."

"I'm sorry about that, sir. I shouldn't have done it, but I wanted Carma's birthday to be memorable."

"Ha," Tucker chuckled. "Believe me, she won't be forgetting that ride anytime soon. It's no wonder they've teamed you up with James Paul. Of course you know him better by his nickname—JP. You remind me of him."

Menza beamed with pride. "JP! I still can't believe I'm traveling out of the galaxy with a true Novem hero. He's the biggest name in aviation history—other than you, of course."

"Yes, JP's a fearless one. I just hope you two thrill seekers bring back our biocraft in one piece."

"Don't you worry about that, sir. Those new airships are barely broken in after a centillion TSA's. Heck, I don't need to be telling you, you designed them."

Tucker nodded. "Young man, you're probably right. The biocraft will probably hold up okay. How about the occupant? Son, are you psychologically and emotionally prepared for this strenuous mission? A year away from home can be a long time if you aren't in the proper frame of mind."

"Yes sir, I'm ready. I passed all the tests without any problems. I scored pretty high as a matter of fact."

Tucker was silent for a moment. "Wisdom isn't obtained from a test score. You know that, don't you son?"

"What do you mean, sir?"

Tucker turned towards the inscribed tablet. "This old rock has been here for a long time, a very long time. I saw you reading it when I walked over here. Tell me son, do you know what it means?"

Menza once again directed his attention to the weathered stone. "I think I've got a good idea what it's all about. Stars are forever, right?"

"And just what does that mean?" asked Tucker. "Why are stars forever?"

"I guess they'll be around forever. They'll last throughout eternity, right?"

Tucker placed his hand on Menza's shoulder. "The true answer is a little more complicated than that. Let me give you a little hint. Time and space, young man—time and space. Unlock those two mysteries and a river of wisdom will swallow you up and carry you away. Look at me, son."

Menza stared up at Tucker. The old man gazed expressionless into Menza's eyes for a long moment. Menza didn't dare look away. No words were spoken, but a message was delivered—and received. It was more than two individuals communicating, more than an intellectual transference of information. This was about spirit and soul. Menza didn't comprehend the message—not yet, but he knew the seeds of truth and wisdom had somehow been planted into his psyche, and they would sprout at their predestined time.

Tucker finally released his mystical hold on his young student with a nod and a smile. "When you return in one year, drop by my office. Then you can tell me why stars are forever."

Tucker turned and walked away.

Menza stood motionless, not moving a muscle, for fear of losing whatever he had just obtained. He knew he would never be the same. Whatever Tucker had instilled in him had soaked his being, and he was fortunate for it. Tuesday he would fly away, leaving his galaxy, headed for some planet the locals called Earth. Now he was more ready than ever to go.

Chapter 2
JP COOL

"Tomorrow's the big day. Are you ready to roll, boy?" JP gave his young copilot a playful poke with his elbow.

"You bet I'm ready!" declared Menza. He looked up at the imposing figure standing before him.

Menza's eyes focused on the dark grey uniform with the bright red JP stitched over the chest, reminding him once again that he would soon traverse the universe with Novem's most famous citizen, an intergalactic legend, the one and only JP.

In less than twenty-four hours, the two of them would be streaking through time and space towards MWG91177-3, the third planet away from star number 91,177 located in a galaxy named The Milky Way. JP would then say goodbye to spend some time on a space station, doing whatever it was that aviation heroes did on space stations, and return to pick up Menza in one year. Life couldn't get any better.

"Whatya say we get a cup of coffee, kid? Carma just brewed up a fresh batch."

Menza pushed his paperwork aside. They were some important last minute items that needed to be addressed, but no one ever said no to JP.

"Always ready for a cup of coffee with you, JP. I'll learn more in twenty minutes with you than a month of studying these dry technical manuals."

JP chuckled. "Yeah, but the stuff you learn from me might not be what the IOS brass want you to know. It ain't all flying and research out there in the universe. Lotta things going on that can bend the mind."

"Wanna expand on that a little bit?" asked Menza. "If you don't mind, of course."

JP poured two cups of black coffee. Cream and sugar were nothing but bothersome frivolities.

"Here's your coffee, kid. I like mine hot, strong and black—just like my women."

Menza laughed. Entertaining comments like these were the reason the media flocked around JP.

"Kid, before we delve into the intricacies of the universe I want to talk to you about genomel."

Genomel—the scary subject everyone was afraid to bring up to one preparing to embark on a journey. Leave it to JP to get right to the point. Genomel was still very much a mystery. Even though it had been under the microscope for millennia it still befuddled scientists. There was one thing about genomel that everyone understood—without it you die.

In one respect genomel was nothing more than a nutrient, a vitamin, a common form of nourishment. But it also contained something that existed outside the physical realm. Genomel contained an element of *emotion*. Genomel fed the soul with joy, passion and love. Without a trace element of raw emotion the soul died. Shortly thereafter the body followed with its own death. Every living creature in the universe required it to survive. Many of the primitive civilizations were not even aware of the existence of genomel. They unknowingly received it through their natural diet. Genomel was found throughout the universe in a wide variety of food products. The common denominator in these genomel-rich substances was emotion.

Studies suggested that the amount of joy, passion and love that went into the creation of a product directly corresponded with the amount of genomel that was present. More emotion meant more genomel. No one really understood the hows and whys behind this magic. Maybe it was the emotion that went into the creation of the product, or possibly that the creator was simply blessed with an abundance of these emotional traits. Some species needed it in larger quantities than others. The more emotion-based a particular species was, the more genomel they required. Novems were high on the emotion-scale, therefore they needed relatively large amounts of it and at regular intervals.

No one needed to be reminded of the consequences of genomel deficiency. History books were full of accounts of space travelers dying from it. Although there were literally millions of substances that contained genomel, there was a terrifying twist that had forever haunted interplanetary travelers. Genomel could not be transported from its planet of origin! It would lose its magical power once removed from its home planet. It would have to found over and over and over again. Maybe the creator of the universe had somehow installed a built-in survival mechanism for love. What better way to ensure eternal love than to make sure the search for it was never-ending.

The search truly was eternal. The story never changed. Travelers would become stranded on a strange planet without a source of genomel. Most of the time the vital substance was right in front of them, but they did not know where to look. Many times when genomel was found it was purely by accident, a stroke of luck. They would ingest a food or liquid substance and immediately feel the unmistakable energy boost that genomel provided. When this happened it was indescribable relief. Life could continue.

The word genomel was thought to be an offshoot of genome. The word genome was described in ancient texts as a life-giving force. I come into being, I am born, I become—these were all descriptions of the mystical substance. Genomel was the lone wild card that defied science. It was joy, passion, love, soul—it exemplified all that was good in the universe. Genomel was life itself. JP knew it.

"Kid, I ain't one for beating around the bush. Most travelers avoid the subject of genomel like it's the plague. Everyone knows you find it or you die. It's that simple. Those undeveloped planets like the one you'll be visiting—they're the worst. You can't ask someone down there where to find it. Even though it's keeping them alive they don't even know that genomel exists. Here's my advice. Get down there and start sampling everything in front of you—every food product, every liquid, even pet food if it comes down to it. Because genomel is an emotion-based substance it might show up anywhere. The good thing is that it hits you like a ton of bricks when you find it, especially if your body's been missing it for a while. You'll know instantly. One hint—if you run across someone down there who's obviously passionate about what they do, what they believe in, what they produce, or just life in general—you hang around that person and eat everything they eat, drink everything they drink, breath everything they breath until you strike it rich. One thing we know for sure, it's there. Where there's life there's genomel. You gotta find it and you gotta find it quick. You got it, kid?"

"Only a fool's not going to listen to you," said Menza, "and I ain't no fool. Thank you, JP."

"You're welcome, kid. Let's move on. You were asking earlier about making sense of what we do, blasting through time and space on our way to the unknown. This much I know. The universe isn't black and white. It's as mixed as this mess of hair perched on my head. Just when you think you've got it figured out, some new information will whack you in the nose—and boom, just like that, you're dealing with a whole new deck of cards. You've added another layer of knowledge that demands cultivation. Everything else you've learned in the past sinks down a level. You store it in the experience department—to be pulled up when you need it. Another reality becomes a false reality and you hope the present reality is the real thing, but it never is."

JP was momentarily silent. "Kid, when I was your age I knew it all, or thought I did. Several years back, I came to the conclusion that the smartest beings were the ones who realized how much they *didn't* know. So, kid, enjoy the ride. But let me warn you, it's going to be a bumpy one. You ain't the type that sticks his head in the sand. You're like me, always looking around the next bend, wondering what's out there. That kind of living ain't easy, but it carries its own type of internal reward. At least there are some girls out there who fancy our style. That ain't a bad thing."

Menza had never really given any thought to intergalactic romance—until now. He had always known he was a decent looking guy. Girls were constantly reminding him how handsome and fit he was. Novem girls were not known for shyness. As a matter of fact, some of them could be quite aggressive. They were constantly flirting with him.

They seemed to like the fact that he was six feet tall. Most Novem males were shorter in height. They also regularly complimented him on his multi-hued eyes that changed colors with his mood. He was even getting used to the more-than-occasional comment about how nice of a butt he had.

JP flashed his legendary smile and held out both hands, palms up. "So how's our ship? Is she ready to go?"

"She's rearing to leave Hammerhead Galaxy, just like me." Menza's eyes lit up at the thought. "The maintenance crew gave her the final inspection this morning. Sixteen more hours and we're off. I still can't believe it. Me and JP traveling the stars!"

"I like your spirit, boy. That's the reason I chose you over the others. The selection committee gave me a short list that included five others. Didn't even look at it—told 'em I wanted to fly with that Menza kid. They didn't give me any friction with it. They must like you pretty well too."

JP smiled at his copilot. Menza was about to burst with pride.

"Well kid, let's go look at our ship. It's gonna be our home for a couple of weeks, so it needs to be right. I've got all the confidence in the world in our staff, but my craft never leaves the ground without my own final inspection. Something has kept me alive over the years and I ain't gonna change things now."

The two strolled towards the hangar past the guards. They didn't dare ask JP and his young companion for credentials. JP's face had been a media mainstay for decades, etched into the memories of millions. Heroes didn't need clearance.

Menza instinctively stayed a half a step behind the master aeronaut. It was all about respect. JP sauntered along with a natural swagger—confident, not cocky. There was no pretentiousness about him. He was who he was—a charismatic galaxy-renowned icon famous for living on the edge. JP was a common man's hero, unapologetic about his freewheeling adventurous lifestyle. He was a media magnet with a built-in audience anxious to hear of his tales from beyond.

JP was the unofficial ambassador for his beloved home. Without him Novem would be just another insignificant planet. JP *was* Novem. He was always spewing out historical facts about her. Because of him most of the galaxy was aware that Novem was an ancient word for the number nine—and nine was a universally lucky number. JP sometimes referred to her as Planet Nine. She was the ninth planet from her sun, her celestial unit number was HG/99999999-9, and she had nine beautiful rings circling her midsection. Planet Nine was indeed lucky—lucky to be the birthplace of JP.

"There she is—what a beauty." JP had seen every aviation craft ever produced, yet he still felt an intense heart-jolting rush every time he laid eyes upon a flying machine. From the primitive to the fantastic, they were all birds of flight. Nothing topped the sensation of lifting off from the doldrums of the known and reaching out to the limitless sky. JP was born to fly.

The ZPB was a standard zeropoint spacecraft that had been modified to be biologically compatible with the operators of the airship. Once airborne it transduced into energy and became completely weightless. This allowed the craft to safely traverse through the time space arcs. ZPB/JM was specifically designed to transport senior pilot JSPL-2519 and copilot MNZA-9716. Anyone else that controlled the aircraft ran the risk of a catastrophic midflight breakup. ZPB/JM had been constructed of a living synthetic material that perfectly matched the two pilots' genetic makeup. It *was* JP and Menza.

"Climb in kid," said JP, already sliding in through the open door. Menza followed close behind.

"First things first. Kid, check the quantflow regulator. They ain't sending me up in one of these birds with a faulty quantflow regulator. We'd last about eight hours before we're turned into universe dust."

The ZPB biocraft came about because of its capacity to endure the shock of entering quantflow, the point where matter/antimatter interaction took place during extreme space travel. Previous crafts were deemed unreliable after several quantflow incidents resulted in pilot fatalities. The ZPB bionics solved this problem. As the craft slips into the realm of quantflow, an organic shift occurs. The craft and the occupants become one biological entity, preventing the aircraft from breaking up. Truth be told, no one actually understood how this process prevented quantflow accidents, but there had never been a fatal biocraft incident. The new technology had apparently resolved the problem.

"Everything's okay with the quantflow regulator, JP," said Menza. "I'll run through the rest of the checklist. I know what you want."

"Atta boy," said JP. "Keep us safe. We're shooting through two galaxies and neither of us wanna be changing tires on the side of the road, if you know what I mean."

"JP, I've got a question for you," Menza said as he methodically ran through the remainder of his checklist.

"Shoot, kid."

"When did you know you wanted to be a pilot—at what age?"

"Oh, for as long as I can remember I've always longed to be with the stars." JP smiled at the thought. "Ain't nothing like getting out there and seeing places for yourself. You can read about places, hear about 'em, see pictures of 'em, but nothing takes the place of *going there*. How about you, kid? When did you decide to get into this business?"

"I'm not really sure, but I think it was the first time I saw a bird. I was so jealous of its ability to soar above us, its wings, its *freedom*. Then it would touch down and begin singing a happy song. I too wanted to lift into the sky, fly free, and come back singing a happy tune."

"Keep going, kid."

"My parents told me that when I was one I would jump off the living room furniture. I don't remember that. I do remember breaking my arm when I was five. I crashed a cardboard glider I had made when I jumped out of a tree. That's when my parents knew I was serious about this flying thing. They've supported me ever since. Now I'm sitting here in a new ZPB that's organically matched with me and you. Dang, JP, I still can't believe I'm flying with you. Tomorrow!"

"Believe it kid, because it's real. In a few days time you'll be in another galaxy. I can't wait for you to see Hammerhead from afar. Our home galaxy really is one beautiful sight. Heck, I'm as excited as you are. Your enthusiasm must be rubbing off on me, kid. Checklist okay?"

"Everything's fine," answered Menza.

"Okay kid—gotta go, I've got some loose ends to tie up before we leave in the morning. Hang around our ship for as long as you like, just make sure you get plenty of rest. No late night at James Café—you've got plenty of time to drink and tell lies when you get back. You've got a big one tomorrow."

Menza laughed. "You own the place, so it would hard for me to sneak in for a drink. Some of your friends might see me in there."

"Friends, hell," cracked JP. "I'd see you. I never said I wouldn't be in there tonight."

Menza watched as JP eased out of the craft and exited the hangar. Outside a television film crew awaited. The media was always trying to pry a salty one-liner from their favorite celebrity. JP was one cool character. Menza pinched himself. It hurt. This was real.

Chapter 3

TIME SPACE ARCS

"Liftoff in one minute. Quantflow check?" JP's tone was all business.

"100 over 100," Menza answered, his heart racing.

"Plasma level?"

"Steady at ninety percent."

"Auxiliary package?

"Perfect."

"Bio-compatible check?"

"Good—three in one."

"Celestial lock-in destination—including the galactic locater coordinates?"

"Celestial unit MWK91177-3—the coordinates are MWK/F-O-L-L-Y."

"Okay kid." JP glanced at his young copilot. Confidence and cool filled the cockpit. "Rev her up to 300 Q's."

"Yes sir."

"400."

"Yes sir."

"500 Q's."

"Yes sir."

"You ready kid?"

"Yes sir, I'm ready."

"Five—four—three—two—roll it!"

SWOOOOLLLL SWOOOOLLLL SWOOOOLLLL. What a wonderful sound—the sound of taking flight. It was nothing more than a whisper in these modern machines. All the readings were normal. Menza glanced towards his left. JP's wink confirmed everything was fine. ZPB/JM lifted upwards, hovering several feet above the ground.

"We'll be outta here soon, kid," said JP, "but first I'm taking her up to 500,000 feet before we sphere it. I want you to see Novem one last time. I don't want you to forget what our beautiful planet looks like—silver Novem."

In an instant JP transported the craft and its two occupants high above their home. Menza peered out his window. Novem really was a beautiful planet, with her sparkling silver oceans and streams, her bright green foliage, and the nine rainbow rings that encircled her.

Menza pondered. What would MWG91177-3, or Earth, as he would soon be calling it, look like with blue oceans instead of silver. That should be beautiful in a different way. Knowing that JP still was so emotionally attached to Novem boosted Menza's sense of pride. JP had seen it all. He had visited planets in six galaxies, passed through several others, yet he still felt genuine affection for his home planet. Novem must truly be a special place.

"Okay kid, let's sphere it." JP pushed back deep into his seat. Menza followed. JP released the sphere safety switch and lightly pushed the sphere button. They were off.

As was the custom, neither pilot spoke for the first hour of the journey. The origin of the tradition was supposed to be health related, the body needed adjustment time, but in actuality it was wrapped in superstition. Supposedly, eons ago, when sphering was in its infancy, two pilots tragically turned themselves and their craft into universe dust. Records showed they were engaged in casual conversation from the point of liftoff until the deadly explosion—exactly one hour into the flight. Out of that tragedy sprouted the traditional one hour of silence ritual. JP wasn't one to be tampering with the ancient custom, and neither was Menza.

Nearly a million TSA's every second over a period of two weeks—Menza had never bothered to do the math, but it would be a heck of a journey. Menza surveyed the inside of the biocraft that was now his temporary home. It had all the comforts, including a plush sofa and two separate sleeping quarters. No expense had been spared. After all, it would be housing the one and only JP. The total area was exactly 333 square feet. The number was no accident. The designers, Tucker being the ultimate decision maker, had an affinity for certain numbers. Nine was one of the most important, hence the triple threes.

The interior was a light cream color, but that would become darker as the flight progressed, something to do with the biological chemistry between the two occupants and the craft. Menza wondered if his own body would do the same. There was little noise, just a slight hum from the zeropoint energy module, quite pleasant actually. The air temperature was comfortable as expected. Everything seemed as it should.

"We're sixty-five minutes into it now." JP was all smiles, doing what he loved more than anything   flying. "It's safe to talk now, kid. So tell me, what do you think?"

Menza followed the voice back to its source. His mind had been drifting and JP's voice shot him back to reality. That *really* was the legendary JP asking him a question. He *really* was off on a one-year mission to a faraway planet in a distant galaxy.

"I'm kinda in awe, to be honest, JP. Copiloting this brand new ZPB with you, the hero I've idolized my entire life—it's a dream come true. Top that off with the excitement of living on a planet that I know very little about—it seems overwhelming at this moment."

"That hero stuff won't last long," JP laughed. "Two weeks sitting beside me and you'll be bolting out of this craft at the first opportunity. Traveling a trillion time space arcs with anybody can be tough, no matter how famous they may be. Ha! You'll be ready to see a pretty face by the time we arrive, that I guarantee. Speaking of that, rumor has it those Earthling girls are pretty things. Whadaya think about that, kid?"

"Well, I guess if I'm gonna live in a strange place for a year, it sure can't hurt to be around some pretty girls. Just how pretty are they, JP?"

"Darn pretty, from what they told me at the space station." JP eased back into his seat. "A couple of fellows from planet Olgan—it's located over in east Hammerhead—spent a month on Earth. One of 'em had a girlfriend while he was there. Came back all smiles, that's all I'm allowed to tell you. You know what they say—us and them come from the same stock."

"Yeah," said Menza. "I did hear a little bit about that. We're supposedly genetically compatible. I know that's why they preferred a Novem for this mission rather that someone from a closer planet. That and the fact that we're nearly identical as far as looks go."

"You're right about that," said JP. "We're more than just genetically compatible. I've been told that we're ninety percent identical, both of us products of some ancient genetic mixing bowl experiment. Somehow our intelligence level ended up eight times higher than theirs. I guess that other ten percent held 'em back in some way."

"That's amazing," Menza stated, his eyes fixated on the blackness outside his window. "You know what they told me during IOS training? They said that the majority of Earthlings aren't even aware that there's life on other planets—can you believe that! What a difference that ten percent must make. Here we are zipping through space at nearly a million TSA's per second while they're sitting there on Earth thinking they're the only beings in the universe. What could have held them back so much, JP?"

"That's what you're gonna find out, kid. The IOS has the same questions as you. They want to know how such a biologically capable species keeps itself in the dark ages. They suspect an elite group of Earthlings, or possibly another foreign species, is controlling the mass population by keeping them dumb-downed, while they selfishly utilize any real technology. That's the working theory anyway. The IOS is hoping you'll bring back some solid answers."

Menza shook his head. "They actually think they're alone in the universe. That's astounding. I guess I've got my work cut out for me down there on Earth."

"Relax kid, you're gonna enjoy it. I wish I could relive my first intergalactic mission. There's nothing like youthful exuberance. It provides the fuel as you slowly acquire wisdom. You'll do a fine job and have fun doing it."

"I hope so, JP. I'm a little apprehensive, nervous actually, about fitting in down there."

"Forget about it, kid. You got your cover story memorized?"

"Yeah, I'm pretending to be a customer support representative who takes phone calls, works on computers, that sort of stuff. That'll explain why I work from home. The IOS has somehow arranged for my living quarters. How they manage those details I'll never know. Anyway, I'll be living in a quadplex apartment building, four units closely bunched together. They said my fellow tenants are a varied cross-section of humans, as Earthlings sometimes call themselves."

"Any details on who your neighbors actually are?" asked JP.

"Yeah, they said the other three apartments will be occupied by a middle aged couple, a young single girl, and another guy who the locals think is crazy."

"You watch, kid. The so-called crazy guy will probably end up being the only one with any sense. How about the young single girl? That's gotta make you happy. It sounds like the IOS is looking out for you." JP smiled mischievously.

"Ah, she'll probably have a boyfriend by the time I get there, which could be for the best. I'm not looking for complications. I've got enough going on already, you know."

"Let it flow naturally, kid." JP gave the gauges a quick read. Satisfied, he leaned back and crossed his arms. "Yep, everything's gotta come naturally, and I mean *everything*. When people start blindly pushing forward, that's when things go bad. Don't get me wrong, progress is a wonderful thing, as long as it's harmonious with the universe. Figure this one out if you can. Time is infinite and space is infinite, yet throughout history fools have always rushed through time to conquer more space. This behavior ultimately culminates in war. Makes a lot of sense, huh?"

"You're right," said Menza. "That seems crazy if you ask me."

"Kid, I've been to a lot of places and seen a lot of things, but I ain't got this universe figured out—not even close. It does seem, at least in the reality I presently believe in, that there's an eternal conflict between good and evil. Good will prevail for a while, evil will find a crack in the door to stick in a corrupting tentacle that spreads like a disease until it's the dominating force, good returns, and the cycle goes on and on. I often wonder if there's a mastermind somewhere that's controlling this whole thing like a giant chessboard. I can picture some deranged power-mad psychopath sitting in front of a computer pushing buttons, alternating between chaos, horror and war—and joy, happiness and peace."

"Do you think there's any hope for the future out there?" asked Menza. "Maybe we should be like most Novems, and just stay home and enjoy the comforts of life."

"You know what?" said JP. "We Novems are universally famous for our song and dance—and being a peace loving planet. I'm very proud of that. I could kick back into retirement tomorrow and probably enjoy it. But I still got a fire inside that keeps me rolling along."

"That's obvious, JP," said Menza. "Might as well do what you enjoy, right? I believe I remember an interview one time where you were describing how fragile life is."

"Probably so," said JP. "Ain't nobody safe—ain't no galaxy, no planet, no species or no being that's gonna totally escape without some pain. I know one thing though. I'm mixing in some fun and adventure in my life. They might knock me to my knees, but I'm gonna go down swinging."

"I gotta agree with you, JP. Sitting home and playing it safe is not my style either."

"I tell you, kid. Our pleasant little planet's security is no more than an illusion." JP looked out the window, peering backwards, as if he could actually see his home planet. "We Novems aren't immune to the evils of the races, as much as I'd like to think otherwise. All you gotta do is look at our past to see that. We've blown ourselves to bits more times than I can count."

"I know we've had our share of growing pains," said Menza. "At least that's what the history books say."

"Yep," replied JP. "Sixteen, that's how many times they tell us we've wiped ourselves out. For millions of years we were trapped—caught up in a suicidal cycle of modernizing ourselves into self destruction. We'd industrialize, only to abuse the technology to destroy ourselves, and start the process all over again."

"Kind of silly, isn't it JP?" asked Menza. "What's the use of technological advancement if it's only used for advanced weaponry?"

"I guess our planet's history characterizes the nature of the universe, kid," replied JP. "Time after time our civilization would rise from the ashes of stupidity to rebuild, each time a little wiser than before. Eventually we achieved a level of societal maturity and realized shooting ourselves in the head over and over again didn't constitute progress. A lot of other planets have gone through the same process. Enough of that—did you know we'll be coming up on Hammerhead Space Station in a couple of minutes?"

"Really," asked Menza. "I didn't realize we'd traveled that far already."

"Take a look at the TSI, that'll show you." JP pointed towards the time space indicator.

"Wow!" exclaimed Menza. "Twenty billion TSA's already. You're right, the space station is just ahead. Too bad we're shooting right past it."

"Ah, that's okay, kid. You're gonna get plenty of opportunities over the course of your career. I must have stopped there a hundred times over the years. I tell you what I am excited about—the Milky Way's central station. I heard it's teeming with interesting characters. I'll be working there, but you can bet I'll also have my share of fun."

"That's a huge station, right?"

"Yeah, their biggest," answered JP. "The Milky Way is a fairly large galaxy with an extraordinarily diverse range of beings. There are plenty of galaxies larger in size then the Milky Way, but I know of no others that sustain such an interesting mix of life."

"Knowing you JP, that's why you're heading there—is that correct?"

"You got it, son." JP was quiet for a moment before looking up at Menza. "You know kid, I've been running all my life. But I've been running *towards* something, not from something, at least most of the time. One thing I've learned is that you can't run from yourself. Yourself will tag along on every journey, dragging along all its smelly garbage with it. So you might as well tend to your messes instead of running from them. When you do that, running becomes a genuine pleasure. Ain't nothing like a guilt-free footloose adventure. That's enjoying life to the maximum in my book."

"JP, you sure know how to live. It's no wonder you're the pride of Novem. You're as cool as they come."

"Kid," crowed JP, "cool ain't cool unless you're true to yourself. You gotta be real or the charm's gonna fade real quick. You're as real as you wanna be. Always remember that."

Menza nodded. "I will, JP, I will."

Chapter 4

MEETING THE NEIGHBORS

"I'm gonna put her down right here." JP's eyes locked onto Menza. "Are you ready?"

"Set her down, JP. I'm ready." Menza took a deep breath before looking down at MWG91177-3, his home-to-be for the next year.

The two weeks had passed as quickly as a lightning strike. JP had been wrong about one thing—the long journey and tight quarters had not worn on his young protégé. JP's tales of his past adventures had only left Menza yearning for more. Soaking in JP's wisdom had been both educational and entertaining. The memories had already been labeled as treasure and locked away in a special place in Menza's brain. They were precious cargo indeed.

Menza looked out the window into the darkness. There was a distant glow from the east. That must be MWG91177-3's sun preparing to pop over the horizon. Unlike Novem's sun which rose from the west, this was reversed. It seemed a bit odd. But so the was the 24-hour day—it was a whole lot shorter than Novem's 52-hour cycle. It all seemed momentarily overwhelming, but he dared not mention it. JP had once mentioned that he had spent time on a planet that had a 600-hour day. 600 hours! Heck, they probably took 52-hour naps on that planet.

"MWG91177-3 is just below us," said Menza, trying not to sound nervous. "JP, I guess this is it."

"You'd better start remembering to call it Earth, otherwise the natives are gonna think you're crazy—or some alien from another galaxy," JP chuckled. "All those letters and numbers ain't gonna fly with the locals. You live on Earth from now on—okay kid?"

"Yes sir, JP. Thanks."

"You got your stack of cash, right? You're going to need a lot of spending money to get through a year."

"Yes sir, JP," replied Menza. "I've got the money with me."

"Kid, I'm also assuming you got your universal communicative transmitter. The IOS will be expecting regular reports from you."

"I do, JP, but thanks for the reminder."

"Kid." JP put his hand on Menza's shoulder. "If you run into any serious trouble you buzz me on my UCT. I can be here in five days to pick you up and get you out of here."

"Thanks, JP, but I certainly hope that won't be the case. I don't want to bother you while you're at the Milky Way station."

"Oh, and one last important reminder—find you a source of genomel quick. I know we talked about it earlier, but it's worth another mention. Follow the passion trail."

"Thanks again, JP. I'll find some. I promise."

Menza glanced out the window one last time. The designated landing site was somewhat of a mystery. They hadn't given him a lot of information about it, only that it was rural farmland situated a short distance from his assigned destination. Whatever—he would be on his own shortly. No longer would JP be around for guidance.

JP lowered the biocraft to within inches of the ground. Menza leaned over and gave JP a hug, followed by a high-five.

"I'm outta here, JP. See you in a year. You be careful on your way to the space station, okay?"

"You got it, kid," JP replied. "Remember everything I told you and you'll be just fine. You just find out what makes those Earthlings tick and send back some IOS reports. Oh, and don't forget to have a little fun along the way."

"Right on, JP." Menza stepped out onto the foreign soil and closed the door. He turned and watched as the biocraft lifted several feet off the ground. JP dipped the craft, giving Menza the traditional goodbye sign, before shooting out of sight.

It would be light soon and there was work to do. First step—find his new home, the small town of Ashmont, North Carolina, United States of America, on planet MWG91177-3. That would be Earth from now on. According to his IOS directive, the town was supposed to be two Earth miles away.

Menza began walking towards the road from the field where JP had dispensed him. Suddenly he heard a squish and felt something wet around his ankle. Then came the smell—a very foul smell. It was the stench of freshly laid cow manure. Menza hadn't been on Earth as much as a minute and he'd already stepped in cow doo. Not only was he an alien in a strange land, but he was a stinky one at that.

Menza walked to the road and looked both ways. To the west were more cow pastures, he certainly didn't want to go that direction. What if a street-crossing cow had left more welcoming patties for him? It was still quite dark and he could easily step in another one. He looked towards the east—city lights! He also spotted a street sign. He strained to read it, *Ashmont—2 miles*. Menza set out for town.

Thirty minutes later he reached the edge of town. A huge red brick structure stared back at him. *Welcome to Ashmont, North Carolina—Where living is easy.* Menza certainly hoped so. He reached into his pocket and pulled out a piece of paper. 412 Twain Drive, Apt. 4—that was to be his new home. Now all he had to do was find it.

Menza looked back up at the town's welcome sign. Incredibly, located at the base of the structure was a map of Ashmont. He quickly scanned the map. Great! He was only a five-minute walk from his new home.

Two right turns later he was there. He knocked on the door of apartment number one, just as he had been told to do. A well-groomed man opened the door.

"Hello there," he said in a friendly voice. "How can I help you?"

"Hi there. My name is Menza. I'm new in town and I was told you have an apartment that might be for rent."

The man smiled. "Mensa? Isn't that some sort of high IQ club? You must be a smart one."

"Not really. I'm Menza with a Z, They probably won't let me in the club since I can't even spell it."

"Ha, that's funny. As far as the apartment goes—number four is vacant right now. Rent is five hundred dollars a month. Is that something you might be interested in?"

"Yes sir," replied Menza. "That sounds like a fair price. Can I take a look at it?"

"Sure you can. By the way, my name's Jim—Jim Dixon. I live here with my wife Joan. Our son Alan owns this apartment building. Menza, where are you from?"

"I'm from Novem," Menza casually replied. Immediately he realized his mistake. He was supposed to pretend he was a customer service representative from Seattle, Washington— not from the planet Novem located in a distant galaxy.

"Novem?" Jim looked puzzled. "Is that near Raleigh?"

"No sir," answered Menza, hoping the conversation would stray elsewhere.

"Novem…that sounds…is that Russian?" asked an inquisitive Jim.

Menza realized this dilemma wasn't going to fade away. "Yes sir, I'm from Russia." His mind shifted into overdrive. Where in the heck was Russia?

"Oh really?" Now Jim was totally enthralled. He stared at Menza waiting for a response.

Menza had to come up with something—and quick! "Jim, let me explain. My town Novem is part of Russia, and Russia is part of Earth. I hope that makes things clearer for you."

Jim looked at Menza, shook his head, and chuckled. "Yeah, things are a lot clearer now. Thank you. Why don't we go take a look at the apartment? Follow me."

Jim spoke as the two of them walked. "Like I said, you'll be in number four. Joan and I are in one, Truman is in two— more on him later, and you've got pretty Marilyn in three. She's going through a bit of a rough time right now. Her mother's quite sick."

"I'm sorry to hear that," said Menza.

Jim nodded in agreement. He seemed to be feeling out his potential tenant. Menza could almost see his mind churning away underneath that cool demeanor.

Jim continued. "We have a good bunch of tenants, quiet and clean, and most important they all pay their rent on time. That is, except for the wife and I. My son gives us free rent in exchange for putting up with his teenage years. That allows me plenty of time to fish—that's my thing. Okay, here we are."

Jim opened the door to apartment four and stepped in. Before Menza could follow Jim stopped him.

"Menza, we really take pride in our clean community here, so I'd appreciate it if you'd scrape that cow poop off your leg before you come in. You must be in the cattle business."

Menza had completely forgotten about the cow manure that encrusted his foot and ankle. Some of it had fallen off during his walk, but the remaining dung had been given new life by the hike into town. The stirring motion seemed to have intensified the stench. Some of the foul smelling excrement had actually soaked through his socks and had taken refuge between his toes. Yuck!

"Oh, Jim, I'm so sorry! On my way into town I stepped in some manure and completely forgot about it. And no, I'm not in the cattle business. I'm actually in customer service."

"Menza, I'll go fetch a water hose while you take off your shoes. We've gotta hose you down good before you go in. Joan just cleaned the apartment yesterday. She'd kill us both if you spread cow droppings everywhere. Oh, look, there's Marilyn!"

As Menza removed his shoes he looked over at the striking blonde standing on the adjoining patio. She was gorgeous! With her flowing locks and beautiful smile and perfectly proportioned body, she topped every Novem female he'd ever seen. JP had been right, these Earthling girls were stunningly attractive.

"Marilyn, mind if I borrow your water hose?"

Jim's voice snapped Menza back into reality—the reality of meeting a beautiful girl for the first time while being covered in cow manure. It wasn't the optimal first impression.

"Of course not, Jim. What's going on?"

Her voice streamed out a smoky sensuality. She walked over to Menza and stuck out her hand.

"Hi there, I'm Marilyn."

Menza was momentarily speechless. Finally he reached out and clasped both of his hands around Marilyn's hand. Her skin was smooth. He wondered if all Earthling skin was like hers.

"Hello, I'm Menza. I'm hoping to rent this apartment."

"Stand back, Marilyn," interrupted Jim. He moved in close with the hose. "I've gotta wash this cow manure off our new tenant."

Jim aimed the hose at Menza's feet and turned the nozzle. For a full minute he sprayed away at his guest. The manure slowly fell away, but some dung particles stubbornly hid between Menza's toes.

"Marilyn, turn it up full blast," Jim commanded. "Our new neighbor's not giving up his cow manure without a fight."

Jim proceeded to blast away at Menza's toes. The dung finally released its grip and fell to the ground, leaving a relieved, but embarrassed victim. Jim was now satisfied that his new rental prospect was clean enough to step foot in the apartment.

"Okay, Menza," Jim said with a chuckle, "now we can take a look at your new living quarters."

"It was nice to meet you and I hope you'll decide to be our neighbor." Marilyn's eyes sparkled as she spoke. "We've all stepped in some messes before, so don't worry about it. See you."

Menza tried not to stare as Marilyn walked towards her apartment. She was as charming as she was beautiful. This Earth mission might not be too bad.

"You couldn't find a nicer neighbor anywhere," said Jim, snapping Menza back to the situation at hand. "That Marilyn's really special. Come on in."

Menza entered into the living room. It was small, but clean and bright. It smelled of fresh flowers. Jim then showed the bedroom, complete with a view of the mountains, and a spotless bath. It really was a wonderful apartment with plenty of room for a single person.

"I'll take it if you'll take me," said Menza. "I love this place."

"Great," replied Jim. "Let's go see the boss, that'll be my wife, and complete some paperwork. You can move right in if you like."

"Sounds good," said Menza.

Menza and Jim strolled towards Jim's apartment.

"Hey Jim," a voice called out. Menza looked over at a man standing in the doorway of apartment two. He had a guitar dangling from a strap on his back. He had a huge grin that seemed to be permanently etched into his face, eyes that were both friendly and distant—soul eyes as they were called on Novem—and both hands were clasped around an incredibly large glass filled with a golden beverage.

"Hello Truman," answered Jim. "How are you today?"

"Not bad—got us a new neighbor?" The man stepped out onto his patio.

"Yep, he's moving in today," replied Jim. "His name's Menza."

"It's nice to meet you, Menza. People call me Truman—crazy Truman when I ain't within hearing distance."

"It's nice to meet you also. I'll be living in apartment four."

Menza took a good look at the man. He was tall and well built, without an ounce of fat on him, and appeared to be in his early-fifties. Menza immediately noticed a certain presence about him, an air of openness and honesty.

"We'll catch you later, Truman," Jim said with a quick wave of his hand. "Gotta get this boy all signed up before he changes his mind."

"Okay Jimbo," said Truman. "Hey Menza, don't be a stranger. You're always welcome for beer and conversation at my place."

Menza threw up his hand. "Thanks for the invitation. You're welcome at my place too as soon as I get settled."

Truman walked back into his apartment and closed the door.

"He seems to be quite the character," Menza remarked.

Jim laughed. "That's an understatement. Those giant two-liter beers don't seem to hurt his body—he's in great shape, but I'm not so sure about his mind."

"What do you mean?" asked Menza.

"You'll find out soon enough," Jim said with another hearty laugh. "Truman runs our local pub, The Jumping Cow. As a matter of fact, Marilyn's a bartender there. Truman's also a songwriter, pretty good one I'm told. There's a reason we all call him crazy Truman. He's one of these conspiracy nuts who believe everything that happens is part of some evil plot. Catch him after a couple of those double liters and you're really in for a treat. He'll get off on his alien spiel. He actually thinks aliens come here from other planets."

A quick chill raced through Menza's body. For the first time he felt the sharp reality of being on a primitive planet. The act was now on. Menza calmly glanced over at Jim and chuckled.

"He is pretty far out there. Aliens from another world—guess all that beer is affecting him."

"Something is—that's for sure." Jim nodded towards his apartment. "Come on in. I want you to meet my wife."

Jim and Menza entered the front door. The apartment was immaculate.

"Come here honey," Jim called out in a pleasant tone. "I've got someone I want you to meet."

A woman emerged from the master bedroom. She was short and a little on the plump side. Her eyes were kind and warm and full of soul. She held out her hand. Menza reached out and gently grasped it.

"I've been cleaning, so I hope you'll excuse my appearance."

"Hi, my name's Menza. I'm hoping to rent one of your apartments."

Joan looked over at Jim's approving smile. The two of them seem to communicate without words.

"Hello, I'm Joan. I'm sure Jim's shown you the apartment already. Did you like it?"

"Yes ma'am, I love it," said Menza. "It's quiet and clean. That's exactly what I was looking for."

Joan's smile seemed to fill the room with warmth and kindness. Someone in the IOS had done an excellent job in finding this apartment. Menza made a mental note to find out who it was and thank them. Jim and Joan were wonderful humans. Menza hoped the rest of the planet's inhabitants would be so friendly and accessible, but he already knew that was too good to be true.

"I'm glad you like the apartment," said Joan. Her words rolled out deceptively slow, but Menza instinctively knew this was a lady of intelligence and class. "Let's go ahead and take care of the paperwork. Would you like something to drink?"

"Sure," answered Menza. "A plodder would be great."

Joan looked over at Jim. He shook his head.

"I'm sorry, honey," she said, "but I'm not sure I know what a plodder is. Is it some sort of a tea or coffee or juice—or maybe a chocolate drink?"

Menza had done it again. Of course they wouldn't know what a plodder was. They weren't Novems. How would they know that a plodder was the traditional Novem welcoming beverage? He would have to wiggle out of another foolish self-inflicted trap.

Menza remained calm and smiled towards Joan.

"Yes, you're exactly right. A plodder is a mix of four equal parts—coffee, tea, juice and chocolate—served steaming hot. I'm surprised you guessed what it was. It's relatively unknown except in my hometown of Novem, which is in Russia, which is located in a different part of Earth."

Joan kept a straight face out for the sake of being polite. Part of Earth? This boy was definitely different. She looked towards her husband for a sign. Jim flashed a sly grin he usually reserved for his poker-playing buddies.

"Well," said Joan, "that was a really lucky guess on my part because I had no idea what a plodder was. It does seem to be an odd mix, but I think I'll try it. Jim, how about you? Wanna try a Russian plodder?"

"What the heck," chuckled Jim. "I'm always up for something from a different part of Earth, as Menza so aptly describes it."

"Three plodders it is then," said Joan. "Does anyone want sugar in their plodder?"

"Not for me, thank you," answered Menza.

"Me either," said Jim. "I'm gonna go like the pro—it ain't everyday we can experience a new drink from a small town in Russia from a different part of Earth."

"Okay, three plodders, no sugar, coming right up." Joan scurried off to the kitchen.

Jim settled back into his chair. "So tell me, Menza. What brought you to Ashmont, North Carolina, of all places?"

Menza's mind kicked into overdrive. With an IQ eight times that of an average Earthling, he had not expected any intellectual challenges, but friendly Jim was a clever one. It was way too early in the game for anyone to begin questioning his background. He had to be very careful.

"Oh, I just needed a change. I've heard North Carolina was a beautiful place with friendly people, and Ashmont was the exact geographical center of the state, so here I am."

"I'm sure it's way different from small town Russia—right?"

"Oh yes," Menza confidently replied. "On that part of Earth we do a lot of things different from you guys." He was trying to keep his answers as generic as possible knowing Jim the fisherman was baiting the hook for information.

"I heard it's kind of cold over there," Jim said, sliding even deeper into his recliner.

"It can get cold at times," replied Menza. Non-committal statements couldn't get him into trouble.

"Yeah, it gets down below zero here in Carolina occasionally. What's the coldest temperature you've ever experienced over in Russia?"

Menza dug into his memory chest. Planetary temperature differences had never been of interest to him. Russia apparently had one of Earth's cooler climes. Jim had pushed him into a corner that required a solid answer. A wishy-washy response wouldn't float with this wily fisherman.

Menza projected an air of self-assurance. "Oh, I don't know exactly—maybe a thousand below zero."

"A thousand below!" exclaimed Jim. "That's the coldest temperature I've ever heard of. Are you sure?"

Menza immediately knew he had made another humongous mistake that needed to be rectified. Yet again he needed to think quickly to dig out of a hole.

"I'm sorry Jim, that's a thousand below zero on our local scale. I'm not sure how that would equate with yours. What's the coldest you've ever seen here?"

"Back around forty years ago it got down to ten below, but that was highly unusual."

Menza laughed. "No wonder you thought I was crazy. A thousand below on our regional temperature gauge would register at approximately forty below on yours. I'm sorry about the confusion."

"Okay fellows, the drinks are ready." Joan walked into the room carrying a tray with three freshly brewed plodders, and not a moment too soon for Menza.

"Here you go, nice and hot—just the way you like it," said Joan, as she dispensed the still-boiling beverages. "And I've also got the leasing paperwork, so we can get that out of the way while we sip our plodders. I hope they're satisfactory for you, Menza."

Menza inhaled a whiff of the steam rising over his cup. "Ahh!" he exclaimed. "The aroma tells me this is a properly prepared plodder. Kudos to you, Mrs. Dixon."

"Thank you," said Joan. "I hope you enjoy it. Here's our simple rental agreement. The first month is free with a one-year lease. If you'll just sign here, the apartment's all yours."

Menza quickly signed the rental agreement. He then took a sip of his plodder, expecting it to be horrible. To his surprise it was quite pleasant.

"Cheers," said Menza, holding up his drink. "To my new home—to my new friends—and to Joan's tasty plodders."

The three of tapped their cups together and proceeded to small-talk the next hour away. Menza was careful not to let the conversation stray into any danger zones. He had already had too many close calls. Joan kept it safe as most of the conversation dealt with her new tenant's lack of furniture. She insisted he take some blankets, a chair, a lamp, even a small TV. She was truly a caring individual. Joan would have been special on any planet, including Novem.

Menza would settle in today, get some much needed rest tonight, and begin work tomorrow. He had only 364 more days to find out what made humans tick. These Earthlings were an interesting species—that much he knew for sure.

Chapter 5

A LOCAL BITE

Menza rolled out of his makeshift bed and looked out the window. The sun was just popping up in the eastern sky. Novem's beautiful sun came to mind. His mind momentarily wandered, recalling memories of a bright orange sun kissing Novem's shimmering silver sea. Menza wondered what his folks were doing back home. Were they worried about him? Were they concerned that their loved one was living with an alien race on a distant planet, in some place called Ashmont, North Carolina. Menza didn't ponder the situation too long—there was work to be done.

Menza's first order of business was to get some breakfast. This project served a dual purpose—researching human behavior and filling his growling stomach. Menza was starving. Jim had mentioned a place called Dixieland Restaurant. It was located downtown and filled with locals. It sounded like the perfect spot to observe Earthlings feeding in their natural habitat.

Downtown Ashmont was only a ten-minute walk from his apartment. Joan had drawn a map for him, marking some historical sites along the way. One of them should be just around the corner—Ashmont War Memorial.

Menza made the turn onto Fayette Street. It was a short unpaved road that led to a cemetery. A huge granite wall stood in front of a graveyard scattered with tombstones of various shapes and sizes. Some looked to be at least two hundred years of age, others appeared to be more recent. Inscribed on the wall were hundreds of names.

Menza took a closer look. The first column on the wall was too old to make anything out. The second column wasn't much better, but in some places it was somewhat legible.

Gerald Adams 1839-1863
A life so short, but you're in our memories forever

Menza went to the next name that was readable.

Brent Prilliman 1835-1862
A proud defender of the Confederacy

Menza scanned the names on the third column.

Roy Jarrell 1929-1952
Korea took you from us
God took you to a better place

Menza quickly reviewed the remaining columns. It seemed to be nonstop death and misery and grief. Humans, many of them young kids, had died fighting in conflicts with such names as World War One, World War Two, Vietnam War, Afghan War and the Gulf Wars. The columns represented an almost continuous timeline of humans killing other humans.

Menza noticed there was enough space left for several more columns of dead soldiers. Backwards as this species were in many respects, Menza gave credit to their foresight. These Earthlings certainly knew how to plan ahead when it came to war. Settling disagreements through violence seemed to be their accepted solution.

Just as Menza turned to walk away, a name caught his eye. At the bottom of the last column was a freshly-carved engraving. Etched in bold capital letters it had grabbed his attention.

William Dixon 1987-2011
Our little pilot now flies in Heaven

Dixon was the name that Jim and Joan went by. Menza hoped it wasn't one of their loved ones.

Menza closed his eyes and said a short prayer, directed to whom or what he didn't really know, for the departed souls whose lives were ripped away by the horrors of war. He then turned and began making his way towards Dixieland Restaurant. Now, more than ever, he wanted to discover the driving force that made Earthlings behave as they did.

Menza almost walked right by it. The old sign in front of the restaurant was barely noticeable. It looked as if it could have been the original, which would have dated it back ninety years. It didn't matter. A place like this didn't require any signage. Dixieland Restaurant was an Ashmont institution, a gathering spot where grandparents would take their grandkids for their first chili-dog, a place where local politicians and business leaders would hash out deals as locals listened in from the next booth, a place where gossip was art.

Once a bit of information made its way into Dixieland it soon became public knowledge. For a fresh-faced curious alien from a distant galaxy it was a potential goldmine of information. It also posed risks. Menza couldn't afford to make any mistakes.

The door creaked as he walked in. The restaurant was packed with the breakfast regulars, along with a table of tourists who were visiting the local zoo. The place was humming with conversation, yet it seemed to gear down a tiny notch with Menza's appearance. It was if the locals instinctively knew when a stranger had entered.

Menza found the lone seat remaining at the counter. He smiled as he eased his way between two very large men. They had to weigh at least 300 pounds apiece. Menza had never seen such girth before. Novems rarely exceeded 170 pounds. Maybe these two guys had some sort of medical problem that caused obesity.

Menza took a quick glance around the restaurant. A couple of the other patrons had the same condition. Then he remembered a footnote from one of the IOS mission memorandums. Some Earthlings were prone to overeating, viewing food as recreation rather than sustenance.

Menza figured the best way to avoid suspicion was to go on the attack, be the aggressor. This crowd would undoubtedly begin inquiring about his background at some point, so why not go ahead and give them something to chew on. He might as well start with his two hefty counter-mates. Food seemed to be a suitable subject.

"Hey guys." Menza greeted each one with a friendly nod. Both men acknowledged him with a nod of their own. Menza immediately felt comfortable in their presence.

Menza turned to the older of the two. "This is my first time here. Any suggestions as to the menu?"

"Well, it depends on what you like."

The man's eyes seemed to light up as he spoke. Menza couldn't have posed a more appropriate question. Food was obviously something he took very seriously.

"You sure can't go wrong with a chili-dog, even for breakfast."

"You talked me into it. I always go with the local advice." Menza stuck out his hand.

"My name's Menza and I'm new in town. Thanks for your help."

"No problem. I'm always glad to hand out advice about our local cuisine. As you can see I'm somewhat of an expert in that field."

He grabbed a handful of his ample belly and gave it a playful shake.

"Kevin's my name. That's my nephew Brian on your other side. How do you like Ashmont so far?"

"I love it," answered Menza. "The people here are very friendly. I haven't been here long, but so far I'm quite impressed by your planet, er, umm, I mean your town."

The two men stared quizzically at Menza. He had done it again. Three minutes in the restaurant and he had already said something stupid.

"What will it be for you this morning, sweetie?"

A relieved Menza turned to the smiling waitress behind the counter. He could have hugged her for coming to his rescue.

"I'll have the chili-dog," said Menza. "My friend Kevin here says they're very good."

"Kevin's had a few, so he should know." She lightly tapped Kevin's arm. "We think we've got the best chili-dog in the county. Would you like some fries with that?"

"Sure—and a plodder to drink, please."

"What did you say, dear?" The waitress flashed her blue eyes at Menza. "What did you want to drink?"

Two critical bumbling mistakes in less than a minute! At this rate he wouldn't last a week on planet Earth, much less a year. It was time for another bailout.

"Water please. A glass of water, thank you."

"Oh, okay," the waitress replied. "For a moment there I thought you said something else. Okay, a chili-dog, fries and water coming right up."

The waitress walked away, Kevin and Brian were both wearing silent smiles. Menza knew he had aroused their curiosity. "I guess all that traveling has affected my speech a little bit. I just arrived from Russia yesterday."

"Russia!" exclaimed Kevin. "I've always wondered what Russia was like during the Cold War."

He stared patiently at Menza waiting for a response.

"Oh, the Cold War!" declared Menza.

Menza had no idea what a cold war was, but he did remember that Jim had told him Russia was very cold. He cleared his throat before continuing.

"The Cold War was cold—very very cold." He placed his arms over his chest and pretended to shiver.

"It was a tough battle, and a lot of people got very cold during the process. The cold fought valiantly, but warmth finally prevailed. We Russians were really happy when the ice began melting."

Kevin let out a burst of laughter. "That's one way to describe it. Actually that's a great allegorical summation of an important time in history. I think I'm gonna like you, Menza."

Menza smiled and nodded. He didn't know exactly what he had done, but he was grateful that his explanation of a cold war had been accepted.

"Ashmont is going to enjoy having you around," said Kevin. "Where are you living, Menza—near here?"

"Yes, very close to here. I've got an apartment over on Twain Drive. Jim and Joan Dixon manage it. They're very nice people."

"Oh yes," said Kevin. "Everyone loves them. Jim and Joan and their two sons...er...son...are well known around here."

Kevin looked down at the floor momentarily. There was a look of sadness about him. Menza made a mental note to himself—two sons? Jim and Joan had only mentioned one.

"Have you had a chance to meet crazy Truman yet?"

Menza turned to his left. Brian had been quiet until now, changing the subject.

"Yes, briefly. I heard he's a bit eccentric, but he was very nice to me."

"He's more than a little eccentric. He's crazy as a rabid bat."

"Oh yeah?" Menza leaned in closer to Brian. "What is it that makes him crazy?"

"Well, for one thing, nothing that happens in the world is ever an accident. According to Truman, it's all part of a vast conspiracy. Wars, terrorism, disease, even the weather— they're all staged by some powerful criminal group that rules the world. Now what kind of a nut is going to believe that stuff? Truman's latest theory tops them all—he thinks aliens from other planets are somehow involved."

"Hey Brian, don't forget the Moon." Kevin was smiling again.

"Oh yeah," said Brian. "Truman thinks the Moon is an artificial satellite and it's hollow inside—and get this, aliens live inside it! He says it's some sort of Noah's ark space station. It's no wonder Truman's been divorced three times. Maybe he should marry an alien next time. She might stay."

Brian and Kevin burst into laughter.

"Wow, he is out there." Menza pretended to be shocked that someone would think moons could be considered habitable. Actually he was shocked—that someone would think moons *weren't* livable locations. Heck, there had been activity on and inside Novem's moon for eons. It served many purposes. That's why the ancients had made it.

"Here you go, sweetie." Menza turned to see a gigantic plate filled with chili and french fries. The waitress skillfully cleared an area with one hand, placing Menza's meal on the counter with the other.

"Thank you so much. It looks great." Menza looked at the server and gazed into her bright blue eyes.

"I guess I'd better introduce myself since I'll probably become a regular here. My name's Menza."

"Well Menza, it's nice to meet you. My name's Betty, but it's Bet around here."

"Bet's got a nice ring to it. I like that name—and I really love your beautiful eyes."

"Oh thank you," said Bet, blushing ever so slightly. "I hope you do become a regular with compliments like that. Oh, and by the way, there is a hot dog hidden somewhere under all that chili. You just have to dig for it."

"Yeah, it is a lot of food," said Menza, "but it'll be fun trying to eat it all."

"Okay, gotta go. Got lots of customers waiting for their chow." In a flash Bet disappeared into the kitchen.

"That Bet's one of a kind," said Kevin. "She's been here over twenty years—only job she's ever had. This place would fall apart without her."

"Yes, she's very nice," said Menza, plowing away at his chili dog. He was surprised at how much he liked it.

"Well, we've gotta be going,' said Kevin, as he and Brian lifted their ample bodies off the tiny counter stools. "We'll be seeing you around."

"Okay," said Menza. "It was really nice to meet you both."

Menza watched Kevin and Brian squeeze through the small doorway before returning his attention to his chili dog. His mind raced as he ate. These simple beings that appeared to be an easy study had something else going on, something that played with their emotions, something that drove them from within, a curious sort of unpredictability about them. Earthlings weren't going to be easy to decipher.

Chapter 6

A BURNING IMPRESSION

She was the most beautiful female he had ever seen. Her eyes, her hair, her smile, even the way she walked—*everything* about her appealed to him. She was fantastic. Out of a pool of seven billion humans she just happened to be his next-door neighbor. How would he ever get any work done? At this point he couldn't decide if Marilyn was a blessing or a curse, but she sure as heck was a distraction.

Menza cracked the opening in the blinds a little wider. Marilyn was washing her car. She was wearing the shortest of shorts exposing her tanned legs, a well-worn loose fitting sweatshirt that displayed a peace logo, and a ridiculously large straw hat that flopped down over her pretty face. One arm was completely lathered in soapy foam all the way up to the shoulder. Everything about her was natural. She was an effortless work of art.

Marilyn walked around the car and began washing the passenger-side door, obstructing Menza's view. He squirmed to his left, his right, his left again—nothing but a glimpse of an elbow. Menza thought about walking away from the window. Should he really be doing this anyway? What right did he have to covertly watch his lovely neighbor wash her car?

Another torturous minute passed. Menza couldn't control himself any longer. She was just too pretty. If he stood on something he could look down over the top of the car and maybe see this magnificent Earthling that so captivated him. Menza grabbed a nearby chair and stood on it. Yes, this would definitely improve the viewing angle! He raised up on his tip-toes and strained his neck upwards. The higher he could get, the better the view of beautiful Marilyn. Menza pulled on one blade of the blinds—nothing, it wouldn't bend. He tried another blade and it also stubbornly refused to bend into place. Finally a third blade met with the same result. Menza's frustrations overcame him as he yanked on yet another blade, this time with force.

CRASH! BOOM! BANG! The blinds ripped completely off their hinges and fell on top of Menza's head. The chair slipped out from under him. Menza slid down the window in what felt like slow motion, wailing away with his arms and legs. Amazingly the glass didn't shatter, but the noise had been thunderous.

Menza looked out the window. With the blinds no longer a factor, he now had a totally unobstructed view of his subject. But Marilyn wasn't hiding behind the car anymore. She was looking directly at him. The noise had alerted her to her new neighbor's apartment. Menza looked at himself. He looked like a wannabe superman with the blinds that were now draped upon his shoulders. Marilyn began walking towards the window. How was he going to explain this one? This Earth stuff was starting to become a real chore.

"Are you okay?" Marilyn cupped her hands around her mouth so she could be heard through the window. Menza nodded to signal he was physically okay. He unlocked the side latch and opened the window.

"Are you okay?" Marilyn asked again.

"Yes, I'm fine. Just took a little spill, that's all."

"I'm glad that you're all right." Marilyn's eyes reflected the morning sun. "The noise was very loud. I thought you had broken the glass and fallen through the window."

"It was a little scary," said Menza. "You can bet the next time I decide to clean the blinds I'll be more careful."

"You must be a very clean person." Marilyn reached over and rubbed the blinds with her fingertips. "These blinds aren't even dirty."

Marilyn then blinked or winked. Menza didn't know for sure.

"Oh yes," answered Menza. "I've always been very hygienic. If I see a speck of dust I immediately go into a cleaning mode."

"That's great. It's unusual to see a man that's so concerned with cleanliness. They usually leave it for us females."

"It looks like you're doing a bit of cleaning yourself," said Menza, motioning towards Marilyn's car.

"Oh yes, Friday is my car washing day. I like to clean it up before I go into town."

"So you go into town every Friday?" asked Menza.

"Yeah, I usually meet some friends and we do something together. Actually, today we're gonna go to the zoo. I must have been there a dozen times, but I still enjoy going."

Marilyn pushed a lock of her blonde hair from her face. Menza tried not to stare at her. Her beauty was beyond description. JP's amatory warning never prepared him for anything like this. A crazy thought raced through his mind— maybe she would like to go back to Novem with him and become his wife. Menza mentally slapped himself on the face.

Daydreaming about impossibilities wasn't a productive use of time. He couldn't let a pretty blonde Earthling distract him from his assigned duties. He had to stay focused on his tasks.

"Menza, are you all right?" Marilyn's sweet voice complimented her beauty and inescapable charisma. Had this pretty human female placed some sort of magical spell on him? She seemed to be assaulting his senses with her hypnotizing charm.

"Yes, I'm fine." Menza snapped out of his trance. "I'm sorry. My mind was drifting a little bit. I've had a lot to think about lately with my move and all."

"I've got an idea!" exclaimed Marilyn. "Go to the zoo with me. You can enjoy yourself, meet my friends, and maybe clear your mind. It'll do you good. Come on!"

Menza thought for a moment. Why not? It would be a great opportunity to observe humans utilizing their leisure time. He would just have to make sure one particularly charming Earthling didn't divert him from his work.

"Okay! You talked me into it. When are you going?"

"I'll meet you at my car in five minutes," said Marilyn. "I've gotta change clothes real quick and I'll be ready. See you."

Menza watched as his pretty neighbor darted off inside her apartment. She sure was friendly towards him. He wondered—would she be so welcoming if she knew he was an alien from another galaxy? Under *no* circumstances could he ever tell a human who he was and what he was doing, but it didn't stop him from pondering the question.

Menza quickly washed his face and combed his hair. He walked outside. Marilyn was already standing by her car. Unbelievable! An on-time female was an anomaly regardless of what planet she originated from. Novem women had been known to stretch five minutes into an hour, an hour into a day, and a day could linger on for weeks. JP had once remarked that the one constant in the universe was a man waiting on a woman—but he also said it was worth it. This cute little Earthling must really be special if she was defying the laws of the universe.

"What kept you so long?" joked Marilyn, opening the passenger door.

"I didn't realize five minutes meant five minutes. Most women turn five into twenty."

Marilyn laughed. "Imagine that, a hygienic blind-cleaning man and an on-time woman living in the same apartment complex. What are the odds of that?" Marilyn ushered Menza into the front seat, closing the door behind him.

Menza watched her walk around the car. Marilyn had an easy confidence about her, an air of knowingness, and a covert sensuality that oozed from within.

Marilyn slipped into the driver's seat. "Oh my, I need to get some fuel. I'm completely empty."

Fuel? Menza was shocked that Earth-dwellers still needed fuel for their personal vehicles. He knew they were a planet behind the universal curve, but still using fuel for individual transportation needs was as primitive as it could get.

"That's okay," said Menza. "I'm sure you've budgeted a little emergency time for any unforeseen challenges, at least the minor ones."

"You already know me pretty well," Marilyn said as she pulled out into the street. "I do like to be prepared. There's a gas station right here at the next corner."

Marilyn eased into the gas station and expertly maneuvered her car in front of the pumps. "I'm gonna go in and pay. Do you mind pumping the gas?"

"Of course not," Menza casually replied, disguising his nervousness. He didn't know the first thing about pumping gas.

"Thanks. I'll be back in a few minutes."

Menza was churning with apprehension. Pump gas? Just the sound of it was scary. The thought of transferring an energy source from one location to another wasn't a pleasant one. How was this procedure done? What sort of safety issues were involved? What if something exploded? What if he blew up the whole planet!

Menza needed answers—and fast. Looking around he noticed a man standing beside a pickup truck. In his hand was a large cumbersome looking hose with a chunk of metal mounted at the end. Menza watched as the man inserted the unwieldy hose into an opening located in the back of the truck.

It looked easy enough. The man certainly wasn't concerned, as he was now petting his dog that shared his front seat. Clad in a set of worn coveralls and hauling gardening tools, he appeared to be a farmer. He continued to occupy himself with his dog as the fuel pump hummed away. If a simple Earthling farmer could pump gas with such ease, then surely an intellectually superior being from an advanced civilization should have no problem.

Menza confidently strolled towards his pump. He lifted up one of two hoses and pushed a button. Then he walked around to the back of Marilyn's car. Sure enough, as plain as day, was a receptacle staring him right in the face. Menza stuck the hose into the hole and latched the trigger down. Now he could hear the same humming noise that was coming from the farmer's pump. It was too easy.

Menza glanced over at the farmer. He was now cleaning one of his side mirrors, paying no attention whatsoever to his gas pump. Menza admired the casualness of it all. Volatile liquids were blasting through pipes everywhere, yet no one appeared concerned. Here was this farmer, surrounded by danger, and all he wanted to do was to wipe some dust from his mirror. It all seemed sort of cool.

Menza was feeling really good about himself. He too wanted to nonchalantly engage in some casual behavior despite the danger that lurked all around him. Showing off a little bit wouldn't hurt anything. Maybe pretty Marilyn would notice how much of a man-of-the-world he was.

Proud as a peacock, he ambled his way over to the farmer's truck. "Hi there, how's it going?"

The farmer looked up. "Everything's going well. Yourself?"

"It couldn't be better," said Menza, poking his chest out with pride. "Just putting a little of that highly flammable gasoline into my car. Not a big deal really."

"Is that your vehicle there?" The farmer pointed towards Marilyn's car.

"Yep, sure is," Menza replied, not even bothering to look back at the car. "I'm fueling her up to the top."

The farmer shook his head. "That's the first time I've ever seen anyone put fuel into the tailpipe. I ain't got much education, but it looks kinda dangerous to me with all that gasoline flooding the parking lot."

Menza looked back at the car. Fuel was spewing out the tailpipe. The area surrounding the car was soaked in gasoline. Menza went into panic mode.

Marilyn finished paying for the fuel and exited the store. Immediately she knew something was wrong.

"Menza! Menza! What are you doing!" Marilyn ran towards the car.

"Help! Your car overflowed! What do I do! How do I stop it! Help!" Menza was running back and forth behind the car with his hands in the air, splashing around in a puddle of gasoline.

Marilyn tromped through the gasoline to the back of the car. She yanked the hose from the tailpipe and turned off the pump. The fumes were overwhelming. She grabbed Menza by the collar of his shirt and dragged him away from the car. They walked to a vacant lot adjacent to the gas station.

"Marilyn, I'm so sorry," said Menza.

"It's okay…but what happened?" asked Marilyn. "Gasoline is everywhere."

"I think I put the fuel into the wrong hole. And it overflowed all over the place."

"Didn't you notice?" Marilyn was remarkably calm considering the situation.

Menza looked back at the gas station. "I was too busy making friends with the farmer. Now it's a big mess. I'm so sorry."

Marilyn put her hand on Menza's shoulder. "Accidents happen. But I'm curious—why did you try to put the gasoline in the wrong hole?"

"What happened is this." Menza cleared his throat. "My family in Russia owns a very old car. Those old Russian-built cars have their fuel tanks installed at the exact location where your tailpipe would be located. So I've spent my whole life putting fuel into that fuel tank, which, by the way, resembles the tailpipe on your car. So you see, it was an honest mistake due to cultural factors."

"Okay, Menza, now I understand," nodded Marilyn.

Menza did not like lying to such a sweet girl, but what were his other options? Tell her he was an extraterrestrial being from a faraway corner of the universe? Tell her he was from the planet Novem located a trillion time space arcs away? Tell her that he had never seen gasoline because he only rode in zeropoint bio-engineered spacecrafts made of material that matched his own DNA? Hadn't she had enough trauma already?

Menza took another look towards the station. The farmer had relocated further away from the danger zone, having moved his truck across the street. He was now in the parking lot of the local fast food restaurant, Burgers and Dogs. Menza could see him relaxing on a chair in the bed of his truck, calmly petting his dog and watching the action.

Nor was he alone. A crowd of nearly fifty people had gathered to watch the possible explosion of Harry's Gas & More. Word had spread like lightning that the new kid in town had tried to put gasoline in the tailpipe. The fool then left it unattended and it had flooded the whole area.

The news ripped through town, gaining embellishment along the way. Harry's Gas & More could blow at any time. The forty-year-old Ashmont landmark was one spark away from doom. The last time the town had seen this much action was the summer of '99. That was when young Tommy Monroe dipped into his daddy's bourbon and slammed his pickup truck through Hedge Hardware.

Burgers and Dogs quickly became the official disaster staging area. The parking lot was lined with ambulances, fire trucks, and other assorted emergency vehicles. Workers were scurrying about installing a makeshift medical tent and burn center. The mayor and city manager were on hand to provide leadership during the crisis.

The entire membership of Ashmont Women's Club had rushed in to comfort Pearl Moore. She and Harry had spent a lifetime at the gas station and now it was in danger of going up in smoke. Senior member Libby Hunt was especially emotional. Pearl Moore had been her best friend since childhood. She wanted to go choke the foolish idiot who was responsible for this horrible event. It took several ladies to physically restrain her from attacking Ashmont's newest resident.

The crowd swelled to nearly three hundred people. A television film crew had arrived on the scene at Burgers and Dogs. The local news anchorwoman, Rebecca Roddin, was interviewing the farmer who had witnessed the entire event. A helicopter flew overhead with a spotlight aimed directly on Menza—the center of attention. The unassuming alien from a distant galaxy who had hoped to remain anonymous had—in a matter of less than an hour—become Ashmont's most famous citizen.

Burgers and Dog's employees were not worried about the lurking danger. They were too busy. All the activity had stirred the local appetites. Hungry workers and bystanders were double-lined ordering hot dogs, hamburgers and soft drinks. The rumor that they all could be blown to bits in a massive gasoline explosion didn't seem to bother them. Burgers and Dog's manager, David Markson, had called in every employee in an effort to satisfy demand.

Two hours passed. After much deliberation the area was finally deemed safe enough for an inspection. An investigative crew was sent in. They discovered that nearly all the gasoline had evaporated from the spill zone. The danger was in the past. The whole situation had been blown out of proportion. As far as gas spills go, this had been a relatively minor one. Everyone could go home.

The crisis was officially declared resolved. Harry's Gas & More was reopened and back in business. Harry and Pearl Moore accepted Menza's sincere apology. He even had them laughing with a charming display of self deprecating humor.

The authorities interviewed the prime witnesses—the farmer, the owner of the vehicle involved—Marilyn, and finally, the instigator and primary subject responsible for the event—Menza, The officials agreed it was simply an act of ignorance, some said stupidity, and there was no malicious intent on his part. Menza was free to go.

Marilyn and Menza were the last to leave the scene. They wanted to make sure Harry and Pearl were adjusting okay after their traumatic experience. Menza did everything he could to put the couple at ease—cleaning up debris from the parking lot, sweeping the floors, even stocking some shelves in the store. After one last apology they both slipped into Marilyn's car.

Both of them immediately burst into laughter. They had barely spoken to each other during the ordeal. They had been too concerned with the situation at hand. Now they could finally take a deep breath and relax. The great gasoline fiasco was finally over. What a day it had been.

Marilyn started the car and perched both hands high on the steering wheel.

"Come on Menza. Let's go to the Jumping Cow. I need a drink!"

Chapter 7

THE JUMPING COW

Menza opened the door and they entered. The Cow was jumping. It was 5 o'clock on a Friday afternoon and the place was packed. Marilyn led the way as they eased through the crowd towards the bar.

Just as they reached the bar a couple left their seats. Marilyn quickly motioned to Menza and they slid into the overstuffed barstools. They felt extremely comfortable, especially after the day they had just been through.

"Truman—I'll have my usual," Marilyn practically yelled over Marshall Tucker's "Can't You See." Friday was the only day that Truman allowed loud music. He always said the primary purpose of a pub was for conversation, not screaming in each other's ears—unless, of course, one or more of those two-liter mugs of beer inspired him to break his own rule, which occasionally happened.

Truman grinned when he looked up and saw Marilyn.

"Hi sweetie, I heard you had a rough day. What'll the new kid have—not something with flames shooting out of it I hope. I'm just kidding you, Menza. Accidents happen."

Truman reached out and shook Menza's hand. "Where are you from?"

"I'm from Seattle, Washington," answered Menza without thinking.

Menza immediately realized the trap he had just laid for himself. Now he was officially from two different places—Russia and Seattle. He hoped the subject of where he was from would never come up at the wrong time. It would surely make for an awkward moment.

"We welcome you to Ashmont. How about a beer? I just brewed up a fresh batch of pale ale."

"That sounds good. I love those pale ales."

Menza was trying to sound confidant. He had never tried this particular liquid before. Novem didn't have beer.

"So what do you think?" asked Marilyn. "The Jumping Cow's quite a place, huh?"

"Yes, it sure is," Menza quickly scanned the bar. "Lots of happy people here, that's for certain. I can see why you like working here."

"I love working here, but I'm glad I'm on this side of the bar today." Marilyn smiled as she waved at a fellow bartender.

"I bet you are after what we went through today. I wouldn't want to be working right now."

"That's for sure," said Marilyn. "Wanna know how this place got its name? Bet you'll never guess."

"I have no idea why it's called the Jumping Cow," said Menza, shaking his head. "Go ahead and tell me."

Marilyn laughed. "It's actually quite funny. Truman writes songs as you might know already—most of them concern hard-to-believe conspiracy type stuff. He's always trying to expose world corruption, secret societies and such. I actually admire him for it. He also writes these simple little rhyming jingles for children."

Marilyn continued. "Anyway, this is what happened. Jim and Joan had another tenant a few years back—he lived in your apartment as a matter of fact—who thought Truman was completely bonkers. He made the comment that Truman would sell one of his silly songs when cows jumped over the Moon. Well, wouldn't you know—Truman actually sold one of those little jingles to a large food manufacturer. They used it to sell a popular kids' cereal. He took his proceeds and opened this place—The Jumping Cow. Kinda funny, huh?"

"Yes, a great story," said Menza. "That was probably embarrassing to the other guy. What happened to him?"

Marilyn lowered her voice. "Don't turn around, but you know what? He's a regular here. He's standing right behind us and looking at us now. John Sheaple is his name and he's a close-minded peabrain. He loves to argue. He's got it down to an art—whatever you are he ain't. He hasn't liked me since I turned him down for a date. You gotta have a personality for me to be interested and he ain't got one. He's not bad looking, but to go out with him—yuck!"

"Here you go. These are on the house." Truman plopped down two pints of beer.

"Oh Truman," purred Marilyn. "You didn't have to do that. Thank you so much."

"It's the least I can do for my best employee. Besides, you're gonna need a couple of beers. This crowd's gonna get on you good when they realize you're here. It ain't everyday somebody tries to set the town on fire."

"Yeah, you're probably right," said Marilyn. "Maybe you'd better get another one ready for us. This can be a tough bunch."

Truman laughed. "If they only knew what was really going on with this planet they wouldn't have time to worry about a silly accident. Governments are making hurricanes and earthquakes around the world and they make a big deal out of a little local gas spill."

"As crazy as that sounds you might be right," said Marilyn. "It seems everything you tell me turns out to be true after I research it."

"Well, you guys enjoy your beer. I gotta go. We're pretty busy here this afternoon."

"Cheers!" Marilyn picked up her glass and clinked it against Menza's. "Here's to friendship and love and peace on earth and the lack of a fire-setting spark today. Ashmont's still standing."

"I'll drink to that." Menza raised his glass and took a sip. It was wonderful—his senses welcomed the flavor. The liquid had a soft sweetness about it, yet seemed to bite back with a tinge of citrusy bitterness. Beer was an intriguing beverage that should exist on every planet—a superb product indeed. He took another long sip.

Then it hit him. A lightning bolt of energy surged through his body. He had found it! Genomel! It was in the beer. Someone's passion and joy and love for what they were doing had manifested inside this wonderful beverage. Menza felt a sense of relief like never before. He wished he could tell JP. There would be no more worrying about locating the life-sustaining genomel. As long as he drank Truman's beer he would survive. It was good that he liked the taste because beer had now become a necessity. The Jumping Cow and Truman's beers would be a daily ritual. Truman's beer was a lifesaver—literally.

"How ya doing? Who's ya new friend?" Menza felt a hand on his shoulder. It was John Sheaple, the guy Marilyn had pointed out earlier. He appeared to be somewhat intoxicated.

"Oh, hi John." Marilyn was trying to put on a friendly face. "This is Menza, my new neighbor. He just moved into your old apartment, of all places. How are you doing these days?"

"I couldn't be better since I moved out of that dumpy apartment complex. Two years there was two too many."

"I'm sorry you didn't like it. Menza and I both seem to enjoy it. So does Truman. And I personally feel that Jim and Joan keep it clean and well maintained."

John gave Menza a quick look-over and smirked. "Menza, huh? Sounds like Mensa—that organization of geniuses. That was a real genius move I heard you two pulled off earlier today. What are you trying to do, blow up Ashmont? And as far as Truman goes—I heard him talking that crazy stuff that our government makes hurricanes and earthquakes, so who really cares what a nutcase like that thinks."

"Truman's not crazy." Marilyn looked directly into John's eyes. "And please don't disrespect him in front of me because he's my friend. If this continues…"

"Hi John," interrupted Menza. "You're right about me. I don't claim to be smart and what I did today was quite stupid. But Truman is another story. He seems to be highly informed. Tell me—have you ever heard of a thing called weather warfare?"

"Weather warfare, what's that?" John seemed momentarily taken aback.

"That's what Truman was describing when he said hurricanes and earthquakes could be created and controlled, and by the way, that's not all. They can also make tsunamis, cause droughts, create floods, target lightning, you name it—they can probably do it. Weather warfare is just what it sounds like, using weather as a weapon of war, and the war is usually not a declared war. It's usually a secret war. It's the ultimate weapon because the perpetrators can say it's an act of nature, claim

God did it—anything except what it really is—a premeditated criminal act. John, would you like to know *how* they do it?"

Menza was on a roll. This John Sheaple fellow had irritated Marilyn with his disparaging comments. He would not stand for it. His Hammerhead Galaxy blood was beginning to warm up. Hammerheads, and Novems in particular, were universally known to be an even-tempered race, but on the rare occasions when they did become angry, it could be an explosion of emotional energy.

Menza decided to knock out his prey with superior intellect, despite the fact he had been specifically instructed not to expose his 800 IQ under any circumstances. It would be especially dangerous to reveal it at this early stage in the mission. To heck with it! This Sheaple character was going to be bombarded intellectually with universally accumulated data. By the time he got finished Sheaple's little brain would explode with weather warfare facts and technical terms. The IOS brass would probably never allow him on another mission after this. But it would be worth it to send head-in-the-sand Sheaple running away confused and intimidated.

"Hi John, can I get you another drink?" a voice rang out. It was Truman. Another second and Menza would have blown his cover wide open. He had been saved at the last moment.

"Sure, oh great songwriter. Go ahead." Sheaple seemed to be slurring his words a little bit.

Truman barely paid attention and started to walk away.

Sheaple continued with his drunken babble. "Before you do that, songwriter man who can't keep a wife, why don't you listen to Menza the genius. He's gonna tell us a little fairytale about how governments make hurricanes and earthquakes."

Truman turned back around. He was amazingly calm considering the circumstances. He leaned in close and began speaking.

"Let me tell you something, John. Weather warfare is no joke. Wanna know how it's done—with electromagnetic waves—among other things. There are several facilities spread out around the world that are capable of creating earthquakes, hurricanes, and so on. The enemy is you, me, and all of humanity, except for the criminal powers themselves. Their motive—keep us all in fear and distracted while they pursue a one world government."

Truman looked around and quickly scanned the bar. "Mr. Sheaple, would you like some examples of weather warfare? Let's start with the flood of '52 in England caused by military planes cloud-seeding the area days before. Hurricane Katrina—created, strengthened, and steered right into New Orleans. The big Pacific tsunami that ripped across Indonesia, Thailand, and other countries—absolutely manmade, you gotta wonder why the important military base Diego Garcia was prepped in advance on that one. The big quake in Iran striking where quakes never strike—think there's any political intrigue behind that one, huh? The Myanmar cyclone—funny how the US navy just happened to be running a long planned disaster relief exercise off the coast of Myanmar when that one hit. The media obeyed their masters and spun that one as ordered. The Haitian earthquake—same ole story, they're coincidently running a Haitian disaster drill in Miami the day before the quake. The military just happened to have planes loaded with pallets of supplies when the quake struck. Funny how the military's still there, huh? The Japanese quake ain't no different. They were running a drill there too. The big China quake—yep, created also. Don't think for a moment that the Chinese and the Russians aren't involved in all this. The granddaddy of them all will be the upcoming California quake. How do I know that one's coming—that's easy, FEMA told me. That's right, the *day before* the September 11, 2001 disaster—this was all reported in the Los Angeles Times by the way—the Federal Emergency Management Agency stated that they're preparing for three emergencies, a terror attack on New York City, a major hurricane hitting New Orleans, and a major quake striking California. You can bet that quake's coming soon. Here's one more thing for you to chew on regarding weather warfare. You know that great flood that the Bible and several other ancient texts mention so prominently—hummmm. Any questions, Mr. Sheaple?"

"Yes, I got a question. When you gonna stop talking and get that drink you promised me? Have your waitress bring it to my table if you don't mind. I'm tired of hanging out with all you crackpots."

John Sheaple then turned and walked back to his table. He pointed back at them and said something to his friends. They all erupted in laughter.

"I guess his friends are about as peabrained as he is," cracked Marilyn.

Truman laughed. "Yeah, they seem to be typical of the state of the world right now. All we can do is try to spread the truth. You two ready for another pint yet?"

"I think I will," replied Menza. "You make some fine beer."

"Me too," said Marilyn. "Thank you, Truman."

"My pleasure," said Truman. "Believe me, I'm glad to have you guys as allies in the information battle. And yes, Menza, I think I do brew up some good beer here. It's natural and unfiltered—keeps in all that yeasty vitamin B."

Truman hustled back to the beer taps to help his staff. The Jumping Cow was now standing room only. Some of the crowd was singing along to an old Jimmy Buffett tune. Everyone seemed to be in a festive mood.

"This is a really great place. Thanks for bringing me here." Menza looked over at Marilyn. He was once again struck by her natural beauty. Her charming personality sometimes made him forget just how attractive she really was. Not to mention her intellect—hiding behind that charming pretty face was a razor-sharp mind to match. She was one beautiful charismatic little Earthling girl.

"Oh, I knew you'd like it. Truman's got a great place. I didn't realize you two had so much in common. Both of you seem to be really aware of certain things going on in the world."

"Yeah," said Menza. "Some things I'm more tuned into than others I guess."

"You know what really amazes me? How a guy who puts fuel in a tailpipe can know so much about things like weather warfare. I hope me saying that doesn't bother you."

Menza looked at Marilyn. Their eyes momentarily locked.

"Marilyn, you could never say anything that would bother me. I could never get upset at such a pretty Earthling…er…I mean girl."

He had made another bumbler despite his genomel-enhanced state. Menza turned up his beer and took in a long gulp. This gave him valuable seconds to catch his cool. His mind raced through the situation. Maybe Marilyn had a point. How could a Novem possessing an 800 IQ continuously do and say stupid things? He needed to start being more careful. This intergalactic travel thing was no piece of cake.

"Oh, funny guy—you're not such a bad 'Earthling' your-self. I kinda like you."

Marilyn's sweet voice was reassuring. Menza relaxed again. Maybe it was the effects of the beer—or maybe it was simply spending an entire day with such a wonderful girl.

"So tell me," Marilyn continued, "what other interesting facts can you share with me about our world?"

"What do you want to know?" asked Menza.

"For starters—do you think there are other worlds out there? I mean real worlds with intelligent life."

Menza cringed inside. Of all the questions she could ask, it had to be this one. Maybe he should be honest and tell her everything—yes, there is life on other planets, and I'm one of them, an alien from outer space, down here to drink beer and chit chat with the natives for a while, take some notes, after which I'll jump back on my spaceship that travels at speeds so fast it bends time and space, arriving back on my nine-ringed silver-oceaned planet—naw, not a good idea.

"Intelligent life? That wouldn't be me after what happened today," quipped Menza, hoping to lighten up the subject.

"Oh Menza," laughed Marilyn. "You've joked around about Earthlings and such—really, what do you think? Do aliens exist?"

Marilyn was not going to let this one pass without some sort of an answer. Menza was going to have to commit one way or the other.

"Aliens, huh? Let me put it this way. There are zillions of galaxies with zillions upon zillions of solar systems with countless planets circling within them—and Earth is the sole source of life in the universe? I don't think so."

Marilyn lightly touched Menza's shoulder. He remembered something his wise grandmother had told him years ago back on Novem—you know a girl likes you when she touches you. This was definitely a good sign. Menza made a mental note to thank his grandmother when he got back home.

"That's what I thought you would say," said Marilyn. "I feel the same way. Sometimes I wish I could jump on a spaceship and zip away to another planet—one far away filled with nice people, fresh air, clean beautiful beaches, no war, no hate, no greed—just peace and love and all around niceness—and maybe a friendly pub where I can work."

"Now that would be my kind of planet." Menza smiled and thought to himself. That *was* his planet.

"Menza, I'm getting tired all of a sudden. I guess it's the beer on top of such an exciting day. Do you mind if we go home after this beer? There's always tomorrow. I'm bartending if you wanna drop by."

"Of course I don't mind. I'm kind of tired myself."

Menza glanced over at the lovely girl that had accompanied him all day. He pictured her sitting on one of Novem's spotless beaches, crystal clear sky overhead, watching the silver waves gently roll in—charming all the Novems with her big warm smile, bright green eyes, and a personality that could fit anywhere in the universe.

Chapter 8

SPRAYING THE SKIES

"They're spraying us pretty good this morning, huh, Menza?"

Truman was pointing up at the sky. His guitar dangled from his back. In his hand was a huge mug of coffee. He seemed to do all beverages in a big way.

Menza had slept great. He had needed it. Yesterday had been one heck of a day.

"What do you mean?" asked Menza, looking upwards.

"I'm talking about those darn chemtrails." Truman had a look of disgust as he took a sip from his enormous coffee cup.

Menza took a closer look at the sky. Two airplanes were flying high above. Thick white trails were pouring out from behind them. They were not normal vapor trails that quickly dissipated. These stayed in the sky much longer and turned into mushy clouds.

"Do you see them?" asked Truman. "They're spraying the whole world with that garbage and everyone is blind too it."

Menza knew exactly what they were. Chemtrails had been used on various primitive planets in the past. They had several purposes, none of which were beneficial to the populace affected. They were definitely bad news. Menza did not want to let on how much he knew about chemtrails—not yet anyway. He would let Truman do the talking for now.

"What exactly are they?" asked Menza, feigning ignorance.

Truman gathered his thoughts before speaking. "I'll tell you what I know is true, what I think is true, and what could possibly be true. One thing is certain—chemtrails are a weapon being used against the entire human population for evil purposes."

Truman pointed at the sky. "Menza, take a look at those planes. What do you see behind them?"

Menza looked upwards. "I see a white trail of what appears to be exhaust from the airplane's engines."

"Now look over there." Truman pointed to a patch of fuzzy clouds. "What do you see?"

"I see what appears to be clouds, but I've got a feeling you're going to tell me they're something else."

"It's really simple." Truman once again pointed towards the airplanes. "If you watch those trails, they will turn into that." He was now pointing at the clouds.

Truman continued. "The naysayers can't have it both ways. It's either a natural cloud or it came from an airplane— it can't be both. It would be obvious if they would take thirty minutes and watch the transformation."

"Who's doing it—and why?" asked Menza.

Truman took another sip of coffee. "The whole planet is being sprayed. That tells me one important thing. This is not a nation against nation program. This is much bigger—global in nature. Do you think China would allow another country to crisscross her skies dumping poison everywhere—of course not. Would Russia sit back while some foreign military scattered toxic chemicals all over her—no way. Is the good ole USA going to put up with an aerial chemical attack—fat chance. All the world powers are not only aware of it, but engaged in it. There is a relatively small group of people, beings, whatever—who work together to control the world. This chemtrail program is extremely important to them."

Menza was impressed by Truman's knowledge. "Okay, so we know a little about who is responsible for the chemtrails. Now—*why* are they doing it?"

"That's the wild card question," said Truman. "It's multi-purpose—that much we know for sure. I've got my own theory if you'd like to hear it."

"Absolutely," answered Menza.

Truman sighed. "Okay here it is. Remember this important fact—the lie is different at every level. Every step up the ladder of knowledge is lined with lies. It's a different lie for every stage of awareness. That's how they control us."

Truman looked upwards at the sky. "The biggest lie is always reserved for the masses, the ones who never question anything. Unfortunately this happens to be about ninety-five percent of the population. Chemtrails—they simply don't exist. That's been the official story for years. Boom, just like that—ninety-five percent of humanity needs no more convincing. It matters not that chemtrail planes fly over them on a daily basis. If the government says they don't exist, they don't exist. This massive group of people will always do as they're told. I could pee on them, tell them it's raining, and they'd believe it."

"That's one way of describing it," Menza chuckled.

"Now on to level two where they start dissecting the remaining five percent—this lie has to be a bit more believable. This is aimed at the first layer of official story nonbelievers, maybe two percent of the populace. They can see the planes spraying above, but they don't want to believe there is any evil intent involved. Through various information sources strategically inserted into the alternative news sources, the government convinces them, without actually admitting it, that the chemtrails are being introduced to fight global warming. Of course, the whole global warming-climate change scare is a total fraud, but it satisfies this bunch. They pride themselves on being more knowledgeable and less naïve than the masses."

Truman looked upward at the planes as he continued speaking.

"Level three—this one grabs another two percent. This group is herded off in the direction of weather control. There is some overlap here with the global warming bone they threw out earlier. As we both know, the government does indeed control the weather, and they probably utilize chemtrails along with their electromagnetic gadgets to modify the climate. The important point I'm trying to make here is this—this group is molded to believe the *primary* purpose of chemtrails is weather modification, regardless of whether it's used for good or evil. This group knows the government does some bad things, including spraying chemtrails, but they think the buck stops at weather control. They have no idea of the *real* purpose of the spraying.

"That leads me into level four—here's where the remaining one percent gets chopped up. Some people think population reduction is the primary purpose of chemtrails. They—let's call them the ruling elite for now—do make public statements calling for a reduced population, so there's most likely some validity there. I think it's entirely possible they'll eliminate as much as ninety percent of the human race at some point. They'll keep a few hundred million of us as slaves. There's no practicality in keeping more useless eaters than they need. 'Useless eaters' is the term they sometimes use for us. Slow poisoning through chemtrails would certainly help them attain their goal. So what do you think, Menza? Do you think I'm crazy yet?"

"Not at all, Truman. It all makes sense so far," said Menza.

Menza was thinking to himself that Truman was actually one of the most aware and sanest people on Earth, just as wise ole JP had predicted.

"Good," said Truman, "because here's where it really starts to get wild. Now I'm gonna tell you *what I think* are the primary purposes of those wicked white streaks above our heads. Number one—total and absolute mind control of the masses. I'm not sure how the chemtrails fit in with all of the other mind control traps they're using on us. I think it's possible that they are going to be used in coordination with all those low frequency microwave towers that are going up worldwide. Most people assume these towers are used exclusively for cell phones, but they're not.

"Now, Menza, I'm going to tell you what I think their number one motive is behind spraying us with chemtrails—to change our DNA structure. Yes, you heard correctly, manipulate the actual building blocks that make up our bodies."

"Can you give me more details?" asked Menza. "You've really got me curious now."

"Honestly, Menza—I don't know the answer. I can only speculate that it's linked to what some call our junk DNA. It seems that at some point in our genetic past someone or something 'unplugged' the majority of this material. I hold the view that this 'unplugged' DNA is what controls our psychic abilities, universal awareness, telepathic communication, that sort of stuff. They cannot, under any circumstances, allow us to regain these powers."

"So what you're telling me, Truman, if I understand correctly, is this is strictly a matter of control. Correct?"

"Bingo! Menza, you've just hit the nail on the head. Something has them running scared. I can sense it. I'm sure you've heard the term 'control freak.' The people running our lives are the ultimate control freaks. Their greatest fear is humanity escaping from their grasps. There's something within us, at the most cellular level, that's got them hustling to contain. They're either losing their grip on something or they're stepping something up, tightening the noose until it strangles us. Either scenario ain't good. What it all boils down to is a bunch of ruthless killers with unlimited resources playing with our DNA."

Menza nodded in agreement. He was amazed at Truman's insight. This Earthling, working on approximately twelve percent of his own mental capacity, was close to capturing the big picture—very close.

"Please continue," said Menza. "This is truly intriguing information."

Truman looked upwards at yet another airplane dispensing its misty cargo upon humanity. He held his gaze until the plane was completely out of sight. Finally he spoke.

"This chemtrail thing is the most important project they've got going on. Can you imagine how much it must cost to fly thousands of airplanes all over the world day and night? Remember now—these ain't tiny one-propeller cracker boxes they're flying—these are massive jets. The world's taxpayers are paying for the planes, the fuel, the pilots—unless the planes are remotely controlled, which is highly possible—and the poison they're dumping on us. You think the masses would be angry if they ever figure this out? They'd want to start stringing people up. Hey, Menza—wanna know why they'll never wake up to all this?"

"Of course I do," Menza answered quickly.

"Their cover-the-grid chemtrail conditioning program, that's why. This program is so organized, so subtle, so complete, so pervasive, so interlocked—that it scares the heck out of me. This actually worries me more than the chemtrails themselves. You know why—because the power and control needed to pull this off is mammoth, gigantic, colossal. There aren't enough adjectives in the English language to describe what's going on here."

"I'm listening," said Menza. "You've got the floor, Truman."

"Let's start by looking at the background for the television 'news' shows. It's all white streaks amongst a blue background. It prepares the viewers for the real chemtrails. It's on the local, national and international shows. Sometimes they'll shoot white steaks across the back even as they're delivering the so-called news. We can only imagine what they're doing to us on a subliminal basis.

"Now let's move on to rest of television. It's infiltrated with images of chemtrails, real ones and graphically-designed ones. They're everywhere. If you start paying attention you'll notice them on entertainment shows, sports programs, kid's shows—especially kid's shows! They gotta get them while they're young and impressionable. They've even taken classic movies and television shows from years back and *added chemtrails in them!* One example is The Sound of Music. Look at a copy that was manufactured years ago and compare it to a recent one. You'll see. Take a look at a few Gunsmoke episodes where they've added the trails.

"Advertisements are probably their most effective conditioning method. Generally speaking, the bigger the corporation, the more likely its advertisement will contain some sort of chemtrail conditioning within it. Start looking at television ads, magazine ads, billboards, even the packaging on your favorite food product. Some are subtle, some are in your face, but they're coming at you with a full frontal attack on your senses, especially the subconscious mind.

"Other methods include corporate logos, some of which have been revamped to include a chemtrail or two. Take a look at an old US twenty-dollar note and compare it to a new one—yep, chemtrailish clouds have been added over the White House. Since it worked with the money, they figured they might as well make up a few chemtrail-promoting postage stamps as well. If you look hard enough, you'll find them out there. Oh, and before I forget, look at the background when you open your computer every morning. White streaks will be greeting you."

Menza shook his head. He was as disgusted as Truman, maybe more so. He knew the terrible consequences of chemtrails, and how they could affect inhabitants of primitive planets. Aerosol campaigns, as they were sometimes termed, truly were tools of evil utilized by evil beings. Menza now had a personal interest in this particular primitive planet, especially two humans who were quickly becoming his friends. He wished he could whisk Truman and Marilyn away with him to the safe confines of Novem.

"Menza, I guess we gotta live with it for now, so let's have fun." Truman had shifted back into his normal upbeat personality.

"Yeah, you're right," said Menza. "We can't let fear control our lives."

"Come out to the Cow tonight. I got a seasonal beer I want you to taste. Have you ever had a bock beer?"

"No, not that I can remember," answered Menza. "I'll try to make it."

"Marilyn's bartending tonight," Truman said with a wink. "Maybe that'll inspire you."

"Good beer and a pretty bartender—Truman, you sure know how to reel in your customers. I'll be there."

"Okay, Menza, see you there. Oh, I almost forgot something. After our talk today, maybe you can add to this song I'm working on about chemtrails."

Truman fished inside the pockets of his weathered jeans and pulled out a crumpled piece of paper. He handed it to Menza.

"You're a smart kid. Give me another line or two. You might just hear our local band play it one Sunday night at The Cow. That would be Terry Tee and the Tornadoes."

"I'll do my best," said Menza. "See you tonight."

Truman then took off jogging. Menza watched him round the corner, guitar bouncing on his back and coffee cup still in hand.

Menza unfolded the crumpled paper.

MADMAN IN THE KITCHEN

I get up in the morning and I struggle to survive,
Trying to stay afloat in the rising tide
I bite my lip until the blood starts to flow,
I try to keep silent like I don't really know
People think I'm crazy when I speak my mind,
Truman's all baked in the bright sunshine
Well, they can talk all they want
And they can think what they may
But they're gonna find out that I'm right one day
Cause there's trouble a brewing
And it won't be long

They're gonna remember the lyrics to this ole song
There's a madman in the kitchen
He's acting real strange
There's a madman in the kitchen
Who's gone deranged
There's a madman in the kitchen
I think he's half drunk
There's a madman in the kitchen
Who's on the brink
The world's gone crazy and we don't even know
That we're sitting on a timebomb ready to blow
When the whip comes down it's gonna hurt real bad
Then they're gonna remember
What ole Truman said
But by then it's too late and the damage is done
They'll be nowhere to go—nowhere to run
There's a cloud of deceit that leads us astray
Herding us to the gallows
Where they can have their way
There's a madman in the kitchen
He's acting real strange
There's a madman in the kitchen
Who's gone deranged
There's a madman in the kitchen
I think he's half drunk
There's a madman in the kitchen
Who's on the brink

Chapter 9

FOOTBALL AND CONVERSATION

It was small town America on a Saturday night. Menza entered the Jumping Cow. He felt surprisingly comfortable. He felt like he had learned so much in a matter of days.

The bar was crowded, but the energy level was not as high as the night before. There were several faces he recognized from the previous evening. Menza made his way to the bar. He slipped in between a senior-aged lady and a young man.

"Menza!" an unmistakable voice called from behind the bar.

Marilyn literally ran over to Menza. She leaned over the bar and wrapped both her arms around him. Menza felt the warmth of her body against his.

"Truman told me you might make it in tonight. I'm so happy you made it."

Marilyn looked fabulous in her jeans and red pullover shirt. A sunflower was pinned on each side of her long blonde hair. There was not a hint of makeup on her face. She didn't need any.

"You look great, Marilyn. How are you?"

"Real good," said Marilyn, as she whirled around gracefully in a complete circle to allow a fellow worker to pass behind her. "I feel great, lots of energy. Can I get you a beer?"

"Yes, please. Truman was telling me today he had a seasonal beer on tap. Maybe I'll try that."

"Good choice," Marilyn chimed. "One pint of bock beer coming right up. Oh, let me introduce you to the lady sitting beside you. You'll have to speak kinda loud too her. Her hearing ain't so good. Don't let that fool you though. She's a retired history professor who's sharp as a tack."

"Luce." The lady didn't respond.

"Luce," Marilyn called out a bit louder. The lady still didn't hear her.

"Luce." Marilyn tapped the lady's hand. The lady turned and smiled.

"Luce, There's someone I want you to meet. His name is Menza. He lives next to me in one of Joan's apartments."

The lady turned her attention to Menza. She looked to be at least 80 years old, but she had zest in her eyes. Menza immediately liked her.

"Oh my!" declared Luce. "He's a handsome one. Marilyn, you had better keep your eye on him."

"Oh Luce!" roared Marilyn. "You're such a character. I'll get Menza's beer while you two get acquainted."

Marilyn bounced off towards the beer taps. Menza stuck out his hand and smiled.

"Thanks for the compliment, but there's plenty of better looking guys in here than me. I'm Menza and it's nice to meet you."

Luce grasped Menza's hand, holding it tight. "So you're in one of Joan's apartments, huh? Joan actually mentioned you to me. She's my best friend."

"Maybe I'm in trouble," joked Menza. "Did Joan give you all the dirt on me already?"

"No, no, no," Luce laughed. "She described you as being a character. That's a plus in my book. Joan and I go back a long way. Her sons and my grandsons practically grew up together."

"Yeah, Joan and Jim seem to be wonderful people," said Menza. "I'm curious, how many sons do they have?"

"I've got a sad answer for you on that one," Luce said solemnly. "William was killed over in Afghanistan fighting that fake war on terror that I so despise. He was a sweet wonderful kid. I miss him so much. Joan and Jim try to keep their pain private, but they'll never get over it. Alan's all they have left now."

"I'm so sorry to hear that," Menza said quietly. "I actually saw his gravesite the other day without realizing who it was. I feel so bad for Joan and Jim."

Luce tightened her grip on Menza's hand. He realized she had not let go of it since they began their conversation.

"You know who's to blame for William's death, don't you, Menza?" Luce gripped his hands even tighter.

"No. Who is to blame?"

"Our own government—or whoever's hijacked it." Her voice now had the vigor of a woman half her age. "That's who murdered William."

Menza was silent. Luce took the opportunity to continue.

"Menza, I don't know how much you know about politics, but I've learned a lot the last couple of years—thanks to Truman. This all started with the events that occurred on September 11, 2001. Three thousand people were murdered by our own government. Then they turned around and blamed it on some innocent Muslims. Immediately they go invade a few countries and strip us citizens of all of our freedoms—in the name of security, of course. 9/11 was an inside job. It's as simple as that. If they want to come here and haul away an 88-year-old woman for telling the truth, then they're welcome to do it. I'll be clawing at their eyeballs as they drag me away."

"Here's your beer, my friend." Menza looked up. It was Truman, smiling as usual.

"Marilyn's so busy she ordered me to take care of you. I guess she's the boss now."

Truman placed the beer in front of Menza. He immediately sensed the seriousness of the conversation.

"Lady Luce, is everything okay with you and Menza?" he asked.

"Yes, Truman, everything is okay. I'm just letting off some steam. I was explaining to Menza that our own government was responsible for 9/11, which ultimately led to William's death. But you know that better than anyone."

Luce took in a deep breath. It seemed to relax her. She was no ordinary 88-year-old woman. Menza liked her now more than ever.

"Yes," commented Truman, "9/11 was certainly an inside job. There's plenty of documentable evidence—bombs in the twin towers, the air defenses standing down, WTC 7 being brought down by demolition, the Pentagon plane hoax, the incredibly hard-to-believe official story of flight 93, the war games on that day that were designed to confuse, the forewarning clues they gave us through their Project for a New American Century, Osama Bin Laden's work with the CIA, the cover up—especially the bogus investigation. I could go on and on for hours with the evidence that proves 9/11 was an inside job. That was just another day at the office for the soulless beings that run our planet. False flag terrorism, where they pull off some horrible event and blame it on someone else, is one of their specialties."

"They also did that Oklahoma City bombing years ago," injected Luce. "Don't forget that one. It didn't seem to matter that they killed babies."

"Oh, there's a list a mile long of false flag events," said Truman. "9/11, Oklahoma City, the London 7/7 bombings with the government coincidently running drills where bombs go off at the exact time and place as the real thing—pure coincidence they say—yeah, right! That's about as believable as when I told my seventh-grade teacher my dog ate my homework."

"Don't forget Hitler," a voice interrupted. Menza turned to the young man sitting to his left. He looked to be around twenty years old. He was wearing a pair of jeans lined with gold stripes, the gaudiest purple jersey imaginable that read East Carolina University, and a gold baseball hat with an extra long purple brim. The hat displayed a logo of sorts—it was the head of a pirate clenching a sword between his teeth.

Truman reached out and shook the young man's hand. "How are you, Meier? I see you're ready for the big game. Let me introduce you two. This is Menza, my new neighbor. Menza, this is Meier, probably the biggest East Carolina football fan around, more so than me. That's pretty big."

"It's nice to meet you," said Menza, "I'm guessing your school colors are purple and gold—am I correct?"

"That's right," said a grinning Meier. "Tonight we're playing the North Carolina Tarheels—gonna stomp 'em too. Go Pirates!"

Menza knew nothing about football. Obviously it was some sort of sport Earthlings played. It must be important if it influenced seemingly intelligent people to dress up like clowns.

"Good luck," said Menza. "I don't really keep up with football, but now I'll be rooting for the Pirates. Your enthusiasm is contagious."

"You'd better be a Pirate fan if you're gonna sit near us tonight," said Truman.

He reached underneath the bar with both hands and brought up what had to be the biggest glass Menza had ever laid eyes upon. It had to contain at least three liters of beer. Truman could barely hold it with two hands. In the middle of the glass was the logo again—the Pirate's head brandishing a sword between his teeth. Truman lifted the glass up head-high and poured an enormous amount of the golden liquid into his mouth.

Truman set the glass back underneath the bar. "That glass is reserved for Pirate games—had it special-made. Once a Pirate, always a Pirate—right Meier?"

'That's right!" barked Meier. "I'm enjoying my senior year there, that's for sure. It ain't changed much since Truman attended there. When was that, Truman—back in the 1800's?"

"Oh, we got a comedian in the crowd tonight." Truman laughed. "I ain't that old. I bet I can still take you in a five-mile run."

"Actually, I'm sure you can," said Meier. "Everyone knows you're an egg white-steamed vegetable eating, five-mile-a-day jogging freak of nature—who drinks beer in a glass as big as a swimming pool."

"Don't go exposing my secret to everyone. The healthy eating and exercise is all a front—it's really the beer. That's enough talk about me. Meier, what were saying about Hitler?"

"Oh yeah," said Meier. "I don't know if you remember, but I actually learned this from you. You guys were just discussing false flag events. Do you remember when you told me that Hitler staged the murder of German soldiers and blamed it on the Poles. This provided him with an excuse to invade Poland."

"Oh yes, you're right about that," said Truman. "Throughout history governments have used these types of staged events to start wars. They know the public won't back a war unless they're provoked. There's a lot of evidence that suggests that the attack at Pearl Harbor was allowed to happen—it sure did get the people all fired up to go to war. Does anyone remember the Moscow apartment bombings in the late 90's? The Russian intelligence agencies were behind those. They blew up high rise apartments, blamed it on the Chechens, and promptly went to war with them."

"I've never heard about that one, but you're probably right" said Meier. "I know how much you research this stuff."

Truman nodded. "Sometimes I wish I didn't know about all this. You know—the ignorance is bliss thing. Unfortunately, this has been going on for a long time. Nero burned his own city of Rome so that he could blame it on the Christians. The USS Maine was blown up by the US government to blame on the Spanish. The assassination of Franz Ferdinand that started World War One was orchestrated by British and French intelligence services. The sinking of the Lusitania drug the US into that same war. The Japanese blew up their own railroad in the Manchurian incident so they could invade China. The burning of the Reichstag was staged by Hitler to blame on the communists. Operations Ajax, Gladio and Northwoods—all of those were false flag missions. The Gulf of Tonkin incident that pushed the US into the Vietnam conflict was entirely faked. The attack on the USS Liberty was an Israeli/American operation designed to justify US involvement in yet another war. One last thing about the World Trade Center towers—does anyone remember when they were bombed in 1993? That was an *admitted* FBI sting operation. How about that?"

Truman was silent for a moment before speaking again. "Okay guys—it's time for a little ignorant bliss—ain't nothing going to spoil the big game. The first Pirate touchdown gets everyone in the house a free drink."

Truman reached underneath and retrieved his beer. He took another long gulp.

"Hey Truman," said Meier. "Maybe after you leave I'll drink your beer and blame it on a Tarheel fan—sort of a beer false flag. Then we'll throw 'em all out of here."

"Ha," Truman laughed. "That won't work because I need them in here spending money. Besides, I'd quickly figure that one out. Only a Pirate fan is capable of drinking a beer as big as mine."

"You're right about that," said Meier. "Swashbuckling pirates ain't exactly got reputations for being teetotalers."

"I'll see you guys in a minute," said Truman. "I gotta go check on the kitchen real quick. Luce, do you need anything before I go?

"Thank you, Truman, but I'm fine. One glass of wine is enough for me. I'm a naturally feisty 88. You don't wanna see me a feisty and drunk 88. I might start a barroom brawl."

Truman laughed. "Luce, you're hilarious. Menza—how about you, need another beer?"

Menza nearly ordered another beer even though he was only halfway through his first one. The magical concoction that provided him with his life-sustaining genomel was not only nutritious—it was tasty.

"I'm okay for now," answered Menza, "but compliments to you on this bock beer. It's great."

"It's actually a favorite of mine. I'm glad you like it. Meier—you okay?"

"I'll be okay when the game starts. It looks like we'll have to watch golf for a while." Meier nodded towards the television above the bar.

"It's only ten more minutes," said Truman. "I guess ole Hunter Ward will have to entertain you until then."

Menza looked up at the television. A man was hitting a little white ball with a thin stick that had a fat head. The ball rolled onto an area with short grass, stopping just short of a white flag. Spectators stood up and cheered. The guy with the stick had apparently accomplished a virtuous deed. He acknowledged the adoring crowd with a wave of his hand. This seemed to silence his horde of fans. Not a sound was to be heard. Then the stick guy changed over to another stick and tapped the ball into a hole. Once again the crowd stood and applauded. The guy with the stick had obviously done something heroic in nature. Golf must be important to Earthlings.

"Everyone knows that Hunter is a great driver, but he's a pretty good putter too—huh, Menza?"

Menza had no idea what Meier was talking about. Golf did not exist on Novem. What the heck was a putter? Whatever—this was no time to appear uninformed.

"Yes," Menza declared confidently, "Hunter can putter very well. He's probably one of the best putterers in golf. Puttering ain't easy either. And you're right—we all know Hunter's one of the best drivers around. He really knows how to drive a car—and trucks too."

Meier was silent for a moment before bursting into laughter. "Menza, you've got quite the sense of humor. Driving cars and trucks—and puttering—you're funny!"

"Thank you," said Menza. "Golf is too serious. I like to keep things light."

"Maybe you're right," said Meier. "These golfers appear so uptight. Look at Hunter on television. You'd think he's a robot the way he acts sometimes."

"That's because he *is* a robot," a voice interrupted, "in a sense, anyway."

Truman was back.

"What do you mean, Truman," asked Meier, "about Hunter being a robot?"

"I've always kind of wondered about him for some reason, so I did a little research. I've been aware of MKULTRA for years—that's a CIA mind control program. Their human subjects, many of them from military backgrounds, are horribly traumatized, resulting in fractured minds and splintered personalities. A little background on Hunter—his father was a special operations intelligence officer in Vietnam. Hunter was programmed from birth, some would say sacrificed, to be a mind controlled super athlete. Most of the trauma-based programming occurred in underground military mind control centers. Does anyone else wonder how he managed to appear on a nationally televised program at the age of two? Suspiciously standing beside him while he hit golf balls was a well known actor who's rumored to have handled mind controlled subjects. Hunter's been controlled by handlers his entire life. Even his caddy during his formative years was a naval psychiatrist. I suspect they took him underground and reprogrammed him after his wife famously took a driver to his face. That entire incident was probably staged. The bottom line—Hunter is a mind controlled robot."

"Wow!" said Meier. "I had no idea. I just thought he was an intensely focused athlete. Mind controlled—unbelievable!"

"It gets worse, much worse," said Truman. "Hunter is a small brick in their wall of total control. The mind control program covers the grid. They want to completely suffocate our consciousness, snuff out all our critical thinking, and do it in such a way that we actually enjoy our servitude. It's brilliant madness on their part."

"That's some eye-opening information," said Meier, shaking his head. "I don't know how you keep from going crazy sometimes. This stuff is insane."

"This helps—temporary relief anyway." Truman once again lifted up his colossal glass of beer and turned it up.

Truman placed the glass back underneath the bar after taking in a long drink. Then he looked at the clock.

"It's Pirate time! Kickoff is two minutes away. Menza, you need to be wearing some Pirate garb. I'm gonna see what I can rustle up for you. You too, Luce. I'll be right back!"

"Now *he's* a character," said Luce, as she watched Truman trot off to his back office. "Truman's the one who got me started researching the 9/11 story. A lot of people think he's crazy, but I just adore him. He's not afraid to speak his mind. The world needs a lot more Trumans."

"I'll tell you what's amazing about Truman," said Meier. "His mind is like a sponge. It just soaks up information and filters out the trash. Sometimes he tells me things that are so wild, so far out, so unbelievable, that I would bet my life he's wrong. Then I research it, apply a little common sense, and it ends up being true."

Menza listened as the two of them discussed Truman. The man really was unique—and would be on any planet. His eyes were fixed on a distant star. He had an insatiable thirst for knowledge and truth. He was genuine and refreshing, a beacon of reality in a superficial world. Menza thought about his own life and how lucky he was. Fate was a funny thing. Who decided who was born where? Why were some granted life on a planet of peace and tranquility, while others were destined to spend their life in a place so tumultuously troubled. What if things were reversed—what if he was the trapped Earthling and Truman was the visiting Novem?

Chapter 10
JIMI WHO?

Menza looked at the clock—ten o'clock in the morning. He had not slept this late in years. It was after midnight when he left the Jumping Cow. It had been a fun night. The Pirates won the football game in an overtime thriller.

Menza personally did not witness anything thrilling about the game itself. Football was a difficult game to understand. He never could grasp the concept even with an 800 IQ. One group of oversized men would bunch up tight in a circle and discuss something. Another group of men would wait patiently a few yards away. Then both groups would gang up around an oblong leather ball. One guy would grab the ball and everyone would pile up on him. This would be repeated several times. Then the other group would take their turn grabbing the ball and running into a pile. This went on for nearly four hours.

Occasionally one player would show affection for another and slap him on the butt. This tender display of affection would temporarily boost the morale of the lucky guy who got his rear rubbed. With a freshly caressed butt he would sprint out upon the field with newfound energy and proceed to tell his teammates how good it felt.

Finally one of the guys wearing a purple shirt kicked the ball between two poles and it was over—or at least everyone thought so. Then someone noticed a yellow rag lying on the ground. One of the guys wearing a striped suit—he must have been on some sort of work release prison program—announced that a purple shirted player had done something wrong. Much discussion ensued. After twenty minutes it was decided that no rule had been broken after all. The Pirates were declared the winners.

Truman celebrated the victory by buying the house a round of drinks—and refilling his own tankard. Then he uncharacteristically cranked up the music and people started dancing. Menza was watching the show when someone suddenly grabbed him by the arm. Marilyn had just gotten off work and was ready to unwind. She literally dragged him out to the makeshift dance floor. The two of them danced for nearly an hour.

Menza felt right at home on the dance floor. Moving to the beat had always come easy to him. Novem was known throughout Hammerhead Galaxy as being a planet of song and dance. Several famous songwriters and musicians had hailed from Novem. Numerous solar systems had borrowed their rhythms. Singing, dancing and playing musical instruments was instilled in their souls.

Marilyn and Menza were the center of attention as they shuffled away on the dance floor. Menza burned up nervous energy that had accumulated since his arrival. He even showed off his triple-joint-boogie, along with a crowd pleasing double high-kick. Menza had not had this much fun since the night he celebrated the IOS announcement of this assignment. That night he had gone out to James Café and danced until the wee hours. At the time he was not aware that the celebrity owner would accompany him on his mission. Maybe fun loving JP enjoyed his celebratory style.

Marilyn drove the two of them back home shortly after midnight. Both of them were exhausted from the dancing. For over an hour they sat in her car talking and laughing like a couple of teenagers. They agreed to go hiking on Carpe Diem Mountain the next day. It was one of Marilyn's favorite places. Finally they decided to go back to their respective apartments. That's when he leaned over to give her a quick goodnight kiss that turned out to be not so quick. Another hour passed. Their intergalactic relationship was definitely heating up.

Marilyn would be knocking on his door soon to take him to the mountain. One thing he had learned about her was that she was always on time. Menza quickly showered and got dressed. Sure enough, right on schedule, he heard a light tap from outside. He opened the door. Marilyn jumped in his arms. She kissed him on the lips, bringing back pleasant memories from last night.

"Good morning, Menza. Feeling okay today?"

Marilyn looked great. Once again she was simply dressed. She was wearing jeans and a lightweight flannel shirt. On her feet was a sturdy pair of walking shoes. She was such a natural beauty that it didn't matter what she wore. Marilyn would look good in a burlap sack. Her bright cheerful smile would shine right through it.

"I'm feeling real good after that kiss," said Menza. "You look great."

"Look what I got!" Marilyn reached down beside the door and brought up a guitar.

The guitar was well worn. The wood was actually slick in certain places. The strings however appeared to be new. There appeared to be something written on it as well. This guitar had not been sitting around in some closet somewhere. It had been used.

"Truman just gave it to me. It's a little worn but I really like it. I mentioned last night that I was experimenting writing some lyrics and would like to put a little rhythm to them. I told him I was thinking about buying a guitar. Then a few minutes ago—this! Here, take a look."

Marilyn held out the guitar. Menza took it and looked it over. He gently rubbed a hand over the slick area. It felt good. It felt real. He carefully plucked one of the strings. A soulful pitch echoed through the doorway. The guitar might be old, but it was a source of spirit and emotion and passion. He could sense it. It had a special presence about it.

"That's a beautiful sound, Marilyn," said Menza, still examining the guitar. "There's no need to go out and buy a guitar when you've got this. This has character. Hey, look at this. This is a right-handed guitar. It's been restrung to be played upside-down by a left-hander. Is Truman left-handed?"

"Yes, and so am I!" exclaimed Marilyn. "No wonder Truman wanted me to use this guitar."

"You and Truman are lefties. So am I! All three of us are left-handed. I've heard we're smarter than the righties. On second thought, after that fire incident maybe we're not."

"I've heard we're more creative," said Marilyn. "Truman certainly is. What's that? What's written there? It looks like someone signed their name there."

Marilyn pointed to what appeared as illegible words on the guitar. They both leaned down for a closer look. It was indeed someone's signature.

"I see a M," said Marilyn, straining to decipher the name. "And an E, and what looks like a D. It looks like it says Jimi Hendrix! It can't be! He's a guitar legend. There's no way this can be real."

Menza did not hear the name clearly. It sounded like Timmy—Timmy Kendricks. Menza had never heard of Timmy Kendricks. He was obviously a very good guitar player. It was time to play along again.

"Timmy Kendricks!" shouted Menza. "No way! He's the greatest! Kendricks rules!"

Menza hoped he was not overdoing the theatrics, but he could not take any chances on this. Apparently everyone on Earth was supposed to know who Timmy Kendricks was. Menza was not going to be the only one on the planet who had never heard of him.

"What did you say?" asked Marilyn. "Did you say Timmy Kendricks?"

"Of course," declared a confidant Menza. "Everyone knows that Timmy Kendricks was the greatest guitar player to come out of the Milky Way."

"Oh Menza, There you go again with your wacky sense of humor. Timmy Kendricks and the Milky Way—where do you come up with this stuff?"

"I just pull it out of the universe I guess."

"Well, it sure is funny," said Marilyn. "But seriously, could this really be Jimi Hendrix's signature? Add the fact that this guitar has been modified to accommodate a left-hander, and Jimi Hendrix played the guitar left-handed—it sure makes things interesting."

"We'll have to ask Truman about this. Surely he'll know."

"Yeah, you're right,' said Marilyn. "I know it's a great guitar regardless. I think I'll take it with us to Carpe Diem. Maybe I'll play you a song at the top of the mountain. Ready to go?"

Menza was more than ready to go. It looked like he had escaped the Timmy Kendricks/Jimi Hendrix fiasco relatively unscathed. He did not want to stir up the pot again.

"Yeah baby," said Menza. "Let's go to the mountain."

Menza turned away to grab a bag he had packed for the trip. He was completely unaware that he had just called her baby. It had been so natural that it just flowed out. The affectionate label did not slip past Marilyn. She heard it loud and clear—and she liked it.

Chapter 11

LOVE ON THE MOUNTAIN

Welcome to Carpe Diem Mountain State Park—seize the day. Marilyn had parked directly in front of the sign. The two-hour ride had seemed like two minutes. They had not stopped talking since leaving Ashmont.

"Seize the day—Menza, do you know what that means?"

"I've got an idea," replied Menza, "but I would like to hear it from you."

Marilyn held both arms high, spreading them wide.

"It means we should make the most of life because our time on Earth is short. It means live each day as though it's the last because it very well could be. It means to enjoy the present. It means to be extraordinary. It means to live!"

Menza looked directly into Marilyn's eyes. "I guess that means I've been carpe dieming for the last twenty-four hours—because I've spent most of it with you. In my opinion that's living life to the fullest. There's nothing I would rather do than spend precious moments with you."

"Oh, Menza, that's so sweet." Marilyn pulled her legs out from beneath the steering wheel. She raised up on her knees and let herself fall into the passenger seat, enveloping Menza with her body. The two held each other tight for a long moment without speaking.

Finally they released their embrace. Marilyn crawled back over into the driver's seat. She reached over and grabbed Menza's hand.

"Menza, I've got something to tell you and I'm going to be direct. I'm crazy about you. I've been attracted to you since the day we met. I don't know what it is or how it happened or why—all I know is that you totally consume me. I've tried not to show it, but I can't hide it any longer. I'm sorry, but I just had to tell you. You make me crazy."

"Baby," whispered Menza, "it's been the same with me. I've been totally captivated since the moment I laid eyes on you. You're the most beautiful, the most charming, the most wonderful girl in the entire universe. I've tried to hide it also, but I probably didn't do such a good job of it."

"Oh Menza, you're making me crazy now. Come on, we'd better get going up the mountain or I don't know what's going to happen. Let's go!"

Marilyn grabbed a backpack from the back seat. She opened a cooler and removed two sandwiches she had prepared. She placed them inside her backpack along with a bottle of wine, a flashlight and a small blanket.

"Oh, I can't forget the guitar. I know it's bulky to be taking on a hike, but I want it."

Menza took a couple of items from his bag and transferred them into Marilyn's backpack. He slipped the pack over his shoulders and grabbed the guitar. The trailhead was straight ahead.

It was a two-mile hike to the top. The rocky terrain and the steep elevation gain made the trekking difficult at times. Menza was amazed at Marilyn's endurance. Not once did she appear to be breathing hard. At times he could barely keep up with her. She effortlessly marched up the steep incline all the while humming a tune.

Marilyn was very familiar with this particular trail. She knew all the interesting places to stop. There was a large hickory tree that had been struck by lightning. An owl had made it his home. Further up the trail and several yards off in the forest was a very active hornet's nest. Marilyn stood directly under it unfazed as the giant wasps whizzed by her head. Once she suddenly stopped in her tracks and motioned to remain quiet. A moment later three beautiful whitetail deer bounced out across the trail. Marilyn was a girl who was in tune with nature.

Neither of them spoke as they neared the top of the mountain. They were too busy admiring the beauty of the natural environment that surrounded them. As they turned a corner the summit came into view. They were almost there.

"Let's cut through here." Marilyn pointed towards a tiny path that veered into some thick brush. "There's a place I want to show you."

Menza acknowledged Marilyn with a nod. He followed her as she expertly peeled back a layer of brush. They slipped through and emerged into an open clearing.

"Oh my, Marilyn. It's incredible."

Menza was stunned by the raw beauty. The sunlight beamed in from the heavens like a spotlight. It lit upon a natural open area covered in bright green grass. The smell of honeysuckle filled the air. Standing in the middle of the clearing was a breathtakingly beautiful oak tree. Its enormous branches majestically draped the entire area. Wildflowers dotted the landscape with an array of colors. A butterfly darted past them. Nearby a gentle stream flowed before emptying itself into a small waterfall.

Marilyn walked out into the clearing and stood under the giant oak tree. A stream of sunlight reflected off her face. For a long moment she stared upwards in a trancelike state. She became one with the tree as it showered her with its grace and beauty. They were both feeding upon each other's energy. Chills ran through Menza's body as he witnessed the powerful connection taking place. The universe was speaking as two wonderments of nature melded together. Finally they each released their mystical hold on the other.

"She's a grand ole lady, don't you think? Some people say she's over 600 years old."

"Yes," replied Menza. "She's magical, just like you."

"Thank you," said Marilyn. "This is my favorite place in the whole world. Sometimes I come up here for hours and do nothing but think."

"I can see why," said Menza. "This place has a spiritual energy about it."

"Yes, it certainly does. Menza, why don't we spread out the blanket, eat our sandwiches, have some wine and relax. Does that sound good?"

"Real good—we're not going to find a better place than this. That's for sure."

Menza opened up the backpack. Together they laid out the blanket and prepared the sandwiches and wine. For over an hour they ate, drank and enjoyed conversation that touched on a variety of subjects. Marilyn picked up her guitar when the topic turned to music.

"I got a little song I've been working on. I've been humming it all day. Now that I've got a guitar I would like to try it out. Wanna hear it?"

"Of course I do," replied Menza. He leaned against the backpack.

"Okay, here it is."

Marilyn lightly strummed a couple of chords. The old guitar rang true. Menza could once again feel a special energy surround him. He could not believe his good fortune. To be lying under an ancient magical oak tree, full of joy and happiness, spending an enchanting afternoon with the girl of his dreams—it could not get any better than this.

Marilyn tapped her fingers on the wood above the strings. The guitar seemed to answer with an echo that bounced around the trees. She strummed a few chords, then a few more, until she established an easy rhythm. She closed her eyes as her left hand coaxed soul from the old guitar. She seemed to fall back into the trancelike zone where she was earlier. Then she spoke softly.

"This one's titled 'Love Song'—and it's for you, baby."

Her eyes still closed, she strummed one more chord. She seemed to be waiting for something. A tear rolled down her cheek. Then she began to purr out her lyrics.

I've tried so many times and I'm always looking,
But I can't ever find it no matter how hard I try
Every time it comes close I reach out to touch it,
But it disappears before my very eyes
I'm looking for that one, that's all I need,
Just one person with whom I can share my life
My dreams and my struggles and just getting by,
Someone to hold onto in the middle of the night
Love is so hard and never seems to last,
It's a passing affair that leaves a wounded heart
You get back on your feet and you try again,
You swim in your tears and make a new start
But I'm getting tired, tired of the game,
There's so many lies and so much deceit
It's all so futile cause it's never real,
It's like a dream where you wake

When you wanna sleep
I circle and spin in a world of pretend,
Where a smile's a disguise—a saving grace
But I can't erase the sadness of being alone,
I can't spin away the tears that mark my face
I'm trapped in a world of endless rain,
Searching for some sunshine to ease the pain
That one and only that'll beam through the night,
And burn up the blackness that blinds my sight
Somewhere there's a star that lights up my world,
Out there in the darkness there's one for me
A big ball of fire that burns from within,
The love of my life that will set me free
I'm looking for a love, a love all my own,
A lover like me who wants to belong
Belong to each other
And make our dreams come true,
I'm looking for a lover—a lover like you
So come to me please and share your heart,
Open it up and set it free
Let it run loose and see where it goes,
Let it run and run til it comes to me
I'm looking for a love that's true, so true,
I'm looking for a lover just like you
So kiss me baby and hold me tight,
Let's take a chance and make it right
I'm looking for a lover that's oh so true,
I'm looking for a lover just like you

Marilyn laid down her tear soaked guitar. Menza pulled her close and held her. He kissed her cheek, tasting the salty tears of raw emotion. They looked into each other's eyes. He wanted her. She wanted him. The late afternoon sunshine unleashed the beauty of her face. Each lay bare their soul to run free and their souls ran to each other. Lust and desire overcame them. Two beings from two different worlds came together as one. The incredible energy of love surrounded them as the rush came. They seized the day as the old oak tree watched approvingly from above.

Chapter 12
TRUMAN'S VIEW

Menza sat down at the bar. It was three o'clock in the afternoon. The Jumping Cow was patronized with a few regulars. He was starting to become somewhat of a regular himself. Why not—the girl of his dreams worked here—his best Earthling friend owned the place—and they brewed up a beverage that was tasty, made him feel giddy, and just happened to keep him alive.

Menza was still floating from the day before. Words could not describe the happiness that was bubbling inside him. Spending the day at Carpe Diem Mountain with Marilyn had been incredible. The connection they had developed was unbelievable. Her feelings for him were as strong as his for her. The comfort level between them was off the charts. Never had he felt so relaxed around a girl—on any planet. The physical connection they had was based in spirituality, but they also each possessed a raw animal attraction for each other. They probably could not turn it off if they wanted to— and they sure as heck did not want to. Being with Marilyn was just plain fun.

Marilyn was visiting her mother, who was having an especially difficult day. The cancer was consuming her and the pain was nearly unbearable. The narcotics did not seem to be helping much. Menza really felt sorry for the both of them. Marilyn truly loved her mother and it was extremely difficult to watch her deal with this situation. Even though it was her day off, she said she might come in later to see him. Menza certainly hoped so.

"Hey Menza—It's five o'clock somewhere, right?"

It was Truman showing off the personality which made him the consummate bar owner. He was always good for a cheerful one-liner, the prerequisite for any bartender.

"Yes, Truman, I guess it is. What's on tap today?"

"I've got a sweet-tasting brown ale you might like, nice and malty. Wanna try it?"

"Bring it on. You haven't let me down yet with those beers you brew. Hey Truman, I got a question for you."

"Oh yeah, what do you need to know?"

"You know that guitar that you gave Marilyn—was it really signed by that Hendrix guy?"

Truman smiled. "I was wondering when she would be asking me about that. As a matter of fact Jimi Hendrix owned that guitar—until he gave it to me. I was ten years old. It's a long story."

"Sounds interesting," said Menza. "I've got the time if you do."

"Sure, I've got time. This is what happened. Both of my parents have always been very musical. One day we're in a guitar shop because my dad is interested in buying one. They end up in the back with the owner looking at some guitar. So I'm kind of just hanging around looking at all the music stuff when a group of people walk in. They all had long hair and you know—the hippie look. Remember this was the late 60's.

One guy seemed to be the leader. He was this black guy, funny and full of charisma. I immediately took a liking to him. We started talking and he told me they were musicians on their way to New York. They were driving by and saw the guitar shop and thought they'd take a look. He picked up one of the guitars and started strumming it with his left hand. Then I *really* liked him. Up until that point I thought I was the only left-handed guitar player in the world.

"I started asking him all kinds of questions. Looking back on it, I was probably bugging him to death. I guess he figured the only way to shut me up was to entertain me. He pulled up two chairs and we sat down together. He had me hold the guitar and he showed me where to place my fingers on the strings. Then he held my left hand and guided it over the strings. Basically, he was giving me a guitar lesson. This goes on for about five minutes. Around this time my parents and the shop owner come wandering out from the back. My parents see me practically sitting in some guy's lap strumming a guitar. I turn around and tell them my friend was teaching me how to play guitar. They took one look at his face and their mouths dropped.

"That's when I learned my friend was Jimi Hendrix, possibly the world's greatest guitar player. It took several minutes for the shock to wear off. Jimi stayed for a while and graciously signed a few album covers for everyone. When it was time to leave he asked me to follow him out to their bus. Of course I did. He went inside the bus for a few moments. When he came back out he handed me a guitar. He asked me to hold it. Then he took out this big black marker and signed his name. Then he told me it was mine. There you have it— that's the story behind the guitar. I don't tell many people. Most of them wouldn't believe it anyway. The story's got kind of a sad ending though. A couple of years later I read that Jimi died over in London. I'll always remember him. It ain't everybody that gets a private lesson from the world's greatest guitar player."

"That's one interesting story," said Menza. "I'm sorry about him dying. I know that was tough. I'm curious—what made you give the guitar to Marilyn?"

"Jimi gave it to me. I learned how to play on it. I knew Marilyn had a genuine interest in learning how to play guitar. So I followed in Jimi's footsteps and gave it to her. I know she'll treat it with respect. I hope that one day she'll send it down the line to another. That's a special guitar and it was meant to be played. Jimi would be proud that it's being used instead of sitting in some museum collecting dust."

"You know what, Truman," said Menza, "I can tell you that Marilyn truly appreciates it. I can't wait to tell her the story behind it."

"Marilyn's been going through some trying times lately with her mother's illness. I thought I'd cheer her up a little. You two seem to be hitting it off pretty well, huh?"

"Yes," replied Meza sheepishly. "We went to Carpe Diem Mountain yesterday and had a really good time. I hope I see her in here today."

"You two deserve each other," said Truman. "Both of you are great people. Maybe you were meant for each other. Hey, you know what? If we keep talking it's really gonna be five o'clock before you get a beer. I'll be right back with that brown ale."

Truman headed towards the taps. What a nice guy he was. Who else would give away a guitar that was so valuable both monetarily and personally? Menza's mind flashed forward to the day that he would depart Earth. It would not be pleasant leaving his friend Truman. Then another thought shot into his mind—Marilyn! He would have to leave her too. In less than a year he would zip away to his tranquil home and leave both of them to fend for themselves on a dangerous and disorderly planet. There wasn't anything he could do about it. There was no way he could stay here. He did not want to stay here.

He couldn't take them with him—or could he? Of course he couldn't. Why would they want to go anyway? And bringing back foreigners on an official IOS mission—the brass would hang him from a rope for that. And what about the biocraft—it would have to be DNA modified to accommodate two humans, otherwise everyone is blown to smithereens. The whole idea was absurd. Menza decided he would not dwell on that depressing subject until the time came. For now he would do what he was supposed to do, gather data and information and transmit it back to the IOS. He would also try to enjoy himself during his stay on Earth.

"Here you go, Menza." Truman plopped down a pint of beer. "I got you a fresh malty brown ale. I hope you enjoy it."

"I will," said Menza. "It's not five o'clock yet. Maybe I'll just pretend it's a glass of milk."

"That's funny," said Truman. "I was just reading about milk this morning. Governments around the world are approving milk that comes from cloned cattle. They say it's perfectly safe to drink milk that originates from a cloned cow. Then they turn around and say no one is cloning cows. Now that might fly with the dumb downed public, but I don't buy it for a minute. I think this cloning thing is much bigger than they say."

"What do you mean?" asked Menza. "Can you expand on that?"

"Here's what I think is going on. The government and the whole military-industrial complex have been involved in cloning for decades—and I ain't talking only about animals. They share a few little tidbits with us here and there, like that tadpole they cloned in the 50's, the famous sheep they cloned several years back, along with a bunch of mice, monkeys, cats, dogs, horses and so on. Wanna know what they're *not* telling us?"

"You know I do," said Menza.

"There are underground biogenetic laboratories spread throughout the world where unbelievable things are going on. If you dig deep enough on the government's own websites you can find a surprising amount of information. Many of these hellholes, commonly referred to as deep underground science and engineering laboratories, or DUSEL, are doing a lot more than innocently cloning a tadpole. You'd better take a good long drink on that beer if you want to hear the rest of the story."

Menza did exactly as Truman suggested. He turned up his glass and drained a quarter of the glass. Menza knew exactly what was coming next and it was not going to be pretty. Underground laboratories were prevalent throughout the universe and some nasty stuff was definitely taking place within them. Truman was a master at researching and using his instincts to decipher the cold hard truth. He knew as much as anyone about what was really taking place on his home planet—a planet that was obviously lost and out of control.

Truman watched as Menza picked up his glass and took another long sip. He motioned and caught the attention of the pretty brunette working with him behind the bar.

"Amy, would you please bring us a couple of brown ales over here."

"Are you thirsty?" teased Truman. "That's either some very good beer or some very bad news."

"It's both," answered Menza. "The beer is excellent and the secret underground stuff is shocking. I've done a little research myself."

"Shocking is right," said Truman. "There are some horrendous experiments going on. They obviously consider secrecy a high priority, but occasionally someone will speak out. It's usually someone who has worked in one of these labs. Many times it's a researcher or scientist with a conscience who realizes everything is upside down. They discover that their research is being used to hurt humanity instead of benefiting the planet. They find out that the people running the show are only interested in power and control."

"What's actually going on down there in those labs?" asked Menza.

"It's a bizarre biogenetic playground," said Truman. "These guys are way past Tadpole 101. That's the aboveground stuff. Most of the laboratories are several layers deep. Security gets tougher with each passing level. Once you get down to some of the lower levels it gets crazy. They've got multi-legged creatures that look like human/octopus hybrids—and maybe they are. There are mice and fish and reptiles that seem to be a mix of all three species. They've got rabbit-like critters that mimic human words. They have cages that contain human children with large wings, gargoyle-type beings that are chained down, grotesque bat-like creatures that are five feet tall. There are rows of humans and human mixtures in cold storage, along with embryo storage vats containing humanoids in various stages of development. There are also humans in cages that have been drugged. These are the future experimental fodder. Tell me, Menza—are you now going to join the Truman-is-crazy club?"

Menza was amazed. Once again Truman was nailing the truth. If anything he was treading lightly. Menza had knowledge of underground bases on other primitive planets in various solar systems. These were the type of things that were actually happening—and more.

"I wish it was that easy," said Menza. "But you know what—it matches what research I've done on the subject. Who's responsible for this? Who's actually running the show?"

"It's the usual suspects. You know—the group that's looking to bring in a global government. Research some of those well-funded genome projects when you get a chance. They sugar coat their objectives, but if you read between the lines you'll find some foul motives.

"Milk," said Menza. "All this started because I mentioned the word milk. I guess I should have kept the conversation on beer—huh, Truman?".

"You should know by now that any conversation with me can turn dangerous. So Menza, do you have a question about brewing beer?"

"No Truman, I was just joking. Actually I want to learn some more about these clandestine underground operations. Where are they located?"

"They're scattered all over the world," replied Truman. "Some of them are massive. It's rumored that there's a large underground city directly underneath Denver airport. I'd bet there's hundreds of them worldwide. I've heard they're also beneath the sea. Many of them are interconnected by electromagnetic high speed trains that are faster than jet airplanes. The tunnels are produced by nuclear-tipped boring machines that melt rock. There are also some weird happenings surrounding the poles at each end of the earth. Some say they're actually entrances that lead into a hollow earth. I gotta say it wouldn't surprise me. I know this sounds wild to the average person. I just wish they would take ten minutes to research it on the internet—while we still have one that contains some truth. That's an entirely different can of worms that we don't have time to open up now."

"I've got another question about these labs," said Menza. "The humans that are down there—who's bringing them in and and how do they get them?"

"Government agencies mostly," replied Truman. "The CIA, FBI, United Nations, Russian intelligence, European Union operatives, the list runs a snaky gamut around the globe—they operate within their secret black budgets for most of these abominable acts. Of course these agencies utilize their corporate partners and criminal contacts and any other sicko that can get the dirty job done. A 'charity organization' was caught a few years back with over 100 African children sitting on a plane waiting to be flown to God knows where. It's happening every day and rarely do these powerful psychopaths get caught. They're smart and they're brutally coldhearted and they have unlimited resources. It's all a game to them."

"You know," said Menza, "it's too bad someone doesn't come out and expose all of this barbaric activity that's taking place."

"It takes courage," said Truman. "What happens is this— these scientists and researchers start out naively thinking they're working for the betterment of mankind. Then they realize that these new technologies are being used to wage wars, create diseases and epidemics, cause droughts and famines, promote eugenics and sterility programs—and on and on. Over the last decade or two a significant number of microbiologists have died mysteriously. I think many of these were going to speak out, or maybe they were just killed because they were all used up and were nothing but a liability. Then it becomes a cold business decision to eliminate them. That's how these ruthless animals think. Hey Menza— quick—look at the TV."

Truman pointed upwards at the soundless television. On the screen was a well dressed man standing in front of a group of people. They appeared to be asking him questions.

"There's our fearless leader," Truman said sarcastically. "That's our puppet president doing exactly what the powers tell him to do. People think he's running this country. Ha! He doesn't tie his shoes without permission. I wouldn't be surprised if he's not a clone—seriously. I heard a rumor that every important head of state has been cloned. It makes sense to have a few backups if you look at from their twisted perspective. You also gotta wonder about some of these bubble headed film stars, entertainers and athletes. They're a big influence on us, especially the youth. I don't know if they're clones or synthetic robots or just heavily mind controlled, but I know something's going on."

"Wow," remarked Menza. "You seem to be aware of so much—and you openly spread your knowledge. Truman, do you ever get scared? You and I both know that the people you're trying to expose are merciless murderers. Are you ever concerned that they might come after you?"

Truman shut down like Menza had never seen before. His eyes became dark and distant. Menza thought he noticed his hand tremble slightly. His face became pale and blank. Menza had obviously struck a nerve that made his friend very uncomfortable.

"Excuse me for a moment," Truman said in a solemn tone.

Menza watched as Truman walked to the far end of the bar. He reached high above to the top shelf and retrieved a large beer stein. He strolled over to the taps and slowly poured himself two liters of beer. He turned it up and drank for what seemed an eternity. Then he placed the stein on a ledge and walked back to Menza.

"Is it five o'clock yet?" he cracked.

At least he still had his customary humor. Menza was glad to see that. Truman handed Menza a folded piece of paper without telling him what it was. Truman then looked him in the eyes and began speaking.

"Menza, I'm going to tell you something and I don't want you to repeat this to anyone—except maybe Marilyn. Over the last year I've been pitching my conspiracy songs trying to find an artist to take them on. I've sent them out to some pretty important players and agents in the business—a lot of Hollywood and Nashville types. I'm sure that's also drawn attention that I didn't really want. For the past six months I've been noticing little things going on. Things like strange noises on my phone, unusual computer glitches, weird things with some of my text messages, a couple of low flying helicopters, that kind of stuff. One time I came home and someone had moved some of my clothes from my bedroom closet to the hall closet.

"I know who's doing it. It's *them*. It became more serious last Tuesday. I'm an early riser as you know. Early last Tuesday morning I walked out of my apartment to go jogging. There was an army-style duffel bag lying in my front yard. I found that to be very strange. I went over and opened it up. Inside was a large dog—dead."

There was a long moment of silence before Truman continued.

"Menza—they're not going to shut me up—and I'm not stupid. This was a major warning and I'm well aware of it. I know they can take me out any time they choose. They have assassination squads that get in and out and leave no trail. Most likely I'd be 'suicided.' They have heart attack weapons and laser guns and who knows what else—things the average person could not fathom in a million years. The bottom line is

I'm stubborn and hardheaded and I might pay the price with my life. I guess I'd rather die on my feet than live on my knees. And yes—I'm scared as hell."

"Truman, I don't know what to say," said Menza. "On one hand I want to tell you to stop everything because I worry about your safety. The other part of me wants you to keep fighting and exposing these evil people. Just remember that you can always ask for my help. Okay?"

"Okay, Menza," replied Truman. "I know we've only known each other for a brief time, but I want you to know I consider you a friend. Thanks. I've gotta go do a couple of things. I'll talk to you later."

Menza was torn. His friend was definitely living on the edge. Powerful people were sending him signals to ease up. If he stopped exposing them they would probably go away. That would be the easy way out. But where would that leave Truman? He would be a shell of the man he is now. Menza tried to picture Truman playing it safe and going along with the corrupt broken system he so despised. There was no way that was going to happen. Truman was going to fight until his last breath. Menza remembered something that JP had said— he was going to go down swinging. That characterized Truman perfectly. He was blessed with intelligence and an ability to put together all the pieces of a puzzled planet. The blessing could also be a curse. Truman was a courageous man fighting for humanity even though most of humanity ridiculed him for it.

Menza still held the piece of paper Truman had given him earlier. He knew exactly what it was. He unfolded it.

THE REBEL IN ME

I don't beg and I don't steal,
I ain't got a lot but at least I'm real
I'm an easy going soul, that's plain to see,
But it's a laid back disguise for the rebel in me
Guts and pride is about all I got,
Nobody but me calls my shots
When you gamble to win, you lose a few,
But I'm gonna do what I'm gonna do
So mind your own business—get outta my way,
Say it to my face if you got something to say
I live simple, I live free,
You'd best not bring out the rebel in me
The rebel in me, the rebel in me,
The rebel in me you don't wanna see
You don't wanna bring out the rebel in me,
Best not bring out the rebel in me
Fittin' in ain't easy—ain't easy for me,
But I gotta survive, gotta be free
Don't tell me what to do, don't tell me who to be,
There ain't no changing the rebel in me
I'm a screw loose original—they broke the mold,
For better or worse, I don't do as I'm told
If you're afraid to look you'll never see,
Ain't no cookie cutter world gonna crumble on me
The rebel in me, the rebel in me,
The rebel in me you don't wanna see
You don't wanna bring out the rebel in me,
Best not bring out the rebel in me

Everybody's want'n to right my wrongs,
It's the price I pay for not playing along
Well the way I see it, you only got one life,
So don't come around here giving me advice
I don't take no crap, I do as I please,
You're playing with fire when you play with me
The rebel in me, the rebel in me,
The rebel in me you don't wanna see
You don't wanna bring out the rebel in me
Best not bring out the rebel in me

Chapter 13
REPORT TO THE BOSS 1

MG/IOS/HG FACILITY—Report 001
Intel/Analysis of Celestial Unit MWG91177-3
(GLC MWK/F-O-L-L-Y)
Prepared/Submitted by MNZA-9716
(HG-131313-8)
Transmitted to the Ministry of Governance
Intergalactic Open Society—25/22/4422/HG

Accumulated Intelligence Summary:

MNZA-9716 reporting from MWG91177-3. A lot has happened in a short time. That is why I felt the need to issue this early transmission. I have a message I hope you'll pass on before I delve into the absorbing traits of Earthlings. Please inform my mother that I have already found a genomel source. I know she worries about me. Tell her that I won't perish on some distant planet. My genomel comes from a delightful beverage known to the locals as beer. Not only does it provide vital nourishment, but it also leaves you with a funny feeling in your head. I kind of like it. I will try to bring back a few bottles when I return.

Now—on to the humans, as they call themselves. At first glance they appear to be simple creatures. While it is true that their intelligence level is quite low they make up for it in other areas. They are an industrious species. Most of them are hardworking and report to a job several days a week. They are highly capable of performing quite complicated tasks. They are not, however, adept at any form of critical thinking. They only want to know the "how" of matters, not the "why." In this way they resemble another species that is prevalent on many planets throughout the universe—sheep. The average human is very gullible, extremely naïve and easily misled. One enlightened human that I met down here described his fellow beings this way. He said that he could pee on them and tell them it was raining and they would believe it. That seems to be the case. Humans fail to see the obvious, although they're capable of rattling off trivial details about matters that interest them. They appear to be extremely interested in the private lives of entertainers, athletes and other assorted celebrities. They know who's dating who and what flavor of ice cream they prefer. Yet if you ask them a question of importance they answer with a blank stare. Like their chromosomal cousin the sheep, humans have a non-questioning herd mentality. This significant defect could eventually lead to their demise.

Humans love television. They herd up in front of one at every opportunity. In no way whatsoever does it hold any educational value. Fifty percent of the airtime is dedicated to subliminal-laden advertising. Humans are mesmerized by the flickering screen that typically displays a scantily clad woman pitching some worthless product. As bad as that sounds, the scheduled programming is even worse. So far I have seen an athletic contest where armored men pile up on each other at regular three minute intervals, game shows where the contestants act like fools after winning a cheap washing machine, and staged talk shows where illiterates throw chairs at each other. The mainstay bread and butter of these less-than-creative broadcasters is the sexy cop show. On any given day there are countless sexy cop shows that all contain the same plot—a sexy female cop with a gun and a sexy male cop with a gun and a criminal that gets caught by sexy gun-toting cops. Their so called prime time programming really takes the stupidity cake. They telecast something they describe as a situational comedy. On these shows canned laughter is provided to the viewer to remind them that the comedy is supposed to be funny. Millions of humans actually laugh at this stuff. I thought we were eight times more intelligent than they are—not eight hundred.

In actuality I'm probably not being fair. The masses are being controlled. By who or what I'm not exactly sure at this point. I've got my suspicions. My next report should provide some details for you. The one thing I am certain of is that most humans are generous and loving beings. They are loyal, kind, and they can knock you silly with their emotions. They also love music. I've actually made two friends already. One is the enlightened guy I mentioned earlier. His name is Truman. Truly informed humans seem to be at a premium down here. He's a lifesaver when I have the need for intelligent conversation. As a matter of fact, he is literally a lifesaver. He's the chap who introduced me to beer—my sole source of genomel. How can I not be forever grateful for that?

My next friend deserves a paragraph of her own. Her name is Marilyn. Let me tell you up front that she and I are involved romantically. Don't worry—I promise I won't be distracted from my mission. Marilyn is absolutely beautiful in every respect. Before I forget—tell JP in your next correspondence with him that he was right. Earth girls are stunning! While you're at it, tell him to send me a quick transmission. I'd love to hear of his adventures on the Milky Way's station. Okay, back to the girl. The last thing I was looking for down here was a girlfriend. You all know me well—I take my work very seriously. Just consider her as part of my job. I promise I will analyze her thoroughly—ha! I'd also like to ask a favor from you. I've met most of you there at the IOS office. It might be best if you don't tell Julie about my love interest down here. For those of you who may not know her, she's the brunette who works in the galactic data department. She's always kind of had the hots for me and it might disappoint her.

My first few days down here have been very productive. I've faced a few challenges but I managed to get past them. There was one incident where I nearly set a gas station on fire and the whole town wanted to kill me. I eventually got them all calmed down. Early on I found myself making some comments that landed me in trouble. I ended up having to tell some of the folks that I hail from Russia, others have been fed the Seattle story. I'm praying that it doesn't backfire on me. Another time I had to bail myself out after mentioning something about plodders. They don't drink those here. Everyone makes mistakes. I think I'm over it now. I fully realize where I am and where I'm not. Another JP relay if you don't mind. Tell him when he picks me up down here to please find a new landing spot. The last one was covered in cow poop.

Let me move on to some stuff of a more serious nature. Weather weapons are commonly used on this planet. Earthquakes, hurricanes and plasma beams (which they call lightning) are used politically against the masses. Virtually no one is aware that they can be artificially produced. I'm hoping that the general public will wake up to all this. Then these terrible weapons will lose some of their effectiveness. As of now they're convinced these are naturally occurring events.

Many of you are aware of the bio-geo-engineering spraying projects that are taking place in various solar systems. Unfortunately this is occurring here. The entire planet is being sprayed on a daily basis. The handful of earthlings who are aware of this know them as chemtrails. Chemtrails and the secrecy that surrounds them are *extremely* important to the controllers of the planet. The program is multi-purposed. The primary goal appears to be total and absolute control of the populace's minds. The chemtrails work in combination with electromagnetic systems strategically located around the globe. In a nutshell the controllers want to reduce the population dramatically, and transform the remaining humans into robotic slaves. They want to control their every thought. The masses cannot see the obvious poisonous trails in the sky due to the conditioning program. The conditioning is an unrestrained across-the-grid attack. In every form of media and communication there are images of chemtrails. I can only imagine what they're getting blasted with on the subliminal front.

The oldest trick in the universe is routinely utilized on Earth—killing your own people and blaming someone else. False flag terrorism events have occurred in major cities around the globe. New York City, London, Madrid, Moscow—these are just a few examples. Probably the most spectacular and politicized false flag attack occurred in the United States on September 11, 2001. This event was planned years in advance by intelligence agencies from several different countries. A group of humans termed "Muslims" were falsely held responsible. The controllers created and currently manage a group of intelligence operatives they term "Al-

Qaeda." This group is the primary patsy blamed for the controller's atrocities.

The controllers have accessed the planet's interior. They have underground laboratories where they perform biogenetic experimentation. Much of this experimentation involves kidnapped humans. Cloning of humans is prevalent. The controllers also have massive underground cities that are connected by tunnels. Transportation is provided through high speed magnetic trains. Most humans are not aware that their planet is but a shell with a cavernous interior. The northern and southern entranceways are fiercely protected by the controllers. The controllers' controlled scientists tell the masses their planet is solid with a molten fiery center. They even tell them they know the approximate temperature. What did they do—send a guy down there in a fire suit with a thermometer and raise up his charred body along with the thermometer? Yeah, right! There is a lot the controller's are hiding on this one. A whole lot.

Well, that's it for now. Tell mom I'm doing well and I miss her. Tell JP I'm working on accumulating some travel tales, but in no way do I ever expect them to top his. Carma— I know you're going to be reading this report because nothing escapes you. I really miss your coffee and I apologize again if I scared you on your birthday flight. And Tucker, if you deem this report important enough to browse over, thanks for the opportunities you have provided me. THE MENZ

Chapter 14

THE ROUTINE

Several weeks passed. Menza fell into an enjoyable routine. Every morning he would rise early and have a light breakfast. Then he would take a casual walk around town. He would explore a different neighborhood every day. It was an excellent form of exercise and a great study in human behavior. Menza witnessed Earthlings going about their daily business. They really were a species rich in emotion. He witnessed children playing without a care in the world. He reckoned that must be universal. Menza would watch a man kiss his wife goodbye as he left for work. The very next house he would hear a couple arguing inside. He observed laughter and joy and crying and sadness. Humans were contradictory and complicated. What they lacked in intelligence they made up for in spirit. Life for them was a struggle yet they persevered.

Menza would usually spend the late morning hours recording his observations and analysis into his transmitter. Then he would have lunch. Sometimes he would prepare something at his apartment. More often than not he would walk to Dixieland Restaurant. This was another opportunity to watch humans. Actually there was another reason he spent so much time at Dixieland. The food was darn good. Menza had become accustomed to southern cooking. Thanks to Bet's homemade biscuits and Truman's beer he could actually tug a little roll around his belly.

Menza was seeing Marilyn nearly every day. They truly enjoyed each other's company. It had developed into a passionate relationship. Once she decided to open up there was no stopping her. Her sensuality was off the charts. Novem girls certainly could not compare. Menza found himself sleeping at her place more than his own. He tried to keep his emotions in check and not fall too deep. He knew this relationship would have to end. There was a sinking feeling in his gut every time he thought about returning to Novem. He wondered how he would tell her when that dreadful day arrived. He tried not to think about it.

Most of Marilyn's morning hours were dedicated to her guitar. It seemed she was learning a new chord every day. She was working at the pub six days a week. Truman liked for her to handle the busy evening shift. She had a way with the customers that put them at ease. She also had a knack for letting someone know they had enough to drink without putting them on the spot. Truman was trying to convince her to be the general manager. Marilyn was resisting taking on the extra responsibility. Now was not the time to add stress to her life. Dealing with her mother's illness was stressful enough.

Menza was now the Jumping Cow's most regular customer. Every day around 4 p.m. he would find a place at the bar. Why not? His beautiful girlfriend worked there and personally served him a tasty beverage that sustained his life. Menza was sure glad the IOS provided him with a wad of spending cash, even if they did suggest that he be as frugal as possible. He wondered what the IOS accountants would say when he handed over his expense report. He could just imagine how old Charlie the budget director would react—what's this $500,000 expense for beer—Menza, get in here!

Menza usually ordered dinner from the Cow's simple menu. Truman was a firm believer in freshness and quality. There weren't many choices available but it was all top notch. Menza liked everything on the menu and rotated his choices. All the staff knew exactly how he liked his food prepared. They took very good care of him. They should—he was not stingy when it came to tipping.

Menza was also becoming popular with his fellow Jumping Cow patrons. He wasn't shy about buying a round for the house. Who didn't like free beer—except for old Charlie. Among the luckiest recipients of Menza's generosity were his biggest competitors for Cow-regular. Todd Pepper and Stan Wright frequented the Cow about as much as Menza. Everyone referred to them by their last names. They had both gone to high school with Marilyn. The three of them had been friends for years. Both of their families were well respected throughout the community. Wright's family was politically active at a state level. Pepper's father was a highly decorated war hero. They were genuinely nice guys and Menza was not concerned about the IOS granting them an occasional beer.

Menza's affable personality and easy going nature won friends easily. Wright jokingly dubbed him Cow Mayor. He somewhat seriously suggested that Menza should run for mayor of Ashmont. There were, however, a few guys who did not care for Menza. They did not like the fact that a stranger had come in and captured Marilyn's heart. How could he ride into town and sweep her away in a matter of a week? Menza had shattered their dreams of one day making Marilyn their own.

There was also the Truman factor. Everyone knew that Menza was on the same page as Truman. They were two conspiratorial peas in a pod. There was nothing they did not agree on. From 9/11 to weather warfare to cloned politicians to aliens living inside the Moon—they were in total agreement. This disturbed some of the townsfolk. Truman was bad enough, but now he had a running buddy backing up his wild accusations. Two beer drinking nutcases posed a double threat to a rigid thinker.

Chapter 15

CAROLINA BARBEQUE

Dixieland Restaurant was buzzing. It was always packed on Wednesdays. That was the one day a week that 84-year-old James Henry worked his culinary magic. He was the undisputed baron of barbeque. James slow roasted his pork for ten hours over open coals of hickory and oak. The result was Carolina's finest barbeque. One day a zoo-visiting tourist made a derogatory racial slur after seeing Henry in the kitchen. He quickly realized he had made a major mistake. Several burly barbeque-devouring construction workers immediately surrounded his table. The stranger was lucky to escape with his life.

Bet was just clearing a table as Menza and Marilyn walked in. She motioned for them to come over. The two of them waited as she wiped down the table. Then they sat down.

"Thank you, Bet," said Menza. "You guys look busy today."

"Lunch always lingers a little longer on Wednesdays. Nobody knows when James is going to finally retire for good. They get it while they can."

"We can understand that," said Marilyn. "That's why we're here."

"Okay," said Bet. "I'll assume two barbeque plates for you, right?"

"You've got it, Bet," said Marilyn. "Along with a couple of sweet ice teas, please."

"Coming right up."

Bet trotted off to place the order. Menza leaned back in his chair. It did not get much better than this—hanging out with his pretty girlfriend and dining on fine Carolina barbeque. Suddenly a familiar voice shattered his mood.

"Hey Marilyn, I see you're still hanging out with Menza. Congratulations. You both deserve each other."

It was that Sheaple guy—the ignorant saphead who had nearly made him lose his temper a couple of months back. He was seated right beside them. He was just finishing his lunch. How they missed him when they came in, Menza would never know. Sheaple was wearing an eye-blinding orange jacket that was so ugly even a clown would be ashamed to be seen in it. His trousers were not any better—they were bright red and he had them pulled up chest high. Menza did not recognize the unfortunate girl that was accompanying the dapperly dressed mental midget. Sheaple's first name escaped him. Memories like him were a waste of valuable brain cells anyway.

"Thank you," replied Marilyn. She hoped being polite to him would shut him up.

"Hey Menza, did you bring your earthquake making machine with you? Sheaple burst into laughter at his joke.

"No, I left it at home today." Menza figured he would try to avoid confrontation. What was there to gain by debating a simpleton?

Sheaple put his arm around the girl beside him. Then he proudly puffed up like a pompous peacock past his prime.

"Marilyn, I think you know Tink. She says you two used to hang out in high school. She's been out in Hollywood making movies. It sure beats pouring beer at the local pub, huh?"

Marilyn certainly remembered Tink. They spent some time together during her senior year in high school. Tink was pretty—and pretty wacky. She could dramatically change moods with no warning. It was almost as if she had multiple personalities. Marilyn eventually distanced herself from her. Some called her Tinkerbell because she was obsessed with the little animated fairy that flew around sprinkling pixie dust. Tink would also repeatedly watch certain movies. Wizard of Oz and Alice in Wonderland were two of her favorites. They seemed to have a grip on her that went beyond fascination. After graduation Tink did indeed move away to Hollywood to pursue an acting career. Early on she had some minor roles in a couple of big budget movies. Her career seemed to have stalled as of late.

"Hello Tink," said Marilyn. "It's been a while. You still look great."

"Thank you Marilyn," replied Tink. "So do you."

Menza had even heard of Tink. One quiet evening at the pub Truman had mentioned her. At the time Truman was discussing the government's mind control program. He suspected that Tink was one of their victims. Tink's father was a career naval intelligence officer. As weird as it seemed, military families would sometimes allow their own children to be traumatized and mind controlled. In their view it was for a greater good. Then the victim could be manipulated in any way the controllers desired. Truman suspected that many film stars and musicians were programmed like robots. They possessed several personalities. These altered identities could be triggered by a handler. Something as simple as a hand sign could signal a personality shift. Triggers were sometimes implanted into movies, television shows and even books.

"So tell me, Menza," barked Sheaple, "What's yours and Truman's latest? Are aliens going to come down and gobble us all up?"

Menza bit his tongue. Sheaple was as obnoxious as the first time they met. At least then his drunkenness provided an excuse. He was actually more arrogant sober than drunk. He dressed better drunk also. His farcical attire probably helped keep the situation from getting out of hand. It was hard to get angry at a woodenheaded buffoon who chose to wear retina-burning garb such as his.

"Yeah, Sheaple," Menza replied calmly, "They'll probably save you for dessert though. The best and the brightest for last—you know."

Marilyn could tell where this conversation was headed. Sheaple would surely follow up with a thoughtless comment that would only escalate the tension. She quickly changed the subject before he had a chance to speak.

"So tell me, Tink," said Marilyn, "What's it like living in Hollywood?"

It took a moment for Tink to respond. She was peering trancelike out the window. A colorful butterfly had lit upon a flower in front of the restaurant. Marilyn noticed that she still had those faraway eyes that seemed to stare out into nothingness. Tink had maintained her fashion model looks, but she seemed so empty, so broken. It was if she had been robbed of her very soul. She watched the butterfly as it fluttered its wings and darted away. Finally she broke from her hypnotic state and turned towards Marilyn.

"I'm sorry, Marilyn. I was watching that butterfly. Those monarchs are so beautiful and fly so free. I wish I could be that free. What was your question again?"

"I was asking you how you liked living in Hollywood," Marilyn repeated.

"Oh, that's right," said Tink. "Hollywood's great. I just needed to get away for a while."

Tink was momentarily silent. Marilyn did not want to provide Sheaple with an opportunity for any more yokelish comments. She needed to keep the conversation on track.

"It must be interesting working in the entertainment industry. You know, being around famous people and all."

Once again Tink seemed to slide off into her own little world. She stared out the window again. She seemed to be searching for the butterfly that was now long gone. Finally she spoke softly.

"Sometimes I feel like I'm a character in someone's dream, that I'm a part of a circus act that goes round and round without a ringmaster. I'm a cat in a cage where the door's always open, but I'm too scared to leave—scared to walk on that checkerboard floor that can set me free. I'm caught up in the pyramid and its all-seeing eye, watching me float away, like a puff of fairy dust in the wind. Mine's a world where pain is pleasure and pleasure is pain and a smile ain't nothing but an upside down frown."

Marilyn was speechless. Menza didn't dare say a word. Even smart-mouthed Sheaple could not manage to issue a statement. All eyes were on Tink as she stared out the window. Suddenly the butterfly reappeared. Tink's body language immediately changed. It was if the butterfly was directing her in some way. Marilyn knew what was coming next. She had seen it happen years ago. Her old friend was switching personalities. Tink's body stiffened and her voice took on a more serious tone.

"Hollywood's a business, just like any other. I'm just in Ashmont taking a break. My agent is working on some projects for me. I feel sure I will have a role in a major film soon. Marilyn, it was nice seeing you again. Menza, it was nice meeting you. John, if you're ready I would like to go now. Thanks for lunch."

Just like that they were gone. Menza and Marilyn remained silent for a moment. They were halfway expecting the loopy couple to return. Those two were capable of anything.

"Wow," exclaimed Menza. "I think Truman's right about that girl being under some sort of mind control. I actually feel sorry for her."

"Yes," said Marilyn, "she seems to be in a worse mental state now than she was years ago. I think she definitely has multiple personalities."

Suddenly two plates of James Henry's finest appeared in front of them. The always cheerful Bet then handed them both a glass of Carolina sweet tea.

"Here you go," said Bet. "I'll be around to refill those teas shortly. Enjoy."

Menza and Marilyn held up their glasses and lightly touched them together.

"To interesting times," said Menza.

"Yes, "said Marilyn, "to interesting times."

Chapter 16

THE WRIGHT DECISION

It was 4 p.m. Menza could not wait to see the smiling face of the girl he had fallen in love with. He opened the door and entered into The Jumping Cow. His favorite seat was available. He sat down. Marilyn immediately came over and planted a big kiss on his lips and plopped a beer in front of him.

Actually the beer had been paid for by Pepper who was sitting at the other end of the bar. Pepper was no dummy—far from it. Buying one for Menza usually meant three coming his way before the evening was up. Menza acknowledged him with a wave and a smile.

Menza was in a good mood. Work was going well. He was filling his transmitter with accounts of his encounters with the aliens he was studying. Every day he was greeted with something new and unexpected. Earthlings were a fun and interesting species. The overwhelming majority of them were caring and kind. It was only a few that wished to inflict pain and suffering upon others.

His relationship with Marilyn could not be better. They were clicking on every level. Marilyn had been in particularly good spirits the last couple of days. Her mother's new medication was helping her deal with the ongoing pain. Marilyn was also becoming increasingly competent playing her guitar. She was writing some pretty darn good songs.

Menza took a sip of his beer, India Pale Ale, one of his favorites. Just then someone gave him a friendly slap on the back. It was Wright. He pulled out a barstoll and sat down beside Menza.

"How's it going my friend?" asked Wright.

"I'm doing well,' replied Menza. "How about you?"

"I'm too busy trying to figure out the universe to worry about my own back yard."

"What do you mean by that?" asked Menza.

"Oh, it's just some family stuff going on. I probably shouldn't be bothering you with it."

Menza could sense his friend was feeling a little down. He caught Marilyn's attention and signaled her to deliver Wright a beer.

"I've got you a beer on the way. Wright, I've known you long enough to know when something's bothering you. Would you like to talk about it?"

"Menza, You know my uncle's an ex-state senator, right?"

"Yes," said Menza. "I've heard you mention that before."

"My father's also been politically involved, election campaigns and that kind of stuff. Well, both of them have been bugging me lately about a political career. They think I should become involved in some local elections and work my way up the state level—and maybe beyond. Basically they want me to follow in my uncle's footsteps. Menza, you know how I'm always joking with you about running for mayor of Ashmont. Well, listen to this. They actually want me to run for mayor in the next election. I honestly don't know what to do. I'm pretty confused."

Menza put his hand on Wright's shoulder. At the same time Marilyn slipped a beer in front of him on her way to a table.

"Wright, I'm certainly not going to tell you what to do, but I will tell you this. With your personality and integrity I think you would make a fine mayor. I also have no doubt you would win if you ran. You seem to know everyone in town. They all love you, especially the girls. Heck, you would win in a landslide with just the female vote alone. I see how they swarm all over you in here."

"Menza, you always make me laugh," said Wright. "You know how to cheer someone up."

"Well, you know it's absolutely true. You know what's special about you? You can genuinely relate to anyone, rich or poor, black or white, working class, whoever. Heck, you could probably charm the socks off of an alien from outer space."

Wright chuckled. "There you go again being funny. Actually my family tells me the same thing—that I'm sort of a natural at making people like me. I guess I do have a talent for making friends. That's really the root of my dilemma. I know I would be a successful politician—but it can be a messy business. Coming from a political family I've seen it firsthand. I'm at a crossroads."

Menza thought for a moment before speaking. "Maybe you should just jump in and go for it. You'll make a great mayor."

"But that's the problem," said Wright. "I'm passionate about everything I do. I guess what I'm trying to say is this. If I get involved in politics I'm going to go all the way. I don't want to stop at the mayor's office. I don't even want to stop at the state level. I want to keep going.

Menza smiled. "President Wright has nice ring to it. You've got to be better than that puppet we've got in there now. Hey, look—here comes Truman. Let's ask him what you should do."

Truman had been chatting with Pepper at the far end of the bar. He walked over to Menza and Wright.

"Looks like I got all my regulars in here today," said Truman. "Between you two and Pepper over there we keep the electric bill paid around here."

"Hey Truman," said Menza, "Wright's in need of your expert advice if you've got a moment."

"Advice from me," cracked Truman. "What do you need to know? How to drink a liter of beer in under three seconds? How to get divorced before the ink's dry on the marriage license? How to get committed to a funny farm? Those are my fields of expertise."

"Yes, Truman, you are definitely qualified to dispense advice on those subjects. We also know your knowledge runs a little deeper than that. Wright's got a major decision to make regarding his future. Wanna hear him out?"

"Go for it, Wright. I'm all caught up around here, so I've got plenty of time."

"Let me sum it up for you," said Wright. "I was just telling Menza that my family is pressuring me to run in the upcoming mayoral election. Frankly, I know I would be a successful politician. It comes natural to me. The problem is this—if I decide to enter into politics I'm going all the way. For better or worse that's the nature of my goal oriented personality. I won't be stopping at mayor, senator, gover-nor—I'm gonna take it as far as I can take it. Truman, here's my question to you. Should I enter into the often times corrupt arena of politics? This is truly a major decision for me."

Truman was momentarily silent. Menza could sense Tru-man's brain churning away as it processed the data Wright had just presented him. The man had an innate talent for analyzing an issue from several different angles simultaneously. Finally he spoke.

"Wright, let me begin by telling you that I admire your honesty, ambition and obvious intelligence. You will undoubtedly be successful in whatever field you ultimately choose to concentrate on. For what it's worth here's my view on politics and power in today's world. I feel I should warn you—this is the stuff that earns me my 'crazy' moniker. Do you think you can handle it?"

"Sure I can, Truman," replied Wright. "It's no secret around here that you have some extreme views. You're not going to scare me away. As a matter of fact I want to hear your opinion on *everything*. Who's running the planet at the very top of the political pyramid? How are they doing it? Is there any room for an honest politician in the current system? What do you foresee in the future? And my last question— should I run for mayor of Ashmont? Truman, I really value your opinion. Shoot it to me straight. I don't care if you tell me a pack of lady bugs from Mars are running the world. I'm ready for anything. Go at it."

Truman laughed. "Lady bugs from Mars, huh? After I finish you'll probably wish those Martian lady bugs really were in control."

"That's exactly what I figured," said Wright. "I was just trying to loosen you up and let you know I'm open-minded about all this."

"You asked for it," said Truman, "so let's go on a voyage from the top of the world political pyramid and work our way down to the local mayor's office. You're gonna find out real quick that I'm not pulling any punches. At the top are the 'controllers.' These controllers have hijacked the human race. They are an alien species that view us the way we would look at ants living in a glass enclosure. The ants are our science project. We are the controllers' science project. We love to watch the ants build their tunnels. The controllers enjoy watching us go about our daily lives. We can close off a tunnel and disrupt the ants. The controllers can herd us into various locations on the planet. At any time we can eliminate or contaminate the ant's food, water and air supply. The controllers can do the same with our food, water and air supply. At any time we have the power to kill one ant or the entire colony. They are at our mercy—unless someone or something more powerful than us intervenes. At any time the controllers have the power to kill one of us or the whole human race. We are at their mercy—unless someone or something more powerful than them intervenes."

"Unbelievable," Wright muttered. "But coming from you I know it's possible. What you're saying is aliens are controlling the human race. Wow!"

"I'm afraid so, Wright. And this particular bunch ain't so nice. The controllers have set up a hierarchy within the human race. At the top is a class of humans that interbred with the alien 'Gods' thousands of years ago. I am in no way saying that these alien 'Gods' are the creator of the universe. I honestly don't know who or what created the universe. That conversation is for another day. My point is that these hybrids, for lack of a better word, are the true rulers of the planet. The faces they present as our rulers aren't necessarily the ones with the real power. Many times the real power remains behind the scenes. They cannot be blamed if they're invisible. They just rotate another public puppet into the mix and continue doing business—and yes, I am saying they control so-called democratic elections. They stage elections with a lot of media hoopla, count the votes via rigged machines and corrupt officials, and declare *their* choice to be the fairly elected winner. The populace thinks they had a choice in the matter. It's easy to make us slaves, but they're taking it a step further. They're manipulating our perception of reality so that we actually enjoy our servitude."

"I must be going crazy," Wright said with a nervous laugh. "I'm sitting here listening to someone tell me that we're controlled by aliens. And I'm believing it! Aliens and alien hybrids run the world. Aliens and alien hybrids are the powers behind the curtain. Aliens!"

"I'm afraid so," said Truman. "They've got us under their thumb because they control the money—little green pieces of paper. Money and power go hand in hand. The true rulers of the planet manipulate the money supply for their benefit. They print the stuff and they hand it out as they see fit. The world's economy is their private playground. They tease us with a boom so they can watch us squirm with the bust. The great depression of the 1930's was an example of asset collection. They broke everyone down and bought everything up for pennies on the dollar. Don't think for a minute that an economic downturn affects these scoundrels. Their mansions and yachts and servants ain't going anywhere."

"Greedy sons of wrenches! It's all about greed and power." Wright shook his head. He did not like what he was hearing, but it was better than going through life with his head stuck in the sand.

"Greed is right," affirmed Truman. "Money allows them to control governments. This in turn allows them to control the world's militaries, intelligence organizations and space exploration programs. When you control governments you control industry and the flow of information. They stage wars and play countries off against each other. That's easy enough—they just sic their media on a targeted leader and declare him to be the new Hitler. Then they send in the troops. The misled public will be waving their flags as the bombs fall on the babies. It's easy to influence the masses when the media is completely controlled."

"Why?" asked Wright. "Why are they doing it?"

"The elite are concentrating all this power in an effort to obtain a one world government. They want absolute power and control over every single human on the planet. They're not bashful about telling us. They spell it out in documents they know few will ever read. They tell us in their political speeches around the globe. You have to listen for their key phrases—new world order, world this, global that and so on. There's a monument called the Georgia Guidestones that openly spells out their goals. Centralized everything is what they're shooting for. One world government, one world economy, one world legal system, one world bank, one world religion—you name it, they're trying to centralize it. You gotta remember that it's much easier to exercise control when everything's under one umbrella. George Orwell's *1984,* Aldous Huxley's *Brave New World* and Yengeny Zamyatin's *We* spell it out for us in novel form. These famous authors had access to inside information. Each of these novels described a planet with centralized government."

Truman was momentarily silent. He instinctively knew that Wright was mentally deciphering it all. Finally Wright spoke.

"So these people—or whatever they are—think it's easier to control us if we're one giant flock of sheep. How are they gonna do it?"

"Now you're getting it, Wright," said Truman. "How will they achieve this one world government? It's a step-by-step process that's been in play for decades. It's all based on fear and threats. One of the Nazi scientists that the US brought over in Operation Paperclip described it this way. He made his statement back in the 70's when the cold war with Russia was in full swing. He said America had an 'enemies' list. First there would be a staged cold war with Russia. That came and went. Then there would be a staged terrorist threat. We're in the middle of that right now thanks to 9/11."

Once again Truman hesitated. Another long moment passed before he spoke.

"Now we start getting a little wild. Lots of people officially mark me off as a wacko with the next subject—Project Blue Beam. This is a four step process that will eventually lead to the implementation of a new age religion with a new messiah as its head. This new religion will be the very foundation upon which the one world government will be based. Now I know this is going to sound like fantasy, but it's real as hell. The first step involves hoaxed discoveries. Artificial earthquakes will uncover the 'error' of all fundamental religious doctrines. Hold onto your hats for what comes next—a *worldwide* space show with laser-projected holograms complete with 'God' speaking in every language and dialect. This will occur at a time when the world is already reeling in chaos from a worldwide catastrophe. Images of Jesus, Mohammed, Buddha and other important prophets will come together as one in the sky. This holographic god will explain that he's the new boss and all the other guys were wrong. Levitation technology will be employed to 'rapture' a large group of people into the sky never to be seen again. The final step in Project Blue Beam is a fake extraterrestrial invasion. This staged event will unite the world to fight a common enemy.

"Can they really do that stuff?" asked a mesmerized Wright. "Can they actually pull it off?"

"Believe it or not the technology already exists to pull off this incredible stunt. It's all alien based stuff and they share it when they feel like it. The satellites are aimed and ready as I speak. If the masses would take a moment to break away from their precious televisions they could see them. All it takes is a set of binoculars and they'd see all those stars aren't stars. The twinkling ones are ready to take a bite out of humanity. But of course Billy Bob and Sally Sue won't bother to look up at the sky. That would entail missing ten minutes of a rerun of their favorite TV show—a *real* tragedy. How are they going to put those big pictures in the sky—that's ancient technology for this group. Hologram technology is alive and well and being refined every day. Some of the UFO sightings are actually holographic tests. Hollywood is heavily involved in that caper. Wright, you wanna here more? Or I have I blown your mind already?"

"Keep going," said Wright. "I want it all."

"You got it," replied Truman. "Now—about the voices that will be projected into our brains. The military has hinted for years about being able to brainwash the minds of enemy soldiers. The controllers are already feeding artificial thoughts into our heads via electromagnetic waves. It's also possible to wipe out past memories and install fake memories. The victim is totally convinced the thoughts are his own. It's happening every day. Many of these alien 'abductions' are actually shadow government operations. As far as levitation technology goes—it's been around for eons. How do you think they moved the stones when they built the pyramids? How about that structure in South America made of massive rocks that weigh several tons each? I can tell you what it wasn't—gangs of slaves dragging around a sled using ropes made from papyrus. Why don't the creators of this fantastic tale try moving a 50-ton rock by this method? That would motivate them to change their official crap story.

"So there you have it. That's the plan they have for us— those of us who survive their depopulation program. I'm hoping someone or something or some force can stop it. That's where I'll answer your final question. Wright, you asked me if you should run for mayor of Ashmont. The answer is an absolute yes. Run and win. Then use this local position to propel yourself into big league politics. Get out there and start swimming with the sharks. Keep your honor and integrity at all times. Be the trailblazer politician who is moral and honest even if it hurts. Admit any faults or weaknesses you may have. Do this *before* anyone questions you about it. This will build credibility. After you attain a certain level of status they're gonna come in on you like hungry hawks. They'll try to blackmail you and squeeze you into submission. If they can't get something on you they'll probably make something up. This is where you make a deposit from the credibility bank. You'll weather the storm because of your reputation for honesty. Your word will actually mean something. Go for it. Let your ambitions take you as far as you can go. The world desperately needs leaders like you. There really is no choice in the matter. If someone like you doesn't take the reins and run with them then we have zero hope of a decent future. Can they stop you? Sure they can—they can kill you anytime they choose. It all boils down to living free or living as a slave. Wright, go back home and tell your uncle and father that you're gonna be the next mayor of Ashmont and you've got your eye on the White House. Let me know when you need some campaign volunteers and I'll be there. I'm sure you can count on Menza and Marilyn too."

"You can count on me too!"

Everyone turned and looked at Pepper. He was sitting two seats away. No one had noticed he had moved closer to them. They had been too engrossed in Truman expressing his interesting point of view. Pepper slid in one seat closer.

"I didn't move over here with intentions of eavesdropping. My father turns ninety next Thursday. I wanted to invite everyone to his birthday party. You guys know where I live, close to the zoo. We're thinking about having it inside the Pig Parlor."

"So you came over to invite us to a party and I sent you to the twilight zone," said Truman. "Sorry about that."

Pepper laughed. "Yeah, I was expecting to join in on a conversation about pretty girls or football or beer. Truman, you know nothing you say ever surprises me. Terry Tee and I go way back and he says you're dead on the truth one hundred percent. I'm open minded about the extraterrestrial thing, but until one lands in my backyard and I can see it with my own eyes, well, until then I'll be a little skeptical. Changing the subject—Wright, you would make a fantastic mayor."

"Thank you, Pepper," said Wright. "And Truman, thanks for the confidence and faith you have in me. You just inspired me more than you'll ever know. I'm going to do it!"

"Don't worry about it," said Truman. "Just don't stop coming to the Cow after you're elected mayor."

"You don't have to worry about that," said Wright. "Not as long as you keep brewing those great beers. As a matter of fact, I think it's about time for Menza to buy us a round. Nah, I'm just playing with you, Menza. This round is on me. Truman, get us all a beer—including yourself. Fill that monster glass of yours to the brim. We're celebrating. I'm running for mayor!"

"You've got it, Wright," said Truman. "The beers are coming right up. Oh, before I forget it—Menza, can you give this to Marilyn. It's some lyrics I've thrown together and I'd like her to put a little rhythm to it. She's getting good on that guitar, as you well know."

"I'll do it," answered Menza.

Menza took the customary crumpled piece of paper from Truman. Later that evening Wright and Pepper engaged themselves in a deep discussion. Menza took the opportunity to read Truman's lyrics while Wright talked strategy with his new campaign manager.

SOMETHING AIN'T RIGHT

The stock market's down, down for the day,
The Yanks are in the cellar—swinging away
Got one eye on the wife and her wandering ways,
The other's on another who's begging to play
Got a teenage daughter driving me insane,
Got a Mississippi habit that's playing with my brain
I'm running myself ragged—I'm running blind,
My head's in the sand most of the time
Something ain't right in the world today,
Something ain't right but I can't say
Something ain't right, something's all wrong,
Something ain't right in the world today
There's scandal in the paper, fear in the news,
Division and revision's keeping us confused
The media's a mess as they peddle their trash,
But they keep on pitching cause trash is cash
Shock and sensation—that's what they cover,
Deep beneath the rubble is the truth they smother
Something ain't right in the world today,
Something ain't right but I can't say
Something ain't right, something's all wrong,
Something ain't right in the world today
They're blowing up the world—a piece at a time,

We look the other way while they take it away
Something ain't right in the world today,
Something ain't right but I can't say
Something ain't right, something's all wrong,
Something ain't right in the world today

Chapter 17
LOVE AT THE ZOO

Menza heard a honk—not the usual blaring blast that one normally associates with an automobile horn. It was more like a soulful tap delivering a cheerful hello. He peered out the window. He already knew who it was. There was only one person who could make a car horn purr with soul. Marilyn was sitting in his driveway right on time. They were going to the zoo—hopefully. The last time they attempted it he almost sat the town ablaze. He hoped she had the foresight to fill her own tank this time.

Marilyn had been at her mother's place all morning. She had been spending most of her free time with her. She knew her mother's days were limited. The doctors were giving her a few months at the very most. They had openly discussed it and both mother and daughter were at peace with the situation. They had decided to enjoy what time she had left. Marilyn was in the process of writing a song for her. Her mom had made her promise she would sing it at her funeral. Menza had heard her humming a few lines of it. It was quite touching.

Menza was exactly five months into his stay on Earth. Seven more months and he would be riding the sky in the ZPB back to Novem. Marilyn's situation with her mother made him realize just how much he loved his own parents. It would be wonderful to reunite with family and friends on his beloved home planet. But the happiness would be offset with a tremendous sadness. Leaving behind the girl he loved would be the hardest thing he would ever do. Marilyn would forever be with him. Every time he looked at the sky he would think of her. She had somehow stolen a piece of his heart and he would never get it back. His emotions were tearing at his guts. Why did Earth have to be a trillion time space arcs away? Why couldn't he have both worlds? Why did everything have to be so complicated?

"Come on, slowpoke. The monkeys are waiting for us."

Marilyn's sweet voice rang through the air as he closed the door behind him. It was a reminder of her philosophy 'seize the day.' Carpe diem she called it. That was exactly what he would do. These were precious moments that needed to be savored. He was not going to worry about an event that was seven months away. He would seize the day with the girl he loved.

Menza jumped into the passenger seat and leaned over and kissed Marilyn. He pressed her body tight against his for a long moment. Finally he loosened his embrace and gazed into her eyes.

"Marilyn, I love you. There are days that pass when I don't tell you so. That won't happen anymore—every single day I will tell you how much I love you. Neither of us knows what tomorrow will bring, so we had better live each day as if it were our last. If it all ended today then so be it. Nothing could be better than spending my last day alive with the girl that I love with all my heart. Let us seize the day, my love."

"Oh, Menza, I love you too."

Marilyn wiped away a lone tear that trickled down her cheek. She leaned over and wrapped her arms around Menza. Neither of them spoke except through the current of love which seemed to flow between them. It was genuine. It was unconditional. It was electric. Menza was sure this was the root source of genomel that was universally treasured. What he was feeling was the priceless emotion of love in its purest form. It transcended the physical realm of desire. It was an intoxicating elixir of spirit and soul—trust and respect. It was caring about someone and knowing they truly cared for you. For two long minutes the two of them held each other. Finally they loosened their grip and once again looked into each other's eyes. It was at this moment that Menza knew they would be together forever. Somehow, someway—the guiding force of the universe would make it happen. He just knew it.

"Come on baby," said Marilyn. "Let's go to the zoo. If we don't leave this very second we're not going at all. You know what happens when you push me over the edge—and I'm sitting there right now."

Menza laughed. "Okay baby, start the car now because I'm ready to give you a nudge that'll send you tumbling."

Marilyn immediately started the car and backed out of the driveway. They were on their way to the zoo. They looked at each and laughed. Menza placed his hand behind Marilyn's neck and gently massaged it.

"To be continued this evening, okay?"

"Absolutely," replied Marilyn.

Marilyn humorously displayed two crossed fingers as they approached Harry's Gas & More. This time they managed to pass it by uneventfully.

"Looks like we're finally going to see some animals," joked Marilyn.

A few minutes later they turned into the parking lot of the zoo. The bronze sculpture of an elephant marked the spot. Marilyn expertly zipped into a parking space.

"What's that!" exclaimed Menza. He pointed towards a man walking beside the oddest animal he had ever seen. It had to be close to twenty feet tall—nearly all neck."

"Oh baby, that's a giraffe. Surely you've seen pictures of them.

Menza had never seen such. Novem had its share of unusual animals, but nothing that resembled this creature. He could tell from Marilyn's tone of voice that this particular animal was one he should recognize.

"Oh, yes," said Menza. "I have seen pictures of these. Giraffes are amazing with their long necks."

"Come on, baby," said Marilyn. "Let's go inside."

Marilyn insisted on paying the entrance fee. They walked through the turnstile and entered the zoo grounds. Menza immediately began hearing strange squawking and howling noises. This time he kept quiet. He would be careful not to make any more mistakes. He would pretend to recognize every animal by sight and sound.

"Look over there—an ostrich," said Marilyn. She pointed at a large bird with yet another long neck.

Menza kept his cool. Here was another mystery animal that had a long neck. Apparently all zoo creatures had long necks.

"That's one of the most beautiful ostriches I've ever seen," Menza casually commented.

Just then Marilyn wrapped her arm around Menza's waist and pulled him close. She kissed his cheek.

"Look at those two chimpanzees," she said.

Menza mentally prepared himself for another long-necked surprise. This time it was two human-like animals locked in an embrace. Then the larger of the two leaned over and gently kissed the other one. They were obviously showing affection for each other. They seemed oblivious to everyone and everything around them. Romance was their only concern.

"It's all about love in this world," said Marilyn. "At least that's what I think. And you know what—I love you."

"I love you too," Menza answered.

She gripped him tighter. Menza swore he could feel a little blast of genomel shoot through his veins. This was the woman he wanted to spend the rest of his life with. She was his dream come true. He would have her forever. Fate had seven months to provide an answer as to exactly how it would come about.

Menza then noticed another loving couple. It was two animals that looked completely different from each other. One was a huge barrel-shaped animal with enormous mouth and teeth. It weighed at least 3,000 pounds. The other was a stubby-legged animal that carried a large shell on its back. Although small in comparison to its companion it looked to weigh at least 500 pounds. The two animals looked very comfortable together as they basked in the sun.

"Oh look," said Marilyn. She too had noticed the odd couple. "There's Sammy the hippopotamus and Sally the giant tortoise. They're famous around here. They've been insepara-ble for six years. Everyone's waiting to see if they ever produce any offspring. Can you imagine the publicity this place would get if we suddenly had a hippotortoise in our zoo?"

A thought flashed through Menza'a mind. This was two completely different species that had come together. They seemed perfectly content together. Why couldn't two beings from different galaxies do the same? Novem and Earth were separated by a trillion time space arcs. Why couldn't they come together? Why not start with him and Marilyn? And what if they had a child between them? He couldn't help but think that it would be the best of both worlds—a perfect little kid.

Menza and Marilyn spent the rest of the afternoon wandering the grounds of the zoo. They saw lions, zebras, crocodiles and kangaroos. They saw reptiles, mammals and birds from around the world. Love and passion was definitely the theme of the day. Birds were whistling love songs, crocodiles were bellowing their low pitched mating calls, even the snakes were entwined in loving embraces. It seemed that couples representing every species on the planet were sending out romantic vibrations. It was as if they were aiming them directly at the enamored human couple patrolling their grounds. Love was in the air and it was contagious. Menza and Marilyn finally headed home for a romantic interlude of their own.

Chapter 18

PIG PARLOR PARTY

"Amy, turn here," said Marilyn. "It's two miles down this dirt road."

Marilyn, Menza and Truman were headed to the Pig Parlor. That is what everyone called Pepper's home. It was originally built by Sir Pepper—that was his father's longtime nickname. He turned 90 today. He earned his name by simply being himself. He was a World War Two hero who was personally decorated for valor *twice* by General Patton. Ashmont considered him as royalty for his work with troubled teens. For three decades he had turned wild running-in-the-street teenagers into upstanding citizens. They included two current city commissioners and one possible future mayor. He always joked that the only teen that he could not tame was his own. There was a hint of truth to the matter. Boy Pepper certainly was not the docile submissive type. Maybe he knew all his father's tricks.

The Pig Parlor was legendary. It sat in the middle of 300 acres of farmland. It was built thirty years previously entirely by Sir Pepper. At the time he was raising pigs for a living. He needed some modest accommodations to accompany the pig house. He built a simple one room shack. Over the next decade he periodically added on to it. Boy Pepper lived there throughout his high school and college years. During this period he threw legendary parties. Some of his New Year's parties were especially wild. One year he was nearly arrested for disturbing the peace. The investigating officer estimated 1,500 people to be in attendance. Terry Tee and the Tornadoes were playing rock and roll on a makeshift stage. Boy Pepper had discovered several vintage machine guns his father had stashed away. At the stroke of midnight half a dozen inebriated country boys began firing World War Two weapons into the sky. It took a call to Sir Pepper to keep young Pepper out of the slammer that night.

Pepper always thought he would eventually move out of the Pig Parlor. It just never happened. He got married and promptly moved his new bride into the Pig Parlor. She promptly left. The Pig Parlor remained the Pig Parlor however. At any given time there was a down-and-out friend staying there trying to get his life back on track. In all likelihood Boy Pepper probably staved off a couple of suicides. The Pig Parlor was a last ditch refuge for more than one troubled soul. Over the years the parties became fewer in number and much more subdued. The Pig Parlor and its permanent resident had both calmed down considerably, but one thing was still certain—a gathering there would be entertaining. The Pig Parlor and its master had reputations to uphold.

Amy had been recruited as a designated driver. No one was taking any chances with drinking and driving. Truman was paying her the equivalent of what she would have made bartending for the night. She enthusiastically accepted, having worked eight straight days without a break. Besides, one never knew who might show up at the Pig Parlor. Several years ago a well known pop star showed up and stayed the weekend. No one questioned why one of the world's most famous entertainers would spend a weekend sleeping on a cot in an abandoned pigpen in Ashmont, North Carolina. His limousine somehow seemed to fit in parked between two broken down tractors. The Pig Parlor welcomed all comers.

"Amy, start slowing down," said Marilyn. "Make a right here. It's an easy turn to miss, but Pepper likes it that way."

Amy turned and drove up the long driveway. Cars were already parked on both sides. Truman motioned for her to continue going forward.

"Back it into the front yard," he said. "I've got to unload this keg. I figured I'd contribute some beer for Sir Pepper's party. That man has done so much for the community. Amy, watch out for the helicopter."

Sitting in the front yard was a dilapidated antique helicopter. One of the blades appeared to be held together with duct tape. The other did not look much better. The helicopter had been sitting there for over three years. One of Pepper's friends had given it to him. The Pig Parlor had always been sort of a graveyard for worn out mechanical devices. Pepper was constantly tinkering with them trying to bring them back to their glory. So far he had left the helicopter alone much to the relief of his friends. This flying machine was definitely not airworthy.

Amy slowly backed Truman's car into the yard. Truman popped the trunk open. Three young men standing nearby immediately took notice of the beer keg.

"Take it away, guys," said Truman. "She's all yours."

They did not waste any time. One particularly burly fellow hoisted the heavy keg onto his shoulder and carried it away. The other two grabbed the tapping equipment and followed him. This crew definitely did not need lessons on how to tap a keg of beer.

"Truman, how are you?" It was the voice of Pepper. "Hi Marilyn, Menza, Amy—thanks for coming."

Everyone greeted Pepper. He seemed to be in great spirits. "I know everyone's been here before except Menza. Would you like for me to show you around."

"I would love to see the place," said Menza. "I've heard so much about it."

"Well, come on then. Let's start with the pig house." The group followed as Pepper led the way.

They walked about thirty yards down a path which opened up into a clearing. There they saw a large dwelling. Pepper opened the door and they went inside.

"Menza, this is it. This is where we used to raise pigs. Nowadays it's just a big open space except for that old Wolseley Hornet saloon car over there. This place was wall to wall people at a couple of those New Year's parties. I'm lucky I escaped those days. Let me show you the other stuff around back."

Pepper walked them through the pig house and exited through a back door. In the midst of overgrown weeds stood a cluster of tiny buildings, some in better shape than others. They were surrounded by an assortment of abandoned vehicles and mechanical contraptions whose purpose was unknown to anyone with the possible exception of Sir Pepper.

"Over here is the old shingle mill," said Pepper. "That hut over there is where we process wild game—venison and boar mostly. That patch of flowers between the two buildings is actually an herb called comfrey. We use it for all kinds of ailments. Pop's had that little garden going for years. He got a little upset when I mixed a different kind of herb in there a couple of years back—wasn't exactly legal if you know what I mean."

Truman chuckled. "Yeah, Terry Tee told me about that one. He said you threw all the blame on him. I guess he does make a good scapegoat for that stuff. He ain't never tried to hide his love for it. I know one thing. It sure doesn't hurt his guitar playing."

Pepper laughed. "Speaking of Terry—he's inside the Pig Parlor now talking to my dad. Let's go see him. It's getting kinda cold out here.

Pepper led them back to the Pig Parlor's living quarters. They could feel the warmth of the blazing fire as soon as they entered the building. Approximately forty people were packed into the small room. Most of them already had a glass of Truman's golden lager in their hands. Sir Pepper was relaxing in a recliner in front of the roaring fire. It was obvious he was enjoying himself. He had lived a life dedicated to helping others. This party was a small payback for his good deeds. Nearly everyone in the room owed at least a small debt of gratitude to the unassuming gentleman who had steered so many lives in the right direction.

"Howya pop?" twanged Pepper. "I've got a few people who want to say hello. You've met Marilyn and Truman before. And this is Amy. I'm not sure if you two have met or not. And this is Menza, the new guy in town that I was telling you about."

Sir Pepper reached out and shook everyone's hand. "Amy, I don't think we've met before, but it's a real pleasure. Menza, my boy's been telling me all about you. I'm glad to finally meet you. Marilyn, it's nice to see you again. Truman, we've howdied, but we ain't shook. It's good to see you. Thank you all for coming out."

"Sir Pepper, we all love you. Happy birthday." Marilyn wrapped her arms around Sir Pepper and squeezed him tight.

"I'm starting to like getting older. I've been getting hugs from pretty girls all day. Seriously, thank you Marilyn. This party means a lot to me. Menza, you're a lucky guy to have a girl like this one. I've known her since she was a little thing. She's a keeper."

"Trust me, Sir Pepper," said Menza, "I'm not letting her get away. I know what a treasure she is."

"She's just like her mama—a good person. By the way, Marilyn, send your mama my love. Tell her to hang in there. I know she's been pretty sick."

"Okay," replied Marilyn. "I'll tell her. That'll mean a lot coming from you."

"Hey, look who's back," said Sir Pepper. "It's the guitar man. Terry Tee, some of your friends are here."

Terry Tee walked over. Menza took a close look at the local guitar hero. It was true what they had said about him. You could practically see music dripping off him. There was no doubt the man was blessed with talent.

"Hey guys, it's good to see you all again. Marilyn, I hear you're getting pretty good on that guitar of yours. Let me know if you ever have any questions. You must be Menza— it's great to finally meet you. Pepper's told me lots about you."

"It's good to meet you too," said Menza. "I've heard all about you too. I can't wait to hear you play one day."

"Ah, I'm not as good as they say," laughed Terry. "That's what friends are for, embellishing the truth. Hey Truman, before I forget it—all the guys like your latest song. We're gonna put into the set list. So—what's new? I've been telling Sir Pepper about some of your conspiracy stuff. He's open to it."

Truman sighed and shook his head. "Sir Pepper, I'm worried that all the sacrifices you and many others made in World War Two ain't going to be enough. I think the insane people running the planet are going to spark off another big one—World War Three. I hope I'm wrong."

Sir Pepper nodded in agreement. "You know, Truman, I've got a sickening feeling in my gut that you're telling the truth—and my gut is usually right. I wish I knew back then what I know now. I would have given ole Patton an earful to carry back to those Washington bureaucrats. Truman, can you tell me what you know? Who's behind it? And why? My boy tells me you have some pretty wild theories. Years ago I wouldn't have believed any of that stuff—nowadays I'm open to anything."

"Sir Pepper, you're a true hero. What you and others did was honorable and virtuous, but I think we're all being played like pawns on a chessboard. You asked for it, so here's my view. Back in the 1800's there was a true insider named Albert Pike. You'll find his statue in downtown Washington D.C. He wrote a document outlining the blueprint for world domination. Some people say the document is a fake, but the naysayers are the fakes. He said there would be three world wars. The first would bring down the Czars in Russia. The purpose was to install Communism as a political tool. The second war would be staged to strengthen Zionism and create the state of Israel. The third war will pit the Zionists against the Islamic world—note 9/11 and other fake attacks wrongly blamed on Muslims. The United States, Russia and China will all join in to turn it into one messy bloody event. The people of the world will be broken down physically, spiritually, morally and economically. Coming to their rescue will be the *saviors* with a global government. The first two wars have gone exactly as planned. The third seems to be on its way. I'm afraid, Sir Pepper, that we're in for some rocky times ahead."

Everyone was quiet. No one dared speak until Sir Pepper responded first. It was all about respect and seniority. Finally Sir Pepper replied.

"Truman, it breaks my heart to hear this, but my heart knows it's true. I think about the dozen or so German lives I snuffed out so many years ago. They never got the chance to live their lives, have families, enjoy growing old—I stripped all that away from them with a bullet to their heads. They were kids, just like me. We all thought we were doing the right thing. Now the same thing is going to happen again if we don't wake up. Innocent people will kill other innocent people because they're told to do so. We listen to a bunch of power hungry madmen pushing their propaganda and beating their war drums. If I could go back and do it all over again I honestly don't know what I would have done.

"Sir Pepper," said Truman. "I didn't mean to get off on this subject on your birthday. I'm sorry. We can discuss something else."

"No, I want to talk about it," answered Sir Pepper. "It's probably good therapy for me."

Sir Pepper was quiet for a moment. So was everyone else—once again, out of respect. He finally spoke.

"I remember the first German soldier I killed. He couldn't have been more than seventeen years old. I had him in my sights and before I pulled the trigger I remember thinking—it's me or him. And then I put a bullet into his brain. I puked my guts up after that. I have nightmares about it to this very day. Killing another human being ain't a natural thing. Most of humanity is people like you, me, and everyone in this room tonight. We want to live in peace, enjoy life and love one another. It's the twisted manipulators with their insane objectives who are to blame. I look back—what if that same kid would have taken my life instead of me taking his? He had his gun aimed at me and no doubt was a split second from pulling his own trigger. Sometimes I wake up in the middle of the night seeing his face in my dreams. But it's not the face of a kid, it's a 90-year-old man. And he's trying to tell me something, but I don't know what. I always wake just as he begins to speak. At that moment—in the darkness of the night—I wish it would have been him who pulled the trigger first. Then he would be the one with the guilt. He would be seeing my face at two o'clock in the morning. I honestly don't know who won the gunfight on that cold Sunday morning so many years ago. He lost his life and I lost a little bit of my soul. I guess we both lost. There are no winners in war. We're all losers."

Another long moment of silence ensued. This time Boy Pepper broke the silence.

"Pop, you can't worry about it. It is what it is. Think of all the people you have helped over the last fifty years. Half of them would be dead, on drugs, or in jail now if it wasn't for you. God pulled the trigger that Sunday morning—not you. You were important enough to keep alive. At least that's the way I'm looking at all this."

"Maybe you're right, son," replied Sir Pepper. "I don't claim to have the answers. Truman, I've got another question for you. I know you believe in aliens from other planets. Well, back in the war I had a very good friend who was a bomber pilot. He came back to the base one day and his face was white as a sheet. I asked him what was wrong and he told me he had been chased in the sky by an orange fireball the size of a football field. At the time I honestly thought he might be losing his sanity. It wasn't long after that when other pilots began reporting the same experience. And it wasn't just the allied pilots who saw these things. The Germans and Japanese saw the same fiery balls of light in the sky. They always seemed to toy with the airplanes before shooting off into space at incredible speeds. These objects earned the name foo fighters. Truman, what were these huge fiery balls that were chasing after airplanes during World War Two?"

"Sir Pepper, I have to tell you I don't really know. The fact that both sides saw these mysterious objects leads me to believe it was some sort of psychological operation. It was probably orchestrated by the same group that staged the war itself. Remember the real war was and is against humanity. Also remember that the controllers of the planet have access to advanced technology. Maybe it was some sort of conditioning program to get the public used to the idea of alien aircraft. The foo fighter story generated a lot of press worldwide. The publicity attached to these incidents is usually no accident. The powers sometimes intentionally leak some information as a form of psychological warfare. There's also the real possibility that an unknown alien species was letting us know they were watching us—sort of a psyop of their own. There were rumors that the Nazis had somehow gained access to alien technology and were working on some anti-gravity flying discs near the end of the war. It all gets a bit cloudy with the espionage behind these subplots—and that's the way they like it. They like to keep us guessing at every level of awareness. That's my take on the foo fighters. But like I say, Sir Pepper, it's only an educated guess on my part."

"Truman," said Sir Pepper, "that makes about as much sense as anything else I've heard. There are two important things I've learned from you. I'm now totally convinced that all wars are staged. I'm also certain that the entire human race is the central target."

"Target is the correct word for it," said Truman. "Have you ever taken a look at the United Nations logo? It looks like a target aimed at the world. I'm sure they'll give you some other fluffy reason why their logo looks like that. Everything these criminals do has a double meaning to it—doublespeak as Orwell described it in *1984*. The United Nations Against Humanity, that's what the real name should be."

"Truman, I could sit here and talk to you all night. You are one interesting and knowledgeable person."

"Thank you, Sir Pepper," Truman said respectfully. "But I feel like I'm bringing you down on your birthday with all this political talk. This is supposed to be a celebration. Can I get you a beer?"

"Actually you can, Truman. I rarely drink these days, but you make some fine beer. I gotta get out to the Jumping Cow sometime."

"You got it, Sir Pepper, one cold beer coming right up. It's funny you mentioned the Cow because I've got your birthday present right here—a gift certificate for two dinners at the pub. Also, here are some lyrics I threw together last night. You were the inspiration behind them. Thank you for everything you've done for so many people. We all love you, Sir Pepper."

The rest of the evening was all fun and relaxation. Everyone sang happy birthday to the man who had changed so many lives. Terry Tee's wife unveiled a huge homemade cake adorned with ninety candles. Each candle resembled a child— a child whose life had been changed for the better. Then she handed Sir Pepper an oversized birthday card signed by ninety well-wishers. Each of them had been touched by Sir Pepper in one way or another. Later that evening as Sir Pepper opened his gifts he finally gave in to his emotions. A stream of tears rolled down his weathered face. All night long he had been treated like the royalty he truly was. Finally the last guest left around midnight. Sir Pepper then took time to read the lyrics Truman had given him.

PRISONER OF WAR

Sometimes I look in the mirror to comb my hair,
But the man looking back don't seem to care
It ain't important if his hair's out of place,
And he don't really care if he's shaved his face
None of that's important
Because he lives in the past,
Years gone by that went so fast
It's all about the war, that's what did him in,
The memories of the killing that just won't end
When you take a life you never forget it,
Cause a man's staring back that ain't gonna let it
He's looking back at you every day,
A reminder of the past that won't go away
I'm a prisoner of war, I'm in my head,
I'm all shackled down and he's all dead
I'm a prisoner of war, I'll never be free,
There's no escaping the prison that's me
That reflection in the mirror, he's damaged goods,
If he could let it all go he surely would
His heart knows he's innocent and he did no wrong,
How he wished his mind could be that strong
But it ain't never gonna happen
Cause there's always more
He ain't never escaping from the prison of war

The mirror never answers the questions I ask,
It just stares back at me reflecting the past
It's an image of a man that's hurt and torn,
It's a constant reminder he's a prisoner of war
I'm a prisoner of war, I'm in my head,
I'm all shackled down and he's all dead
I'm a prisoner of war, I'll never be free,
There's no escaping the prison that's me

Chapter 19
TRUTH TALK

It was 7 p.m. There was only one seat available at the bar. Wright slid his seat over to allow room for Menza to slip in. Menza was running a little off schedule due to some extended observations. He had spent the entire afternoon monitoring humans in a place called Paxmart. Truman had mentioned the fact that the giant retailer was a CIA operation from top to bottom. Menza seemed to agree after spending several hours wandering the aisles of the megastore.

"Hi Menza,' said a jovial Wright. "What's going on with you?"

"Oh, I've been out doing a little shopping. How are things with you?"

"Real good," replied Wright. "But it'll be better in about thirty seconds. Marilyn saw you walk through the door and she's getting us both a beer. She said you're buying! I don't even have to wait for you to buy'em anymore—just automatically goes on your tab. Damn, that's funny!"

"I'm going to have a talk with that girlfriend of mine before she breaks me," Menza laughed. "Nah, Wright, you know I enjoy buying you a beer."

Marilyn arrived with the beers. Before sitting them down she leaned over and kissed Menza.

"Hey baby, how are you?"

"I'm doing well. I've been shopping at Paxmart. I bought you a little surprise gift. I'll show it to you tonight."

"Thank you, baby. I gotta go. As you can see we're pretty busy right now. Here comes Truman. I'm sure he'll keep you entertained."

"Okay, I'll talk to you later when it slows down."

Truman walked over to his two regulars.

"How's it going, guys? Menza, you're a little late today. You didn't find a new pub, did you?"

"No Truman, you know I'll never find a better brew than yours. I've actually been shopping at Paxmart. You're right, that place seems a little weird."

"That's a CIA operation," barked Truman. "That's why it's spooky. It's full of spooks."

"Can you tell me a little more?"

"Sure," replied Truman. "Paxmart is part of the overall centralization plan. It's like this. They build a Paxmart and the low prices bring people in. The smaller local businesses cannot compete and they eventually fold. Paxmart then has control of a large portion of the consumer goods market. They dictate the availability of products, the pricing, and the quality of the goods. This becomes especially important when we're talking about food products."

"I heard something about that," said Wright, "that much of what we eat is what they call genetically modified foods."

"You're exactly right. Governments are increasingly taking over the world's food supply. Food is a weapon. Believe it or not, they're going to outlaw private gardens in the near future—all in the name of public safety of course. Yeah, right.

Genetically modified foods are already the norm. God only knows what garbage they're putting in there."

"Wow!" exclaimed Wright. "They're not even going to allow us to grow our own food—unbelievable."

"That's right," said Truman. "They'll grow it for us. The world government is stashing seeds in a 'doomsday' seed bank in Norway. Once again, they say it's for *our* benefit. Sure—sounds like the standard pee on me and tell me it's raining trick. They say the raw genetic materials are there for *us* when climate change or food and water shortages or disease pandemics affect our food supply. First of all—there is no climate change except for their electromagnetic induced weather manipulation. The scientists who tell us there is climate change are living on money provided by the elite's foundations. Wanna take a guess at who's going to cause the food and water shortages?"

Wright sighed before answering. "The machine that is our government, right?"

"You're correct. It'll be the good ole world government who will squeeze us to the point of starvation. They've already started. Take a look at the artificially induced rising food prices. As far as disease pandemics—those same bad guys make the diseases and unleash them upon us whenever the need arises. All these flu shots everyone lines up for are full of poisons and who knows what else. It wouldn't surprise me if they're injecting microchips into our bodies. The nanotechnology is already being used. At some point they will let loose a disease, hype it up with their spineless media, and force inoculations on everyone. Those of us who refuse will be sent to the FEMA camps they've already built to imprison resisters like me and you."

"You're right," said Menza. "They're really playing hardball when they control our food. Hey, Truman, you know what happened at Paxmart today? They were showing videos at the checkout lanes telling shoppers to report any suspicious activity to the nearest law enforcement officer. Guess what they classified as suspicious activities—paying cash for your purchases and glancing at the surveillance camera. Guess who paid cash for his purchases and looked at the surveillance camera—me! You should have seen the stares I received after that. One bored soul actually followed me out to the parking lot and watched me get in Marilyn's car. I saw him writing down her license plate number. I guess she's in some terrorist data base now."

"Yeah," said Truman. "I can see the headline now, 'Bartender Bomber Pays Cash for Oatmeal Cookies—Plots to Blow Up Universe.' Seriously, both of you are now permanently registered in their terrorist data file. You're both considered potential homegrown terrorists. What's happening now is a repeat of what occurred in Nazi Germany. Hitler had the whole country spying on each other. Germans were snitching on their neighbors for dropping a candy wrapper. Propaganda and fear are age-old weapons that turn humans into sheep."

"You know what else I saw at Paxmart? Those hidden surveillance cameras were *everywhere*. There wasn't one inch of the store that wasn't covered."

Truman nodded sagely. "Let me tell you how deep this goes. The CIA set its sights on Paxmart early on in the company's growth. They made the founder incredibly rich—but make no mistake about it—the spooks were calling the shots. Paxmarts across the country are being prepped to become neighborhood crisis centers. At some point they will attack humanity with bird flu, swine flu, or whatever they decide to name their next homemade disease. Paxmart will be the location where they'll forcibly shoot us up with their poison. Paxmart will be their control center when they make their next big earthquake or hurricane—and I mean *control*. We are going to have absolute chaos in the streets after a total economic collapse or a major false flag terror attack. Paxmart will play an important part in imposing martial law. The stores will be used as FEMA processing centers to lock up us bad apples. Hey, do you guys wanna hear a tall tale regarding Paxmart?"

"Of course we do," Wright quickly answered.

"I'm sure everyone remembers the devastating Asian tsunami. It was planned well in advance. The controllers made sure everything was in order before they set off their underwater quake. They always plant their media in strategic locations to record and sensationalize whatever angle they're presenting to the sheep. Well, listen to this pack of lies. Paxmart *just happened* to have a top executive vacationing in Thailand exactly when the tsunami struck. He was the company's director of *global procurement security*. Now what are the odds of that—a global disaster security expert sipping his umbrella-topped cocktail on the beach when one of the biggest 'natural' disasters strikes. Wait—hold onto your hats—the fantastic plot thickens. Just like in the movies this guy heroically lifts his wife and two children up a ladder to safety. Immediately after hoisting the second child out of danger he is tragically swept out to sea. A Reuters photographer *just happened* to photograph the event. Calculate the odds of that occurring and you'll be calculating all night. Now keep in mind that Reuters is one of the largest news providers in the world. The photograph is shown worldwide. The executive's parents see the photograph and notify Paxmart's corporate headquarters. Paxmart immediately goes into action. Through a series of highly unlikely events the executive is rescued and revived. Everyone else who is swept away by the killer wave dies. But not this guy, he lives to tell his incredible tale. Kudos to the writers of this imaginative work of fiction."

"Wow!" exclaimed Wright. "You know what that tells me? That is clear evidence that the tsunami was planned in advance. Heck, they probably staged that photo weeks before the disaster."

"It fits the mold," added Menza. "They like to have their people in place during these important events. Truman, I remember you telling me about the 'heroic' public official who directed the rescue operations in New York after 9/11. He *just happened* to be visiting London during the 7/7 subway bombings. I guess they needed more 'heroic' leadership to 'control' the situation."

"Yep, I think you've got these guys figured out." declared Truman. "Government and big business work hand in hand. You don't get any bigger than Paxmart."

"It sounds like Paxmart is an actual arm of the government," said Wright. "Truman, what do you think?"

"I can tell you this. They have the largest private computer system in the world—only it's not private. It's tied in to the CIA and pentagon. The bond between Paxmart and government intelligence agencies runs deep. One of the heirs to the Paxmart fortune died in a plane crash. He was involved in covert special operations in the Vietnam War. He specialized in psychological warfare. That's a red flag as far as I'm concerned. Things can get truly psycho when you're the eleventh richest person in the world and you've got associates that specialize in murder and deception. Eighteen billion dollars floating around with a dead owner might provide a little motivation for someone. I would bet the plane crash is the result of four scenarios, none of them being a true accident. A—It was flat out murder for money. Chase the money trail to solve that one. B—It was a murder to keep him quiet. I'm sure he knew all the secrets. Of course you should always add the money factor into this one too. C—He was a sacrifice. I have a theory that some of the rich and famous actually sell their souls for their glitzy rewards. Payback could be a family member's life. Include some famous entertainers along with the very rich in this one. Who's collecting the dark debt of death here is someone or something very powerful, possibly beyond human. D—He staged his own death for whatever reason. Anything is possible here including him going underground, the Moon, Mars, or some space station where the elite go to escape all the pain and suffering the rest of us are forced to endure."

"So Paxmart is a bigtime player in all this nutty stuff going on in the world," said Wright. "Who would have ever guessed?"

"It depends on how you look it," said Truman. "Paxmart is actually chump change when it comes to the military-industrial complex. I've been discussing them only because they're a company with a public face. Millions of people shop there regularly and Paxmart is ingrained into our culture. The reality of corporatism is that it's fascist in nature. Every major corporation has been infiltrated by intelligence agencies. Once they reach a certain size they have to pay to play. Many an entrepreneur has learned that lesson the hard way. Freedom and fair play is thrown out the window when the government thugs come knocking. They will buy you out or burn you out. Every large corporation worldwide has to fit into their control grid. Most of the general public has never heard of the biggest corporate players. They operate with the trillions of dollars siphoned out of taxpayer money that fund the black budget operations. All the dirty stuff flies under the radar."

"I think I know what you're trying to say," said Wright. "Big business and government are one and the same, right?"

Truman nodded in agreement. "Have you ever noticed the cycle of certain high level government officials? They're in office during a certain administration, they disappear for a while, then they're back. Guess where they were? They were the go-betweens for the military-industrial complex. They command huge salaries connecting the blood stained dots of so-called national defense and security. Members of this exclusive club shuffle taxpayer cash amongst themselves. Did you ever wonder why the government pays a thousand dollars for a two-dollar hammer? It's because a member of the club makes $998 on the deal. He runs the company that sells the hammer. Apply that logic to a billion dollar weapon deal. Your calculator will start smoking from the corrupt numbers it spews. The black budget stuff is off the charts—and it's been going on for a long time. Go on the internet and listen to President Eisenhower's warning about the military-industrial complex in his farewell address. He knew the dangers of misplaced power because he lived with the snakes. They slithered around him seeking raw power and control. They're relentless in their greed and ambition. They'll stomp any president they don't own. Look what happened to Kennedy."

"How in the heck can they get by with it for so long?" asked Wright. "Can't anyone stop it?"

"The answer to that is rule by secrecy. Let me go back to Kennedy. He too made a significant speech. He warned America and the world about secret societies. You can find this important speech on the internet also. Listen to it now before they yank it off the web. Kennedy was assassinated not long afterwards."

"What was in that speech?" asked Wright.

"Just the truth," replied Truman. "But they don't want the truth exposed. Kennedy told members of the press that secret societies were dangerous in a free and open society—and he was right. Any elected public official who has taken an oath of secrecy to an organization is tainted. Where will his loyalties lie—with the public he supposedly represents or his secret buddies? Needless to say there is a conflict of interest."

"I've heard of Skull and Bones," said Wright. "Isn't that a secret society?"

"Yes, you're correct. Skull and Bones is a secret society based at Yale University. Several presidents have been members. Other major secret societies include Freemasons, Rosicrucians, Knights Templar, Bilderberg Group and a handful of others. Basically it's the same ole story—the powerful elite are conspiring to gain total control over humanity."

"Which of these groups are the most powerful?" asked Wright.

"That's a good question, Wright. They are so intertwined that no one group takes precedence above the others. However—I have a theory. I personally believe there is a super secret society that directs the others. They're a group few in number but concentrated in power. They harbor the secrets of the past—and the future."

"Who makes up this secret organization?"

"Wright, it is my belief that it's basically other-worldly—a select group made up of aliens, human/alien hybrids and a few good old fashioned humans. I think they hold the answers to the planet and the universe. We've definitely had previous technologically advanced societies on this planet. Atlantis was real—and there have been others. Those civilizations were destroyed, but the technologies survived. By the way, the theory of evolution is an absolute lie—monkeys we aren't."

"That's fantastic stuff," said Wright. "But you know I'm open to just about anything. Please tell me more."

"Sure," said Truman with a short laugh. "Right now a John Lennon quote comes to mind. He made this statement just before he was murdered by the CIA. I remember it word for word. 'Our society is run by insane people for insane objectives. I think we're being run by maniacs for maniacal ends and I think I'm liable to be put away as insane for expressing that. That's what insane about it.' You can bet John Lennon knew what a twisted world we live in."

"They shut him up, that's for sure," said Wright, "Tell me, Truman, just how crazy is it? This secret society group that you say rules the world—what's their agenda?"

"Another good question—one that I don't know the answer to. Once again, I'll speculate. It's possible that this ultra-secret group, club—whatever you may call it—holds the answers to the biggest of the big questions. Who are we? Where did we come from? What is the history of our planet? They're not about to let us commoners in on their private stash of information. We're considered to be cows and donkeys in their eyes, replaceable beasts. We're an inferior race, created solely to serve them as slaves, born and bred for licking their feet. We could become dangerous to them if we're armed with the truth. They keep us occupied with silly things like sports, entertainment and gossip. They supply us with a fake history and trick a bunch of Piled High and Deep's—that's an accurate description of certain tunnel-visioned PhD's—into intellectually jargoning their pack of lies until they sound believable. They play us like we would play with a windup toy."

Wright looked away and sighed. "So what you're saying is that they're the ultimate secret society—the true controllers of the planet, even to the point of controlling other controllers, other secret organizations—right?"

"Yes," replied Truman. "And it's all based on knowledge. Keeping us stupid is of major importance to them. A secret society ain't secret when the secrets get out—know what I mean?"

"I guess that makes sense," said Wright. He looked over at Menza.

"Menza, you've been mighty quiet over there. What do you think about all this? What's your take on Truman's theory of an alien-based secret society running our planet?'

"Maybe we're all aliens," Menza joked. He smiled and held up his empty pint glass. "I think I need another glass of Truman's beer to keep my alien blood flowing."

"I'll second that," chuckled Truman. "Let me go get us one. These are on the house."

Truman reached underneath the bar and pulled out a legal pad. He tore off the top sheet and handed it to Menza.

I GOT A SECRET

SSSSHHH—don't you say a word, you gotta swear
I'm gonna tell you something and you don't dare
Say a word to anybody and I mean no one,
Or I'm gonna tell your mama bout you and Tom
SSSSHHH—I got a secret, I share it with a few,
I got a secret, yes I do
Promise to keep quiet
And I'll share my secret with you
SSSSHHH—yes I will—SSSSSHHH
Something's going on
They won't look me in the eye,
Every time I ask they tell me a lie
Yeah, the whole town's a whispering

Bout you and me,
They got a secret that we can't see
SSSSHHH—I got a secret, I share it with a few
I got a secret, yes I do
Promise to keep quiet
And I'll share my secret with you
SSSSHHH—yes I will—SSSSSHH

Chapter 20
REPORT TO THE BOSS 2

MG/IOS/HG FACILITY—Report 002

Intel/Analysis of Celestial Unit MWG91177-3

(GLC MWK/F-O-L-L-Y)

Prepared/Submitted by MNZA-9716

(HG-131313-8)

Transmitted to the Ministry of Governance

Intergalactic Open Society—11/33/4422/HG

Accumulated Intelligence Summary:

MNZA-9716 reporting from MWG91177-3. Hello to everyone on our beautiful planet. I miss you all. It has been several months since my last report. All is well. I still have unlimited access to my genomel source and my health is fine. I have settled into a routine here on Earth. It took me a while to acclimate socially. I am very careful about what I say and how much I say. As you know, a person learns a lot more from listening than he does speaking.

I have become attached to the occupants of this planet. Humans have captured my heart. I have personally witnessed numerous acts of kindness and generosity. I just want to mention a few of them to give you an idea of their basic nature. Let's start with my landlord. Her name is Joan Dixon and she has a heart of gold. Yesterday I was sitting on my front porch. The clouds were blackening and a light rain was beginning to fall. I saw an elderly man walking on the street in front of my apartment. He was carrying several paper bags that appeared to be loaded with groceries. Just then I saw a car stop in front of him. It was Joan. She spoke to him for a moment, after which he stepped into her car. At that very moment the skies burst into a downpour. Joan took the man home. It was just a small act of kindness, but it came from the heart.

Here's another example of human generosity. A few days ago I was researching human behavior at a large retail establishment. I was standing in front of a bench in front of the store. A man who appeared to be homeless was sitting on the bench. He was holding his jaw and groaning in pain. I asked him what was wrong. He replied that he had a terrible toothache. Another gentleman overheard the conversation. It just so happened there was a dentist's office directly across the street from the store. The stranger told the homeless man to follow him. He told him he was taking him to the dentist and would pay the bill. I watched them both walk in the office. I am certain the man was well taken care of. What a wonderful human being that stranger was.

I could literally list hundreds of instances of humans helping humans, but this report would go on forever. Here is one last example of the human spirit. It's sort of double-edged. After the 9/11 false flag terror event there was a tremendous fund raising effort led by two ex-presidents. After the devastating manmade earthquake in Haiti there was also a well publicized relief effort. It too was directed by two ex-presidents. In both cases millions of dollars poured in to help the unfortunate people affected by the disasters. Donations flowed in from all classes of grief stricken humans, rich and poor alike. In both cases the bulk of the money was stolen—stolen by the same people who planned and carried out the two events. The naïve masses are allowing their corrupt leaders to have their way with them. A handful of bad apples are causing the whole basket of apples to rot.

Good against Evil—this appears to be the nature of the universe. I guess Novem is an exception to the rule right now. At this stage of our history we're all about peace. Let's hope it stays that way. On this particular planet the Goods vastly outnumber the Evils, but the Evils have the upper hand right now. I hope the Goods ultimately prevail.

My observations of Earthlings have resulted in many answers—and many more questions. One thing I know for sure—Earth is a prison planet. It appears to me that a malevolent species have hijacked the human race and taken control. I see evidence of hybrid walk-ins. I will expand on this later on in the report. I feel sorry for the good humans who are caught up in this takeover. They are wonderful emotional creatures with hearts of gold. What I would like to do is put ninety percent of the population on a super biocraft and fly them the heck out of here.

The mind control program being used against the humans is off the charts. I touched on this in my previous report, but I feel it is necessary to mention it again. Basically it amounts to a mutation of the entire species. It is a total assault on their senses. They are attacked from the moment of conception and the onslaught continues until they die. Their "reality" consists of television, movies, music, sports and other forms of "entertainment." I'm glad none of you have to witness what I see here on a daily basis. I truly pity them. Humans are such a magnificent species and they're being destroyed. The most incredible aspect of this across-the-grid mind control program is that *they like it*. They love being indoctrinated to the point of numbness. Earthlings float through their short little lives occupying themselves with trivial pursuits. They spend their entire lives chasing nothing which they think is something. By the time they realize their something is nothing it's too late—a wasted life. It's a shame and it makes me want to cry. Their minds are not their own.

Who's truly in control here? I have been analyzing the situation down here trying to figure it out. This is my working theory. This could change as I learn more. Alien intervention is definitely a factor down here. That much I know. Here's how it might be playing out. I think there is a war going on between two or more alien groups. Like everything in life there's lots of grey here, no clear good guys, no clear bad guys—although I do think that one group is considerably worse than the other. Both sides desire total control of humanity. Most likely there is a more powerful faction of aliens that are dictating rules for this war. The reason I say this is because physical destruction is kept to a minimum. Either side could totally destroy the planet with high tech weaponry at any time, but they don't. This war seems to necessitate free will. The battle is for the human mind, spirit and soul. These are the spoils of this war.

Earlier in the report I mentioned walk-ins. I think this is all part of the ongoing war. The alien invaders are disguising themselves as humans. They inhabit human bodies in an effort to hide their covert activities. I suspect they're using cloaking technology, teleportation, clones and other means of deception to trick the humans. It's an age old trick of the universe—they create a character out of nothing and place him or her in a position of power—be it political, economic, whatever. They then use the human body as a shell to deceive the public. They even create entertainers, fire up their publicity machines, and shoot them to the top of the fame game. Then the entertainers acquire influence over the population, especially the youth. The bottom line is all about gaining power and control over the masses. Earth is a battlefield. A war is raging all around the humans and they are completely unaware of it. They're surrounded by aliens as they sit around and debate the possibility of life on other planets. It's a very sad situation indeed.

Let me quickly update you on my interpersonal relationships. I'm still seeing the same girl down here—sweet Marilyn. I told you about her in my last report. Marilyn is a very special human being. She's going through some difficult times right now. Her mother is dying of cancer. The health care program down here is a total joke. The controllers of the planet have a secret serum that cures cancer, but it's not available to the masses. It's an absolutely ruthless strategy. They prefer to keep the population in check by allowing people to die. It's truly an upside-down planet. No means yes, white means black, war is peace and lies are the norm.

I see Marilyn nearly every day. Her presence makes my stay here more bearable. I miss my beautiful planet and my friends and family, but I've got to tell you—this girl really lights my fire. I'm talking *really really* lights my fire. She's beautiful, charming, musical and hotter than a supernova. It's all I can do to keep my emotions in check. I'm really going to miss Marilyn when I leave.

Remember my friend Truman? We're still hanging out together on a regular basis. He's the one who makes beer. That's the stuff that keeps me alive down here, my genomel source. He's been teaching me a little bit about the art of brewing beer. You can bet your tail that I'm gonna learn how to make it. I'm gonna talk JP into serving it at James Café. Wait until you try beer. It's darn tasty stuff. One more note about Truman. I'm still very concerned about his well being. His life has been threatened. The controllers don't appreciate him exposing their secrets. He's being harassed on a daily basis. I don't like those buttdompers messing with my friend!

I've also made several other friends since I last communicated with you. One of them—Wright is his name—aspires to become involved in the politics of the planet. Wright is honorable and trustworthy. My first impulse was to persuade him to stay out of this dangerous game. There is a very good chance the controllers will murder him when he starts to ripple the political waters. After giving it some thought, I decided to keep my mouth shut. This planet is in desperate need of leaders like Wright. It's better to die for what you believe in than to do nothing. I admire Wright's courage. May luck be with him. I ask all of you to pray for him and Truman. They need all the help they can get.

Wright has enlisted a mutual friend to jumpstart his political career. His name is Pepper. He is another wonderful human being. The three of us spend much time together at Truman's genomel/beer establishment. Pepper and his father have become close friends of mine. Pepper is typical of the human race in the fact that he is skeptical of the existence of extraterrestrial life. He says he will believe it when he actually sees a spaceship land in his front yard.

I apologize if I seem a little down. It's just that I see the writing on the wall and it's not good. The outlook is dismal for Earth. It sickens me to think about the future. Marilyn, Truman and all my other friends are going down on a sinking ship. I know I should not have become emotionally involved with my subjects. It's the first thing you learn in IOS training—do not let your emotions interfere with your task at hand. Well, I have failed miserably in that area. I *love* these humans that I interact with on a daily basis. If it did not go against all IOS regulations I would send Tucker a direct transmission. I would beg him for help. I would convey the desperation of the situation down here. My friends are dying a slow death. A powerful snake has wrapped itself around humanity. It won't release its cold blooded death grip until it has squeezed out the entirety of the human spirit.

Maybe I am weak—I don't really know. All I know is that I'm frustrated watching this beautiful planet self destruct. Humans are having their very souls sucked out of them. I wish I could sit down and have a one on one conversation with the creator of the universe. I would ask him why—why are you doing this? Why do you put my friends through so much pain? Why are you slowly killing them? I know he must have a valid reason—but I don't understand it. All I see is misery and suffering and despair. I would tell him that most humans are kind and gentle. They are full of soul and passion and emotion. I would explain to him that Earth is a special place, a mother lode of love. I would show him that this planet is overflowing in genomel. There is so much love residing here that it's inevitable. Humans are creatures of generosity with feelings for one another. They have a presence about them. They are *real*. There's too much raw emotion for it to be any other way. I wish I could have one brief moment to plead my case to the creator. I would lead him to a stream of pure passion that flows into a sea of endless love. He made this place. His building blocks were love and spirit and soul. Earth is a masterpiece that's being ripped into shreds. Why is he destroying such a beautiful place filled with gentle souls? Why?

I have to go now. Tears are falling. I will close this transmission with some song lyrics. Truman and Marilyn wrote this song together. I think it pretty much sums up the situation here. Tell everyone there hello. I miss you all. THE MENZ

GOTTA BE A BETTER PLACE

Out there in the night, dancing among the stars,
There's got to be a light that's better than ours
One that's honest and true, and not ruled by greed
A world where love is the rule, and rulers do love
A place of peace and understanding
Compassion and trust
Where smiles are the currency and everyone's rich
Where you help one another and there's no police
Gotta be a better, gotta be a better,
Gotta be a better, place than this
Yeah, there's gotta be a better, gotta be a better,
There's gotta be a better—place than this
Come take us away, away from this place,
This place of emptiness, of broken glass
We're nothing but prisoners paying our toll,
And our soul's the toll for them to control
So if you're out there and listening,
I can whisper or shout
But please take a moment, please hear me out,
We're desperate down here, down and out
We're caught in a crossfire
Of hopelessness and doubt
We gotta get away, and escape with our soul,
I'm pleading, I'm begging, I'm bearing it all
Fly us away, to your shimmering refuge
Glistening in the dark
Away from this evil, away from the pain
Gotta be a better, gotta be a better,
Gotta be a better, place than this
Yeah, there's gotta be a better, gotta be a better,
There's gotta be a better—place than this

Chapter 21
MOON TALK

It had been a slow night. Tuesdays were like that sometimes. Truman was closing down relatively early at 11 p.m. Marilyn had worked the evening shift as usual and had just finished her cleaning duties. Menza stayed until the end, being the loyal customer he was. Of course his pretty blonde girlfriend might have had something to do with it. Marilyn especially needed some comfort this evening. Her mother's condition had worsened. She had been crying off and on all day. The three of them stepped outside as Truman turned the key to lock up.

"The Moon sure is bright tonight," commented Marilyn.

Truman looked up. "Yeah, and it's full too. They're probably having a big party up there tonight. There are a lot of things going on up there."

"Like what?" asked Marilyn. "I've always been curious about the Moon."

"Well, for one thing, there are aliens and humans up there."

"Really?"

"Sure," replied Truman. "The world government—utilizing the U.S. and Russian space programs mostly—moved a bunch of equipment up there in the early 60's. They called it Operation Whiteout. The humans are working with the aliens on various projects, most of them having to do with controlling us little peons down here on Earth."

Menza remained quiet. He wanted to learn the extent and accuracy of Truman's knowledge. Once again the wizard of awareness was proving to be accurate. The depth of Truman's perception was amazing.

Truman continued. "The Moon is an artificially constructed spaceship—and it's hollow. The bought off science boys are desperate to provide an answer as to where the Moon came from. Even professional liars such as NASA can't come up with a plausible theory that sticks. The Moon is a custom-built satellite of Earth. The extraterrestrials designed it perfectly to be synchronized with the Sun. It's 400 times smaller than the Sun, and at a solar eclipse it's 400 times closer to Earth. This makes the Moon appear to be the same size as the Sun. Nice coincidence, huh? That's about as coincidental as the fact that the Moon rotates at the exact speed necessary to coincide with one rotation around the Earth. Do you know what that means? That means we never see the 'dark' side of the moon. Hummm…I wonder what's on that back side that we're not allowed to see."

That's some amazing information," said Marilyn. "If we went to the Moon in the early 60's, then why did they say we first put a man on the Moon in 1969?"

"That gets a little complicated. Let me explain it. There have always been rumors that we never actually went to the Moon. NASA *wanted* those rumors out. They thrive on conspiracy theorists wallowing in confusion. The first official landing on the Moon was a complete fraud. It was all faked—

it was nothing more than a movie. A famous American film director staged it in a studio. The world government had been flying to the Moon for years with 'flying saucer' technology. No one went to the Moon in that tin can of a spacecraft they showed us on television. That rusty old piece of crap wouldn't make it to the corner store, much less a quarter of a million miles to the Moon. The Moon landing hoax was nothing more than an expensive Hollywood production. It would have been much easier to actually go to Moon than to fake it. It was another fine use of taxpayer money—expensive foolery to keep the sheep asleep."

"What's going up there?" asked Marilyn. "You mentioned earlier that they are controlling us from the Moon. How are they doing that?"

"The Moon is sort of a second home for a certain race. They were here on Earth before our species arrived. In their mind they are the true caretakers of the planet. They live underground on Earth and in the Moon. Yes—*in* the Moon. They zip back and forth as they please. Both of you look up at that big bright ball in the night sky. As we speak there's some spooky things going on up there."

"Tell me, Truman," said Marilyn. "What! What are they doing?"

"They're having a party—and we're their entertainment. They're sitting back pushing buttons playing us like a video game. The Moon is their turf. They run a good portion of their mind control program from the Moon. They also base a lot of genetic experiments out of there. You know—the same kind of stuff that's going on in the underground labs down here, but maybe a little more geared towards the fine tuning and finesse details. They gotta tune up their new bio toys before they put them in the streets."

"What kind of mind control can they do from so far away?" asked Marilyn.

"A few years back Hollywood clued us in on that one. They made a big budget movie starring a top actor and a fake Moon. The main character—who has the same name as me by the way—is being controlled from the Moon. That movie is another example of them exposing a piece of reality through 'fiction.' My theory is this. I think they're transmitting electromagnetic waves directly from the Moon into our brains. They can attack us collectively or individually—the planet, one nation or one person. Combine that with brain-rotting television, throw in some good old fashioned subliminal stimuli, mix in some nutritious chemtrails—and we're looking at a mind control cocktail that leaves us the mentally wounded zombies that we are. Yep, there are some strange things originating from that big white ball in the sky."

"It kinda makes you wonder," said Marilyn. "What else is going on? Just look up there. As far as you can see there are stars and more stars. There must be zillions of them."

The three of them stared into the endless sky. The Moon seemed to stare right back at them. Menza felt uneasy for a brief moment, a feeling of intrusion. A chill raced through his body. It was if the Moon was reading his mind. Maybe it was.

"Get outta here," snapped Truman. "Did you guys feel that? I think the boys running the show up there just sent us a message."

"Yes, I felt it," answered Menza.

"Me too," said Marilyn.

"It's gone now," said Menza. "I think you're right. They just let us know that they're watching and listening."

"You know what?" said Marilyn. 'Here we are, looking at one moon circling around one planet that's circling around one sun—and this crazy stuff is going on. Can you imagine what else is going on in that vast universe? It makes me question the very nature of reality."

"You might be on the right track," said Truman. "Is reality real—or has some advanced species made us their special science project? Are they creating our perceived reality? Are we microscopic pawns on an insignificant planet—and the planet itself is nothing more than a tiny square on a giant chessboard? Could we be nothing more than a study, an experiment, maybe nothing more than a source of entertainment—who knows?"

"All I know," said Marilyn, "is that there's lots of stuff floating around up there. Suns, stars, planets, moons, asteroids, satellites—space is a busy place."

Truman scanned the night sky. He seemed to be looking for something. He focused on one particular cluster of stars.

"Menza, do you remember something I told you a few weeks ago? All the stars aren't stars. Many of them are ancient space stations. The sky is full of them—clusters of space stations teeming with life. Look up there. Do you see what we commonly call the Big Dipper? There's not one star there. It's entirely composed of artificial space stations. Many of them are massive in size. Intelligent beings constructed them and inhabit them. There are cultures in Africa where they refuse to look at the Big Dipper. They claim it brings bad luck. They say the controllers of the human race live there. Grab some decent binoculars and look at the Pleiades. It's more of the same. Take a look at the International Space Station. There are websites that track its daily position. They tell us it's the brightest object in the sky now, brighter than Venus. Then look at the sky. Do you see some stars that have a similar reflective quality about them? Yep—you guessed it—those are space stations too. Who's operating them? Well, that's anybody's guess."

"Star wars," said Marilyn. "I bet that is what's going on. There's an infinite amount of space up there, yet everyone's fighting over it. Ain't that crazy?"

"You could be right, Marilyn. As a matter of fact I think that's exactly what's going on."

Truman gazed towards the heavens. Once again he seemed to be searching for something in particular. Then he began pointing towards various stars scattered across the sky. He finally focused on one particularly noticeable one.

"I want you both to look over there. Do you see the star that seems to be twinkling. If you look real close you can see flashing lights on it. With binoculars the lights appear more vivid. That's actually some sort of satellite or spaceship or weaponry. It's definitely no star. There are lots of those in the sky. Take a look over there. It's also flashing some bright colors. And look at those three 'stars' that seem to be lined up in perfect symmetrical order. They all have colored lights. Do you see that odd looking group of 'stars' over there—same thing, flashing multicolored lights. There are two more just east of the Moon. I could show you several more, but my point is that they're everywhere. Something is going on— something *big*."

"So what are you trying to say?" asked Marilyn. "Do you think that's some sort of star war technology?"

"Absolutely," answered Truman. "Those flashing objects are relatively close to us. They're focusing on our planet and our planet alone. They're not several light years away like real stars—no, no, no. Those things up there are big league instruments of war and control and surveillance. Let me explain this with a top-down approach. First of all, there is a war going on. Humanity is the target. The technology that is sitting above our heads is fantastic science fiction stuff, incomprehensible to most of us. That much is certain. That leads us to two big questions. Who is doing it—and why?"

"Well…Truman," muttered Marilyn. "I've never known you to be shy about voicing your opinion. Who do you think is doing it? And why?"

"You're right, Marilyn. I definitely have an opinion. First of all, let's dispense with the Propaganda 101 level of lies that the government's going to eventually throw out there. The purpose of this space weaponry is *not* to defend America from Russia, China from America, Russia from China, or any of that nonsense. That's the popular excuse the powerful world government conspirators love to circulate to the masses. The trusty old divide-and-rule trick has worked for millenniums. The dumb-downed sheep fall for that one every time. So that's what it's *not*."

Marilyn took a deep breath and slowly exhaled. "Okay, Truman. I'm emotionally ready to handle it. Tell me what it *is*."

"There are four possibilities. Number one—the human elite are working alone using this incredible technology to control humanity. Let's give that one a ten percent chance. Number two—the elite and an alien race are working together for the same objective. I'll give that one a twenty percent chance. Number three—a single alien race *is* the elite. They have disguised themselves in human bodies. They are using their advanced technology to maintain control over humanity. I'll go thirty percent on that one. Number four—there are two or more alien races battling it out for control of our minds and souls. They are operating from space and utilizing technology that even science fiction writers cannot dream up. This goes beyond the standard teleportation, cloning, plasma beams, invisibility cloaking, deleting memories, implanting false memories—all those are kindergarten toys for this bunch. Stealing souls is the name of the game. I mean *literally* stealing souls. It's not enough for them to maintain absolute control of our thoughts, emotions and everything else it is that makes us human. Their prize is the soul itself. I'm sorry to say, but I'm giving possibility number four a forty percent shot at reality. I'm afraid we're caught up in something so fantastic that it exceeds our imagination."

Marilyn shrugged. "I was expecting something wild and you delivered. The scary thing is you're usually right. Aliens are fighting a war in the skies over control of our souls. Wow! *Our souls.* We trudge around down here occupying ourselves raising kids, paying mortgages, dreaming of new cars and houses, and trancing ourselves out watching television. Meanwhile a bunch of aliens are sitting in spaceships pushing buttons and directing us like a Broadway play. Truman, please tell me this. Is nothing as it seems?"

"Marilyn, you've hit the nail on the head again. Nothing is at it seems. They're placing and replacing characters just like a Broadway play. I wouldn't be surprised if every major political and entertainment figure was either a clone, synthetic robot, an alien in a human disguise, or at minimum heavily mind controlled. Do you remember Shakespeare's frequently quoted phrase? 'All the world's a stage,' his character so famously said. He compares the world to a stage and life to a play. Well, we humans are the big event. We wander around chasing trinkets while the world burns all around us. You can't help but laugh at the fact that Shakespeare himself was a hoax. He was a sometime amateur actor hired to distract from the true playwright, an insider who couldn't afford to write about his powerful political friends. Sometimes I wish I didn't know this stuff. Is it any wonder that I have to drink beer out of a 55-gallon drum to keep my sanity? Oh my! Noooo!"

"Take a deep breath, my friend," said Menza. "It's better to know what's going on than to walk around in a fog believing everything is peaches and cream. They'll eventually find out their peaches are rotten and the cream is spoiled. Maybe I should just manifest a spaceship and haul us out of here. We'll leave all the sheep to fend for themselves. What would you two think of that?"

"You got my vote!" exclaimed Marilyn.

"Count me in," Truman agreed. "Just make sure my beer making equipment fits inside the spaceship."

"I'm glad you're back, Truman," said Menza. "I thought we had lost you. I want to hear more wisdom from you."

Truman laughed. "Sure, why not? We haven't discussed the planets in our solar system. Everyone's always bringing up the possibility of life on Mars. Occasionally someone will discuss possible life on Venus and Jupiter. I personally think there's intelligent life on all three of them. But you know who I think the granddaddy of them all is—Saturn."

"What's different about Saturn?" asked Marilyn.

"Take a look at it with a telescope. Saturn is spectacular. Those beautiful rings around it are something else. By the way, they ain't made of ice—that's another official lie for the masses to munch on. Saturn is the second largest planet in the solar system, several times larger than Earth. It has a multitude of moons revolving around it. Most likely they're all hollow and bustling with life inside. The same with the planet itself—and the rings! Just imagine living and working inside one of those stunning take your-breath-away rings. Wow!"

"It sounds like you have quite the fascination with Saturn," said Menza. "Tell me more."

"Sure, I could go on all night about my favorite planet. I would bet that Saturn is the intelligence center of the solar system. It's probably a real destination—for business and pleasure. How would you like to take a holiday riding one of those luxury moons around that magnificent planet? Can you imagine what those glorious rings must look like from a point so close? I can just picture it now—kicking back in a comfortable Saturn-produced recliner, sipping a cool brew, admiring the splendid breathtaking views as my five-star moon slowly rotates around the ringed beauty that is the jewel of the universe. Oh yeah, that's just what I need—a nice long Saturn vacation."

"Maybe you should add in there a beautiful girlfriend from Saturn," kidded Menza. "You would make a nice interplanetary prize for a single Saturn girl on the prowl for a mate. Those Saturn girls would probably take a liking to you, a handsome Earthling with a brain that actually functions. What do you think, Truman?"

"Why not!" cracked Truman. "With three ex-wives from three different continents, I might as well try one from a distant planet. Maybe an alien could put up with my weird ways. All my human wives certainly couldn't handle me. Truman and his new wife from Saturn—it certainly has a *ring* to it. Ha!—my feeble attempt at humor."

Marilyn laughed. "Truman, you are funny when you want to be. You're actually a little bit of everything all mixed up— and that's good. That makes me think of something. What star sign are you? I've never thought to ask you about your zodiac sign."

"I'm an October Libra," replied Truman. "I'm supposed to be balanced, but I'm not so sure about that. A lot of people would say I'm the most imbalanced person on the planet— Oh, that Truman, he thinks 9/11 was an inside job and he believes in aliens! Pity poor unbalanced Truman!"

"That's funny," said Marilyn, giving Truman a playful poke in the ribs. "You know you really are a very balanced person. I personally believe in astrology. I think there's something to it. I've seen some amazingly accurate birth charts. Maybe whoever or whatever is controlling us is doing it through the stars. There has got to be some kind of connection we have to the stars—there's just gotta be."

"Absolutely," remarked Truman. "There are some very powerful people who won't make a move unless the so-called stars are lined up. It's all about secret knowledge and appeasing the controllers. We have been led to believe that all those bright lights up there are stars. Well, it just ain't so. Many of them are of intelligent design—and I do mean *intelligent*. They're ancient space stations full of life forms that would blow the human mind. When you walk the halls up there you're hanging with the powers. They're in charge of spirituality, consciousness, the supernatural—chew on those key words and you'll begin to get the picture. They can shake up a soul with a psychic earthquake to merge the unconscious into consciousness. Yep, they've got some numinous tools up there. They're beings of spirit and soul, but however big they are, they're still taking orders from others bigger than they—and the ladder reaches even higher. It's one crazy universe, huh guys?"

"It certainly is," replied Menza. "So what you're basically saying is that the beings on those space stations have a major influence on you humans…er…us humans…down here on Earth, right?"

Truman continued, but not before giving Menza a quick glance—and what possibly could have been a wink—one without a hint of surprise or shock.

"Yes, Menza, they act as sort of a steering wheel for humanity. Go with the flow of the stars and the road rides smoother, the bumps are a little smaller, and life's destination seems a little easier to reach. Go against the grain of those starry space stations and things can get rocky real quick. Why did the wife of a popular American president check with the stars before her husband traveled? Why does NASA not make a move until the star charts give them the go-ahead—even though they deny it. Why do numerous celebrities and world leaders have personal astrologers? Why do masses of people religiously check their horoscope every day? Carl Jung, the extraordinary founder of analytical psychology, was quoted as saying, 'Astrology represents the summation of all the psychological knowledge of antiquity.' Just think about that for a moment. That's a pretty strong statement. What he's trying to tell us is everything that's ever been rides on those spaceships—every tidbit of knowledge, every secret unbeknownst to man, every mystery that's yet to be unraveled, everything that stirs our soul, guides our spirit and steers our path. That's powerful stuff."

The three friends were quiet for a moment, each one in their own world of thought. Finally Truman broke the silence.

"Look at you, Marilyn. You're shivering from the cold. Let's all go home. It's chilly out here this evening."

"Yes, it is a little nippy out tonight. I'm pretty tired also. At least we've all got some light to guide us back to our cars—thanks to full Moon. I don't like walking in the dark."

"Just remember this," said Truman. "Darkness is the light you cannot see. You can take that two ways. I know you're going through a dark period dealing with your mother's sickness. There's a light in the middle of that darkness. It might be a faint glow, but it's there. Find that ray of light and hope, follow it, track it to its source—and fire up the power behind it. Turn that dim little glow into a roaring fire that lights up that blackness that is consuming you. Turn the corner on sadness and find your light. It's out there and it's burning bright."

Truman turned to Menza. He said nothing, but he did not have to. Menza read his eyes and understood the message loud and clear. His friend was telling him something he already knew—he was the bright light that Marilyn so desperately needed.

"Marilyn," said Truman in a calm voice, "here are some lyrics that need a little help from Jimi's guitar. You and that star guitar give 'em a little life."

Marilyn took the paper from his hands. She walked over to Truman and wrapped her arms around him, squeezing him tight. For a long moment she held him. Tears streamed down upon his shoulder soaking into his coat.

"Thank you, Truman—for being a friend."

GUITAR ECHO

When everything's gone crazy,
And you don't know where to turn
And you just want to say screw it and walk away
When the world's turned cold and cloudy,
And your candle's all burned
And all your hopes and dreams
Are a thousand miles away
When everyone's speaking sign language
And it don't make sense
Their words come out
But they don't make any sound
Just when you're at your breaking point
It all comes through
It's a guitar's echo
And it's so full of soul and desperation
Softly calling the names

Of those who have lost their way
It's a guitar's echo
Coming in with soulful respiration
It's calling your name and it's got a lot to say
Cut away the fray and the jealousy
The envy and the malice
It's telling all truths to come out from hiding,
It is what it is and there ain't no denying
The guitar's echo rings clear and clean,
She's an echo bouncing back
From a real bad dream
She's that way cause she's a little bit like you,
Both of you sing to a different tune
Her echo's soft but sure—and oh so true,
She's a whispering echo reflecting off you
She's a round trip message coming back home,
She's hope and promise wrapped in a song
You're an echo away with your star guitar,
Ain't nothing done that ain't been done before
You'll be stars in the morning til the sun rides in,
Soon as he leaves you're back out again
So hang in there tough when you're feeling down,
Cause things can change on a guitar's sound
One minute you're cold and distant,
And your face is in the ground
Then you're off like a rocket to the promised land
She's a guitar's echo—that's what they say,
A guitar's echo's just a breath away.

Chapter 22
ZOO JUMPER

Menza zipped up his jacket. It was cold and a brisk wind chilled the air even more. Marilyn had just tapped her horn and was waiting in the driveway. The two of them were going to the movie theater. Menza closed the door and raced the cold to the car. He jumped into the passenger seat. It was toasty warm inside.

Truman had recommended that they see "Stone Dance." He thought the film contained some telling clues about a possible future false flag terror event. Prior to the 9/11 attacks the powers placed many clues in movies and television shows. It was their idea of an inside joke. Some people theorized that telling the public beforehand offered some sort of satanic value. That could very well be true. The people or beings that ran the planet were definitely into some very dark stuff. They were certainly deranged enough to preview the blueprints of their murderous schemes. They had proved that with 9/11. They were undeniably a demented bunch that was into some sick kicks.

Marilyn turned the corner onto Highway 440. The movie theater was located in a shopping center two miles away. The zoo would be coming up soon on the left. Marilyn loved to look at the massive bronze sculpture of the elephant at its entrance. Although she must have seen it a hundred times she still loved it. As they passed by she noticed a commotion of sorts. A large crowd had assembled on the west end of the parking area. Marilyn immediately knew something unusual was going on.

"Wow," said Menza. "The zoo must have added a new animal or something. Look at all the people here."

"No," replied Marilyn. "Something else must be going on. The zoo's never this crowded on a weekday like this. I'm gonna see what's going on."

Marilyn quickly made a U-turn. They entered into the zoo parking lot.

"Look at that!" exclaimed Menza. "There's a guy dangling from a tree—and there's a large animal underneath him."

Marilyn took a closer look. Menza was right. There was a man hanging from a tree. He was entangled in a parachute. Apparently he had been skydiving and misjudged his landing zone. An obviously perturbed giraffe had its long neck stretched to the limit trying to get at the man. The man would desperately kick up his legs up every time the giraffe took a nip at him. The giraffe was missing him by mere inches.

"Look," said Marilyn. "There's a helicopter parked near the tree. Who's that guy with the broom? He's headed for the giraffe! What the heck is going on?"

"That's Pepper!" shouted Menza, "and he's going to take on the giraffe with a broom. Let me out. I've got to help him."

Menza jumped from the car and ran over to help his friend. He fought and pushed his way through the crowd. Finally he reached the epicenter of the activity. Pepper was directly in the middle of it. He was valiantly trying to divert the giraffe's attention to himself and away from the man in the tree. Pepper would rush in every time the animal would approach the unlucky paratrooper. He would issue a gentle poke towards its hindquarters with the broom handle. The animal would snap back at Pepper giving the skydiver a temporary reprieve.

"Pepper! What's going on? How can I help?"

Pepper looked over at Menza. "We've got a problem. This giraffe's trying to eat Meier. They're normally mild natured creatures, but somebody accidently let it out of its cage. Now it's confused and angry. We gotta get it away from here."

"What's the deal with the helicopter," asked Menza.

"There's no time to get into that now," replied Pepper. "I'll tell you later."

"Okay. Hey! It's a female giraffe! I've got an idea. Pepper, keep her off Meier with the broom. I'll be right back."

Menza ran into the midst of the onlookers. He was looking for Luce, his 88-year-old friend that he knew from the pub. He had seen her when they pulled into the parking lot.

"Luce!" he called out. He remembered she was hard of hearing. "Luce!" he yelled out again. There was no answer. "LUCE! Where are you? It's me, Menza!"

"I'm over here," Luce cried out. She was standing just a few feet away.

Menza ran over to her. Yes! She was wearing what he had thought she was wearing. Due to the unusually cold weather, she had a large blanket double-wrapped around her body. The blanket was tawny-beige in color with dark-reddish circular blotches. It looked remarkably similar to the fur on the giraffe.

"I'm sorry, Luce," said Menza, "but can I borrow your blanket? It's an emergency."

"Of course," answered Luce. "Take it."

She quickly unwrapped herself and handed the blanket to Menza. He grabbed it and raced back to the center of the storm. The situation had deteriorated. Pepper was now holding off the giraffe with half of a broom. The angry giraffe had bitten it and broke it in half. Meier had actually slipped a little lower in the tree. The giraffe had already pecked away both of his shoes. Things did not look good. Meier was on the verge of becoming a human hors d'oeuvre for the disturbed long-necked animal.

"Pepper!" cried out Menza. "Cover yourself with one end of this blanket. I'm slipping under the other end."

Pepper gave Menza a strange look—but fulfilled the bizarre request. This was no time for debate or explanations. Pepper was now completely hidden except for his legs poking out from beneath the blanket. Menza slipped in under the other end of the blanket. Now it was completely draped around the both of them. Only Menza's head was exposed. Menza reached down and picked up the two pieces of the broken broom. He slid the wooden handle underneath the blanket.

"Pepper, take the broom handle and stick it out your back end. Make it look like a tail. We're gonna pretend we're a giraffe."

Pepper dutifully did as he was instructed. The last thing he wanted to do was humiliate himself by parading around as a giraffe. That behavior should be contained to the five-and-under crowd. But what the heck—he didn't have any better ideas—and there certainly wasn't any time to spare. Meier could be chomped down upon by an angry 1800-pound giraffe at any moment.

Menza looked back at Pepper's end of the blanket. He had done a good job. He had used the sharp broken end of the handle and pieced a hole in the blanket. The handle was visibly protruding from the buttocks of the makeshift zoo creature. It was a short little tail, but it would suffice. Pepper was portraying a giraffe butt as well as could be expected.

Menza was now satisfied that the rear end was in order. He proceeded to take care of the front end. He grabbed the other piece of the broom. Following Pepper's lead he too ripped a hole into the fabric using the jagged edge of the wooden end. He pushed his arm through the hole. He brought the broom handle out from inside the blanket and placed it bristle-end up in his hand. He stuck out his arm as high as it would reach. His outstretched arm with the broom handle extension was certainly not as long as an actual giraffe neck—and the broom head surely did not resemble a giraffe head—but it would have to do. Hopefully they resembled a lusty male giraffe on the hunt for a mate.

Now came the hard part—getting the female giraffe's attention. Menza hoped she was feeling amorous. It certainly did not appear that way at the moment. All her attention was focused on the amateur parachutist just above her reach. She was still nipping at the heels of the young man dangling from the branches. Meier was fighting her off with weak kicks while screaming at the top of his lungs.

Meier's piercing screams had apparently awakened every animal on the premises. His squeals were being echoed by what sounded like the entire zoo population. It seemed every mammal, reptile and bird in the zoo was wailing in on the chorus. The cold blooded and warm blooded alike were in on the symphony of wildlife calls. The airwaves were filled with grunts, screeches, squawks and howls that represented every faction of jungle life. Even the insects were in on the action as they chirped along to the beat. The monkeys and apes were an especially vociferous bunch as they banged on their cages for added rhythm. One baboon appeared to be the maestro conductor of the whole orchestra. He had escaped from his cage and was waving a stick appearing to control the tempo. An elephant seemed to be in charge of the cheerleading section. He would blast a loud trumpet every time the giraffe struck at Meier. Every member of the zoo community would then cheer in unison with their distinctive calls. Who they were rooting for was anyone's guess—the giraffe or the human. The smart money would be on the long-necked one.

It was now or never. Menza prepared himself for action. He had read somewhere that male giraffes made a loud coughing sound when trying to entice a mate. He would imitate it the best he could.

"Pepper, follow me! Make your tail look as real as possible. Try your best to be a giraffe butt. Come on!"

The two of them crept up directly the angry female giraffe. They were dangerously close to her deadly hind legs. Menza poked his head out from underneath the blanket. What he saw was horrifying. Meier was slipping out of his parachute. Another minute and he would fall directly into the gnawing molars of a wrathful beast.

"CROUGHHH! CROUGHHH! CROUGHHH!" Menza stood still and waited. Nothing! The cough wasn't working. What now! Then—poooff. He passed some gas. The pressure of the powerful coughs must have loosened up something in his system and produced a little flatulence. What else could go wrong?

"ARGCRUUUCCCHHH! ARGCRUUUCCCHHH! ARGCRUUUCCCHHH!" Menza! I'm going to kill you for stinking it up under this blanket. The smell is stuck here. You should be the butthole—not me! ARGCRUUUCCCHHH!"

Just then the giraffe turned her attention away from Meier and towards the direction of a familiar sound—a calling male looking for love. That was it! Pepper's sneezing, coughing, moaning—whatever the heck is was—was enticing the lusty desires of the female giraffe. This opportunity could not be lost. They had to steer the angry animal away from Meier.

"Pepper! Make that noise again! It's working!"

"I can't," replied Pepper. "I don't know how."

At times like these alien intelligence was required. Menza knew how to extract that valuable cough from Pepper. He gritted his teeth and closed his eyes. He squeezed his stomach muscles as tight as they would go. He contracted them until he thought he would burst from the inside. Finally—poooff. It brought an immediate reaction from Pepper.

"ARGCRUUUCCCHHH! ARGCRUUUCCCHHH! Menza! You stinked it up again. You just wait until we get out of here. I'm going to get you! ARGCRUUUCCCHHH!"

Menza took a few steps back. Pepper trailed behind, glad to get some circulation in the air. The giraffe hesitated for a brief moment. Then it began following this strange looking representation of her species. Menza and Pepper turned and methodically walked towards the main entrance of the zoo. The curious giraffe continued to follow. Occasionally the curious giraffe would stop and glance back at Meier. That's when Menza would resort to his secret malodorous weapon. He would release a little flatus to induce another mating call out of Pepper.

The plan worked. Several poofs and coughs later they were inside the grounds of the zoo. Once inside the giraffe seemed to lose interest. She quickly wandered over to the section of the zoo that housed a real male giraffe. Why bother with two stinky idiots wrapped in a blanket and holding broom handles when she could have the real thing?

Menza peeked out from the blanket and watched the animal walk away. The coast was clear. He pulled the blanket off of himself and his irritable friend. Pepper was definitely not a happy camper.

"Whewwww! Whewwww! Whewww! Fresh air! God—I thought I was going to suffocate under that blanket. What the heck are you eating that makes your insides smell like that? Are you some kind of bean fanatic? Menza, you need to seek medical attention! Whewww!"

"Come on, Pepper. There's no time for chit-chat. Let's go check on Meier."

Pepper reluctantly agreed. They both raced back towards the tree where Meier had been lodged in his parachute. A crowd of at least one hundred people were gathered around it. The parachute was swinging from the tree limbs, but there was no sign of Meier. Then they looked at the base of the tree. Meier was leaning against it. He appeared to be shaken, but unharmed.

"Thank you!" rejoiced Meier. 'You two saved my life. That beast was going to eat me alive. Pepper, I don't know where in the heck you learned that giraffe call—but I'm darn glad you knew it. It made her forget about me—thank God!"

"You don't wanna know how I came up with that," answered a still perturbed Pepper. "Menza and I are going to have to discuss that one later. The important thing is that you're safe."

"That brings me to an important question," said Menza. "Can you two tell me how in the world Meier ended up in dangling from a parachute in a tree with an angry giraffe snapping at his heels? And what's the deal with the helicopter over there?"

"Ah, I guess it was my fault," professed Pepper. "Do you really want to hear it?"

"I think I deserve some sort of an answer. I just risked my life pretending to be the front end of a randy giraffe. The least you guys can do is to tell me how this happened."

"Okay," Pepper replied sheepishly. "This is what happened. Pop's been getting on to me about cleaning up some of that junk around the Pig Parlor. The first thing that he said had to go was the helicopter. He told me to haul it off to the salvage yard. Well, you know how stubborn I am. I was determined to show Pop that the copter was not junk. I was going to *fly* the thing to the junkyard just to prove my point. I tinkered with it a little bit and finally got it running. I was getting ready to lift off when Meier showed up. Of course, he wanted to ride with me. Really, when you think about it— Meier was the cause of all this."

"Whoa," interrupted Meier. "I'll pick up the story from here, otherwise I'll be made the scapegoat. Yes, I wanted to ride in the chopper. What Pepper is neglecting to tell you is that the helicopter was designed to carry a designated weight. Overloading it can become dangerous—as in crashing. Okay, here's the way I look at it. The thing has two seats, right? Surely it can safely carry two passengers. That sounds logical. Menza, do you agree with me?"

"Sure," answered Menza. "Two seats, two passengers—that's what it's designed for."

"I'm glad you're with me, Menza. Now—listen to this key bit of information. There's something very important that Pepper forgot to tell me about. Pepper was not only carrying a passenger with him, but also a load of junk. In his mind the helicopter was a moving van. Underneath a blanket in the rear of the chopper was 600 pounds of weight lifting equipment. That dusty old barbell set has been at the Pig Parlor since time began. Pepper figured he would save a trip to the dump in his truck and just carry it in the chopper. Menza, do you see where this story is leading?"

"I'm afraid so," said Menza. "You're overloading the helicopter when you add that extra weight. Go ahead with the story."

"Gladly," bayed Meier. "So we take off in that ancient piece of aviation history. The salvage yard is five miles away. Well, the first mile went okay. Then the engine began to stall. Pepper then casually mentions to me that he's got 600 pounds of steel in the back and the helicopter might crash—unless I jump out! Did you hear me? He wanted me to jump out! Then he hands me this knapsack that looks like it came over on Noah's ark—that's how old it was. He tells me it's a parachute and that I'm supposed to strap it on my back and jump out the window. Well, guess what I did?"

"I'm guessing you jumped," said Menza. "Am I correct?"

"Unfortunately you're right. Pepper here, well, he didn't leave me many choices. Either put on that rat-chewed dirty ole parachute and jump out—or die in a fiery helicopter crash. Not a lot of decent options there, if you know what I mean."

"Oh, it wasn't as bad as you make it to be," crowed Pepper. "It worked out okay, right?"

"Yeah, sure," replied Meier, "if you think jumping out of a dilapidated overloaded helicopter wearing a thousand-year-old parachute with a million holes in it and landing crotch-first into a tree with a giraffe under it that wants to eat me is OKAY—well, yes, it worked out just fine."

"Okay," admitted Pepper, "it was a stressful event that should never have occurred. I'll have to agree with you on that. I will tell you this though—you got the better end of the deal. At least you weren't held hostage under a blanket forced to inhale toxic fumes. A whiff of one of Menza's bean blasters and you'd be jumping back into that tree—giraffe or no giraffe. I'm surprised you don't smell me now. I don't know if this stuff will even wash off."

"Okay, Pepper," cracked Menza. "You're exaggerating a little bit, aren't you? The bottom line is we're all safe and sound and able to laugh at it."

"I've got an idea," called a voice from behind them.

It was Marilyn. She had heard the entire conversation. She was grinning from ear to ear.

"Let's go to the Cow," she said. "I just called Truman and told him what happened. He's got a beer waiting for all of us. Menza, we'll go see the movie another day. Come on, guys."

"That sounds like a darn good idea," chimed Meier. "I don't wanna take any chances on that hot-tempered giraffe coming back for round two. Let me yank this so-called parachute out of the tree and let's go."

"I'll go as long as you two sit between me and Menza," said Pepper. "I need a little buffer zone in case he stinks up the joint."

"He won't do that to me," laughed Marilyn. "I promise you we're safe."

"Oh!" exclaimed Pepper. "What about the helicopter? I can't just leave it here."

"I was gonna tell you about that later," answered Marilyn. "While you guys were busy trying to mate with a giraffe I sold your helicopter for a hundred dollars."

"What!" cried Pepper. "You sold it?"

"Yep," said Marilyn. "Johnny Johnson wanted it. You know he collects vintage planes. Now he's got a helicopter. I wasn't about to give you an opportunity to fly it out of here. Pepper, you just made a hundred dollars. Drinks are on you!"

Pepper shook his head and smiled. "You're right. Beers are on me. Let's go."

Chapter 23

OUT FOR COFFEE

"I'm gonna park at the back of the parking lot. You don't mind a little exercise, do you, Menza?"

Truman was making a stop at Ashmont Mall. Menza had come along for the ride. He needed to pick up a batch of Ecuadorian specialty coffee. Luce and her "lunch ladies" were expected at the pub this afternoon and he was fresh out of the good stuff.

"Of course I don't mind a bit of walking." replied Menza. "I'm not a fitness nut like you, but I do like to stay in shape."

"Yeah, I like walking and running," said Truman, "but I actually prefer swimming. Now that's a perfect workout. It's just that it ain't easy to find a pool that's warm, clean and available at my odd hours."

Menza let out a short laugh. "I'm surprised you don't fill up a backyard pool with beer and swim in it. That way you can exercise and drink beer at the same time. Of course you would have to refill the pool every day because you would drink it all."

"You're a funny guy today, aren't you? Hey Menza, I want to point out something. Look at that car there."

"Yes, I see it," said Menza. "What about it?"

"This is his second go-around looking for a parking spot. He could park back here with us and walk thirty yards to the mall entrance. Instead he'll circle around several times like a vulture hunting down a prime spot near the door. Watch him."

They stood and watched as the car circled three more times. Finally a spot became available near the entrance. The driver smiled like he had won the lottery. He pulled into it and got out of his car. He walked ten yards towards the mall entrance. Then he turned left and entered a door adjacent to the main entrance. It was a gym. Unbelievable! He was going to work out. He was getting ready to do strenuous exercise, yet he couldn't walk twenty extra yards to get there.

"How about that," mused Truman. "He spent seven or eight minutes stressfully driving around in circles and burning up precious fuel to find that prize parking spot—all to save approximately twenty yards of walking. And he looked to be as healthy as a horse! And he went to the gym! Human behavior never ceases to amaze me."

"I've got to agree with you, Truman. It doesn't seem logical, but a lot of things on your—er—our planet don't add up."

"That's for sure," said Truman.

Truman had replied without missing a beat—but not without that blink or wink or whatever it was. That had become his trademark every time Menza put himself in hot water with an ill-advised comment. He never commented, never asked any questions—just that winky blinky stare that lasted for a fraction of a second. Truman could have been a world class poker player. You never knew what cards the man was holding. Was he bluffing with a pair of threes or was he hiding a royal flush? One thing was certain—he never asked

Menza about his past history or background. Did he not care or did he know better than to ask?

"Hey look," said Truman. He pointed to a motorcyclist dismounting his bike. "Just by looking at him you would think he's one tough character, right?"

"Well, yes," answered Menza. "He just came in on an extremely loud motorcycle that vibrated the parking lot. He's big and burly with long hair and a beard. He's dressed in black leather and wearing a bandana. Yes, I would say he might be a tough guy."

"I've got a story about that guy. A couple of years ago, my second wife—Pata is her name—was riding on her little motorbike. She's the Thai wife I told you about. Well, Pata practically grew up on one of those tiny bikes in Bangkok. That's how they get around the horrendous traffic over there. Anyway, she's riding on a street in the outskirts of town. That guy there just happens to broken down on the side of the road. His bike had vibrated some parts right off of it. They were spread out in the middle of the road. Pata has a heart of gold so she stops to help her fellow motorcyclist. She asks him if he needs a lift to the parts store."

"Wasn't she scared?" asked Menza. "Didn't you tell me she only weighed 100 pounds? This guy looks pretty rough."

"Absolutely not," said Truman. "I know for a fact those boney little legs of hers carry a mean kick—and they hurt!"

"Ha, that sounds like you've been on the receiving end of them. I won't pursue that one. So—what happened?"

"Well, tough guy here starts out trying to maintain his bad boy reputation. He makes some wise comment about Pata's little scooter. She politely says goodbye and starts to ride away. I guess the guy wised up at that point and realized he could wait forever for another ride. He quickly changed his tune and hopped on the back of Pata's scooter. She took him into town to the parts shop. I'm sure he looked pretty comical. Here was this huge bearded guy all decked out in his macho attire, riding on the back of a miniature scooter with his arms wrapped around a thin little Asian girl. It probably embarrassed him to death."

"How did it all end?" asked Menza. "Did he get his parts?"

"Yes, everything worked out fine. He bought his parts and parked his big butt back on Pata's scooter. She rode him back to his bike. She even waited to make sure he got it running before she left. I run into him occasionally, but I've stopped saying hello. He knows I know the whole story and he doesn't like to talk about it. I guess it doesn't fit with the image he wants to project. He's a wannabe rebel who's afraid of his own shadow. If somebody said 'boo' he'd leap into Pata's arms and beg her to protect him. Actually he's a very nice guy. I just wish he'd loosen up a little bit."

"People are strange, huh, Truman?"

"Yeah, they sure are. But you know what? Most of them are conditioned to be like they are. Take the parking lot circler for example. He has no idea that he could park back here with us and avoid the hassle and stress of vulture circling. That thought never occurred to him. Grandma circled, mama circled, he circles, his kids will circle, and their kids will circle. It's a circle of mind conditioning. It's the same with biker man over there. If you own one of those machines you gotta put on a tough guy face. You gotta dress the part and fit in with the rest the group. It's quite funny actually. They're all playing the part of rebels, but the only rebel in the group would be the one who has the gumption to ride a quiet bike and dress normally. Once again, it's all a matter of conditioning. We humans are a mental mess, myself included. Mass mind control has us all under their thumb, whoever *they* are."

"Count me in too," said Menza. "I'm sure I'm categorized as a mental mess. I don't have the answers, only questions."

"I'm with you on that on," agreed Truman. "Why don't we go inside and get that coffee we came here for."

Truman and Menza walked into the mall. Menza caught himself looking at every person, wondering what they were doing and why they were there. Truman seemed to be doing the same thing. The trip had turned into some sort of people-analyzing expedition.

"Here we are," declared Truman. "The finest coffee in the Americas—at least in my opinion."

Menza looked above his head. The sign said it all. *The Ecuador Store—Coffee and More.*

"There's my friend, Luis," said Truman. "He's the owner. Come on, let's go inside."

"*Como estas, amigo*?" Truman asked with a perfect accent.

"*Muy bien, gracias.*" replied Luis.

"I'm back for some more of your Andes Blue Roast. That's some excellent coffee."

"You got it, Truman. I'll run in the back and get it. In the meantime sip on this. I'm giving away free samples. It's a new blend I'm working on."

Luis handed over two cups of freshly brewed coffee. It was dark and rich with an aroma to match. They both took a sip.

"Superb!" chanted Truman. "It's a keeper."

Menza and Truman sat down at a corner table by the entrance. It was a perfect location to watch people as they wandered by. They both relaxed in their chairs.

"We might as well hang out for a while, huh, Menza?"

"That sounds like a good idea, Truman. The coffee's great. And this is a great spot to just kick back and observe aliens—er—humans in their—er—our natural environment."

Truman wasted no time. This time it was a double winky blink aimed at Menza's coffee cup. Truman's facial expression did not change in the least, but that split second thing with his eyes relayed a message—but what was the message? What was he trying to communicate with a flicker of an eyelid? Was he teasing? Was he penalizing? Could it be just some sort of natural physical reaction that coincided with his friend's oral blunders?

Truman possessed that cool. It was cool with a soul—an imperturbable cool that sprouted from confidence and knowledge, a cool that pierced and charmed and captured everyone and everything in its presence. It was a world class cool that Menza had seen once before. JP had it. Now there were two.

"Yeah," drawled Truman, "this coffee is good. It's got a Seattle flavor with a universal kick—kinda like you. At least that's the way I would describe you. Hey, check them out. Isn't that little boy cute?"

Truman pointed towards an elderly gentleman accompanied by a little boy. The blond curly-haired boy looked to be about three years old. They were sitting in the food court. The old man was contentedly sipping his coffee. The little boy sat happily beside him licking an ice cream cone and swinging his little legs in the giant chair that encompassed him. Everyone that walked past them would point and smile. It really was an adorable sight. Menza wanted to take it all in and fully appreciate it, but his mind was churning away on something else.

Truman had done it again. The minister of cool had interjected a contemplative statement, before masterfully changing the subject. Menza looked to be engrossed in the charming pair, but his mind remained stuck on Truman's last comment. He had likened him to "a Seattle flavor with a universal kick." What did he mean? Menza had mentioned to him early on that he was from Seattle. Other townsfolk had been told he was from Russia. Had Truman discovered the discrepancy? And what was with the word "universal?" Did he use the term generically? He couldn't have meant it literally— or could he?

Menza decided not to dwell on it. Truman was his good friend. The two of them shared a similar belief system. They had total trust between them. It just so happened to be that one of them was a human and the other was an alien from a faraway galaxy. Sure, it was an unusual situation. But it was what it was—whatever *it* was. Cool Truman chased away any awkwardness by changing the subject yet again. He leaned in close to Menza.

"Those two women over there," whispered Truman, "they're locked in an interesting conversation. Listen to them."

He motioned with his pinky finger towards the table directly beside them. Menza casually glanced towards them. Two females were engaged in a hearty discussion over coffee and pastries. Both of them were well dressed and appeared to be in their mid-sixties. The chunky blonde one seemed a little perturbed about something. Maybe she was frustrated that the much thinner redheaded lady had a big piece of cake covered in whipped cream while she nibbled on a low fat croissant— or maybe it was something more serious. Menza picked up a magazine and pretended to thumb through it. The conversation got hotter.

"Now don't take this personally," the blonde said sharply, "but I can't trust a Republican."

"Well, I guess that means you don't trust me," the red-head snapped. "You Democrats are the arse of this nation.

Why do you think a donkey is your symbol? That's no accident."

"Let me tell you a thing or two about Republicans," the blonde blurted out. "You guys are responsible for everything that's wrong with our country. There are two things you have to watch out for in this world—a rattlesnake and a Republican. Speaking of symbols, your symbol is a big fat elephant that never gets anything done."

"Oh my!" shouted the redhead. "I wouldn't go around calling anything fat if I were you. Have you looked in the mirror lately? You ain't exactly no beanpole."

"Oh, the nerve of you!" snorted the blonde. "At least I don't spend a fortune on a gallon of red hair dye every week. Do you think that big red slab of bird's nest sitting on the top of your head looks good? It's no wonder you can't find a husband. He'd be afraid to touch your hair for fear of stirring up a cubby of quail."

Menza could take no more. Something had to be done. These two ladies were on the verge of a physical altercation right in the middle of a coffee shop. He stood up and walked over to their table.

"Ladies! Ladies! Calm down. I couldn't help but overhear your conversation. Surely this isn't worth fighting over. Now what is the problem here?"

"She's a Democrat," sulked the redhead. "They're the problem."

"She's a Republican," gloated the blonde. "They're the problem."

"I gotta be honest with you ladies," said Menza as he shook his head. "I'm not really political and I'm ignorant of the differences between the two groups. Can either one of you pretty ladies enlighten me?"

"Yes!" both women exclaimed in unison.

"Okay," said Menza in a calm voice. "Let's go one at a time. Both of you will have an opportunity. Who would like to go first?"

"I'll go first if it's okay with her," whined the blonde.

"Sure, go ahead," the redhead groaned.

"It's like this," said the blonde. "Republicans think they're hot stuff. They wander around the world looking for hair dye instead of doing anything to improve anything. They go around talking about how bad the Democrats are. They…"

"Whoa!" interrupted Menza. "That kind of stuff is not what I'm looking for. I want to know what the differences are between the two groups. What is a Republican? What is a Democrat? If it's worth fighting over, then certainly there are some *real* issues that you are disagreeing on. I ask you once again—what are the differences between a Democrat and a Republican?"

"I…I…I don't know," stammered the blonde. "I just know Daddy always said Republicans were no good. They think different from us. They're bad! That's the difference."

"Okay, Republicans are bad," surmised Menza. "And I take it that Democrats are good. You've got nothing concrete to back up those statements—but for now that's the way we'll leave it. Okay, now I would like to hear the opposing view. Pretty lady, you have the floor. I ask you the same question. Can you please explain the differences between a Republican and a Democrat?"

"Gladly," crowed the redhead. "Democrats think they're better than us. They stuff their faces with fatty foods instead of fixing our nation. They waddle around with their chest poked out like they rule the world. They go around talking about how bad the Republicans are. They…"

"Hold it!" cried Menza. "You're doing the same thing as your friend. What I'm looking for here is very simple. I want to know what the *real* differences are between Democrats and Republicans. You two nearly came to blows over it just a minute ago. Surely there are fundamental differences between the two parties. I'll give you one more chance. Now tell me, what are the differences between Democrats and Republicans?"

"The differences are…I mean…they are…darn it! They're just bad. That's the difference. Mama always told me Democrats were bad. Republicans are good. That's the way it is!"

Menza looked at both women and shook his head. The women were silent. It was obvious neither of them knew what they were fighting over. Truman rose from his chair and approached the two women.

"Ladies," he said, "let me tell you what's going on here. Both of you need to get in tune with the truth. The truth of the matter here is neither one of you know the differences between the two political parties. The colder harder truth is that it doesn't really matter."

"What do you mean when you say it doesn't matter?" asked the blonde. "Maybe you're right. My friend and I are probably not real informed on the subject. But that doesn't change the fact that we disagree. The whole country is torn on this issue. It's not just us. There's got to be something that's keeping us divided."

"You're exactly right with that statement," agreed Truman. "Yes, there are some subtle ideological differences between a Democrat and Republican. They're placed there to keep you arguing about moot points. They want you to debate issues that they could care less about. While the nation sits around coffee shops arguing over a drop of spilled milk they're killing all the milk cows. Both parties are actually controlled by a higher, more powerful group. They're dividing you to conquer you.

"What?" muttered the redhead. "Are you saying they're tricking us?"

"Exactly," answered Truman. "They've got you two and most of the nation on a wild goose chase. You chase the goose while they tighten the noose that's wrapped around your necks."

"Who's doing this to us?" the blonde asked. "Who's in control?"

"There's an elite group of extremely powerful people that run the country—actually the world if we get down to it. They control the political arena with an iron fist. They own the players the same as you own your cat. The elections are totally rigged."

"Oh my," said the redhead. "And I actually thought our votes meant something."

"Not to these fraudulent bozos that are captaining our sinking ship," said Truman. "They'll place a Republican in puppet power for a term or two. This riles up the Democrats. Change, change, change, they'll all shout. Then they'll stick a Democrat in office. That little do-as-I'm-told yes man will fizzle out after a few years. In comes another Republican. Their political merry-go-round keeps us kids occupied while they run the circus. They repeat this cycle over and over. We sit around spinning our wheels on distractions while they race down the highway at full speed. When they hit the finish line it will be too late. Ladies, do you understand?"

"Yes, I think I do," said the blonde.

"Me too," agreed the redhead.

"Okay," said Truman. "We've made progress. Now I want you ladies to make up and apologize to each other. You said some pretty harsh words while ago in the heat of the moment. Can you do that?"

"I sure can," said the blonde. "Cindy, I'm very sorry for what I said. I didn't mean it."

"I apologize also," echoed the redhead. "Sharon, I shouldn't have said what I said."

"Great," said Truman. "Just remember what we talked about. Research it yourself. There's a lot of information out there once you start digging. Don't let them divide you up into factions fighting with each other. Join forces and beat those fat cats at their own game."

The women hugged each other and thanked Truman once again. He gave each of them a card redeemable for a free drink at the pub. They left the coffee shop enlightened with a new perspective on American politics—but it didn't last long.

"Lard butt Democrat!" a voice echoed throughout the mall.

"Bird hotel head Republican!" another voice shouted back.

They were arguing again as soon as they left the coffee shop. The split-and divide Democrat and Republican conditioning had rendered them damaged goods. They were permanently entrenched in a state of unyielding ignorance.

Truman sighed and shook his head. "There's another example of just how deep this runs. "It's another case of mind control. Those two women have been conditioned by society to pick a side on the political front. Just like the parking lot circler and the wannabe rebel on the motorcycle, they've been programmed. That's just the subtle end of the mind control business. If they knew about the other hard core stuff they'd blow a fuse."

"You're probably right," said Menza. "The powers seem to be on a mission to dirty up our minds so they can have their way with us."

"Yep, it sure seems that way. The underground trauma labs, the chemtrails, the brain numbing fluoride in our water, the MKULTRA programming, the cell phone towers, all of those and more—they're part of a master plan to control our thoughts. It's no coincidence that the frequency band for cell phone use matches the second order waves that affect thought transmission. In other words they can put thoughts in our brains and we think they're our own. Menza, *that* is some serious mind control."

"Don't forget their number one weapon," said Menza. "Good old-fashioned television rots more brains than everything else combined."

"Right you are, Menza. TV is a total propaganda tool. When they wanna push a war they advertise it on the tube like it's a new brand of shampoo. The eggheads just eat it up. And those subliminals stick into our subconscious like glue. We think we're free when we're not even able to control our own thoughts. It's downright sickening. Of all the nasty things going on in this sad world I think this one hurts the most. I don't know about you, Menza, but I wanna keep my mind. I'm gonna put up a fight to keep mine."

"Me too, Truman—me too."

"Let's grab the coffee and head back," said Truman. "Would you mind giving this one to Marilyn and tell her to work her magic?"

Menza took a quick look at the paper Truman had just handed him.

Sure, Truman—I'll give it to her. Yeah, let's go."

DON'T PEE ON ME

Well, I'm running down the road,
And I'm watching the show
It all seems such a sight to me
They're bickering and a squabbling
And clashing and a quarrelling
Living in the land of the free
Well, I ain't gonna fall for your little tricks of control
Keeping the sheep distracted
While you steal their souls
I'm not so blind that I can't see,
You're telling me it's raining while you pee on me
No, no, no, don't you pee on me,
No, don't you do it, I'm gonna stay free
No, you'd better stop your peeing, peeing on me,
No, no, no, don't you pee on me
You're a fussing and a cussing
Over a petty bunch of nothing
Thinking that you're all so cool
With a mess that surrounds you
And stress all around you
You're looking like a bunch of fools
Well, keep on doing what you're doing,
While they hose you down
Yeah—enjoy that golden shower
As you lie on the ground
No, no, no, don't you pee on me,
No, don't you do it, I'm gonna stay free
No, you'd better stop your peeing, peeing on me,

No, no, no, don't you pee on me
It's a dog and pony show playing with our minds,
It's all smoke and mirrors to keep us in line
I don't see any clouds and I don't hear thunder,
But I see a yellow rain that makes me wonder
So put it back inside and zip it up,
Go pee on yourself, I've seen enough
No, no, no, don't you pee on me,
No, don't you do it, I'm gonna stay free
No, you'd better stop your peeing, peeing on me,
No, no, no, don't you pee on me

Chapter 24
AT THE HOSPITAL

Menza entered the lobby of Ashmont Memorial Hospital. Marilyn had called him an hour earlier sounding very distraught. The doctors had told her to prepare for the worst. They didn't expect her mother to last another 48 hours.

Menza took the elevator to the fourth floor. He walked over to room 412. The door was cracked open. He could hear his baby sobbing. He wished he could take a chunk of her pain and make it his own. Marilyn loved her mother more than anyone or anything on the planet. Watching her die was ripping her insides apart.

Menza took a deep breath as he prepared to enter. Something made him wait. It was the familiar sound of Marilyn's guitar. She was lightly strumming a peaceful melody. He had never heard her play better. She was one with the guitar, resonating soul and passion—pure straight-from-the-heart love. Then he heard the sweet voice of his lover and friend.

"Mom, listen to me. I want you to pay attention for a few minutes. You've been telling me something over and over for the last six months—not to cry, that everything is as it should be. Well, I haven't always been able to do that, but I'm trying. Listen to me, mom—then you can go back to sleep, okay? I wrote this song for you. It's called 'Don't Cry For Me' and it's about you and me. Mom, I love you."

Marilyn looked into her mother's eyes. Neither of them had to speak—their eyes said it all. Life and death—it was the way of the world. You come in and you go out and you hope you make a difference. You love, live and laugh until it's time to go away. It goes quick and you wish you had more time, but you sure don't want to do it all over again. Mother and daughter were expressing their love for each other for what could be the final time. Their bond was so strong that even death could not break it apart. They would meet again in a different place—that was for sure, but until then there would be only memories to ease the ache in Marilyn's heart.

Marilyn warmed up the star guitar with a single strum. Then she began to pour out her heart and soul to her dying mother. Her soft voice echoed down the hallway. It was so full of soul and love you could almost see it.

> *Don't cry for me—no, don't you cry,*
> *Don't you cry my baby, don't you cry for me*
> *No my little baby, don't go crying for me,*
> *Cause you know it's the way, the way of the world*
> *So don't you go crying unless they're tears of joy*
> *You're gonna see me again, that you should know,*
> *Go ahead and live your life, push on through*
> *You know you're my baby,*
> *You're my flesh and blood*
> *You know I'd stay if I could*
> *But that ain't the way, the way of the world,*
> *So don't you cry unless they're tears of joy*

Don't cry for me—no, don't you cry,
No my little baby, don't go crying for me,
My soul's ready to rest, she's at peace,
She's gonna smile when I put her to sleep
So don't you go cry, don't you go weep,
Those memories are there for you to keep
It's time to go, that I know,
So goodbye my little baby, you carry on
Shed no tears, for your time will come too,
You'll say goodbye to the ones you love
No my little baby, don't go crying for me,
Don't go crying, crying for me
Don't you go crying, crying for me,
No, no, no—no crying for me

Marilyn closed her eyes for a long moment. When she reopened them her mother was fast asleep. That was okay. She knew her mother had heard the song. There was no doubt. A great burden had just been lifted from her heart. Writing the song was a release of sorts, but not until she played it for her mother was it complete. There was something therapeutic about writing songs in general, but this one was truly special. The words and music had originated from somewhere else. It was if the song had been channeled through to her by a higher power, a soul doctor on a mission to heal a grieving daughter. Someone or something felt her pain and had lent a helping hand.

Menza pressed against the door and entered the room. Marilyn stood up and they hugged each other tight. For a long moment neither of them said a word. Finally Menza gazed into Marilyn's eyes and spoke.

"I heard your song. That was beautiful, baby. I know your mother enjoyed it. You put her at peace. Look at her. She loves you, baby."

"Oh, Menza, this is so hard," Marilyn said in a soft voice. "This is the hardest thing I've ever had to deal with in my life. I just don't want to see her go. She's really not that old. I know there's a reason for this, but I don't know what it is. I feel like she—and me—have been cheated. She should have had twenty more years on this Earth. She doesn't deserve this. She's a saint, an angel, and her life is being taken away. There are thieves and murderers that live long lives. And my mom, who's never even hurt a fly, barely sees sixty before it's all taken away from her. It just ain't fair."

"I know, baby," said Menza. He reached for her hand and held it tightly. "Everything's going to be okay. I promise."

There was a light knock on the half-open door. It slowly opened. It was Truman.

"Hi guys. Marilyn, I just wanted to drop by and see if you needed anything. Menza told me what was going on. How is she?"

"She's resting comfortably, Truman. Thanks for your concern. They've got her pretty doped up, but when she's awake she's aware of what's going on around her. How are things with you?"

Truman sighed and shook his head. "I'm doing well. I've got a couple of little problems here and there, but overall everything's okay."

"What's wrong?" asked Menza. "I know you well enough to know when something's bothering you. Go ahead and tell us."

"I don't really want to get into it. You guys have enough troubles without hearing mine."

"No," said Marilyn. "We're fine. You're our friend. So tell us—what's wrong?"

"Oh, it's just more of the same. I came in this morning and opened up the pub. Everything seemed normal until I went into my office. Someone had taken a bucket of red paint and splashed it all around the room. I checked all the doors and windows. There was no sign of a forced entry. And there was nothing missing. It's pretty obvious who did it. That red paint symbolized blood—mine."

"Government people," said Menza. "Right?"

"Most likely," answered Truman. "A better answer would be the people who hijacked the government. I think I know what led to this latest incident. An article I wrote was published in a small paper about a month ago. It touched on a subject that they're pretty protective of right now. There's no need to go into the details, but it referenced a certain group that's deep into this crazy stuff. They control everything, at least as far as humans are concerned. The article, and me, was recently mentioned on a popular radio show. Since then it's garnered a lot of attention on the internet. I think that made some people nervous—so they sent me another message."

"What are you going to do," asked Marilyn. "Aren't you scared?"

"Of course I am," replied Truman, "but what am I supposed to do? I can't stop being me. It's pretty much out of my control. There's a force that's bigger than me that keeps pushing me. I couldn't stop if I wanted to—and I don't want to stop. So it is what it is and I'm along for the ride. Just remember if I come up dead and they call it suicide that it ain't so. I ain't gonna take my own life. The same goes for some freaky accident. Most likely it won't be an accident."

"Tell me, Truman," asked Menza, "is there any real hope of defeating these criminals? They seem to have their hands in everything. Do we have any shot at all of winning this war? Or are they just going to have their way with the world and turn us into total slaves?"

Truman nodded sagely. "Honestly, short of a total overhaul of the political, economic, military, media and intelligence systems worldwide—no, we don't have a chance. But I'm never going to give up hope. There's always the chance of a miracle. You gotta have faith that good will prevail. I'll keep believing until they chunk me in the grave."

"Oh, Truman," said Marilyn. "Please don't let it come to that, please. This situation with my mother has really got me to thinking about what's important. It ain't things, it ain't money, it ain't about impressing people with your big house or fancy car, it ain't what you're wearing or who you're hanging out with—none of that matters. That's just crap for people to fight over after you're gone. What matters in this life is friendship and honesty and trust. What's important in this life is love. There's all we're gonna take away from this place—love. Look at mom lying there. She's leaving this plane of existence and I'm going to miss her so much. Truman, please, please, be careful. Please! I can't afford to lose anyone else that I care about. You've got some bad people that want to hurt you. Oh, God, I'm so torn up I don't what to do."

Marilyn burst into tears. Menza smothered her with his body and held her tight. Truman walked over and stretched his arms around the both of them. The three of them remained as one. A minute passed, maybe five—no one was counting. Marilyn finally regained her composure and the sobbing slowed to a sprinkle of tears.

"I'm so sorry," she said. "Truman, I know how much this all means to you. Stopping those people is your whole life. It's what you live for. I have no right to tell you to stop. I'm sorry. I'm really sorry. I just love you both. I don't want anything to happen to either of you. I guess I'm just emotional because of what's going on with mom."

"Marilyn, look at me." Truman wiped a tear from her cheek with his shirt sleeve. "There are things in life that we're not meant to understand. I don't know why I'm obsessed with seeking the truth. I certainly don't gain anything except for the knowledge itself. I'm ridiculed behind my back. People laugh at me and call me crazy. Yet I still go out and stir up the pot trying to spread my message."

"But why, Truman, why?" Marilyn sniffled. "That's all I ask—why?"

"A higher power is behind me—there's gotta be. I've thought about it and thought about it and it's the only logical answer I can come up with. Someone or something is making me do this—and I truly feel I'm being protected by this power. I believe an angel is watching over me. I was put on this planet for a reason. All of us were. Yes, I'm scared, but there's a force that shields me from danger. That force is always close by and always will be, at least until my mission is completed."

"How can you be so sure?" asked Marilyn. "What if you're wrong? What if there is no protective angel and those bad people get you. Then we're crying at your funeral and you're gone forever, someone that we love—gone forever. Truman, what if there's no angel?"

Truman looked down and stared at the floor. That is what he did sometimes when he was in deep thought—and deep thought for Truman had no limits. His most shallow thoughts could burn a hole through concrete. When he was in analyzation mode there were no boundaries. He was an open door where you entered at your risk. His intellect could strip you down and dress you back up and you'd never even know you've got a new set of clothes. Truman's mind was a diamond-tipped drill piercing though time and space—sifting through history, sorting out truths and lifting out lies— flushing out the future where the clues do hide—and once he has enough pieces to the puzzle he puts them all together and hangs it on the wall for all to see, bringing insight to the seekers and fueling the fools with bits of truth they'll never comprehend. Truman's mind was like a thoroughbred racehorse that was too tough to tame, a winner in waiting in a game gone lame. It was a mind that was bright and bold and commanded respect, like the first bolt of lightning that rips across the sky in a thunderstorm. At this moment it was in high gear.

"Marilyn, you ask about angels. Do you two have a few minutes? I'd like to share a story. You guys know that I'm essentially a private person. Sure, I'll joke around with the best of them, but it's pretty much a social charade. I really don't feel comfortable sharing my innermost thoughts, but you are my two best friends."

"Truman, you're…" Menza stopped for a moment. He was choosing his words carefully. "You're a mentor and a role model to me, but above all you're my friend. I know Marilyn feels the same way. I would feel cheated if I missed out on your opinions and beliefs—and your unique perspective of the crazy world that we live in. So—we've got nothing but time, tell us your stories. I'm sure we'll be better for it. My friend, please share your thoughts."

"Thank you, Menza. Those are nice compliments. I'm going to open up a little bit. It's like this. I've always felt like I'm different, but I never could figure out why. All I know is I'm being trained for something. Who's actually training me and for what I don't know, although I do have suspicions. This much I'm certain of—at some point it will be my time to shine, but it'll probably come in the midst of chaos and turmoil, of great change. For sure my success won't come wrapped in fame and fortune."

Truman hesitated. Once again he stared down upon the floor. His presence filled the room as his mind raced. Then he continued.

"I'm going to tell you why I believe I'm protected. Angels, extraterrestrials, spirits—I don't know what's watching over me, but something sure is. When I was twenty years old I was a senior in college. One evening I went to a party. I was an inexperienced drinker and I got drunk on whisky—very drunk. Then I did something very stupid. I jumped in my car and drove home—only I didn't make it. I made an unscheduled stop in Lake Monroe. Yep, I drove my car right into the lake. Witnesses said I was going at least eighty miles an hour. At the last second I turned the steering wheel and the car rolled over and smashed upside down on the sea wall. Of course I didn't have my seatbelt on. I felt myself ricochet off the ceiling of the car with a terrific force. I remember feeling like I was going to smash into something and die. But I never stopped. I just kept going and going and didn't hit anything. My body was shooting like a bullet to somewhere out of my control. The car bounced up and splashed down forty yards out in the lake. I was thrown from the car and smacked into the water on my back. The breath was knocked out of me. I sunk down into the water. It was at least twenty feet deep. I don't remember anything about sinking into those dark waters until I finally took in a deep breath—and water filled my lungs. I've always been a pretty good swimmer, so I pushed myself back to the surface. I looked across the lake and saw my car underwater with the headlights still on. I had been thrown thirty yards from the car. I managed to swim back to shore. Within moments rescue workers and police were on the scene. They sent in a diver who hooked up the car and they drug it back in. The car was crushed like a soft drink can. Although my back was sore for weeks, there wasn't a visible scratch on me. Does that sound miraculous?"

"Yes, it does," answered Marilyn. "You were one lucky kid."

"Well," sighed Truman. "That ain't the miraculous part. Listen to this. Of course everyone had to look at the car when they pulled the car in from the lake. Although it was all smashed up, the doors were still all closed. The windows were cracked, but they were still rolled up and they were intact. The front and back windshields were still in place. There were no holes in the crushed metal. The fact of the matter was there was no explanation for how I exited the car."

"Wow!" exclaimed Marilyn. "Then how did you get out of the car?"

"I know exactly how, but I've never shared it with anyone—until now. They all think I'm crazy enough as it is. *I went through the car.*"

"What!" cried Marilyn. "You went through the car! How?"

"There are two aspects to it. One is scientific and the other is spiritual. Believe me, I've put a lot of thought into this one. I should have died that drunken night."

"Now you've really got me curious," said Menza. "How in the heck did you go through metal and glass without getting a scratch on your body?"

Truman took a deep breath. "Surviving that horrible accident changed my life forever. Of course I learned to never drink and drive. It doesn't take a genius to figure that one out. But I also became interested in what we are—what we *really* are. I read everything I can get my hands on about the science behind our bodies. You'll *never* get mainstream science to admit it, but our bodies are basically nothing but energy. I'll tell you what happened that night. My body transformed into raw energy and traveled through the car, then rematerialized on the other side. I was back into my full physical realm when I hit the water. In a nutshell, that explains the science behind my miracle. The spiritual angle of the equation is trickier to explain."

"Don't stop now," blurted Menza. "I know you, you've got some theories. Please share them if you don't mind."

"Sure, Menz," shrugged Truman. "As far as I'm concerned a protector intervened and saved my life. An angel, extraterrestrials, a spiritual being—someone or something deemed my life important enough to keep it hanging around this Earth for a while longer. If it was extraterrestrial in nature, then they probably employed technology that breaks our bodies down into energy blocks. They broke me down for a couple of seconds to get me out of that car. I would have drowned in there. There's no doubt in my mind. I'm sure it's similar to the science that's applied to the teleportation that goes on around the universe—and here on our planet, truth be told."

"And if it was not alien in nature?" asked Menza. "Then what was it?"

"Now we're delving into the true spiritual side of things. Did an angel save me from death that night? Was it a ghost or spirit protecting me? Did an almighty God save me? Those are questions for which I have no answer."

"Truman, I have a question for you," inquired Menza. "Are you religious?"

Truman took a moment to gather his thoughts before he spoke. "I'm not a believer in any one religion. I look at it like this. Geography is the major determinant of what religion you support. Just look at the numbers. If you're born in a country where Buddhism is the primary religion, odds are you're a

Buddhist. If you've grown up in a Hindu country, you're most likely supporting that religion. If you're born in a country where Christianity is the major religion, you'll probably go down that religious path. It's the same thing with Islam, the Chinese religions, the African religions, and so on. People are born into and molded by the culture that surrounds them. Of course there are exceptions, millions and millions of them. People have free will to choose any religion they desire, or no religion at all. There are practicing Hindus in Buddhists countries, there are practicing Christians in Islamic countries, there are mixed pockets of different religious beliefs all over the world. I'm only speaking in *general* terms here. I'm trying to convey the big picture—billions, not millions."

"I think I'm getting your point, Truman," Menza speculated. "What you're trying to say is that it's unfair to discriminate against someone because of their religious beliefs. That individual had no choice regarding the country they were born into and the culture that swayed them. Am I correct?"

"Exactly," nodded Truman. "Here's an example describing what you just mentioned. You guys have heard me talk about my second wife. Pata is the sweetest, kindest, most caring and loving person I have ever met—smart too, smart enough to leave me. Ha!"

Marilyn and Menza laughed at Truman's self-deprecating humor. Marilyn thought she even noticed a trace of a smile on her mother's face. Truman continued.

"Pata grew up in Thailand as a Buddhist. I lived over there for a while. The kindness and generosity of the Thai people tops any place I've ever seen. They are wonderful people—and primarily Buddhists."

"I have a Buddhist friend also," Marilyn commented. "She's such a good hearted person."

"Yes," said Truman. "Most of them are. Let me tell you a story about Pata and a Christian friend of mine—who is also a wonderful person. We were all having a conversation one evening and the topic turned to religion. My Christian friend inquired about Pata's religious beliefs. She replied that she was a Buddhist. My Christian friend then proceeded to explain to her that, unless she accepted Jesus Christ as her savior, she was going to Hell. My sweet little Pata—burning in hell! I have a hard time believing that God would send such a caring individual to burn in Hell eternally. God rewards good behavior, right? Apparently many Christians whole-heartedly believe that all non-Christians are doomed. If that is true, then two thirds of the planet's population is automatically headed to the fiery pits of Hell. Maybe my Christian friend is right. But if the majority of humans are going to spend eternity in hell because of where they were born—well, it certainly doesn't seem fair."

"You're making a valid point," agreed Menza. "And I'm sure that exclusivity applies to other religions as well."

"Oh, yes, it probably does," said Truman. "I was just using that as an example."

"Truman, what is your honest opinion?" asked Menza. "Is there one 'God' that rules us all?"

"Like I touched on earlier—I simply don't know. I would like to think so. I would hope that he doesn't delegate Hell according to religious beliefs. If so, it could get pretty crowded down there. I'm glad I'm not the one who decides who goes to heaven and who goes to Hell. I'm in the same boat as everyone else. Sometimes I look at all the beauty and the love existing in the world—and attribute it to God. Then I see all the evil in the world—and ask why God allows it. I only have questions. The answers evade me. I wish I knew. I'm a bit skeptical of those who say they do know."

"Okay, back to the car accident," said Menza. "You think that something, be it God, extraterrestrial beings, angels, spirits, whatever—protected you that night. Something intervened and saved your life. Earlier you mentioned that you thought maybe you're here for a purpose, that you're on a mission. Do you have *any* idea what that mission is, what your purpose might be? Also—are you scared that your protective force may one day abandon you?"

"I can tell you this, my friend," answered Truman. "My purpose will be made clear when the time comes, and not before. As to your question about whether I'm scared—I alternate between periods of fear and faith. Sometimes I'm scared out of my pants and other times I feel so shielded that it borders on cockiness. Maybe I'm crazy, but sometimes I feel like I could step out in front of a train and it would pass right through me. But there are other times, like right now for example, when I'm fearful of losing my life. I'm not afraid to admit that those threats scare me. I don't wanna die. I want to stick around and laugh and joke and drink good beer for a long, long time."

"Maybe you could calm down just a little bit," said Marilyn. "You know, not really stop what you're doing—just stop being so in-your-face with the information you're pushing. I don't know what I'm trying to say. I just want you alive. That's all I want."

Truman opened his mouth to speak, but he caught himself before any words came out. Again he stared towards the floor. Again the room became silent. No one dared disrupt the thoughts whirling through the head of their beloved but troubled friend. Truman lifted up his head and looked at the two of them.

"I haven't been completely forthright with you guys. You're my best friends. You deserve to hear everything.

Besides I'm aching to tell someone before I lose my mind. There's something I haven't told you—something very strange."

"I thought there was something else bothering you," Menza stated solemnly. "Tell us, it'll be good for you to get it off your chest."

"I'm sure it will," replied Truman. "You remember what I told you about this morning, right? I'm talking about the red paint splashed all over my office."

"Of course," said Marilyn. "It must have been horrible to open your door and see that."

"Well," said Truman softly. "There was more to it than just the paint."

Truman pulled out his wallet and removed a piece of paper. He unfolded it and held it up. Something was written on it in red ink. Menza took a closer look. He read a few lines. The writing itself was childlike in nature, but the words certainly were not. It was written with intelligence.

"What is that?" Menza asked. "It looks like song lyrics. Did you write that?"

"You're right," said Truman. "It is song lyrics, but no—I didn't write them."

Well…who did?" asked Menza, almost afraid to hear the answer.

"I found it taped to my office door this morning," said Truman. "And that's not red ink or red paint. That's blood. It's lyrics to a song and it's written in someone's blood. I gotta admit this scares me, way more than the dead dog they threw in my yard a few weeks back."

"Who?" stammered Marilyn. "Who wrote that? The government?"

"I'm guessing so," said Truman. "You certainly gotta figure whoever poured the paint also posted the paper on the door—but…"

Menza had never seen Truman so ruffled. He was always so sure of himself regardless of the situation. Truman still maintained a cool exterior, but deep inside he was genuinely scared. An acquaintance would never notice it—but a friend would.

"But what?" asked Menza. "Tell us."

"Do you remember the other night—we were talking outside the pub? We were discussing the possibility that certain stars might actually be space stations. We theorized that the habitants of those stations might be controlling the Earth. Do you remember those weird chills we all felt simultaneously? We all felt like someone or something was sending us a message—letting us know they were listening to us. Well, when you read these lyrics it raises a possibility. Maybe this blood stained piece of paper originated from the conveyers of that chilly message…or…or…the Devil. I would really like your opinions after you read it."

"Keep…on," murmured a weak voice.

It was Marilyn's mother. She was speaking She lifted her head up. Everyone moved closer towards her.

"What?" blurted Marilyn. "Mom, what did you say?"

Marilyn placed her hand underneath her mother's head.

"Mom, what are you trying to tell us?"

"Tell   Truman…to…keep…fighting.   He…can   win. He…"

She closed he eyes and fell back into unconsciousness. Her message had been clear. She wanted Truman to keep fighting the fight. She did not want him to give up. Never in her life had she commented on politics or the state of the world. For some reason she chose to speak those words as she lay on her deathbed. Truman took them to heart. He handed over the blood soaked piece of paper. Together Menza and Marilyn read the words.

I'M YOUR MASTER

High above where you can't see,
There's something going on you'd never believe
It's a game of chess and I make all the moves,
I play both sides and I never lose
The game's been on for a very long time
I made you and I shaped you,
And you're mine all mine
You're my morning duty, a punch of the clock,
Don't think you're important cause you're not
You're a stitch in time and nothing more,
You ain't nothing but a daily chore
I'm your master, I'm your master,
I'm the master over you
I'm your master, I'm your master
You know it's true
I'm your master, I'm your master
What you gonna do
I'm the master, I'm the master—the master of you
You're under my control and you do as I say
I tell you when to war and I tell you when to pray
When you're praying to your God
You're praying to me
I'm the power that rules—a power that feeds
Sometimes I listen and sometimes I don't

I don't give a damn what you might want
Cause you're weak and pitiful and so full of fear
I cull you out and shed no tears
I'm the power behind the puppets that you all see
I'm the force that rules you from behind the scenes
I slaughtered Carthage and made them all slaves,
The Romans were a tool to have my way
I was there at Hastings and Marathon
And Waterloo too
Watching the blood flow as I sacrificed you
I brought those buildings down in New York Town
Licking my lips as they fell to the ground
I'm all about power—power and control
I control your essence, I control your soul
So get down on your knees and bow to me
You're my slaves and you'll never be free
I'm your master, I'm your master
I'm the master over you
I'm your master, I'm your master
You know it's true
I'm your master, I'm your master
What you gonna do
I'm the master, I'm the master—the master of you

Chapter 25

SURPRISE GUEST

Menza looked at his watch—3 p.m. It was a little early to be having a beer, but what the heck. It was Friday and it had been a rough week. A little extra shot of genomel was probably what he needed. He was too distracted to get any work done anyway. All he could think of was the pain his baby was going through. Marilyn was still at the hospital by her mother's side, as she had been for the past 48 hours. Her mother's condition was the same as it was yesterday. Marilyn knew where to find him if she needed him.

Menza took a deep breath before entering the pub. Worry number two was his good friend. Truman had opened up yesterday like never before. There was no doubt that the threats were wearing on him, but Menza knew his rebellious friend all too well. There was no way that Truman would ever change his ways. He was going down swinging.

Menza entered and headed for his customary corner. The pub was surprisingly crowded for 3 p.m. Then he remembered—Ashmont Art Festival was taking place in the city park across the street. The pub would probably be busy for the next three days. Menza looked around. There were the usuals—Pepper, Wright and a couple of guys from the office building next door. He saw Truman on the other side of the bar chatting with some new faces. He seemed to be in a good mood. That was a good sign. Truman had seen him come in. He quickly came over to greet him. On the way he stopped at the taps and filled up a pint glass. He plopped it down in front of Menza.

"Hi Truman, put her on the tab," said Menza. "That's a dark beer. What kind is it?"

Truman shook Menza's hand as he replied. "Oh, that's an unfiltered stout that I just turned loose from the tanks—darn tasty too. Don't worry about paying for it. That guy over there says he's an old friend of yours. He said to put it on his tab."

Truman nodded towards the corner seats at the far end of the bar. Menza noticed two guys standing. One was ole Freddy Tucker. There was no way he would have paid for the beer. He was the town tightwad—a nice guy, but prying a penny from him was like pulling teeth. The other guy standing looked a little familiar, but he certainly was no old friend. Who could it be that had sent a beer his way? There was one more gentleman sitting down. Menza strained to get a closer look. Freddy finally moved his large frame over and opened up a direct line of sight. The man had his back turned to Menza. Then he twisted his chair back towards the bar.

Menza looked at the man. The hair, the face, the smile, the unmistakable demeanor—no way! Absolutely no way! Menza looked away for a moment and rubbed his eyes. He collected his thoughts. He closed his eyes and turned his head back around. Then he slowly opened his eyes.

JP! That was JP sitting at the bar! It was not an illusion. He was not hallucinating. JP was in the Jumping Cow drinking beer! What in the heck was he doing on this planet! He was supposed to be off swashbuckling away on a space station.

What could have brought him to Earth? The coolest of the cool—JP—was in the house.

Menza tried to keep his head and remain calm. He could not let Truman see him rattled. His wise friend would start putting the pieces together and suspect something. Menza needed to act as if nothing was out of the ordinary. JP was just an old friend from times past. That's all, just a friend from good ole planet Earth—not from Novem, a planet a trillion time space arcs away. He could pull it off unless…unless Truman was already onto the scent. Menza looked back over towards JP. This time the Hammerhead legend was looking right at him. JP motioned for him to come over.

"Truman, please excuse me for a moment," said Menza. "I'm going over there. I think I do know that gentleman."

Menza grabbed his glass and walked towards JP, trying not to appear too excited. It was not an easy task for his body was flushed with anticipation of seeing his friend. The excitement was also fused with a bit of nervousness. There had to be an important reason why he had come. Heroes had a reason for everything. He still could not believe it. JP was *here*! *Now*!

JP was now standing. His wide grin seemed to permeate the entire pub. He had not changed a bit in the last few months. He was still the same happy-go-lucky bundle of self confidence that he always was. Menza looked into JP's eyes. They flashed calmness and peace. At that moment he knew everything was okay. JP's journey had not been crisis-based, it was not some sort of an emergency situation, it was not a mission of heartache. Menza felt a sense of relief, but a question lingered. What *did* he come for?

JP and Menza hugged. For a split second their energies greeted each other like the true friends they were. Again an overwhelming sense of calm descended upon Menza. Just being in the presence of such confidence put him at ease. JP had prepared a seat for him. They both sat down.

Menza disposed of a short laugh. "Well, JP, the first question is the obvious one. What in the hell are you doing here!"

"The beer," roared JP. "You've bragged so much about this stuff in both your transmissions that I thought I'd have a taste."

"Come on, JP," bayed Menza. "What's the real reason you're here?"

JP reached for his beer and took a long pull. After draining every drop he motioned for Truman to bring him another one.

"You got it, JP!" howled Truman. "I'll be right over with another one—same kind?"

"Yeah," replied JP. "Another one of those pale ales, please. Thank you."

"Wow," declared Menza. "It sounds like you two are well acquainted already. Give you another day and you'll be running the whole town."

"Seriously, kid," said JP, "I gotta give you credit. You really know how to pick 'em when it comes to a genomel source. I can't say I've ever felt more refreshed so quickly after a long journey. I can see why you like this beer stuff."

"Come on, JP! I'm begging you—tell me why you're here. What the heck is going on?"

"Okay, kid," winked JP. "I guess I've played with you enough. Do you want to know why I'm down here on Earth? I'm here to save the planet—pure and simple."

"JPeeeee. What are you talking about?"

Menza instinctively knew when JP was kidding and when he was serious. He was serious. Something was going on— something big.

"I'll tell you in just a second," said JP. "Here comes Truman with my beer. First things first, ya know."

"Here you go, guys," said Truman. "Menza, I went ahead and brought you another one too. It's on the house. I've got a feeling you guys are going to be here a while. Old friends always have to catch up on things."

Truman placed the beers in front of them and quickly left, but not before aiming a well-timed wink or blink, or whatever the heck those things were, directly at Menza. He did not have time to dwell on that right now. At the moment Menza had more pressing issues that needed answers. He turned his attention back to JP after Truman was safely out of listening range.

"Okay, JP," said Menza. "Spew it out. Save the planet? What's going on?"

"Here's the story, kid. You might as well sit back, relax and listen. You know those transmissions you sent back to IOS? Well, both of them found their way into Tucker's office. The last one you sent, rumor has it, made him cry like a baby. Between that song that your friends wrote and the sad situation you described so vividly—well, you made a huge impression on the old man. A week after your last communication I got my own transmission, straight from the IOS brass. I was to leave Milky Way Central and come down here. They told me to get down here and start setting some things up, make some preparations for something huge."

"You're starting to scare me a little bit, JP. I know you're not kidding me. Please continue."

"Sure, kid." JP went on. "Here's what's happening. The IOS has decided to turn this planet around. They're going to use technology that you and me won't even believe—fantastic inter-dimensional stuff that's fresh out of the experimental phase. Now you know as well as I do how tight-lipped the

IOS is about any new technology. They've got to have a real good reason to be pulling out all the stops—a *real* good reason. There are zillions of planets throughout the universe that are in trouble. Many of them are in far worse shape than this one. Your emotional appeal in those transmissions spilled over into the IOS boardroom. The fat cats decided to save planet Earth—thanks to you."

"Wow," exclaimed Menza. "I'm in shock. This is unbelievable. I've got so many questions that I don't even know where to start. I guess my first question is—why are they making an intergalactic effort to save one planet? That just doesn't make any sense. I know the IOS better than that. There's more to it—right, JP?"

"You're as sharp as I thought you were, kid," chimed JP. "Yes, there's more to this than just saving little ole Earth—a whole lot more!"

"Okay, I'm sharp—big deal," said Menza. "So quit teasing me and tell me. Give me the big picture."

"I'll lay it out for you, kid. As I said earlier, your reports captured Tucker's heart. That last one was a knockout punch. He took it straight to the board members and read it word for word, including the song lyrics. From what I heard you had 'em all in tears."

"Oh my," gasped Menza. "When I wrote that report I had no idea it would affect people like that. And the song—I'm so glad I decided to put that in there."

"Well, you won't believe what happened next," JP said sharply. "Tucker made a formal recommendation to the IOS. He suggested that the free will clause be removed from the intervention policy."

"What!" shrieked Menza. "That's been in effect for eons. As long as anyone can remember the free will proviso has been a given. Only in extreme cases has the IOS intervened in planetary squabbles. What are you trying to tell me?"

"You know what I'm going to say next, kid. The board took a vote and it passed. It passed! Now I'll let you tell me what that means. Tell me, kid."

"It's huge!" bellowed Menza. "The implications are massive, at least in theory. What that means is that the IOS can finally throw out the criminals that are screwing up civilization. They'll no longer be able to hide behind the fine print. There are countless species of intelligent beings inhabiting our worlds. Most of them are good, but like always, a few bad apples spoil the whole bunch. I wish the IOS was able to clean up the whole universe. I know that's a pipe dream and will never happen, but at least they're going to help the poor souls trapped on this planet."

"Hold your horses," said JP. "Not so fast. You're gonna love what I'm going to tell you next. They *are* going to clean up the universe—the whole universe. Did you hear me? The IOS is going to kick out the old and ring in the new, seek out the bad guys and run 'em out of town, smoke out the evildoers and send them running with their tails between their legs. If that ain't good enough news for you—well, it gets even better! Are you ready?"

"I'm totally in shock," answered Menza. "Shoot—go ahead and tell me the rest."

"Let me give you an analogy," said JP. "It'll be the best way to explain it. A lot of times before you rent an apartment, they'll show you around a model apartment, right?"

"Sure," replied Menza. "That makes sense. They want you to see their best product—a nice, clean beautiful apartment. It's the best of the best. So, go ahead."

"Earth is going to be the model apartment of the universe! Did you hear me, kid? There are zillions upon zillions of planets out there that need help. They are going to start with Earth and use it as a model to clean up the universe. Every available bit of technology is going to be utilized. The bad guys don't stand a chance. It's going to be a quick bloodless battle. Once they realize they're outgunned they'll run as fast as they can. Then the IOS will position its own people in place—and just like that—Earth will be transformed into the showplace of the universe. Earth will be maintained in glorious pristine condition for all to see. All of this is because of you, kid. You were the spark that will change the entire universe forever. You!"

Menza reached for his beer and took a long drink. Swallowing this information was not easy. A little chaser of alcohol and genomel would make it go down easier. The knowledge JP was passing on to him was astonishing. Coming from anyone but JP he would not even believe it. Earth was going to be saved! It would be used as a model planet to save the entire universe! And it all came about because of his little report! Menza took another big swig of beer. Then he closed his eyes. He pinched himself—hard! He opened his eyes. Yep, JP was still there.

"Oh, one last note," JP casually mentioned. "Ashmont's going to be the designated governmental center of Earth. All major decisions will be made here. Oh, and one more thing—since Earth will be the model of universal change, Ashmont will house a brand new IOS building. Actually it will be more than a building. It'll be a massive office complex—one of the largest in the universe, nearly as large as their main headquarters."

Menza was speechless. He closed his eyes again. It seemed to help the information absorption process. His mind was racing, utilizing every single one of his 800 intelligence quotients. Was JP finally finished? What else was he going to pull out of the hat? Stunned and shell-shocked—that was the best explanation for his current condition. He had a million questions for JP and he could not mutter a word. Who wouldn't be—it wasn't everyday you received news that you were personally responsible for saving the entire universe.

Menza reached for his beer with his eyes still closed. It was gone. He opened his eyes. A fresh full beer was sitting near where the old one had been. It seemed that Truman had brought over a new round while he had been trancing out. Truman had even filled his own trusty two-liter glass. He and JP were locked into a conversation about hummingbirds— hummingbirds! The entire universe was about to be rescued from evil and JP is discussing the mating habits of humming-birds. That's about what should be expected from the two coolest beings in the universe.

"We thought we had lost you, Menz," laughed Truman. "You were in a world of your own for a couple of minutes. I'll leave you two alone again to catch up. I gotta serve Pepper over there before he sets fire to the place. Good chatting with you, JP."

Truman trotted off to the taps. Menza could not believe how he and JP seemed to be best of friends. They had met only an hour ago. But then again—it was JP and Truman. Nothing else needed to be said.

"Kid," joked JP, "I thought I was going to have to throw that beer in your face to bring you back. All this is a little overwhelming, huh?"

"I'll say," said Menza. "You didn't have to surprise me this way, you know? You could've given me a little warning. How did you think I'd handle it? I come into the bar like I do every day and see you in here! You knew in my wildest dreams I wasn't expecting to see *you* anytime soon."

"Oh, kid," snorted JP. "You know I like to make things fun. You gotta learn to expect the unexpected. It keeps you on your toes—know what I mean?"

"Maybe so," said Menza, "but the last thing I expected was for you to come jetting in here. Speaking of jetting—where is the biocraft? That ain't an easy thing to hide."

"Oh, I parked it across the street," said JP. "Look out the window and you can see it. The last time I looked a bunch of kids were playing on it."

Menza laughed. JP had to be kidding. He was always the jokester. You just don't go around parking alien biocrafts in plain view. So—where did he hide the spaceship?

"That's a funny one, JP. But seriously, where is the craft? This is a small town and there are not a lot of options. Now I'm really curious—where's the spaceship?"

JP lifted his beer for another long pull. Then he rose from his stool and walked over to the window. He gazed out before turning back towards Menza.

"Yep, it's still there. There's a pretty large crowd around it now. It must really be getting the attention. Come see for yourself."

Menza stood up and walked to the window. It was obvious he wasn't going to get a straight answer out of JP until he completed his little joke. Menza chuckled, then turned and peered out the window. He almost had a heart attack!

There was the biocraft!—in plain sight!—with all the lights blinking! It was parked directly across the street in the park. 333 square feet of alien technology was being showcased in downtown Ashmont. It was parked smack in the middle of the park. And to top it off, this weekend was the biggest event of the year—the Ashmont Art Festival! A thousand people would be wandering the grounds of their quaint little city park all weekend long, admiring the local arts and crafts—along with a time space bending spaceship from another galaxy. JP could not have found a *more* conspicuous place to put his spaceship. It was surrounded by a couple of dozen people. There were children playing on top of it and *inside* it. People were posing in front of it and taking snapshots. Had JP gone insane?

Menza stumbled back to his chair and sat down. He was white as a sheet. His stomach was in knots. He was so dizzy he could barely walk. Was this real—or a real bad dream? Did he have too much to drink? Did someone put something in his orange juice this morning that had made this whole day one big hallucination?

"Kid, you don't look so good," said JP. "You gotta learn how to relax."

"Relax!" cried Menza. "How can I relax with a spaceship sitting in the middle of Ashmont? Look out there, JP! That's our ride back home—you've turned it into a tourist attraction. You even left the lights on! I guess it wasn't enough to park the latest model of an alien biocraft in downtown during the busiest weekend of the year. No—that wouldn't get enough attention. You needed to add flashing orange and blue and green lights! And you left the door open! JP—take another look out there. There are kids inside the craft pushing buttons on the control panel. What if they start the damn thing up! What are you trying to do—send them flying through time and space to destinations unknown! JP—have you lost your mind!"

"I'm telling you, kid relax," JP said with a chuckle. "Don't worry. I've disabled all the systems. Kid—I want you to look at something. Do you see that huge banner strung out in front of the park?"

"Yes! I do! So what?"

"Can you read it to me? What does it say?"

Menza peered out the window again. "It reads Ashmont Art Festival. That's what it reads. So what?"

"Okay," said JP in a calm voice. "The biocraft is a work of art—nothing more, nothing less. All those people out there are admiring a work of art. Take another look. Do you see the sign I posted on the craft? I stuck it right under the window. Read that to me if you would."

Menza strained his eyes. Yes, there was a sign under the window. He leaned against the glass for a closer look. He read it.

Futuristic Space Craft
Soon to be Seen in the Air
Art by JP

Menza felt sick again. He went back to his chair and plopped down into it. He gathered his thoughts. This was no nightmare. This was as real as real could be. JP was in the Jumping Cow drinking beer and there was a spaceship sitting out in front of the bar. Those were the facts and they could not be undone. Now was the time to dig into that 800 IQ again and figure something out. JP seemed to have used his all up.

Menza's mind raced at lightning speed analyzing the situation. The past was over and done with. The situation was what it was. There were no viable options for wiggling out of the outrageous predicament that JP had thrown him into. There was nothing left to do but go with the flow. If the IOS wanted to ruin his career over this fiasco of a mission, then so be it. He would go down in flames alongside the longtime hero of the galaxy. Hell, maybe JP knew what he was doing. Anyway—it didn't really matter at this point. That spaceship sitting out front wasn't going away anytime soon. Hell, he might as well just have another beer and let JP run the show.

"Hey, Truman," barked Menza. "Can we have another round over here? I'm going to be here with my artist friend for a while. Did you see his spaceship out front?"

JP laughed so hard he nearly fell off his stool. "Now you're coming around, kid. Now you're getting it. Sometimes you gotta go with a whopper of a story so big and outlandish that no one would ever believe it could be true. Think about it, kid. That spaceship out there can't be real—ain't no way. Ain't no real alien gonna put his flying saucer on display for the whole world to see. That's nothing more than a piece of art by an eccentric old man—just a crazy old man. Ha!—a crazy old man."

Chapter 26

I'M AN ALIEN

C hannel 6 was on the scene. The reporter held the microphone up to JP's face. The Ashmont Art Festival was in full swing. Saturday was always the busiest day of the three-day event. This year was turning out to be the best one ever—thanks to the "spaceship from Jupiter." That's what the press had dubbed it. It was the biggest, boldest, most outrageous piece of art the festival had ever displayed—a giant flying saucer. An outsider from Seattle, Washington had trucked it in for the show. At least that was the rumor. No one knew for sure where he was from. One thing was for certain—he wasn't from a planet named Novem in a faraway galaxy named Hammerhead. That's the tale he was weaving to the kids that constantly surrounded him. The outré artist went by the name of JP. The flamboyant storytelling raconteur had been dazzling the crowd with fantastic fabrications of space travel. The children were especially enthralled by his tales of traveling the universe in his spaceship.

"It was ten years in the design phase," said JP to the young blonde female reporter. "Then I started traveling around the universe in it. I took it to the Milky Way's central space station, Jupiter, Pluto—now, honey, that Pluto's one nice place. Would you care to join me for lunch up there one day? I can have you back in time for tea at three."

Menza stood out of camera range and watched the master reign over his subjects. The crowd laughed. No doubt the television audience joined in as well. It was JP the jokester at his best—only they weren't jokes. It was all true and the unsuspecting public was eating it up. JP had spent a lifetime being interviewed. This kind of stuff was old hat to him. Fans adored him everywhere he made an appearance. It seemed as if Earth would be no exception. JP was as comfortable in front of the camera as he was kicking up his feet in his own living room, maybe more so. It was obvious he loved the attention. Only a cool cat like JP could pull off a stunt like this one.

Menza's mind was all over the board as he watched JP work his audience. The spaceship situation was apparently solved, at least temporarily. The craft was such a hit that the festival director had practically begged JP to leave it there for the duration of the event. JP agreed that he would leave it on display through Sunday. Then he would "truck" it out later that evening.

What was especially amazing about JP's entertaining performance was the fact that he had not slept a wink. Actually neither of them had slept. They had both stayed up all night in JP's hotel room discussing strategy for the takeover of Earth. JP had originally planned on sleeping over in the craft. Through dogged persistence Menza finally persuaded JP to take a hotel room. The Sir Robert Hotel was the best accommodations in Ashmont, but it could not hold a candle to the comforts and conveniences of the biocraft. JP agreed to stay at the Sir Robert through Sunday. After that he was back in the craft. There would be no debate about it.

Menza's head was spinning. Saving a planet that would save the universe was a big responsibility. But all the worries in the world could not wipe the smile off his face today. He had just made his baby the happiest girl in the universe. He saved her mother's life! Last night JP handed over a very special gift from a very special person. It was a tiny vial of liquid from Tucker. Inside that little bottle resided a cure for cancer. Marilyn's mother was to ingest a drop a day for ten days and the cancer would dry up. It was that simple. Marilyn was so happy that she did not even bother to ask how Menza came about possessing a cure for cancer. That question would undoubtedly pop up in the near future.

That prompted Menza to consider how he was going to break some other important news to his girlfriend—that he was an alien visitor from another galaxy! How would he do it? It wasn't something you could casually bring up over dinner. It wasn't as simple as "sweetie, could you please pass the salt, oh, and by the way, I'm an extraterrestrial from outer space." How would Marilyn take the news that her boyfriend was not from this planet? He would find out soon.

Then there was the man behind the bar. When and how was he going to tell Truman? He had not seen him all day. It wasn't something he was looking forward to. Menza was sure he would have some piercing questions relating to his flamboyant artist friend. This alien disclosure thing was beginning to be a pain in the neck. He wished he could be more like JP and just let things flow. Everything always mystically fell into place for the midnight sky rider. Nothing ever seemed to faze him. JP could crash his spaceship into a mound of dodo and come out smelling like roses. Like right now for example—JP was standing on top of his spaceship posing for a photograph. Squeezed around him were all twelve members of the Ashmont City Council. The picture was going to be on the cover of next month's Ashmont Today Magazine.

Menza glanced across the street. Several patrons of the Cow were standing outside the pub taking in all the activity. They would undoubtedly go back inside and give Truman a full report. Truman would then be armed with more background information for the inevitable quiz session. It didn't really matter how tough Truman's questions were. As a matter of fact there was no reason for the interrogation at all. Menza should just walk in and spill it all out—everything. He should tell Truman straight up that he was an alien, that Earth was about to be taken over by extraterrestrials, that his primitive backwards little planet was about to become the model of utopia for the entire universe, that civilization as he knew it would be changed forever—and that *he* was to be an integral part of the process.

Menza's head was all over the place. Preparation for a planetary takeover was no easy task. There were so many things that needed to be done. Last night's conversation in the hotel had been enlightening. He and JP had not stayed up all night discussing hummingbirds—although that was the newly tagged term for the entire affair. JP had laid out the whole plan.

At this very moment there was a massive IOS space station orbiting the Earth's equator. Inside it were 7,700 operatives. Each one had a specialized skill. They represented 52 different galaxies. They had all been prepped and briefed and could slide into action on a moment's notice. All they needed was a green light from JP and the takeover would commence. 111 of the latest model ZPB's were lined up ready to transport them to their destination—a desperate troubled planet named Earth.

Operation Hummingbird would be a three-stage procedure. The first step was covert in nature. It was so secret that JP knew few details about it. This much he did know. He had been told to prepare a clandestine landing zone large enough to accommodate eleven ZPB's. This first stealth phase of the operation would involve only a handful of operatives. JP had hinted that this group might be multi-dimensional programmers. JP theorized that their mission was to lay down several layers of false dimensions. This was deemed necessary to confuse the enemy, who themselves were inter-dimensional. JP thought the covert stage of the operation would last no longer than one week.

The second phase of Operation Hummingbird was essentially an eviction process—of soul intruders. A vile race of beings was ruling the planet through surrogate leadership. Earth was under their control. Thousands of world leaders currently perceived to be human were in fact an alien species or alien controlled. They included politicians, bankers, industry magnates, military and governmental officials, intelligence operatives, religious leaders and entertainment figures. Many of them were humans whose very souls had been seized. Some were clones or synthetic beings created specifically to occupy a certain position of power. Others were merely mind controlled.

Replace and erase—that was the complex strategy that was to be employed in taking over approximately 5,000 human bodies. Those humans whose souls had been invaded were to be freed. The heinous elements enslaving their bodies would be ejected. Their minds and emotions would become their own again. The clones and synthetic robots would be humanely reprogrammed and reintegrated back into society.

The mind controlled subjects were to be transported to the space station for deprogramming. A special technology would permanently erase all trauma memories associated with the programming. They too would regain control of their minds. Decisions would once again be free from the influence of others.

Stage three was the nuts and bolts finale of Operation Hummingbird. All positions vacated by the malevolent alien presence would have to be filled. A joint advisory board of premier trusted humans and foreign selectees would be formed. This group would be responsible for temporarily appointments of all power positions. The appointees would then establish a chain of command to fill all mid-level and grass roots level ranks. Earth could then begin to heal from its deep wounds. The malefic presence of the longtime evildoers would be wiped away forever. A new era would begin.

Menza's attention once again drifted towards his trusted friend. There was a reason that Truman needed to be informed of the big picture as soon as possible—genomel. JP had relayed some more critical information last night. 7,700 beings were currently orbiting around the planet. Earth would soon be their new home. Every single one of them would require a genomel source. The origin of their genomel was to be Truman's beer. The decision was final. There would be no time to piddle paddle around seeking out another source. There might not even be another genomel-laced product on the whole planet. It was entirely possible that the Jumping Cow was Earth's sole producer of the life giving force that sustained the universe. The IOS had decided to take no chances.

7,700 beings would require a massive amount of ge-nomel—and that was only the beginning. The IOS was to construct a governmental complex. Thousands of foreigners would permanently be based on the future model planet. Each and every one of them would also require regular doses of Truman's beer. Tucker and the board had allocated unlimited funds for the purchase of property to house a massive brewery. The brewery would be built immediately. Truman would be the sole owner and operator. He would oversee every batch of suds that came through the place. After all it was his soul and passion and love that sired the genomel. Sure—the IOS could recruit a highly schooled brewmaster from a giant corporate brewery to make the beer. They could hire anyone they wanted. Money was certainly no object. But they were not about to risk some passionless egghead mixing up the frothy substance that would keep their personnel alive.

And it wasn't only about sustaining life—the stuff was good! Menza's reports had praised the gustatory attributes of Truman's beer—the tantalizing delicious flavors, the fragrant aroma of the hops, the ambrosial lingering of the sweet malts that lit up the olfactory sensors. Beer was truly the nectar of the Gods. Truman made the best beer on the planet—and it had been designated to satisfy the cravings of thousands of visitors. It would soon make its way to the saviors from the stars.

Now was the time. There would be no more beating around the bush. Menza decided to just walk into the pub and get it over with. He would tell Truman everything. He would stroll into the bar and order a beer. After a long pull from his glass of courage he would spill his guts. There really was no other option. He wasn't accomplishing anything standing out here. JP certainly did not need any help from his nervous little homeboy.

Menza took another look at the universal celebrity who had so shook up his world. JP seemed to have things well in hand. He was now inside the spaceship holding court.

Another local TV station had arrived on the scene. Channel 2 wasn't about to miss out on the action. Yet another young blonde was conducting a live interview with the master showman. Menza cupped his ears to listen in on the conversation that was being beamed to a hundred thousand viewers. He overheard JP flirting with the pretty reporter. JP was describing the intricacies of the time space indicator. JP told the amiable blonde that he had traveled a trillion time space arcs just to see her. The crowd laughed in unison at the humorous artist who had wandered into their town dragging a spaceship.

Menza walked across the street and entered the pub. It was humming with conversation. Of course the major topic was the spacecraft that was parked across the street. David Markson and several other senior citizens were sitting at a table sharing a pizza. Menza overheard one of them commenting about JP. He thought JP might be an eccentric billionaire who had lost his mental marbles. Another speculated that JP might be a foreign spy on a mission to bomb Ashmont. Still another thought JP was a CIA agent. Finally David joked that JP was probably an extraterrestrial hell-bent on taking over the planet. That one cracked up the whole table.

Menza slipped into a chair at the bar. Truman hadn't spotted him yet. He was busy taking an order at a table. He had been doing a little bit of everything as of late, personally taking up the slack in Marilyn's absence. She had asked for a few days off due to her mother's condition. Truman had taken it upon himself to replace her—which was quite the chore.

Amy came over and brought him a beer—on her. She reminded Menza to thank his friend again for the generous tip from the night before. Apparently JP had left an over-the-top gratuity for every employee last night—including the ones that weren't working! Menza guessed that JP was looser than himself when it came to parting with IOS cash. No one would ever have the nerve to question JP's expenses. Throwing away money was part of his job. That's what salty-tongued celebrity heroes were supposed to do—fly around running up outrageous bar bills and leaving insanely large tips. It was worth every penny to the public just to hear the stories he came back with.

Here came Truman rounding the corner—and he had his eye on Menza. He gave the food order to the kitchen before meandering back over. He had a twinkle in his eyes and an indecipherable smile on his face. Truman began with a little small talk before he went in for the kill.

"Hi there, Menza, it's still quite chilly today, huh?"

"Yeah, Truman, it's still coat weather. That's for sure."

"You know what it is," drawled Truman, "it's the wind. That darn wind will freeze you worse than the cold. So, Menz—how's JP today?"

The dagger was in and Truman was preparing to twist it. Truman would get the truth one way or the other. He almost seemed telepathic at times. Now was the time to let it all fly. Menza took a deep breath.

"Truman, we've been friends for several months—real good friends, right?"

"Yes, Menz, you're actually the best friend I've got right now. Most people either don't understand me or think I'm crazy as a rabid bat. You seem to have me figured out."

"Maybe I do," said Menza, "but how about you? Do you have *me* figured out?"

"That's a tough question, Menz. You know I've never asked you a prying question. That's your private business. I just figured you'd tell me what you want to tell me when you want to tell me—it's that simple. I've always found that you actually get more information when you *don't* ask for it. People seem to trust you more."

"Tell me, Truman," said Menza, "is there anything you would like to know about me? Is there anything you want to ask me?"

"There's nothing burning at the moment. When you first moved here I was curious if there was a city named Seattle—in Russia. I checked and couldn't find one."

Menza winced. In the back of his mind he had always wondered about that early stumble. He knew that sooner or later it would come back to haunt him. So Truman was aware that Menza had two separate background stories floating around town—what else did he know?"

"Yes, Truman, I'm getting ready to explain that one, along with some other things. I know it's pretty busy in here, but why don't you take some time and let's have a beer—on me. You'd better get your big glass. You might need it."

Truman didn't say a word. His patented winky blink said it all. He reached under the bar and retrieved his glass. Menza watched as he patiently filled it to the brim. Then he filled a glass for Menza. He slowly walked around to the other side of the bar and pulled up a seat alongside his friend. Both of them took a long draw off their beers.

"Shoot," said Truman calmly. "Tell me want you want me to hear."

"Truman, I'm going to need your help soon—for something very important."

"You're my friend," said Truman, "a very good friend. I'll do everything I can to help you. What is it you need?"

"It's about me—and JP. Do you see that spaceship out there?"

"Of course I do," chuckled Truman. "The whole town's been talking about it for two days. I can only imagine that's what the real thing might look like. I keep waiting for your friend to crank her up and fly her to the stars."

"Oh yeah," said Menza. Well, if you ask him he might just take you for a ride."

Truman remained unfazed. He took a long sip of beer. He held his enormous glass up and let the light stream through it. The golden liquid shined like the evening sun. He seemed to be admiring it as if it were a fine work of art—which it was. He let the precious wetness remain in his mouth for a few seconds, savoring it before he swallowed it. He finally sat the glass down.

"Now that's a good batch of brew," he said casually. It was as if Menza had never mentioned the fact that he might be able to fly in a spaceship. Truman's feathers didn't ruffle easy. Menza tried again.

"Yeah, Truman, she's a fine spacecraft. And you know what—she flies."

Truman's eyes seemed to soak in the words before transmitting them to his brain. Truman was always using his eyes for more than sight. They were his weapon of survival in a world gone mad. They gleamed of intellect and emotion, they expressed passion and pain, they were the path to his core. He seemed to use them as a first line of defense against the outside world. They filtered out the craziness and let the harmony flow through. Truman's eyes were the bridge between reality and hope. They were the conduit to his soul.

"So she flies, you say," Truman said calmly. "Can we fly away and leave the suffering and pain behind? Can we escape the insanity of a world ruled by cruel tyrants? Can we leave this place of fools and let them drown in their own misery? Can we jump in that spaceship and break loose from all this wretched evil that surrounds us? Tell me we can, Menza—and I'll jump on the spaceship right now and go."

Menza looked into Truman's begging eyes. Then he spoke. The words rang like a Sunday morning church bell.

"As a matter of fact, Truman—we can get on that spaceship and leave. We can do it tonight if you like. I can fly you away to a place of peace and tranquility, a place where love rules, a place you would never want to leave. Maybe one day you'll decide to do that very thing. Maybe I'll be with you. Yes, you can go to that heavenly place of peace and love tonight, but you won't go. You know why—because what I'm getting ready to tell you will change your mind. You will decide to stay right here on your own planet."

Truman's inquiring eyes beamed back at Menza. "And *why* will I stay? Tell me, my friend—tell me."

"Because you're going to save the world," answered Menza.

Truman said nothing. He didn't have to because his eyes said it all. They gleamed with hope.

"Truman, listen to me," said Menza. "I am not who you think I am. I'm from another planet. My home is located in a star system far away from here. I came here to research your planet and study your behavior. Something miraculous has resulted from my stay. Even today I still don't understand how it actually came about—but I do know it's real. My people are going to rescue your troubled planet."

Menza waited for a reaction, a laugh, a scream, an eviction from the pub with a warning to never come back, anything—but there was no obvious emotional response. Either Truman truly was the coolest trooper on the planet and absolutely nothing fazed him or …*he knew already*. Truman's eyes continued to serve as communication. They exalted joy and excitement, and they were craving more of the same. Menza continued.

"JP is one of my kind. He came here to inform me of a takeover. There are 7,700 of us orbiting the Earth as we speak. When JP gives the word they're going to kick into action. That should occur very soon. You're probably wondering how 7,700 beings can save the planet. Well, they've got access to technology that's beyond fantastic. Creating layers of false dimensions, bloodless soul transfers, time separation and splicing—that's the kind of stuff that's going to free humanity. Are you with me so far?"

Truman was still letting his eyes do the talking. They let it be known he wanted to know more. This time he added a nod of the head.

"We're calling it Operation Hummingbird. It's a three stage affair. From start to finish the whole process should take about a month. It will be completely nonviolent and no one will get hurt. The beings that are currently running your planet will have their choice—conform or run to another planet. If they opt to run they'll eventually have to face the same situation. My people are cleaning house on the whole universe, starting with your home—Earth."

Truman was still remarkably calm. He picked up his beer and took another long drink. Menza did the same. There was a long moment of silence, but it was not an awkward silence. It was simply two intelligent beings gathering their thoughts. Finally Truman decided to speak.

"Menza," he said, "What you're describing is incredible to say the least, but I believe every word you're telling me. You might be wondering why I'm not running around here in a fit of hysteria. After all you just told me that you were an alien— an alien!"

"Well, yes—I'm actually stunned that you haven't called in the white coats to haul me outta here and lock me away at the funny farm. So tell me, why haven't you?"

"Menza, to be completely honest with you, I've had some suspicions for a while. Let me explain. I've always believed there was a plethora of species existing out there amongst the stars. It would be foolish to think otherwise. Why would Earth possess the only intelligent life in the universe—if in fact we are intelligent? If an outside race were to judge us solely from our behavior we would probably be deemed a race of fools. They would see that we're a short sighted breed of beings that seem hell-bent on destroying the planet and each other. If you ask me, that's not a sign of intelligence. Planet Folly—that's the name I'd give us. That's the name we deserve. We're a bunch of beings that have yet to reach puberty status on the universal scale. We're a planet of onions growing with our heads in the ground and our feet in the air. Oh, Menza, I'm getting off track here. My point is I've always believed there was intelligent life out there in the universe."

"Go ahead," said Menza. "Tell me more. I'm still trying to figure out why you're not bouncing off the walls after what I just told you."

Truman wiped a bead of moisture from the side of his glass. "I guess my mind's been primed for this since childhood. I've always expected some sort of disclosure statement from the ones in the know. Then when one the Pope's spokespersons came out and endorsed the possibility that aliens existed—well, I kinda figured they knew a bit of inside information. That was the nail in the coffin as far as I was concerned."

"Okay, so you've always believed there was life out there," stated Menza, "but that doesn't explain *me*. What was it about *me* that made you think I might not be from this planet?"

"A gut feeling, that's all," said Truman. "There was the Seattle/Russia thing of course, but it was a whole lot more than that. You seemed too…too…too darn intelligent for one thing. Then there's the way your eyes light up when you gaze into the stars. It's as if you're looking…searching…longing for something. And I noticed certain little things that didn't seem to fit, things that you should've known about, but didn't—you know, like football, golf, world famous entertainers, popular culture type stuff. I couldn't figure out if you had lived a somewhat sheltered lifestyle and just weren't aware of all that stuff or…or you were from…from somewhere else. Menza, I've spent a lot of time analyzing, thinking—trying to figure you out. I knew you were too smart to not know certain things…unless you had never been exposed to it. That's the only logical explanation I could come up with…that you were…were from somewhere else. I kept fighting it and fighting it because I didn't want to believe. Even now I don't want to believe it. I mean—you look like us, you talk like us—who would ever suspect you're not who you say you are? I'm halfway wishing you would tell me right now that you're joking. One part of me would be relieved. You know what? Remember that night a while back when you and I and Marilyn were all looking at the stars? We were in deep discussion trying to figure it all out…the meaning of it all. Well, that evening, I *almost* asked you point blank if you were in some way connected to those stars that were puzzling us so. I think the fact that Marilyn was with us stopped me. I didn't want to put you on the spot and force you into a corner where you'd have to lie. But I'll tell you what—I sure was getting a strong feeling that night that you were bonded to the heavens in some way. Anyway, yes, I'm shocked with what you're telling me. It's damn near unbelievable. And this other information that you're piling on me—WOW!"

"I'm sorry I've got to throw all this stuff at you at once," said Menza, "but I didn't really have a lot of options.

Everything's going to start happening soon—and when it starts there will be no turning back. I just needed you in the loop. Tell me, Truman, what do you *really* think about all this? What's going on in that computer mind of yours?"

"I've got a million questions for you. I guess the first one is this—where do I fit in? Earlier you mentioned that I was personally going to be a part of this rescue mission. What the heck can I do? Ha!—I can tell you right now that I am not a time-splicing technician—nor have I ever laid down a false dimension. I'm also not very skilled at transferring souls. Now—if your guys need a frosty glass of beer I can accommodate them, but I seriously doubt that's the case."

Menza laughed. "Truman, it's funny you should mention your beer. That's *exactly* where you are going to fit in. Your beer will literally be the lifeline that will enable our team to set your planet free."

"I'm sorry," said Truman, "but I'll need a little elaboration on that one. You're telling me that you highly advanced aliens can splice time and create dimensions, yet you can't produce a glass of beer—Menza! And why do you *need* beer in the first place. Hell, I thought I was the only being in the universe that *needed* beer."

"It's a little more complicated than that," replied Menza with another laugh. "Here it is in a nutshell. It's not beer we need, it's *your* beer we need. Did you have any idea that without your beer I would have perished months ago? I would have died—literally."

"Join the club," joked Truman. "So would I—when's the last time you saw me go more than a few hours without the stuff."

"No, seriously," said Menza. "Your beer carries an element that exists outside of the physical realm. I can guarantee you the big breweries' products don't contain it. It's called genomel. It's an emotional element that feeds our bodies and souls. It's a byproduct of joy, passion, love and soul. My friend, you possess those traits and they channel through to your beer. Those 7,700 saviors would not be floating around this planet if it weren't for the safety net of your product. So there it is, Truman—we're going to need massive quantities of your beer. Can you supply 7,700 needy soldiers with beer?"

"7,700!" exclaimed Truman. "How in the heck am I going to brew enough beer for 7,700 people—excuse me, beings?"

Truman took in a deep breath. Then he turned up his glass for a long drink. Menza knew what his friend was doing. He was letting this blast of information settle. Menza tried to put himself in Truman's position. Ten minutes ago his life was much simpler. Cook a couple of pizzas, pour a few beers, tell a few jokes—that's all he had to do. He had been doing that for so long that he could do it in his sleep. Then, suddenly, out of nowhere—his best friend tells him he is an extraterrestrial. As if that wasn't shocking enough, his friend then tells him that there are thousands of aliens currently circling the planet—waiting to invade Earth! Then his friend tells him not to worry because the aliens are going to splice time, create fake dimensions, move people's souls around, and God only knows what else—which will chase away *another* bunch of aliens that have been hiding *inside* human bodies. Just when he thinks there might be a respite from the mental and emotional assault his friend has laid upon him—there's more! Who would have thought that *beer* was the vital ingredient needed to sustain all life forms? What happened to good old fashioned water? Apparently the universe would crumble unless he could miraculously supply all its inhabitants with beer. World peace would not be accomplished until his tiny brewing system metamorphosed into a mega-brewery capable of pumping out a zillion gallons of frothy liquid per hour nonstop until the end of time. Yes—Menza felt sympathy for his shell-shocked friend. Truman looked up at Menza.

"Menza, you're not answering my question. How am I going to supply 7,700 'people' with beer? You know as well as I that my little backyard brewery isn't capable of that production."

"Don't worry," Menza said confidently. "We've got that all worked out. You're aware of that 5,000-acre parcel of land that ole Roy Johnson has been trying to sell for the past year, right?"

"Yes, I am," replied Truman. "That's a nice piece of property. If I had ten million dollars I'd buy it. What in the heck does that have to do with producing beer?"

"It's like this, Truman. JP was instructed to purchase that land. He's already offered full price and Roy accepted. Monday morning you need to head down to Lisk Mortgage Company and sign the papers. You're going to be the owner of that land."

"*I'm* going to be owner—what's going on, Menza?"

"The land will be yours to keep," explained Menza. "You just need to use a portion of it for our needs. We're going to throw up a makeshift brewery utilizing some of those old buildings on the property. I've already ordered the equipment. You need to get some batches rolling as soon as possible. That should meet our immediate needs. In the meantime we're going to construct a large modern brewery on the property—you'll be the owner of course. We're going to need the larger brewery to fill the needs of the future. An organization called the Intergalactic Open Society will be making Ashmont one of their universal bases. Lots of beings from throughout the universe will be relocating here. Every one of them will need beer to survive. I guess the bottom line is this—Truman, you're going to have to work your tail off making lots of beer, but at least you'll be rich from selling your product and land holdings. Not to mention the satisfaction of knowing that you rescued the entire universe from evil. Any questions?"

"Only about a thousand of them," answered Truman as he shook his head. "But first let me refill these glasses with some of that—what do you call it, genomel?"

"Yep, you've got it right. Genomel is what keeps the universe humming along."

"Oh, I do have one quick question before I go grab our genomel."

"What is it," asked Menza.

Truman chuckled. "Have you told Marilyn you're a space alien? That oughta rock her world!"

"That's tonight," Menza winced. "And I'm not looking forward to it—believe me."

"Ah, she'll be okay," said Truman, "at least after she gets over the shock. Oh, one more thing. Check out these lyrics I wrote after seeing you guys in the hospital the other day. I think they've suddenly become appropriate."

Truman reached under the bar. He handed Menza a yellow pad plastered with the customary scribble. Then he gathered up the several beer glasses spread out across the bar and strolled towards the taps, shaking his head the whole way.

PRESENCE

Mama always told me that life can knock you down
She said claw your way back,
Get your butt off the ground
Climb out of that hole
Cause it don't really matter,
That they kick you when you're down

They're ignorant fools in the presence of a king,
Searching for his crown
You gotta be around when they come to call
Cause the truth's gonna pour
When they unlock that door
It's waiting for that day,
When they can't hide it anymore
It's going to flood the gates of lies,
That guard the secrets so true
That's your time to shine, my boy,
They're going to need you
So when they come a calling,
You'd better be prepared
It'll be a brand new world,
Full of leaders who dared
They're coming from the stars,
And they're wearing big shoes
They're gonna stomp out the old and put in the new
There's going to be changes, all brand new,
A brand new presence, a brand new you
Yeah, a whole new world's coming—coming for you

Chapter 27
TELLING THE GIRL

Menza took a deep breath. One down, one to go—but this was the big one. He was going to tell the love of his life that he was not who she thought he was. Sweet little Marilyn would soon learn that the man with whom she had been sharing her bed was not from this world. He was not a customer service representative from Seattle, Washington. He was not an immigrant from a small town in Russia. Nope—he was an extraterrestrial being from a distant galaxy. Menza took another deep breath. Then he tapped on her door. She opened it and immediately jumped into his arms.

"Baby!" cried Marilyn, "I'm so glad to see you. I've got great news. Mom's getting better!"

"That's wonderful!" said Menza.

"I did just what you said. One drop that's all I gave her. I woke her this morning and put it on her tongue. Baby, you won't believe it! She was actually sitting up in bed this afternoon. And she's asking for some real food. What is that stuff? Where did you get it? Oh, baby, I'm so happy!"

"Oh, Marilyn," whispered Menza as he held her tight. "I'm so happy for you. I know you love her so."

"Thank you, baby—thank you so much! It's all because of you and that…that liquid. What is that? Tell me, baby!"

Menza grasped Marilyn's hand and led her to the sofa. "Come on over here and let's sit down. There are a few things I want to explain."

They both sat down. Menza gazed into Marilyn's bright eyes. They were filled with joy and happiness. Maybe her mother's turnaround would soften the blow of what he was getting ready to tell her. Maybe it would make it all a little easier to swallow.

"So, are you going to tell me or not?" asked Marilyn. "What in the world is that stuff and where did you get it?"

"Marilyn, do you love me?"

"Of course I do, baby," answered Marilyn. "You know that."

"Yes I do know it," said Menza, "and you're going to need all that love to help you through this. I'm going to share my deepest secrets with you. It's about me, my life, my being here in Ashmont—it's not as it seems. Baby, I'm different from you. That medicine that I got for your mother, it came from a place far away from here."

"I don't understand," said Marilyn. She grasped his hand. "Tell me, baby."

"Look deep into my eyes, Marilyn. Try to relax. Baby, do you remember that night you and I and Truman were looking at the moon and the stars? We were trying to make sense of it all. We were wondering how the human race fit into the big picture of the universe."

"Yes, I remember it well," answered Marilyn. "So…"

"Marilyn, that medicine came from out there. Out there amongst the stars there exists a cure for cancer. It was delivered from the heavens, not from God, at least not directly—but from a species that looks and talks and acts exactly like you do. You told me one time that you believed there was other life in the universe. Well, I'm here to tell you that there is life out there. There are beings out there with similar traits as humans. They are kind, caring and compassionate. They want to help, not hurt. They laugh, they cry, they have the same emotions as you. That is where the cancer medicine came from. I know this may seem incredible, but it's true. An extraterrestrial race saved your mother's life. That vial of liquid was a gift from the stars—a gift of life. Someone out there decided this was not your mother's time to go. You keep giving her that medicine just like I told you to do—one drop a day. She's going to recover completely. It will be as if she never had cancer. It's all because of a friend that you'll probably never meet. His name is Tucker. He's an extraterrestrial."

Menza waited for a reaction. He was intentionally breaking the news of his alien origin in two steps. He hoped divulging the source of her mother's miracle medicine as extraterrestrial in nature would smooth the way for his own personal revelation. The business of alien disclosure was not an easy task. It was proving to be hell on the emotions.

"My God," stammered Marilyn. "Aliens saved my mother—aliens! Menza, I need a minute for all this…this…whatever it is. Hold me, baby."

Menza pressed her body against his. Her breathing was short, deep and intense. He could also felt another connection of sorts. Her thoughts, her emotions, her innocence, her very essence was beaming into him. It was powerful and real and it stripped Menza down to his core. Marilyn was exposing her soul. It pierced his body and streamed into his own soul. It was warm and bright and it felt really good. It was soulshine. They were one. Suddenly everything seemed okay.

"Marilyn," whispered Menza. "I've got something else I need to tell you."

"What is it, baby?" Marilyn asked softly. "Tell me, tell me anything. Just don't tell me you're going to leave me. That's the one thing I can't handle. You are my miracle man. I find myself bursting with happiness when I'm around you. Tell me whatever you want, but don't you dare tell me you're leaving me. That's all I ask."

Menza's mind flashed ahead. He had never bothered to ask JP what would happen after all this was resolved. Would he still be leaving after his one-year assignment on Earth—or did this takeover situation change matters? Damn it—it didn't matter anymore. Menza's innate stubbornness was kicking in. He would never leave the love of his life. The powerful IOS would bend some rules if they had too. He would take Marilyn back with him to his own planet if that was the only option. Maybe JP could pull some strings and help him out. Somehow, someway, he would make sure they would be together forever.

"No, baby," said Menza. "I will never leave you. That much I promise you. Baby, you know that race of beings that saved your mother's life. I belong to that race. I am one of them. We are a completely benevolent species. We mean no harm to anyone. We only want to help your planet. Baby, I'm from the stars. I'm from a place very far away. I'm from up there."

"Oh my!" uttered Marilyn. "Oh, God, I wasn't expecting this! Oh baby, I need another minute. I need to think. Oh my!"

Menza expected Marilyn to pull away from him. Instead she grasped him tighter than ever. Menza could feel her heart racing. He gently stroked her shoulders as she lay against him lightly sobbing. Time passed—two minutes, five minutes, ten minutes, maybe more—neither of them knew or cared. Finally Marilyn loosened her grip and lifted her head. She looked into Menza's eyes. Her own eyes were filled with dogged determination and unbending stubbornness. Menza had seen that look before. Once she made up her mind about something you could set it in stone. It was final—no questions asked. Marilyn had reached a decision. What was it?

"I don't care!" cried Marilyn. "I don't care who you are. Menza, I love you more than I've ever loved anyone. I don't care! All I care about is *you*. I want you forever. I want to spend the rest of my life with you. I want to grow old with you. I can't live without you. Don't you *ever ever ever* leave me! Do you hear me? This changes nothing! Oh, baby, just hold me. Please hold me. Oh, baby!"

Marilyn pressed her head hard against Menza's chest. She squeezed him so hard he could hardly breathe. It didn't matter. What mattered was that Marilyn had accepted the situation for what it was. What a special girl she was. She had so much love inside of her. Even learning that her boyfriend wasn't from this world couldn't shake the love loose from her soul. Marilyn was as real as real could be. She was morning sunshine, beaming in and warming the day with honesty and purity. When she gave you her word you could stand by it. Marilyn was a very special girl—*his* girl.

Chapter 28
CHANGES ARE COMING

It was Sunday morning. Marilyn was sleeping. Menza leaned over and gave her a gentle kiss on the lips. Neither of them had slept more than an hour or so. They had been too busy sharing their love with each other. They had become one in every sense of the word—physically, emotionally and spiritually. It had been a long night of sharing pleasure, releasing emotions and baring their souls to each other. The revealing of Menza's long held secret had actually brought them closer together. They were both riding the crest of a wave that would never break. It would roll on forever. It was an eternal wave made of trust and faith and everlasting friendship.

"I'll see you later at the pub, baby. I've got some things I need to do. You sleep some more. Get your rest."

Menza gently slipped out of Marilyn's bed. She quickly fell back asleep. Menza dressed and quietly exited her apartment. Menza felt as though a huge weight had been lifted from his chest. He had told Marilyn everything. She now knew about JP, the spaceship and the saviors in the sky. She had practically begged for details of Operation Hummingbird. She knew it all and she was in it for the long haul. She was a lot stronger than he had given her credit for. He would never let her go. He didn't care what corner of the universe he ended up in. It didn't matter as long as she was by his side. She would be his girl forever.

Menza had a busy day ahead of him. He mentally went through the checklist in his head. There were literally a hundred things that had to done before the IOS could send in their covert operatives. Most of them would be relatively easy to resolve, but there were some immediate issues that needed to be addressed.

Number one on the immediacy list was the biocraft—where in the heck was he going to hide it? The art festival would be ending this evening. JP would have to slide in after dark and fly her away to somewhere—but where? Menza had a few potential solutions in mind, but once again they would involve a bit of disclosure. People are just naturally going to be asking questions when a spaceship appears on their front lawn. That nasty ole tell-people-you're-an-alien predicament always seems to pop up. Sometimes it was a real pain in the neck being an extraterrestrial.

Menza hoped he could permanently resolve the parking crisis. Procuring a safe haven for JP's craft was only the beginning. In a matter of days there would be 11 more spaceships that needed to be hidden away. Secrecy was critical during the all important first phase of Hummingbird. He needed help from someone who could keep their mouth shut. He could not afford some loose-lipped louse bungling the operation after a few beers. He needed someone he could trust.

Then there was the matter of the main fleet. Immediately after the groundwork stage 100 more ZPB's would be swooping in. They would require an Earth-based hive for at least one month. They would be shuffling personnel and materials back and forth from the space station base. That meant that 111 additional spaceships needed a home.

The first piece of business was to check on JP. Hopefully he went to his hotel room last night and had gotten a good night's sleep. Menza laughed to himself. A fat chance of that! He was probably in the Cow until the wee hours hanging out with all his new friends. That would be the better bet. Super heroes don't need sleep. They can't leave their legion of admiring fans for the comforts of a hotel bed. It's simply not their nature. JP couldn't hide even if he wanted to. He would be too easy to locate—just follow the spotlight until it ends. There you will find JP's smiling face.

This was the final day of the art festival. JP's face had been splashed on the local news shows all day yesterday. A huge turnout was expected today due to all the publicity. Everyone wanted to catch a glimpse of the "spaceship from Jupiter" and its charismatic captain. News reporters were telling people to car pool to the event due to limited parking. JP was the only being alive that could change the order of the universe with a joke and a smile. His powerful personality had a way of permeating people's souls.

Menza headed out on foot. It was only a fifteen minute walk to the festival grounds. A walk would do him good. There were so many things floating around in his mind. He could still hardly believe what was going on—the IOS was rescuing Earth! It all seemed like a dream. Just a few months ago he was a wet-behind-the-ears kid who knew little of life outside of his own solar system. Now the great big world was coming to him. A couple of hastily written IOS transmissions had propelled the governmental giant to change the universe. They had discarded the age old rule of free will. Freedom and tolerance would still be the guiding force of government. That much would not change. It was just the criminals who were abusing the system who would be affected. Never again would anyone have free rein to harm others. Inflicting pain and suffering upon others would become a thing of the past. The universe would live in harmony. Love and peace would become the sustenance for the newly freed souls long held captive by greed and the lust for power. A great change was coming and an inconsequential planet named Earth would be at the center of it all.

From universal salvation to the personal—there was so much going on. Menza's mind strayed back to Marilyn. She now knew that he was not from her world and she had accepted it. There was no turning back with the love of his life. He had to figure out a way to keep the two of them on the same planet, whatever planet that might be. What about Truman? What did the future hold for his good friend? He hoped nothing would happen to him during the critical time before the rescue mission slipped into full gear. Truman had made some very powerful enemies. Hopefully his angel would protect him until the bad guys were kicked out of town. What about JP? Ha! Menza laughed at himself for even entertaining the thought of worrying about JP. That one was easy. JP would continue being JP.

Menza almost missed her. Joan Dixon was kneeling in front of a tombstone. Every time he walked by Ashmont War Memorial he scanned the headstones. It was a habit he had intentionally instilled upon himself. He never wanted to forget the horrors of war. To forget would not be fair to the departed souls who gave their lives for something they truly believed in—regardless of whether it was right or wrong.

Menza slowly walked towards her. She had her eyes closed and was praying. Menza read the tombstone at the head of the grave.

William Dixon 1987-2011
Our little pilot now flies in Heaven

Menza turned to leave. He would leave the grieving mother alone. Nothing could undo what had been done. William was gone and he was never coming back. He had been a victim of a needless war.

"Don't leave me, Menza," a voice called out.

Menza turned back around. Joan stood up and motioned for him to come to her. He walked back to her and put a hand on her shoulder.

"Menza, I still love him so," said Joan, as a tear rolled down her cheek.

"I know you do," whispered Menza. "He gave his life for something he believed in. He's in a better place. He's at peace."

"It's never going to end," said Joan. "Just look at all these headstones. So many kids died for nothing—for nothing! Look at that empty space over there. There's room for a hundred more of these things. More mothers are going to have to bear the same pain I'm going through. We're savages, all of us. Our race isn't happy unless we're killing each other with guns and bombs and God knows what else. Menza, I'm just so sad."

Menza placed another hand on her other shoulder. He shook her ever so slightly to get her full attention. She looked into his eyes.

"Joan, I want you to listen to me. I'm going to tell you something. It won't make sense now, but it will soon. In a few weeks you'll know what I'm talking about. These graves that are filled with the bodies of brave men and women—they do mean something. Your son sacrificed his life, but it's not going to be in vain. He and everyone else who's lying in this graveyard made an impression on someone, someone very powerful. That person has the power to stop all wars, now and forever. There are going to be some huge changes coming. Don't ask me how I know this, but I do. I want you to always remember that your son played a part in bringing permanent peace to the world. Always know that! Your son was and still is a hero. William's spirit will live forever. His presence will be felt by those who will live in peace, free of the death and destruction brought on by those senseless wars. Peace is coming, Joan—and it's coming soon."

Joan wiped away another tear. "I hope you're right, Menza. I truly do. If that miracle did truly happen…well…then I could have some peace in my own heart. Thank you, Menza. If nothing else, you've made me feel a lot better about my son. You're right, he didn't die in vain. There had to be a reason for God to take him from us. He was too good to die for nothing."

"I'm going to go now," said Menza. "I'll leave you alone with William. You take care and have a good day. Tell Jim I said hello."

Joan turned her attention back to her son's resting place. Menza slowly walked away. He knew that in some small way he had just helped Joan. It also inspired him. The wars could not stop soon enough. Every day that passed brought another mother down to her knees. Every day there was a knock on someone's door delivering the horrible news of a loved one's death. The wars needed to end soon. He would do his best to make it happen.

Menza continued his walk. He rounded the corner at Piedmont Street. Suddenly cars were everywhere. Ashmont's art festival was bringing them in from all corners of the state. Menza noticed some out of state plates. Some attendees had driven in from as far away as Virginia, Georgia and even New

York! There was no doubt in Menza's mind as to who they came to see. That would be the pied piper himself, good ole JP.

Menza looked at the banner strung over the highway announcing the festival. He did a double take. Someone had strung another banner underneath the original. The new one was much larger and in bolder print. Apparently it held more importance.

Welcome to Ashmont Art Festival
HOME OF THE SPACESHIP FROM JUPITER
CAPTAINED BY JP—UNIVERSAL
TRAVELER

Menza just shook his head and laughed. He entered from the side gate. This was the last day of the festival. Sunday was normally the most tranquil day of the three day event. This year was proving to be an exception. The "spaceship from Jupiter" was a popular draw.

The place was packed with new faces—smiling faces. Good cheer was the order of the day. Everyone seemed to be in exceptional spirits, especially the children. Most of them were crowded around the flying saucer from outer space. In the middle of it all stood its charismatic commander. Kids surrounded him as he spun yarns of intergalactic adventures. Menza sneaked in closer and cupped his ears with his hands. He wanted to hear the latest from Ashmont's celebrity aeronaut. It proved entertaining.

"It's your world. I'm just passing through it," JP's confidant voice echoed. "Kids, I've ridden this spaceship through 77 galaxies and visited 910 planets. Nope, I'm sorry, make that 911 planets. I forgot about your lovely piece of celestial heaven—Earth. She's a beauty, a real gem of the universe.

You should be proud of her. She'll be getting a little spring cleaning soon and she'll be prettier than ever. I'm going to send a hundred more spaceships down here and we're going to freshen up your planet. Yep, a hundred more flying saucers are coming your way very soon. Each spaceship will have a whole bunch more aliens in it. They'll be thousands of us. Kids, this place will be *swarming* with aliens. We're gonna take over the planet and make Earth better than ever. We're going to haul away any garbage you may have and brighten up the place. We're going to put on a shiny coat of fresh paint and polish her up good. Your planet will be the glistening model of the universe, the envy of the stars. Me and my alien friends might just make a home here. Do any of you kids want to meet some more real aliens?"

"YES!" the children all answered. They were spellbound by JP's tales of imaginative fantasy. He narrated them with such enthusiasm and intensity. It was as if he actually believed his own fairytales. JP continued amusing his young subjects.

"Kids, when all of my friends come down in their flying saucers I don't want any of you to be scared. My friends are very nice aliens. Maybe, if you ask real nice, they'll take you for a ride in one of their spaceships. Would anyone like to ride in a spaceship?"

"YES!" the youngsters cried together.

"Okay, I'll see what I can do about that. I promise you I'll make sure each and every one of you get to ride in a spaceship. Maybe I'll personally take you all to the Moon. Who wants to go to the Moon?"

"I DO! ME! ME! I DO! ME!" The thought of traveling to the Moon sent the kids into a frenzy. Some of them were begging to go at this very moment. Several parents had to physically restrain their children back from entering the spaceship.

"Whoa, kids," barked JP. "Calm down. You'll get your chance later. I promise. There will soon be plenty of spaceships down here. Then we can take you all to the Moon—and Mars too. Your parents are welcome to come also. If you like, one day I may take some of you to my home planet. Novem is a very special planet. It has nine beautiful rings around it. All the aliens that live there look just like you. You will love the kids that live on my planet. They're just like you. They like to play and have fun. So be patient, kids. Soon you'll get your chance to go to outer space."

Menza could barely contain himself. Everything JP was telling the delighted crowd was absolutely true. He was packaging truth as fantasy, reality as an illusionary bubble for children and adults alike. Maybe JP really was an artist. In a few weeks these people would look back and think about this moment. That eccentric ole artist would not seem so crazy then. They were unknowingly witnessing a piece of history. Time would soon burst the bubble of fantasy and free the truth. JP would then be deemed a prophet, a soothsayer of all that was to come. His amusing witticisms were a clever disguise for a foretelling prophecy. JP was teasing his audience with a gift of truth, all wrapped up in fancy fiction and tied with a colorful bow.

Menza chuckled to himself. So this is how he did it. This is how JP had managed to become the darling of the universal media. This was the method by which he had achieved intergalactic celebrity status. Menza wondered—how many other planets had he charmed off their axis like this one? JP had just scored another triumphal conquest to plaster on his remarkable resume. Earth was putty in his hands.

Menza left JP to entertain his troops. He could use a little time clear his head. He spent the next two hours sauntering through the festival grounds. There were endless rows of booths showcasing the works of the local artisans. North Carolina-produced paintings, sculptures, ceramics and the like could hold their own anywhere in the universe.

Menza looked at the big picture. Earthlings were creating all of this fine art despite the troubled state of their planet. It was only going to get better. The residents of this wonderful planet would soon be free to do as they please. No longer would they be required to slave away at monotonous jobs just to foot the bill of the military-industrial machine that tore through their tax dollars. No longer would the majority of their hard earned money go towards murdering their fellow human beings. In a matter of weeks war would become a relic of the past. Peace was the future.

Menza gazed towards the heavens. He couldn't see it, but it was there. The IOS space station was tracing the equator of the planet, circling the globe high in the sky. It was filled with the skilled and they were rearing to go. Soon there would be no more Joan Dixons crying over the graves of dead soldiers. Soon there would be peace.

Menza took a deep breath. The tranquil walk through the aisles of art had been refreshing. It was time to go to work. Trusty Truman awaited him. Menza needed a little Earthly advice from his newly enlightened best friend. A little genomel boost certainly couldn't hurt matters either. Hopefully his pretty girlfriend would be there. Marilyn had mentioned she might come in for a late lunch before going to work. He strolled across the street and entered the pub.

The Jumping Cow was doing a brisk business. The JP induced crowd had overflowed into the pub. The stinging guitar riffs of Jimi Hendrix swept through the air. "The Wind Cries Mary" had always been a favorite of Truman's. That was the song Jimi had personally showed him how to play.

Despite the near capacity crowd the pub was running like a fine tuned machine. Nearly every employee had been called the day before and asked to work. Truman had baited them with double pay for accommodating him. He was a master at handling employees. Rarely was there ever friction between him and his staff.

Truman had the foresight to predict a hectic day. It wasn't really a difficult decision. All a person had to do was look out the window and see the spaceship sitting across the street. Spaceships always attracted people. It didn't hurt that JP was instructing his followers to go inside the Jumping Cow. Every hour on the hour he would interrupt one of his captivating tales of space travel to make an announcement. He would inform his throng of admirers that the Cow had the best pizza on planet Earth. The beer was even better—the finest in the Milky Way. There was no better product endorser than JP. In three days time he had already branded himself as an intergalactic authority on all there was to know. His loyal disciples reckoned he knew what he was talking about.

Menza quickly scanned the pub. Suddenly someone grabbed him around the waist from behind. Instantly he knew who it was. It was the touch of his lover. Marilyn squeezed him tight before finally releasing her grip. Menza turned around and Marilyn attacked him with a huge wet kiss to his mouth.

"Wow!" exclaimed Menza. "That's some kind of greeting. I could get used to that."

Marilyn flashed her big beautiful smile that had so impressed Menza from day one.

It was sexier than ever. Then she whispered in his ear. "You'd better get used to it because that's what you're going to get every day. That and a whole lot more."

"I'll take it," said Menza. "You can bet on that."

"Come on over here, baby," said Marilyn as she grabbed his hand. "I just finished having lunch with Truman."

She led him to a corner table. Truman watched them with a wide grin as they walked towards him.

Truman stood and shook Menza's hand. "Howya doing, spaceman? Welcome back to the Cow—the source of all life."

The three of them laughed. Truman was an expert at using his offbeat brand of humor to put people at ease. It even worked on aliens.

Menza blushed slightly. "Yeah, it does feel kind of strange knowing that you both know…you know…that I'm not from here."

"Be happy with it," said Truman. "You must have something us humans don't have. Just look at that smile on Marilyn's face. A lowly human male is not capable of creating that. Just wait til you hear of the beer she named after you."

It was Marilyn's time to blush. "Oh, Truman, let's not get into that now. Please!"

"Okay, we'll save that one for later," chuckled Truman. "Seriously, Menza, I think we're all three feeling pretty good. Oh, that reminds me. Marilyn, tell him about your mother."

"Yes! How can I forget!" cried Marilyn. "Mom's walking around her hospital room demanding they let her go home. The doctors can't believe it. Of course they don't know about the medicine I'm giving her. She got her second drop this morning. She actually wanted to come with me to the pub today to personally thank you. I don't think she's ready for that yet, but who knows, maybe by tomorrow she will be. Oh, Menza, thank you so much. Baby, I love you!"

Menza felt a calm warmth overtake his body. It was similar to what he had felt the previous evening. It was an energy that fed his soul. It derived from love and trust and friendship. It was a prodigious presence that had taken on a life of its own—born of the collective consciousness of three friends. There were all operating on the same frequency level. Their vibrations were in tune with each other. Menza was sure they were feeling the same unexplainable sensations. He didn't have to ask. He could see it on their faces. He could feel it in the air.

An invisible force had seeded within each of them an uncommon strength, unwavering confidence, and a measure of universal wisdom. They were no longer from different worlds. They had become emancipated from the shackles of bias and ignorance. They were three enlightened beings to whom fate had delivered a common mission. They would rescue their troubled planet from the grips of iniquity.

They were a team. Each would use their specific talents to make it happen. Menza would be the communication lifeline between the knowing and the nescient, the primitive and the advanced, the stars and a trifling planet known as Earth. Truman would be Truman—an extraordinarily decent man with an innate ability to sniff out the lone drop of truth in an ocean of deceit. Marilyn would be the guiding force of consciousness, an overseeing spirit protecting those who dare, the soulshine that would see it all through.

Menza felt chills racing through his body. He could actually see the hair standing on Marilyn's arms. For sure Truman was experiencing the same sensations. No one spoke for fear of disturbing the powerful presence that surrounded them. Finally the force released its grip on the trio of friends.

"I'm not even going to ask," said Truman, shaking his head in amazement. "I know you guys felt the same thing I just felt. What a powerful sensation that was. It was like…like a…telepathic stream of some sort. It's still sending shock waves through me."

"I felt it too, Truman," said Marilyn. "But you know what? I'm not even going to try to figure it out. All I know is that it's good, it's happy, it's something to smile about for a change. I'm going to run with it. I'm going to run with it as far as I can go. I'm going to ride it as far as it will take me. The last two days have been full of surprises, BIG surprises. Maybe this is a dream and I'm going to wake up tomorrow and find mom back in her hospital bed. Maybe Menza will tell me this has all been a joke and he's just been pretending to be from another place. Maybe the world is not going to be saved. Maybe I'll go back to my life as it was 36 hours ago, but I hope not. I pray that this is real, that mom is getting better, that my boyfriend *is* from another world, that the planet will be spared from the evil that now consumes it. It's unbelievably crazy, but I like it, I want it, and I know both of you want it too. Menza, please make this be real. Please!"

"It's real, baby. Your mom *is* going to be completely cured, I *am* who I say I am, and there *is* a shipload of extraterrestrials sitting just above us. I'm so happy that you guys are accepting this so well. Trust me, as soon as JP gives the word things are going to start happening."

"Ha," cracked Truman. "Speaking of JP, he was in here til closing last night. You should have seen everyone hounding him for autographs."

Menza nodded his head in agreement. "Yeah, you ain't seen nothing yet. I know it's kind of hard for you guys to understand, but he does this kind of stuff all over the universe. There are some planets where he is literally worshiped. I'm not kidding you."

Truman laughed. "Oh, I certainly don't doubt it. He's already looked upon as a God in here. Let me tell you what he did last night. Before he left I offered to pick up his bar tab. There was no way he would have any part of that. He threw down two thousand dollars and told me to keep the change as a tip. Two *thousand* dollars! I'm spreading it out amongst all the employees. Marilyn, I guess that means you've got a couple of hundred dollars coming your way, thanks to JP."

Marilyn smiled. "You know what? A couple of days ago that would have excited me like nothing else. I'd be doing a dance right now after hearing that news. I guess my shock tolerance is off the charts right now. When your boyfriend cures your mother of cancer, then he tells you he's an alien from another galaxy—well, I guess a couple of hundred dollars falls a little short on the shock meter. As I say this I'm looking out the window looking at a spaceship. A spaceship!"

Truman placed his hand on Marilyn's shoulder. "Marilyn, you're not alone. I'm as overwhelmed by all this as you are. I still can't believe it either. Every time I think it might all be a dream I walk outside, and, sure enough, it's still there. There's a *real* spaceship parked across the street."

"That brings me to an important subject," said Menza. "Maybe you two can help me with this. As you know, this is the last day of the art festival. That spaceship out there needs a home as of tonight. JP's planning on slipping out there around midnight and flying her out. He needs somewhere to park it, somewhere safe. We need someone we can trust who will keep their mouth shut. Like I've told both of you, the first week or so of the operation is the most crucial. I've got someone in mind and he's sitting right over there. What do you guys think?"

Menza pointed directly towards Pepper. He and Wright were sitting at the bar together.

Truman sighed and nodded his head. He said nothing. Menza knew exactly what was going on. Truman was analyzing. He was scanning his cerebral databank, sorting information, applying that information to the situation at hand, weighing the pros and cons. Not until that cognitive process was complete would he issue a statement. It didn't take him long.

"I've got to agree with you," said Truman. "Pepper's our best bet. We trust him, he can keep a secret, and the Pig Parlor is the perfect hiding spot. We can park it right in the old pig house. There's plenty of room available. However, bringing Pepper into the loop will also present some special challenges. You both are well aware that he's a skeptical sort. Pepper's told me on many occasions that he's not totally convinced of my conspiracy theories. He's a solid evidence type of guy who wants mainstream approval before he signs on to anything. I respect that about him. At least he's honest. As far as extraterrestrial life goes…well, it's like this. He always comes back with the same line. 'When a spaceship lands in my front yard I'll believe it.' Well, guys, maybe it's time to land that spaceship on his front lawn. What do you think?"

"I'm glad we're on the same page," said Menza. "I've racked my brain for two days on this. I think Pepper's our best option."

"I think he's our *only* option," agreed Marilyn. "This is a small town. It ain't easy finding alien hiders around here. Ha! Listen to me! I sound like an extraterrestrial myself. Menza, what have you done to me!"

"Don't worry," said Truman. "You ain't alone. Sometimes I feel like I'm in the twilight zone myself."

"So, I'm guessing that we're all in agreement," surmised Menza. "What's next?"

"I'll tell you what's next," replied Truman with a mischievous grin. "I'm going to the bar. I'll be right back with four big beers and one soon-to-be-enlightened alien skeptic. Get ready to have some fun."

They watched as Truman, still wearing his schoolboy grin, stood up and walked towards the bar. After motioning for Amy to pour four beers, he casually struck up a conversation with Pepper and Wright. A couple of quick jokes later he was making his way back with a beer-toting Pepper in tow.

"Hey guys, how ya'll doing?" drawled Pepper. "Truman here's making me earn a free beer by delivering yours over here."

"Hi Pepper," said Marilyn. "It's good to see you."

"Yes, it's nice to see you," echoed Menza. "Pepper, please take a seat if you have a moment. There's something I'd like to discuss with you."

Pepper grabbed a chair from the adjacent table and sat down. "I've got plenty of time. What's on your mind?"

"I've got a favor to ask from you—a big one."

"No problem, Menza," replied Pepper. "I guess I really do owe you one after that zoo incident. I have to admit your quick thinking got me out of a jam, even though you did stink me up pretty bad. What do you need?"

"It's actually for my friend, JP. No doubt you know all about him. He's the one that brought in that spaceship sitting across the street."

"Of course I know about him," answered Pepper. "The whole town's been talking about him and his space art for three days. He even bought me a beer last night. He seems to be a great guy. What does he need?"

"He's decided to stick around town for a while and he needs a place to park that spaceship for a few weeks. I was wondering if you had room for it at the Pig Parlor."

"Absolutely," stated Pepper. "That's no problem at all. I can even put it on the back of pop's flatbed truck. We can haul it out of here today if you like."

"That won't be necessary," Truman calmly interjected. "JP's gonna fly it over there."

"Haaaa, haaaa," laughed Pepper. "Truman, you're getting wilder every day with that offbeat humor of yours. Maybe it's time you started drinking regular-sized beers like the rest of us. Those big ones are eating at your brain."

"No, Truman's absolutely right," said Menza. "He's not kidding. It really does fly. JP's gonna fly it over around midnight if that's okay with you."

"Get outta here!" cried Pepper. "It's a piece of art. That thing doesn't fly. You guys are trying to pull a big one on me. Marilyn, pull the plug on their joke. Tell me they're kidding."

"No, Pepper, I'm afraid they're telling the truth," Marilyn said casually. "It really does fly. This is no joke."

"Oh, come on!" wailed Pepper. "Who here has actually seen it fly? Tell me!"

"I haven't," replied Truman, "and neither has Marilyn. Menza's a different story. Not only has he seen it fly, but he's ridden in it."

"Truman! Menza! Marilyn! What kind of trick are you guys trying to play on me? If that thing flies, then where are the wings? What's the power source?"

"It's a special quantflow technology," said Menza. "It's difficult to describe, but essentially it runs off of a zero point energy base."

"Now it's really getting deep," Pepper said with a laugh. "I think you've been watching too many of those alien conspiracy shows. What did JP do—reverse engineer technology from a crashed alien craft? Are you guys still serious? You're seriously telling me that thing flies! Come on!"

"Pepper, it's like this," Truman chimed in. "That thing really does fly. If you think that's crazy you're really not going to believe what Menza's going to tell you next. Can I make a suggestion?"

"Please do," answered Pepper, "because I'm beginning to think the three of you have been dipping into Terry Tee's stash bag. You're all acting crazy."

Truman laughed. "Let's do this. JP really does need that thing moved. Let's assume for the time being that you're right—it doesn't fly. Can you do this for us? Can you show up here at the pub at midnight tonight with the flatbed truck? JP will be here. All you guys can relax and have a beer while I close down the pub. Around 1 a. m. we'll move that art…that spaceship…whatever you want to call it. We'll either fly it out or truck it out. How does that sound?"

"Okay, I'll be here," said Pepper. 'Then you guys can get a good laugh when you finally admit this is a practical joke. I gotta admit, you're going all out on this one. Truman, thanks for the beer. I've earned this one! Okay, I gotta go. Wright's gonna wonder what happened to me."

"You're welcome," said Truman. "Oh, Pepper, one more thing."

What is it?" asked Pepper.

"I know you really do think it's a joke, and that's okay. But could you not tell anyone about this, at least not yet?"

"Sure, Truman," Pepper replied cynically. "I don't want any more people in on this joke, believe me."

Pepper walked back and took his seat at the bar. The three of them watched him for a moment. Even though Pepper thought the whole thing was no more than a practical joke, he was cool about it. He began talking sports with Wright. The secret was safe. Tonight he would have the surprise of his life.

Chapter 29
TRIP TO THE MOON

J P reared back in his chair. "Most of my money I spent on beer and women. The rest I wasted."

The late nighters roared with laughter. For four hours "Captain" JP had been regaling them with accounts of his interplanetary adventures. The Cow was sporting several new faces amongst a sprinkling of regulars. Many of the newcomers had followed JP from the festival into the pub. They hoped to hear more from the charismatic artist with the magnetic personality. JP didn't disappoint.

"Okay, gang," called Truman. "Let's wrap it up and get out of here. We're closing soon. Nobody needs to worry about their tab. JP here has picked it up for the whole bar."

The clock on the wall showed straight up midnight. The crowd slowly filtered out the door. Most of the out-of-towners were walking out wearing Jumping Cow souvenir T-shirts autographed by JP. Truman locked the doors after a final inebriated guest walked out to his taxi. Truman sat down beside JP at the bar. Menza and Marilyn stood alongside them.

"What do you think?" asked Menza. "It's after midnight. Is Pepper going to show up?"

"He'll be here," responded Truman. "I guarantee it."

Just then they heard a tap on the door. Sure enough, Pepper's face was peering through the glass. Truman unlocked the door and let him in.

"Pepper, welcome to our private party," said Truman. "Have a seat and I'll get us all a beer. Pepper, I don't think you've had the pleasure. This is the one and only JP."

JP stood and gave Pepper a firm handshake. "It's nice to meet you, Pepper. I'm JP."

"It's a real pleasure to meet you, JP. The entire town's been talking about your unusual piece of art for three days now. I'm glad to finally see the man behind the art."

"Thank you," said JP. "She flies, you know."

Pepper laughed. "That's what they're telling me. You guys don't need to worry. When the joke's all done I'll haul her away for you. I've got the flatbed parked right beside the "spaceship." I ain't figured out the motivation behind these pranksters yet, but they're sure trying to pull a big one on me. I'm just gonna let it play out and get the last laugh."

JP flashed his famous grin. "I guess it don't really matter how it gets to your place. Flying it would be a lot easier than trying to push it up onto that truck, but we'll move it by any method you choose. The main thing is that it gets there. We really appreciate you letting me keep it at your place for a few weeks. Menza tells me you're a fine fellow."

"That's the reason I'm here," said Pepper. "Everyone here is a friend of mine. Believe me, I wouldn't go along with a charade like this for just anyone. I'm here because I believe you really need a place to store your art. I've got the room for it and I'm willing to truck it over there for you. I'm just a friend helping a friend."

"Well, thank you," said JP. "Tell me, Pepper, have you ever been to the Moon?"

Pepper burst into laughter. "The Moon! No, I can't say I've ever been to the Moon."

"Would you like to go—tonight? It's a beautiful evening. I'm sure the view of Earth would be spectacular from up there. Come on. Let's all of us go right now. I can have us there in ten minutes."

"Alright!" cried Pepper. "I can see this farce won't end until I cave in. Yeah, I'm ready to go the Moon—right now! Let's go through the motions, finish out the play, everyone can get a laugh, then I'll haul that sculpture or whatever it is out of here."

"Truman," barked JP. "Can you put those beers on hold? We're all taking a quick trip to the Moon."

Truman stopped halfway through a beer and pushed back the tap. He looked at JP. Menza shrugged his shoulders. Truman then realized this was no joke. JP really wanted to take a trip to the Moon. He wanted everyone to pile into the spaceship and go on a midnight cruise to the Moon—the Moon!

"I'm game!" declared Truman. "Marilyn? How about you? Haven't you always been fascinated by the Moon? Well, now you have your chance. You wanna go?"

"What the heck!" howled Marilyn. "My whole life has been turned upside down the last two days. I guess a trip to the Moon would just top it off. Why not—let's go!"

Pepper looked around at his friend's faces. They were good—damn good. They were all putting on one heck of an acting job—or were they? For the first time Menza noticed an extra sparkle in Pepper's eyes. Was it excitement, doubt, fear, or a combination of the three?

"Super!" exclaimed JP. "We're all in agreement. We're going to the Moon. Come on, guys, follow me."

Everyone did as JP had instructed. Menza couldn't believe JP was going through with it. But then again, JP was always full of surprises. He probably instinctively knew it was the best way to convince Pepper—just throw him right into the fire. At some point in the very near future he would have to be apprised of everything. Why not just get it over with? Then there was Truman and Marilyn. Neither of them had ever ridden in a spaceship before. The whole experience sounded like a lot of fun—and fun was what JP was all about.

Everyone filed out of the pub. Nervousness and excitement filled the air. Pepper still thought it was an elaborate prank and was trying to figure it all out. Truman and Marilyn knew JP was completely serious. Both of them felt more alive than at any point before in their lives. They were going to fly to the Moon! Menza was simply going along with the master's flow. JP always seemed to make the right moves at the right time.

They walked across the street and marched past Pepper's truck. Menza looked around in every direction. There wasn't a person in sight. JP opened the door to the biocraft and they entered one at a time. JP sealed the door behind them.

"Alright, Menza," commanded JP. "You know the routine. Let's get her going. Everyone back there, please take a seat."

Menza slid into the copilot's seat. It felt good. He hadn't taken flight in months. He did not realize how much he had missed it until now. He had forgotten how much he liked to fly, how he *needed* to fly.

Marilyn and Truman sat down in chairs located in front of the largest window. Pepper crouched down just behind JP and Menza.

"Should we buckle up?" asked Marilyn.

"No, baby," Menza answered. "It's not necessary. We're only going to the Moon. There's no sphering involved."

"Menza, you went all out on this, didn't you?" said Pepper. "Sphering—what science textbook did you dig that term out of? You guys are really trying to get me good."

"I doubt you'll find the word sphering in any textbooks around here," replied Menza in a calm voice. "JP's machine is the only thing capable of that, at least around here. Sphering is only necessary when you enter quantflow. That's where matter and antimatter interact and everything becomes energy. These ZPB biocrafts and their occupants become one biological entity. JP couldn't take you guys along on a sphering journey without configuring the craft with your DNA. The craft could break up in midflight. Luckily we're only going to the Moon, so we're all safe. He'll only be utilizing his solardrive system. It's a relatively slow mode of transport, but it'll get us there."

"Oh, my God," cried Pepper. "What did you do—take a molecular structure course for this joke? What the heck have you guys been smoking? The four of you…"

"Menza, serious business here," interrupted JP. "Monitor the gauges."

Menza snapped to attention at JP's businesslike tone. "Okay, JP."

"Liftoff in one minute. Quantflow default valve check?"

"100 plus 60," Menza answered.

"Plasma level?"

"Steady at eighty percent."

"Auxiliary package?

"Running at full capacity."

"Bio-compatible check?"

"Good—three in one, with a double fallback."

"Celestial lock-in destination—including the galactic locater coordinates?"

"Celestial unit MWK91177-3-S1. The coordinates are MWK/F-O-L-L-Y-S1"

"Okay kid." JP glanced back at his passengers. "Push her up to 100 Q's."

"She's there."

"200."

"You got it."

"300 Q's."

"We're at 300."

"You guys ready back there?" asked JP.

"We're as ready as we'll ever be," answered Truman.

"Five—four—three—two—roll it!"

SWOOOOLLLL SWOOOOLLLL SWOOOOLLLL. The soft whisper of takeoff filled the craft. JP lifted the craft several feet of the ground.

Pepper's face turned pale. "GOD ALL MIGHTY! What in the hell is going on? We're off the ground. Menza! Truman! Marilyn! What's happening?"

"Everyone please be calm back there," said JP with a wink towards Menza. "I'm not used to flying these things drunk. I don't want to crash another one."

"Drunk!" Pepper roared. "Crash *another* one! Menza, it's time you finally told me what's going on. I ain't riding in no flying saucer with a drunk pilot. Menza!!!"

Menza was laughing so much that his sides hurt. JP was having a little fun at the expense of his now not-so-skeptical passenger. Yes, JP was a bit tipsy, but it was nothing to be concerned about. Yes, he had crashed a couple of experimental crafts in the past. So what? That's why they're called test flights. Menza wasn't the least bit worried. He felt more comfortable flying with JP at the helm than anyone he knew.

"JP, can you hold the craft here for a few seconds before you take her higher?" asked Menza. "I need to calm Pepper down. You've got him all riled up."

"Sure, kid. Go ahead and get him under control."

"Pepper," Menza said in a soothing voice, "As you can see, this thing really does fly. And we really are going to the Moon. We're just going to ride around it and take in the view. We're not even going to stop. Now listen to me, there's absolutely nothing to worry about. Okay? In twenty minutes time we'll be safe on the ground back at the Pig Parlor. Then you can say that you've been to the Moon. I guarantee you not many people around here can claim that. Try to relax. It'll be a beautiful flight. Just stretch out on that comfortable sofa and look out the window. Can you do that for me? When we get to the Pig Parlor I'll explain everything to you. Okay?"

Menza's talk seemed to have an effect. Pepper regained some color in his face. He followed Menza's suggestion and took a position on the sofa. There would be no more arguing the point. He had accepted the very real possibility that he was headed for the Moon. He even flashed an uneasy smile towards Marilyn and Truman.

"Okay, JP," said Menza. "He'll be alright. We'll just have some serious explaining to do when we get back here. We're ready when you are."

"Great," replied JP. "Okay, guys, here we go. I'm going to take her up to a million feet so you can get a different look at the planet."

In a split second the biocraft was transported high above the planet. Menza looked down upon it. Earth was a beautiful planet in its own special way. It had a rough-edged rawness about it, much like its people. It didn't possess the resplendent brilliance of Novem with its silver rings and shimmering oceans. Earth exhibited more of a rugged beauty exemplified by its snow-peaked mountains and luminous urban centers. The planet seemed to resonate with toughness, an unwavering spirit of survival. It damn sure was a lucky planet. It just didn't know it yet.

Menza peered back at his passengers. They were all gazing out the window at their home below.

"What the...how in the heck did that happen!" gasped a wide-eyed Pepper.

"Wow," Marilyn muttered. A dreamy languor had over-taken her. She was in a world all her own. She stared down at her world two hundred miles below. It was a troubled place, but oh so beautiful. Earth was a prison of sadness, sorrow and despair, yet it still beamed with a ray of hope. Humanity was hanging by a thread trying to survive. That thread needed to hold out just a little longer because help was on the way. Sitting high in the sky in a spaceship was all the proof she needed. This whole scene wasn't a dream. Menza, JP, and the flying saucer were real. The rest of the story was real too—beings from a distant world were coming to the rescue. She just knew it. A thin smile began to crease her face. Salvation awaited the denizens of a planet that had strayed off course. Change was coming.

"This is truly unbelievable," said Truman, gazing through the broken clouds that surrounded Earth. There it was—home, sometimes sweet, home. She sure looked different from way up here. There was more to it than just physical separation. There was also a sense of invigorating liberation that was both scary and exhilarating. Everything seemed to fall into place from high in the sky. He would never look at his home planet the same again as the rules had changed forever. Earth had become a valuable piece of the massive interlocking universe. Imagination had replaced knowledge as the building blocks of reality. The new reality was humanity's release from bondage. It was all about being free. Freedom wasn't something that came easy. It had to be taken. With a little help from some friends that would happen soon.

"Okay guys," barked JP. "I'm taking us to the Moon. It's about a three-minute ride. Enjoy the view."

"Oh God," moaned Pepper.

The passengers braced themselves for the force of acceleration. It never came. Instead the craft remained quiet and stable. Looking out the window they saw the stars whizzing by. Earth was becoming smaller with every passing second.

"Wow! Look at that!" Marilyn's eyes were fixated on the big white ball glowing ever brighter by the moment.

"The Moon," whispered Truman to no one in particular. "We're going to the Moon."

Three minutes passed. JP slowed the craft down before finally settling at 200,000 feet above the Moon's surface. The spellbound space travelers were speechless.

"What do you think, Pepper?" bellowed JP. "Now do you believe us?"

"Yeah…yeah…I do," Pepper stammered. "The Moon! I'm on top of the Moon!"

"Just look at those craters," muttered Marilyn. "They're so huge, so magnificent. Wow!"

"What's that!" exclaimed Truman. "Over there…what is that?"

Truman pointed to a darkened section of the Moon's surface. There appeared to be a structure of some sort. It actually looked like several artificial constructs lumped together. The whole area looked to be enclosed in a miles-high crystalline dome.

"Let's take her down for a closer look," said JP. He instantly lowered the craft to 10,000 feet.

"Oh my God," yelped Pepper. "It's a city—under glass!"

"Unbelievable," Marilyn uttered.

"This is just what I suspected," said Truman. "I figured there was something big going on here. I'll be damned. Menza, JP—who is it!"

"Truman, I'll answer that for you in just a second," said Menza. "Before I do I'd like to do something else. I think it's time we told Pepper what's going on—everything!"

"Yeah, why don't you!" cried Pepper. "I come into town expecting to load up a piece of metal on my truck and thirty minutes later I'm on the Moon! How in the hell did JP get ahold of a real flying saucer? Are you going to be able to get me back home? What in the hell is going on!"

"Pepper, look at me," Menza said calmly. "I'm going to tell you something that you might find difficult to believe."

"Oh God," whimpered Pepper. "Here I am hovering over the Moon in a flying saucer and you're going to tell me something *more* difficult to believe! Oh, God, please help me!"

"Pepper," said Menza, "I'm just going to put it out there, straight up. I'm not from your planet—and neither is JP. We're aliens. We come from a planet called Novem. Truman and Marilyn know all about us. Earth is in serious trouble and we're going to rescue it."

"Oh—damn! That's just great!" Pepper threw up his arms in surrender. "I'm floating around the Moon in a spaceship filled with aliens! I could be home sleeping away in my comfortable bed, but noooooo! I had to be Mister Good Samaritan and help my buddy move a piece of art. Now my buddy turns out to be an extraterrestrial—a damn alien! Excuse my language, Menza, but I'm a bit overwhelmed right now. You're an alien…Menza's an alien…he took me to the Moon…everything is fine…everything's okay…relax, Pepper, relax."

"Ahh, Pepper," chuckled JP, "you'll get over it soon enough. Just enjoy the show. Believe me, it gets a lot more interesting than this."

"Why the hell not!' snapped Pepper. "What's the worst thing that can happen—me and my alien friends crash our flying saucer into the Moon? I guess there's worse ways to go. Okay! So Menza—what are those buildings doing on the Moon and who put them there? More aliens I would presume!"

"Pepper, you're taking this pretty well," said Menza. "Much better than I expected. And yes, extraterrestrials had a handshake in those structures on the Moon. It was actually a joint venture of sorts between an alien race and humans—but not your current society. An earlier technologically advanced human civilization is responsible for these strange structures and the glasslike dome. They had help from another race of beings that's now long gone."

"You ain't seen nothing yet," interrupted JP. "Pepper, there's a whole lot more to the Moon than meets the eye. Right now there are being*s inside* the Moon—and they're watching us. As a matter of fact, we'd better get the heck out of here pretty soon. Some of the same people responsible for making that mess down on Earth reside inside the Moon. Actually it's a consortium of humans and two other races that rule their nasty little empire from here. This is their main mind control center. They send electromagnetic waves directly into human brains to create thoughts—and you guys think they're your own. Those chemtrails they spray you with every day condition your brains to act as receptors for the waves. Then it's goodbye to your free thought. The bottom line is some bad stuff is originating out of here. The good news is we're kicking 'em out. A month from now they'll all be gone and this place will be a tourist site. I'll show you around again then. For now—let's get outta here!"

"Please do!" exclaimed Pepper. "I would really appreciate it if you would get us out of here—now!"

JP turned his attention to the control panel in front of him. He pulled a lever, pushed a button, pulled another lever, then another button. Nothing happened. Then he began frantically pushing buttons, pulling levers and twisting every knob in sight. Menza noticed a silly grin on his face. He knew what was coming next from his fun-loving friend.

"Damn!" cried JP. "I drank so much beer back at the pub that I can't remember where that plasma defrobulator constrictor valve is. If I can't activate it we'll never get out of here. Where the heck is it!"

"Menza!" yelped Pepper. "Help your drunk friend! Get us out of here! Please!"

Menza burst into laughter. "JP, that's enough. You're going to give Pepper a heart attack. I think he's already had enough trauma for one evening?"

"Okay, I guess you're right," JP laughed. "Pepper, I'm sorry, but I just had to try that one. I promise they'll be no more funny stuff from me. You're one of us now. You're gonna help save the world. Come on, guys, let's get outta here for real. I'm going to take her back to Earth."

JP flipped a switch, this time with results. The craft hesitated for a moment allowing a final opportunity to view the Moon's brilliant surface. Then it clicked into solardrive for the short journey back home.

Once again stellar landmarks rushed by as they peered out the window. Earth was dead ahead and calling for them to come back. No one spoke a word. They were too busy soaking in the entire experience. One never knew when another opportunity for real space travel would present itself again. Earth appeared larger with each passing second until it seemed it would swallow them up. They were going home. It was all so surreal.

JP broke the silence. "Menza, please give me the LLS reading for the Pig Parlor. I've got it plugged in already."

"MWK91177-3/MWK/F-O-L-L-Y/X," Menza answered in one long breath.

JP nodded. "Okay, that's where we're headed. Pepper, that's your official intergalactic address. Menza tells me it'll make for some fine spaceship parking. Would you mind if we parked a hundred or so of these things around your place—just for a little while?"

"A hundred or so—what! Are you kidding me? I never know anymore. What have I got myself into? You are kidding, right? I mean…you've got more of these things? No way…no way you're serious."

"I'm very serious," JP replied. "I guess we forgot to mention to you that aliens will soon be invading your planet. I thought we had told you about that. Sorry—well, now you know."

"What! Aliens invading!" clamored Pepper. "You mean that comment earlier about me helping to save the world wasn't a joke? Oh, God, this just keeps getting worse by the minute. Oh God, please help me! Wake me from this nightmare!"

JP laughed. "Oh, relax, you'll be okay. Take a look down below. That's your home. That's the Pig Parlor. It looks to me like there's plenty of room to park a hundred of these ships. Hell, we could probably squeeze a thousand of them in there if we had to."

"Please land this thing…please!" moaned Pepper. "I'm ready to set my feet down on my planet and never leave again. I don't ever want to see another flying saucer as long as I live.

But I know that won't be the case. I know this ain't going away. You're going to park this thing at my place right now. I'm going to have to look at it every single day. Then you're bringing a hundred more of these spaceships over here—huh—OH GOD!"

"Ahh, don't worry," said JP. "The takeover of your planet will be over with within a month. Then we'll bring in all the IOS crafts. Now, let me tell you—they've got some whopper ships. They're gonna need a home too. How many acres did you say you had here?"

"None!' snapped Pepper. "I'm selling off all my acreage tomorrow. I don't wanna be in the alien spaceship hiding business. I'm going back to raising pigs for a living. JP, please sit this thing down!"

Truman gave Pepper a playful poke in the ribs. "Pepper, I've got a deal for you. You probably haven't heard the news yet, but I'm getting ready to be the largest beer producer in the world. Yep, these guys are buying Roy Johnson's property for me tomorrow and we're building a massive brewery there. If you go along with this for us I'll give you free beer for life. Heck, I'll even make you president of the company. How does that sound? Free beer…huh?"

"Okay…Okay!" cried Pepper. "I'll do whatever the aliens tell me to do. I have no choice, right? You're going to invade my planet either way. I might need all that free beer. Drunkenness might be my best avenue. Sure—let's all ride around in space-invading flying saucers and stay drunk all day. What the hell, bring a million spaceships and park 'em all over my property. Turn it into an extraterrestrial parking lot. I don't care anymore. I don't know what my daddy will say about all this. Maybe he's an alien too! Hell, maybe we're all aliens!"

"Great!" exclaimed Truman. "We've got a deal. Come to the pub tomorrow to start drinking your free beer forever. JP, go ahead and set her down. Your spaceship's got a home."

"That's just what I want to hear," said JP as he hovered above the Pig Parlor. "Pepper, where do you want me to put her?"

"If its gotta be, its gotta be. I guess just park it inside the pig house, right beside the Wolseley Hornet. It'll look good sitting alongside an old saloon car. The doors are open. Just fly her right in."

JP expertly lowered the craft down inches above the ground. He slowly guided it into the pig house. Then he parked it beside the antique car and shut down the power source. Everyone filed out of the craft.

"Ain't bad, ain't bad at all," remarked JP as he walked around his spaceship. "She'll be happy here. Don't you let any birds do their business on her, okay Pepper? I like to keep her clean."

"Sure, JP," replied Pepper sarcastically. "I've got a rule here at the Pig Parlor—any extraterrestrial spaceships parked on the premises gotta be clean as a whistle. I don't allow a speck of dust on my spaceships. That's why all my alien friends wanna park their flying saucers here."

Truman laughed. "Pepper, this alien stuff has been hard on all of us. But you know what—you get used to it quick. Marilyn and I just learned about it and we've already accepted it. It's real and it's here to stay. You should be glad you're in on the ground level. Tomorrow you'll feel a whole lot better. I promise you."

"Yeah, if you say so," Pepper said with a sigh. "I can tell you this. Tomorrow morning when I wake up I'm walking out here to the pig house. If this flying saucer is still sitting here, well, then I'll finally accept that this crazy night has been real.

If it's gone then I'll consider it all a bad dream that I hope never recurs."

"That'll work," said Truman. "But don't get your hopes up, because this spaceship's gonna be here in the morning. It ain't going anywhere unless JP decides otherwise. Sleep on it, Pepper. You'll feel better in the morning. One more thing—how about driving us back to the pub in your car? We don't have a way back. We'll get the truck back to you tomorrow."

Pepper took one last look at the silver chunk of metal parked in the middle of his pig house. An hour ago it was an unusual piece of art created by an eccentric old man. Now it was an alien-owned spacecraft that had just flown him to the Moon. The truth was sinking in. He turned back towards Truman. His eyes conveyed acceptance. He knew his life would never be the same.

"Yeah, I'll take you. Let's go."

Chapter 30
THE WRIGHT LEADER

Marilyn raced past the bar, but not before placing a beer and a steaming plate of sweet potato fries in front of him.

"Thank you, baby," Menza said quickly.

Marilyn bounced off to another table. She had been working double shifts the last three days, yet her energy level was off the charts. Her coworkers were in amazement. Nothing could erase the smile that seemed to be permanently etched into her face. She attributed her newfound vigor to the alignment of the stars. Her mama was back, her boyfriend loved her, and the world was wonderful—and it was all due to the planets and the stars. Some thought she was becoming what they termed "Truman loony." One night she even dragged Amy out to view the night sky. Marilyn claimed that a whole corner of the universe had reoriented just for her. Amy agreed that all of the brightest stars in the northern sky seemed to spell out a big M. She began looking for an A so as get some of what Marilyn had.

Menza took a bite of his fries. A week had flown by. It had been seven days of immense pressure. He had never worked so hard in his life. JP had not wasted any time. Immediately after parking the biocraft at Pepper's he had sent a transmission to Tucker. Operation Hummingbird commenced the following day. Pepper was instructed to make room for eleven more biocrafts. At exactly noon the next day eleven spaceships floated through the open doors of the pig house.

The preparatory stage of Hummingbird had gone off without a hitch. For seven days IOS specialists flew around the world doing whatever it was they needed to do. From their Pig Parlor base they conducted covert missions that spanned the globe. JP didn't even know exactly what was going on. It was that much of a secret. Pepper turned out to be the perfect accomplice, leaving the operatives alone to do their job, yet fiercely protecting the stealth operation. Only his father sensed anything unusual. Sir Pepper knew his son was up to something, but couldn't pinpoint it. The sixth sense that had kept him alive through four years of war told him to let it be. He had faith in his wild-streaked son. Answers would come soon enough.

Keeping a keen eye on Hummingbird wasn't the only project occupying his time. There was the genomel situation. Truman was busy constructing a temporary brewery on his recently purchased property. The town was abuzz with rumors as to how he came up with the three million dollar down payment.

The biggest scuttlebutt floating around had Truman operating an international drug ring. The chatter was that Truman would be setting up a clandestine landing strip on his recently acquired property to fly in planeloads of illicit drugs. Then there was the story that Truman had scored big in the music industry with several of his songs. Truman had actually engaged Marilyn to intentionally get that one circulating around the pub. It didn't take long to make its way into the mainstream gossip. Another piece of hearsay had Truman working with a radical terrorist group. They were going to use the newly purchased land to set up a training facility for militant extremists.

Finally there was the fourth rumor. Somehow a story was on the loose that Truman was an extraterrestrial being. He and his kind were on a mission to take over Earth. He was developing the Johnson property into an alien base which would be used for an invasion. The idea was marked off as ridiculous idle prattle by nearly everyone. Menza was keeping his eyes and ears open on this one however. Enough people were taking it seriously to make it worrisome.

Truman had been working day and night since the purchase. Permits were in the works for the construction of a major brewery complete with a massive distribution center. Within 48 hours he had installed a primitive but working brewing system in the old barn. He already had several batches of beer in the fermenting tanks. He was also ramping up production in the brewpub to its maximum output. Several thousand alien visitors would soon need their regular blasts of his life-sustaining liquid nourishment. Genomel Brewing Company, as it was aptly named, would be there for them.

Another project that was keeping Menza busy was administrative in nature. Tucker had made it clear to him that his duties would not cease after Operation Hummingbird. As a matter of fact his role was to be a major one. Immediately upon Hummingbird's completion a global guidance board would be established. It would be named the World Advisory Council. It would consist of only three official representatives. Menza, Truman and Marilyn would be the sole members. JP would be an unofficial fourth representative. They would serve as a semi-official link between the IOS and the planet's new hierarchical political structure.

Tucker had personally placed Menza in charge of setting up a global governance system. Menza was instructed to handpick every member of a new organization. It was to be called the Participatory World Cabinet. This group of approximately five individuals would lead the soon-to-be freed world into a new era.

The world was to be completely overhauled. Military spending would cease to exist. Humanity would concentrate on coexisting in peace instead of pursuing warfare. A worldwide healthcare network would be put into place. The education, agricultural and financial systems would be revamped. All energies would be focused on improving the physical, emotional and spiritual health of humankind. Prejudice and hate would become a thing of the past. The world would simply be a better place. Menza needed a handful of people to lead the planet into a harmonious future. He needed people he could trust.

Menza had managed to allocate a bit of time for the love of his life. Every evening they were sharing dinner together, even if it was at the pub. Marilyn was a walking talking bundle of upbeat confidence. The world was hers to do as she pleased. The big M in the sky was all the proof she needed. Life was for living. The fact that her boyfriend was an extraterrestrial didn't seem to faze her in the least.

Marilyn's mom was completely healed. The cancer was in complete remission. Doctors were now calling it a miracle of the highest magnitude. Marilyn had sent a heartfelt transmission to Tucker expressing her gratitude. He responded with a promise to personally meet her mother one day. He would be bringing along a liter bottle of the magic cancer potion as

Marilyn had requested. She was determined to cure every case of cancer worldwide once the rescue was complete.

"Hello, Menza, how's it going?" a voice called from behind, accompanied by a slap on the back. Menza turned around. Wright slid into a seat beside him.

"Hey, Wright," replied Menza. "I'm fine. How about you?"

"I'm doing well. I've been working on my political signs for the mayoral election—alone I might add. It seems my campaign manager has abandoned me. Pepper's always too busy to help me lately."

Menza chuckled to himself. He knew why Pepper had neglected his political duties. He was too busy saving the planet. He was guarding the Pig Parlor because it housed eleven ZPB spaceships and a bunch of beings from a mix of galaxies. But he certainly couldn't tell Wright that—or could he? He had been racking his brain about how he should approach Wright about a certain matter. Heck, maybe now was the time.

"Wright, are you still passionate about the mayor's race?" asked Menza. "I mean…you know…really into it?"

"Absolutely," answered Wright. "I can't wait to run, to win, and to start some new projects that will improve our town. I'm going to try to make a real difference. I don't want to be a big puff of political hot air. I'm in this to get something done."

"How far along are you on the signs?" asked Menza.

"Oh, I'm coming along pretty well. I'm about halfway done. I'd probably be finished by now if Pepper would get his butt over to help."

"Oh, don't be too hard on Pepper," said Menza. "I'm sure he's got a good reason for not helping. You know what—why don't you just stop that sign-making project?

Forget about running for mayor. I think I've got something better for you to do."

"What are you talking about?" asked Wright. "I've already filed the papers and put tons of time into this. You want me to drop out now? Why?"

"Wright," said Menza solemnly, "how would you like to be President of the World? How's that for a title?"

"Menza, how much have you had to drink?" laughed Wright. "You're talking out of your head. President of the World—yeah, the Chinese and Russians are gonna vote me right in. I'm sure they want a grit-eating, ain't-saying southern boy running their countries. And since when has there been an official office called President of the World? Menza, let me buy you a cup of coffee. You need to sober up."

Menza looked directly into Wright's eyes. "My friend, I want you to listen to me. I'm sober as can be. This is all going to sound pretty wild, but hear me out. Huge changes are coming soon. The world as you know it will not exist. The new world will be kinder and more humane. It will be a place where leaders actually care about their fellow man. This new world will require a new breed of leadership, leaders with integrity, leaders who care, leaders who aren't afraid to do what's right—leaders like yourself. Tell me, Wright, will you do it? You have the perfect personality for the job. You have the ability to unite the world in peace. You're a good man, Wright—a very good man. Will you be President of the World?"

Menza awaited a response. Installing Wright as President of the World was something he had been thinking about for a couple of days. He had planned on approaching Wright about the idea at a more appropriate time, but somehow the timing just felt right. He had no idea how Wright would react to his spontaneous disclosure, and that was just the tip of the iceberg. He had not even touched on the extraterrestrial takeover of the planet. That was sure to be a shocker.

Wright remained remarkably calm. "Menza, if I didn't know you better I would think you've completely lost your marbles, but I do know you better. I think you need to tell me exactly what's going on. I know something's up. Pepper's avoiding me, Truman's buying up millions of dollars worth of property, Marilyn's walking around here like she's floating on a cloud, now you're telling me the whole world's gonna change—what in the heck is going on? Tell it to me straight."

Menza momentarily collected his thoughts before speaking. "Wright, do you remember that day you and me and Truman were sitting right here in these very chairs? It was when Truman convinced you to run for mayor."

"Of course I remember," answered Wright. "Truman's full of some wild ideas, but I'll always respect his opinion."

"That's what I'm getting to," said Menza. "That day Truman speculated that another race of beings might be controlling the planet. You know—not human. Do you remember?"

"Yes, I do. That's a pretty far out idea, but I think it could be possible. There's some very strange things going on, that's for sure."

"Wright, look at me," said Menza. "I'm getting ready to tell you something that's going to be difficult to believe. What Truman told us that day was the truth. I know that for a fact. Aliens exist—and they're roaming the planet as we speak."

"Maybe they are," Wright said quietly. "But if they are here, why can't we see them? Why aren't they walking among us?"

"The answer to that is a bit complicated." stated Menza. "The ones that have been here for a while are very skilled at concealing themselves. All that is getting ready to change.

There's a new race of extraterrestrials that are coming in, several races as a matter of fact, and they're not going to hide anything. They are totally benevolent. They are here to help us, to rescue us, to clean up the planet. Within 48 hours the skies will be full of alien spacecraft."

Okay," nodded Wright. "So aliens are coming to Earth to rescue us. I'll need some time to let that sink in, but for the moment let's assume that's true. Tell me, Menza, how do you know this? How did you come about acquiring all this information? What makes you special?"

"Wright, I want you to do something. Very casually turn and look at the corner table over there. Then tell me what you see."

Wright did as Menza suggested. Sitting at the table were Charles and Samantha Jordan. They were a married couple who often frequented the pub for dinner.

"I see Charles and Samantha," said Wright, "just as I've seen them in here many times before. They're both wonderful people."

"What's different about them? You know, what is it that makes them not like us?"

"Well, they're black," replied Wright, "and we're white. That's the most obvious difference. So what's the big deal about that? People come in different colors—always have, always will."

Menza took a deep breath. "That's the point I'm trying to make. You think nothing of the color of their skin. It's because you're mentally conditioned to accept it. You've been exposed to black people your entire life. That's the only difference between a black person and an alien. A year from now everyone on the planet will be as accepting of extraterrestrial beings as you are of Charles and Samantha. Wright, do you think you could maintain a trusting relationship, a real friendship, with an honest-to-goodness being from another planet?"

"Yeah, I guess I could be friends with an alien," replied Wright, "but what are you trying to say? You still haven't explained how you know this stuff. Tell me, where do you fit into all this?"

Menza rested his hand on Wright's shoulder. "You haven't been aware of it, but you're already friends with an alien. You are my friend, right?"

"Menza! Come on! Are you insinuating that you're an alien—that you're not from Earth? Yes, you're my friend, but you hardly look like an alien. Menza!"

Wright awaited a reply from Menza, maybe a slap on the back or a hearty laugh that would acknowledge his joke. It never came. Menza stared back at him stoically.

"Wright, it's true," Menza said calmly. "It's somewhat of a long story, but I'll sum it up for you. I came to your planet on a research project. The information I uncovered led to the upcoming rescue mission. Pepper, Truman and Marilyn are also aware of this. That's why they all seem to acting strange lately. They—along with you I hope—will have instrumental roles in the upcoming healing process of the planet."

"Menza…I've never known you to be a joker, but this is crazy. Tell me you're joking!"

Menza was silent. He wanted Wright to realize just how serious he really was. Wright was a different personality than Pepper. Hard cold facts and a shocking dose of harsh reality had convinced Pepper. Silence was the weapon of choice in dealing with Wright. It worked.

Wright lowered his head into the palms of his hands. "Damn," he muttered to himself.

Menza remained silent. Wright was still holding his head with his eyes closed. Every few seconds he would utter an unintelligible word or two. Menza knew better than to disturb him. On several occasions he had witnessed something similar with Truman, albeit at warp speed. Wright was processing data, converting what seemed to be fiction into fact, and generally just trying to pull it all together emotionally. Finally he lifted his head up and spoke.

"I'll do it," he calmly said. "I'll take the position of President of the World. I feel I'm the best man for the job. Hell, who else is best friends with a head honcho alien? I had no idea I had such political connections."

Menza chuckled. "Yeah, I'd say you're universally connected. Wright, I know you're going to have a million questions for me. Why don't you take some time and let this all sink in. You can go home and make a list. Come back and we'll take a couple of hours and work out a plan. A week from now you'll be President of the World."

Wright momentarily burst into laughter.

"What's so funny?" Menza asked.

"My uncle...and my father," answered Wright. "I can't wait to see their faces when they learn of this. A short time ago they were complaining about my lack of ambition. In a few days their misguided nephew and son will be the leader of the entire planet, the President of the World. The look on their faces...oh...what a sight that will be."

"Here's two for you," a voice interrupted. Marilyn plopped down two fresh beers.

"These are from JP. He just walked in and bought the house a round. Gotta go, guys, I'm super busy."

Marilyn sped off in the direction of the Jordans' table. Wright looked at JP sitting at the opposite end of the bar.

"What a character that JP is," Wright remarked. "He's a true original."

"Oh, I forgot to tell you," said Menza. "He's an alien too. We're from the same planet."

Wright shook his head and calmly took a sip of his beer.

"I should have known," he sighed. "I guess I'd better get used to it. Everybody's an alien. Oh, Menza, what have you done to me?"

Chapter 31

THE BOSS DROPS IN

"I think I see it." Frank Nance called.

"Yes, it's coming in from the south," said Tommy Swing, squinting into his binoculars.

"Mommy, another spaceship is coming," said three-year-old Olivia Green. "It's got more spacemen in it."

Tucker would be arriving soon. It was supposed to have been a secret, but word had leaked that a leading IOS official would be dropping down into Ashmont. Now the whole town awaited his arrival.

Three weeks had passed since JP's first ZPB slipped inside the Pig Parlor. Stage two of Operation Hummingbird was now coming to a conclusion. Earth would never be the same. A few weeks ago the majority of the world laughed off any talk of extraterrestrial visitation as fantasy. Now there were seven billion believers.

Pepper was well on his way to becoming a genuine Milky Way hero. With Sir Pepper's approval he had allowed 100 more biocrafts to be housed at the Pig Parlor. Thousands of beings of all shapes, sizes and colors had made it their temporary refuge. They all took a liking to the accommodating human who kept them constantly supplied with refreshing sweet iced tea. Pepper made a point to keep the pretty female extraterrestrials' glasses especially full. His intergalactic flirting seemed to focus on one particularly attractive visitor from a planet named Amare.

The situation had actually been worse than anyone could have imagined. It was somewhat of a miracle that humanity had survived at all. A renegade Draco race and several subordinate species were found to be in complete control of the human race. It had been thousands of years in the making. They played God from their control centers, which were located deep underground, in space stations orbiting high above the planet, and inside the Moon. Earth had evolved into a private playground for the power-mad lunatic beings. The planet was nothing more than their perverted video game—literally.

The IOS rescuers wasted no time in working their magic. Working from their Pig Parlor base they identified their soul-stealing targets. It was determined that every country was under the control of at least one body-snatching alien. Rarely was a head of state lucky enough to remain a true human. The larger countries had hundreds of illicit raiders. All of the true power positions were filled by "contaminated" forces. The major political, banking and economic chieftains were exclusively alien-controlled robots. Their unknowing human underlings had no choice but to obey their powerful bosses.

Once they were identified it was all over for the squatters. All were given the opportunity to leave the body they had invaded. Most vacated immediately. The ones that didn't were "pushed" out with a well-guarded revolutionary technology that sent them running for their lives. All in all over 5,600 foreign dwellers were methodically expelled from their human containers. Stripped of their evil internal controllers, humans became human again. They were interrogated and tested to evaluate whether they were still fit for current leadership roles. A remarkably high percentage of them remained in their positions. It was a testament to the character and nature of a true human being. Once freed from their captors humans proved themselves to be an ethical and honorable race. The IOS was amazed at the overall integrity of the species.

Stealing souls had been the demented weapon of choice in the bad guys' war on humanity, but none of their misery-inducing technologies went to waste. They used it all. Humans, synthetic beings and clones were shuffled around the planet like pawns on a chessboard. Genuine humans were considered emotionless creatures of no significant value. Humans were ants and their dwellings were anthills to be crushed on a whim. They were a bunch of pitiful nothings wandering aimlessly on the surface of the Earth. In the eyes of their controllers they were nothing more than bumbling voyeuristic diversions from daily life. Sicko psychopaths watched as humanity squirmed.

Misery brought high ratings. The human race became a twisted source of entertainment to be watched on sophisticated multidimensional televisions. Horrific events were actually scheduled for sadistic viewing pleasures. Viewers took delight in watching humans scatter after a particularly bloody bombing, a manufactured earthquake or an unfortunate "accident." It was real life primetime prop-your-feet-up and grab-a-bag-of popcorn entertainment. You could even personally contribute to the midweek amusement if you desired. Human beings were the blip on a screen of a real life video game. Control of humanity was an interactive process complete with buttons and a joystick.

For thousands of years a mind manipulation game had been played on humanity. The last hundred years had been an over-the-top smorgasbord of artificial reality. The layers of lies and deception were piled so high even the deceivers had trouble keeping track of the truth. "Perception management" ensured the current version of reality melded with the overall agenda. Truth was an irrelevant issue as propaganda was ingrained into every aspect of daily life. Humans were taught who to date and who to hate, who to adore and who to abhor, when to kneel and when to kill.

Mind control had been the key to enslavement. Humanity gradually turned over its collective mind to the controllers with little or no resistance. Things got serious with the emergence of the television. Trance-induced slaves would sit in front of their flickering propaganda machines for hours on end. It was the perfect brainwashing tool. The stupefied public would literally drink poison if the controlled talking head on the television instructed them to do so. It was that easy. The mind-numbed masses fell into line like cattle headed for slaughter.

Television primed the slaves' brains for bigger and better forms of controls. New technologies were employed that allowed direct manipulation of the brain. The human body became an active receptor for electromagnetic thought waves. The controllers could actually instill thoughts into their subjects' heads. A subject could be made to perform any task and they would actually think it was their own decision to do so. Past memories could be wiped out and fake memories installed. Anything became possible. A person could make war, make love, or jump out of an airplane without a parachute, all on a controller's whim.

No stone was left unturned when it came to control of the masses. It was all about foolery and pretense and making something out of nothing. Entertainment figures and sport heroes were made-to-order creations designed to impress the young and impressionable. The majority of them were the product of mind control techniques, cloning procedures, DNA mixing or any combination of the three. It was even worse when it came to politicians. They were molded to do as they were told. Sign here, sign there, talk about this and keep your mouth shut about that—that was the life of the powerless governors of nations. The making of laws and sausage were two things better left unseen, especially laws.

All of that was in the past. The planet was now free. That was not to say that the process was complete. There were plenty of loose ends that needed to be tied up. The most challenging hurdle was the complex issue of trust. Few humans totally trusted their alien liberators. Humanity had been enslaved for so long they no longer knew what real freedom was. They had grown accustomed to enslavement and some even enjoyed their servitude. A change of attitude would not occur overnight. It would take time to earn the Earthlings' trust. The IOS would pull out their secret universal weapon in the battle for acceptance—love. They would win over humanity with kindness and compassion and a big huge chunk of unadulterated love.

Little Olivia hugged her mother's leg. "Mommy, the spaceship is real close now."

The crowd moved back allowing room for the incoming craft. This spaceship looked different than the others. It was larger and darker in color. It also carried a different insignia located on the bottom of the craft rather than the side. The other spaceships had a colorful IOS emblem prominently displayed on both sides. This one wasn't so much in-your-face as it was authoritative. It reeked of raw power. Whoever was going to step out of this craft was important. There was no doubt about it.

The spaceship lowered to eighty feet before hovering silently. A small door slid open from the bottom of the craft. A bright beam shot down from it extending to the ground. There was a collective gasp as the startled crowd pulled away from craft. All the previous spaceships had landed directly on the ground. This one continued to hover above the ground. None of them had ever projected a beam of light. Some of the townsfolk quickly speculated it was some sort of plasma beam weapon. Maybe these aliens weren't so good after all. All eyes focused on the beam that reached to the ground. Just then a figure stepped out from the light as the beam slowly faded away. It was Tucker.

Menza and JP were there to greet him. JP reached out and shook his hand. He had one eye on Tucker and the other on the spacecraft.

"How was your journey? That's a heck of a craft you've got there."

"That's the new Tarbio model. She's comfortable, that's for sure. Fast too—double the TSA's of a regular biocraft."

"Damn," uttered JP as he shook his head. "Damn."

Tucker laughed. "Don't worry, JP. I've got one on the way for you. It'll be here in a week. I knew you'd be bugging me about it."

JP flashed his famous smile. Nothing excited him more than flying a new airship for the first time.

"There's a catch to it though," said Tucker. "You've got to hand your old one over to Menza here."

Menza's eyes lit up. JP's biocraft was no slouch in the airship department. There were worse ways to get around the universe than your own private biocraft.

"Thank you, Tucker," said Menza respectfully. "That's a dream come true. My own biocraft—from JP, no less. I can't thank you enough."

"You've earned it, son," answered Tucker. "Your work here changed the universe forever."

"It was nothing," said Menza. "I was only doing my job."

"Come on," said JP. "Tucker, you're looking mighty thirsty. Let's go inside the Jumping Cow. It's right across the street."

"That sounds great," Tucker replied. "I want to try one of those beers you guys have been raving about. I want to meet that Truman fellow too."

The crowd parted as they slowly strolled across the street. They whispered and pointed as the three aliens entered the pub. The world had certainly changed since the visitors came to town.

"Hey, Truman," bellowed JP. "I got somebody I want you to meet."

Menza steered his mentors towards a corner table. He pulled out chairs for both of them before seating himself. Truman walked over to them with Marilyn close behind.

He stuck out his hand. "Hi there, I'm Truman. You must be Tucker. I heard you were coming."

"Yes, I am," nodded Tucker. "I hear you make a helluva beer here. I'd love to try one."

"You got it, sir. Marilyn here will bring it right over. I'm sure Menza's told you all about her."

Tucker stood up and clasped both of his hands around Marilyn's hands. "Young lady, I would like to personally thank you for saving the universe. You captured Menza's heart and it resulted in this. That love is some powerful stuff."

"No, sir," said Marilyn. Tears began to fill her eyes. "I want to thank you. You saved my mother's life. That's the greatest gift you could ever give me. *You* are the special one here. Thank you so much. Mama's here today because of you."

"Don't worry about it," said Tucker as he looked deep into her eyes. "We're going to save a whole lot more lives before this is over. I've got a five-gallon container of cancer-remission fluid out in the craft. We'll get it later and you can get started curing the world. How does that sound?"

"Oh, Tucker." Marilyn wrapped her arms around Tucker and embraced him. Tucker said nothing. The energy of love flowed between them. They each gave and they each received. Finally Marilyn released her grip and pulled away.

"I'm going to go get those beers for you guys," she said as she wiped a tear from her face. "I'll be right back."

Tucker watched as she walked away. "She's a needle in a haystack. Menza, you'd better not let her slip away. You hear me, son?"

"Yes sir," answered Menza. "No way will I ever do anything to jeopardize our relationship. I love her more than you can imagine."

"That's good, because she's a keeper. Now, let's take care of some business. JP, Menza—update me on the rescue mission."

"It's going real well," said JP. "Sum it all up for him, kid."

Menza smiled. "Sure, throw it all on me. Seriously sir, it is going well. Stage two is near completion. The final cleanup phase will begin soon. As you know, Truman, Marilyn and I are running everything—along with JP of course. We make up the World Advisory Council. We've got our Participatory World Cabinet in place. They're all solid trustworthy individuals.

"They're an important group," said Tucker. "Tell me more about them."

"Sure," answered Menza. "Let me start at the top. We couldn't have picked a better person to lead the planet into this new era. The President of the World is a guy named

Wright. His head and his heart are in the right place. Marilyn's known him for years. He comes from a political family and he genuinely loves people. He's open minded and he's got a magnetic personality—full of charisma. Women especially adore him. I'd trust Wright with my life."

Tucker nodded. "He sounds like a good man for the job. What about the others?"

"They're all fine people," Menza replied. "Wright's chief of staff is a guy named Pepper. He'll be advising on policy decisions. He's sharp as a tack and a real team player. You've probably heard about him. He's the guy who supplied us with a secure operating facility for the biocrafts. He's a real character, loves to flirt with the girls—at least he used to. Now he's fallen for a pretty little brunette from Silvercake Galaxy. We can count on Pepper. He's proven himself over and over."

"Great," said Tucker. "Keep going."

"Jim and Joan Dixon are dear friends of all of us here. They manage the property where Marilyn, Truman and I stay. We've decided that Jim should be in charge of all things environmental. Jim is the world's greatest fisherman and has a true love for the outdoors. I can tell you from experience you can't get anything over on him. He's as cool as they come, except maybe JP and Truman here. With Jim in charge you can rest assured the air is fresh and chemtrail-free, the water's sparkling clean, and the food's safe and pure."

"He sounds like a great choice for that position. More…"

"Jim's wife has to play a part in the healing of the planet. Joan Dixon is the kindest human I've ever met. She puts everyone else's needs ahead of her own. We've decided to make her the head of an organization we're calling Second Helping. It's designed to feed upon itself exponentially. Every recipient will be required to help two others in need once they're on their feet. Trust me—Joan will make sure it works. She's tiger-tough underneath that sweet exterior."

Tucker stroked his chin. "It sure sounds like you guys have put a lot of thought into your selections. What else do you have going on?"

"There are a couple of other important positions we've filled," declared Menza. "We needed someone to place in charge of planetary healthcare. That one was a no-brainer. Marilyn's mom is champing at the bit to cure the world of sickness. Since you cured her of cancer she decided to dedicate her life to helping others. We're going to set her loose starting with that cancer-remission fluid you've got for us. They'll be no stopping her. I guarantee you she'll make sure every corner of the planet has access to hospitals and medicine."

"Anything else?" asked Tucker.

"Yes, there's education. We're putting another friend of ours to head that up. Her name's Luce and she's one of a kind. Luce is an 88-year-old retired history professor who takes no crap from anyone. She's tired of the bought off academia lying about the past. What's happened is that the history experts mold the so-called facts to fit the agenda. Earth's history has been rewritten so many times even the mythmakers have forgotten the truth. The planet's educational system is going to be revamped and wiped clean of the lies that stain it. Luce will see to that. Another stick in her craw, as she aptly describes it, is gossip and celebrity worship. Education will cease to be entertainment and kids will actually learn something for a change."

"Now that's a lady I want to meet," remarked Tucker. "I think I'd like her. What else do you have for me?"

"Well, there's one more appointee," said Menza with a smile. "His name is Meier and he's yet another character.

Truman and Marilyn have known him for years. We're going to put him in charge of all that's fun. Meier's official title will be the Entertainment Czar. He'll make sure humanity has a good time. Movies, television, music, sports, you name it—it'll all be under the supervision of Meier. He'll make sure it's not contaminated with brainwashing subliminal messages. Meier's all about fun—honest pure fun. Earth had better buckle up for some good times ahead."

"That sounds like a good job, one I wouldn't mind having myself. Is that all the cabinet members you have for me?"

"Yes, sir," answered Menza, "at least for now."

"Well," nodded Tucker, "it sounds like you guys, and girl, have sunk a lot of time and energy into this process. I'm sure it will all work out just fine. Good job."

"Thank you," said Truman, "and speaking of the girl— here she comes. Marilyn's bringing the goodies."

Tucker turned as Marilyn placed an enormous tray in front of him. It contained at least forty small glasses of beer.

"Tucker," smiled Marilyn, "I wasn't sure what type of beer you liked so I brought a sample of each for everybody. I've got the brewpub's regular selections along with all of Truman's new beers. A pizza is on the way. Enjoy!"

"Wow," said Tucker. "I wasn't expecting all of this. Thank you, darling."

"You're most welcome. You're a very special guest. Besides, you need to be thanking JP. He paid for it all."

"Ha!" laughed Tucker. "Yeah, we know all about JP's spending habits. The IOS needs a printing press to keep up with him."

"But I'm worth it," bellowed JP. "Somebody's gotta fly around and check things out. That kind of living ain't cheap."

"Truman, did I hear Marilyn say these are some of your new beers?" Menza asked.

"That's right," answered Truman proudly. "These beers will be the mainstay products of Genomel Brewing Company. That's what I've decided to name it. By the way, Tucker, I haven't formally thanked you for setting me up in the bigtime brewing business. I really appreciate what you and the IOS have done for me."

"Nope," Tucker quickly replied, "it's us who should be thanking you. You'll be supplying us visitors and locals alike with a tasty product that keeps us alive. You know we've got to have our genomel to survive. JP and Menza here love the stuff."

Truman held up one of the glasses. "Let's have a toast. Here's to our guest—Tucker."

Menza picked up a glass. "Before we drink I think Tucker needs to be educated on the fine art of drinking beer. Truman—what are we drinking here?"

Truman put his nose to the glass. He tilted it and swirled the liquid in the glass. Then he held it high allowing the light to filter through it. Truman had probably made a million beers in his life, had personally quaffed well over 100,000 glasses of the stuff, yet the love of his favorite drink hadn't diminished in the least. If anything, he had become more obsessed with the world's oldest alcoholic beverage. Beer was his passion.

"Just look at that beautiful pale amber color—what a sight. This will be Genomel Brewing Company's flagship beer. I'm calling it Cosmic Pale Ale—coming soon to a galaxy near you. Everyone pick up their glass."

Tucker chuckled. "That's catchy. I like it. Now let's give it the taste test."

They raised their glasses and tapped them together in a show of friendship.

"To my new alien friend," Truman rejoiced, "the one and only Tucker. Cheers!"

Five friends from two different galaxies drained their glasses. Smiles appeared all around.

"Whoa!—that's good stuff," exclaimed JP. "Truman, you outdid yourself on this one. That Cosmic Pale Ale is now my favorite."

"That is good," echoed Tucker. "Now I see what all the fuss is about. Menza and JP weren't kidding—beer is an extraordinary beverage. Kudos to you, Truman."

"Thanks, guys," said Truman. "Let's try another one. This is Marilyn's favorite."

Marilyn blushed slightly. Truman gave everyone another glass of beer. This one was deep golden in color with a foamy head. The sweet aroma drifted from the top of the glass.

"Truman, what did you name this one?" asked JP.

"I didn't name this one. Marilyn gets the credit for this. It's called Alien Sex Lager—it's out of this world."

"Maybe Menza should get the credit for that one," cracked JP.

Everyone laughed, including a red-in-the-face Marilyn. They once again turned up their glasses and finished their drink.

"Marilyn might have named it, but you sure did a superb job brewing it," said Tucker. "That's as good as the first one."

"I've got to agree," said JP. "Alien Sex Lager *is* out of this world. I think I'll start keeping a few cases of this on board as I travel around the universe. The girls will love this one."

"What else is new?" asked Menza. "Truman, what other beers have you been conjuring up that I don't know about?"

"You're gonna love the next one," said Truman. "Menza, you were the inspiration for this one. I know the India Pale Ales are your favorite style of beer. It's called Supernova IPA—taste the explosion. Tucker, I've got to warn you on this one—it's loaded with killer hops that I grew indoors under lights. It's hydroponically hopped for an extra blast of flavor. Just look at that gorgeous peach-copper color. Let's all give it a shot. This toast is dedicated to the best friend I could ever ask for—Menza!"

The pungent aroma of fresh hops seemed to leap out of the glass. It was a redolence of floral citrusy pine. This was no beginner beer. These were hops grown indoors under perfect conditions in a controlled environment. The result was an over-the-top product that Truman equated to hops on steroids. To his knowledge no one had ever done it before. He was the groundbreaker in the indoor hop growing business. Others were sure to follow. Everyone tapped their glasses together in a toast.

"To Menza, my friend," said Truman.

"To my copilot and little buddy—Menza, you're the best," chimed JP.

"To my baby, my eternal companion, the love of my love," Marilyn said softly.

"To Menza—the IOS thanks you," said Tucker. "Good job, son."

Simultaneously they all drank from their glasses. Only Truman could finish the contents of the taster glass. Menza managed to drink half of his. The others could manage to down only a half ounce or so. This was a sipping beer—a brew that fought back. Only a battle-tested palate could appreciate the intense attack of this hoppy concoction. Untrained taste buds were easy prey for this super-flavored predator.

Marilyn's face cringed. "Oh, my God, that's extreme!"

"Wow!" exclaimed Menza. "That's unbelievable. Those hops are incredible."

"That oughta cure the universe of all its ills," declared Tucker.

"Damn, Truman," barked JP as he took another sip. "I don't know what in the hell you have in there, but I like it. It's like a woman that lures you in to chew you up—but you keep coming back for more."

Truman laughed. "I thought you guys would be impressed. You have to give partial credit to Terry Tee. Without his indoor growing expertise I could never have grown these hops. He showed me how to put the nova in the Supernova IPA."

Tucker picked up one of the remaining glasses on the tray. "Truman, I'm almost scared to ask, but I've gotta know. What's this dark beer? It looks more dangerous than the last one."

Truman laughed. "No worries, that one is relatively harmless. It's called Paranormal Porter—a beer too good to explain. It might look intimidating with its dark color but it's a very drinkable beer. Come on, everyone give it a try."

They all reached for their tasting glass containing the mahogany colored ale. They held it to their noses. The fragrance was sweet and smoky, not at all overpowering. They turned up their glasses. This one went down smooth and easy.

"Oh yeah," admired Marilyn. "This is my kind of beer."

"Yep, I gotta agree," said JP. "She's dark and smooth—just like my girlfriend back in East Hammerhead."

Everyone laughed. JP was being JP.

"HAPPY BIRTHDAY TO YOU, HAPPY BIRTHDAY TO YOU, HAPPY BIRTHDAY TO TRUMAN, HAPPY BIRTHDAY TO YOU!"

The whole bar had secretly congregated and descended upon the table. Approximately fifty people surrounded the five surprised friends. Standing next to Truman was Amy. She was holding an enormous cake lit up with 54 candles. In the center of the cake was a decorative figurine. It was a man holding a huge beer glass in one hand and planet Earth in the other.

"The whole bar chipped in and bought you this cake," said Amy. "We know your birthday's actually tomorrow, but we decided to give it to you now. It just seemed the perfect time."

Truman blushed. He hadn't told anyone of his upcoming birthday. Someone obviously was aware of it. The most likely suspect was a suspiciously quiet Marilyn.

"Thank you all so much. You know I'm not much on formal celebrations, but I really appreciate this. You really got me on this one. I'm truly surprised. Each and every one of you is a true friend. Thanks again."

Amy began cutting the cake into pieces as everyone congratulated Truman. He didn't seem quite so crazy after what had occurred over the past few weeks. JP leaned over and tapped Truman on the shoulder. Truman turned towards him. JP smiled and spoke.

"Happy birthday, my friend. You and I are going to Saturn tomorrow."

Truman dropped his glass on the floor. It shattered and the precious golden liquid spilled across the floor. It took a lot to distract Truman enough to drop his beer glass. JP's birthday trip to Saturn was enough to do it.

Chapter 32

SATURN CELEBRATION

J P checked the gauges one final time. "The flight to Saturn should take just under an hour. It's too bad the craft isn't biologically compatible with you. We'd get there in under a minute."

"That's all right," said Truman. "I don't think I'll complain about an hour trip to Saturn. It takes me longer than that to get to Raleigh."

"Well, birthday boy—are you ready?"

I'm as ready as I'll ever be," answered Truman. "I still can't believe I'm actually going to Saturn."

"I'm as excited as you are," said JP. "Don't forget, I've never been there either. The guys at Milky Way Central told me it was a heckuva place. Let's go find out for ourselves."

JP reached underneath his seat and pressed a small button. A red light flashed overhead for a brief second. Then they were off.

The flight took exactly 54 minutes—a minute for each of Truman's years. JP took the scenic route, slowing down as they passed by Jupiter, two large space stations and a bright orange comet. Truman learned from JP that comets weren't ammonia, methane, carbon dioxide and water—not even close. That was the official lie the space agencies were promoting. They were actually interstellar space taxis that dropped off and picked up "digital immigrants." JP didn't get into the details, but he did mention a few names. The famous author Mark Twain had been a digital immigrant during his stay on Earth.

JP slowed as Saturn came into view. What they saw rendered them both speechless. Spectacular rings encircled the yellowish planet. Truman counted 33 rings, each one sporting a different color. There was red, green, blue, orange, pink, purple and colors he never knew existed. The ring system had an order about it of intelligent design. One thing was for sure—they were not made of gas or ice or space debris or whatever was the latest lie that the space agencies were floating around.

There had to be at least a hundred moons orbiting their celestial mother—and they were only seeing one side of the planet. The moons varied in size, shape and color. Some of them were round, a few were oblong, and others were triangular shaped. One moon looked to be a perfectly proportioned square—a floating box in the sky. Yet another looked like a piece of weaponry used during medieval times. It resembled a metal ball with several spikes protruding from it.

The planet itself was a breathtaking spectacle. The cosmic wonder that was Saturn dazzled even seen-it-all done-it-all JP. Green and orange stripes wrapped around its midsection like a belt. A bright light beamed from a hole at the top of the planet shining through fluffy green clouds. It was if someone had opened a door from inside the planet. JP noted that several million beings resided inside the huge planet, along with the billion or so that lived on the planet's surface.

"Truman, I'm going to set her down right over there." JP pointed towards a large pyramid-shaped structure. "First I've gotta go through their version of a customs check."

In an instant JP transported the craft to within a few feet of the pyramid. It appeared to be a solid rock structure, yet JP slowly eased his airship *through* the solid mass and emerged from the other side. A green light issued an all-clear signal. The whole process took less than five seconds.

"Okay, Truman," said JP. "We're free to roam the planet and all its moons. How about we go celebrate your birthday?

Truman was trying to hold it together. He was free falling into a new reality. It was one thing to hear tales of other worlds amongst the stars, but it was another to actually visit one. Even the coolest of the cool would have a hard time digesting Saturn. No wonder JP was such a character. Visiting Saturn was just another day at the office for him. Decades of interstellar adventuring had undoubtedly transformed him into an experience junkie. Truman could only imagine what JP had seen and done over the course of his career. The man had lived a full life and showed no signs of slowing down. One thing was for sure—he wasn't a white picket fence and 2.2 kids type of guy. That wouldn't cut the cake for fun loving JP.

"I'm gonna park her right here." JP glided the spaceship between two other crafts in what appeared to be a galactic parking lot.

"It'll be safe here," JP said. "Come on, Truman, let's go have a drink."

JP opened the door with a push of a button. They stepped out of the craft. Truman took in a deep breath.

"The air…it's so easy to breathe here. This is amazing."

"It's the added oxygen," said JP. "Your governments tell you Saturn is an uninhabitable gaseous planet. Ha!—take a look at that beautiful girl walking there. She looks pretty habitable to me."

Truman turned to see who JP was referring to. He was right. A girl was walking past them and she did look good—darn good. She could pass for human with her perfect curves and flowing brown locks. Other "Saturners" were walking behind her. Truman studied them as they walked past. It was a mixed group of males and females, young and old. They seemed healthy, happy, vibrant—so full of life and energy. Truman suddenly felt at ease. Here he was walking around Saturn and he felt relaxed—SATURN! He was uncomfortably comfortable. Maybe having JP by his side made him feel safe, or maybe he was just going crazy. What the heck—happy birthday to himself.

"Follow me," instructed JP. "We're going to the Red Ring—that's the entertainment ring. I've been told it's the hottest place on Saturn."

Truman walked alongside JP. He was headed towards what appeared to be a public transporter of sorts. A sign read *Red Ring Express.* Twenty or so "people" at a time were climbing inside clear tube-like cars. Once they were seated the car suddenly disappeared and an empty one appeared in its place.

"Welcome to Saturn," said a well-dressed attendant. "Have a good time visiting the Red Ring."

Truman followed JP inside the transporter. A large group was already seated inside. JP and Truman took the last two seats available. Truman tried to soak it all in as the door closed. The unfamiliar surroundings, the other-world technology, the Saturners themselves—it was like living inside a dream. His senses were on fire. These memories would be treasured forever. Truman couldn't afford to take any chances. He may or may not ever visit another planet, so he had better assume this was a once in a lifetime treat to be savored. He still could hardly believe he was playing the role of tourist—on Saturn.

Literally in the blink of Truman's eyes they were transported to their destination. No sense of movement, no sound, nothing—one moment they were in one location and the next moment they were somewhere else. Truman looked at JP, who remained unfazed by it all. Apparently being beamed around planets was something he was accustomed to. They stepped out of the transporter.

"Truman, I've got a surprise for you," announced JP. "It's supposed to be right around the corner. Follow me."

Truman was still living inside a dream. Futuristic was too tame of a word to describe the world he had entered. In all his travels he had never seen anything like the Red Ring of Saturn. It was a mix of Bangkok and Amsterdam, with a smither of Paris and Moscow thrown in, all forwarded a thousand years into the future. The street was wall-to-wall packed with bars, restaurants, shops and girls—lots and lots of girls. Some things never went out of style.

"Wow, this is unbelievable," Truman muttered. "I can't believe everything is written in English. I can read everything."

JP laughed. "It's not in English. It only appears that way to you. To me it's written in my language. To that fellow over there it appears in his native language. We're in an interlanguage zone. It's a technology that's been around for millennia. It works for speech also—you speak to someone in English and they hear it in their native tongue. Pretty cool, huh?"

Truman just shook his head and chuckled to himself. It was going to that kind of evening—there was no way around it. He had better get used to it. Laughter would be the best medicine for dealing with the shock of interplanetary tourism.

"Okay, JP, I'll let my questions concerning interlanguage slide for now. Tell me, what's my big surprise—as if I need it?"

"Look right over your head," answered JP. "This is your birthday present, part of it anyway."

Truman looked up at a sign—in English of course. It brought a smile to his face. *Red Ring Music Hall & Brewpub— Home of Good Music and Saturn's Best Beer.* The sign itself was a guitar-shaped beer mug overflowing with the sudsy stuff.

JP led the way as they entered the premises. The place was filled to capacity with mostly a younger crowd. They quickly grabbed two seats at the bar that a couple had just vacated. They were plush and comfy. Truman wondered if he could import a few of them to Earth. He laughed at the thought—importing goods from Saturn. His life had certainly changed over the course of a month.

"JP, how did you find out about this place?" asked Truman.

"Ah, some guys at Milky Way Central told me about it. To be honest, I never gave it any thought until I had your beers. Then I realized I had to come here one day. Now I'm here with the brewmaster of the universe. I'd say it worked out pretty good."

"Yes, JP, it's a heck of a birthday present. I'm just happy to find out that beer exists somewhere besides Earth."

"What will it be, guys?' asked the bartender.

"Give me the hoppiest beer you have," answered Truman, "something that bites back."

"I'll have what he's having." JP pointed to a guy across the bar nursing a black-as-night beer."

"Coming right up," said the bartender.

Truman watched as the bartender poured the beers. "JP, what is the meaning to all this—I mean life itself? You've probably seen more of the universe than anyone. Why are we here? What's our purpose? What is the big picture?"

JP took a deep breath before laughing softly. "The meaning of life, huh? Let me think—here, now, you, me, living for the moment, trying to do the right thing, compassion for others, being true to yourself, and knowing that you can never stop seeking the truth even though you know you'll never find the answer. In other words, Truman, what I'm trying to say is—I don't know the meaning of life."

"So that's it, huh?" Truman said quietly. "It's that hard to figure out. Even someone who's traveled the corners of the universe doesn't understand it. Wow."

"Truman, the problem is that everything is in motion all the time. Nothing is constant. It's fluid and ever-changing, confusing even the greatest minds. You may think that because Menza and I have 800 IQ's that we know more than you. Well, we don't. We're searching just like you are. The dynamical elements always keep us guessing. Is there a God that's running the show—don't ask me because I simply don't know. All I know is we're both enjoying ourselves today. We're sitting here on one of Saturn's beautiful rings having a good time. Who knows what tomorrow will bring? I certainly don't, and I'm not sure I want to know."

"JP, does *anyone* know the answer?" asked Truman. "Or is the entire universe stuck in the search mode?"

"I can only speculate on that," replied JP. "Years ago I met an old man at Hammerhead's old central space station. I was really just a kid. We had a brief conversation, probably no more than fifteen minutes. To this day I still remember every word of that conversation. He told me something that I'll never forget. I was asking questions similar to what you're asking me now. He summed it all up in a way that…well…somehow it made sense."

"Would you mind sharing that with me?" asked Truman.

"Not at all," said JP. "This old man had spent most of his life on Veritas. That was his home planet, a lovely place. The point is this—his answers didn't come from travels and experiences. They came from somewhere deeper. They came from his soul. He told me to seek and find inner peace. That was the foundation of our existence. He said that was the greatest truth, no, the *only* truth I would ever find. Everything else was an illusion, a fake, a counterfeit, a fraudulent reality. He said there was only one reality and that it resided inside my soul. He told me to find myself—then be true to myself. He told me to be kind to others and help them when I could, but that I also had an *obligation* to live my own life. Do the things you want to do, go to the places you want to go, and see the places you want to see—he told me to *live*. Do not grow old and look back at life with regrets. For some reason that old man made a lot of sense to me. He'll never know how much he influenced some wet-behind-the-ears kid. Thanks to him I realized that it's the journey that's important, not the destination. Imagine the horror of finally reaching your destination to find out it's not what you thought—and you've sacrificed your entire life to attain it. At least if you enjoyed the ride it makes it a whole lot easier to swallow. I'm enjoying my ride."

"Here are your beers, guys—enjoy," said the bartender, placing two pints before them. They each picked up their glasses.

"Here's to enjoying the ride," said Truman.

"Here's to my friend from planet Earth—on Saturn," said JP. "Happy birthday!"

They tapped their glasses together before sampling their beers.

"That's not bad," commented Truman. "It's got an unusual flavor. Maybe it's the Saturn hops."

"This one's pretty good too," said JP, "but it doesn't compare with your brews. Yours are in a league all their own."

"LADIES AND GENTLEMEN—PLEASE GIVE A WARM WELCOME TO THE SATURN STARLETS."

A lone guitar chord echoed through the room. It hinted of rock and roll—Saturn style. JP and Truman turned towards the main stage. Five pretty girls were prowling the stage, each holding a guitar. They all appeared to be in their late twenties. Three of them were clad in skimpy silver dresses that climbed high above the knees, the other two were wearing silver hot pants that went even higher. They all wore white calf-high go-go boots. Another silver attired beauty sat high on a perch behind a set of drums. One of the girls stepped to the microphone.

"We're the Saturn Starlets and we're going to rock the house—ARE YOU READY!"

The crowd erupted in what could only be described as frenzied hysteria. Apparently the Saturn Starlets were a very popular band. Several people scrambled to be closer to the stage. A different girl strolled up to the microphone. She struck a chord on her left-handed guitar and pointed it towards the huge amps. The feedback screamed momentarily and ended as abruptly.

"Our first number's gonna be the rockiest version of Happy Birthday you've ever heard. There's a beer drinking rock 'n' roll lover who's having a birthday today. Happy birthday to you, Truman."

A giant spotlight beamed down upon Truman. The crowd cheered amid chants of happy birthday. Truman looked over at a grinning JP. There was little doubt as to who was behind this scene. Truman should have known JP would throw a little something extra into his birthday celebration—as if a trip to Saturn wasn't special enough.

The girls launched into their guitar-laced revved up attack on the most popular song in the universe. They were raw energy as they patrolled the stage that was their turf. They danced, jumped and pranced their athletic bodies all over the stage, whipping their audience into a frenzy. Halfway through the song a seventh member of the band appeared, a petite hot pants-wearing saxophone player. She knocked out the audience with a high energy solo.

True to their word they rocked up Happy Birthday. Jimi Hendrix couldn't have spiced it up any more than the Saturn Starlets. They were on fire as they took turns bending the high notes. The girls were seasoned entertainers extraordinaire, but they also had real talent. Truman knew a good guitar player when he heard one. They were all masters at squeezing out sounds that Truman didn't know existed. There was one more thing Truman admired about the five pretty guitarists—they were all left-handed.

Four minutes of Happy Birthday was nothing more than a warm up to the energetic entertainers. After the song they spread out covering every corner of the stage. The sax player and one of the guitarists kept up a steady rhythmic beat while the other girls teased the crowd with their sexy dancing. One of the girls approached the microphone. A male member of the audience threw a cowboy hat onto the stage. She picked it up and placed it on her head.

"I guess I'm a beer drinking cowgirl tonight," she cooed as she took a sip from a beer. "This next song is called Live Your Life. The lyrics are from birthday boy and the music is from us. We ARE the Saturn Starlets and we're here to rock you through the night. Enjoy!"

Truman was stunned. How did these girls get the lyrics to a song he hadn't given to anyone—except Marilyn! He quickly processed the situation. There was only one logical answer— JP was behind it! He had undoubtedly sniffed them out from Marilyn. Then he worked some alien magic to somehow get them in the hands of one of Saturn's hottest bands. Now he was going to hear his song performed by the sensual silvery performers—on Saturn! One glance at his friend's impish grin confirmed it. JP was indeed the culprit.

The five guitarists lined up in the center of the stage. One struck a chord with her left hand and held the note. Then a second one did the same. The others followed. The drummer tapped out a light beat. The sax player came in behind the drums. Cowboy hat girl stepped back up to the mike. She belted out the first line.

"Go and do what you wanna do—ain't nobody gonna live your life for you."

The four remaining guitar girls surrounded their lead singer as their instruments simultaneously erupted. Hot rhythmic lava flowed from the speakers—visible sound waves! Truman could *see* the gigantic storm of energy as it swept over the audience. The pinkish currents of energy turned red hot just before they reached their live targets. It was raw energy in its purest form. It was get-out-of-your-seat and leave-your-troubles-behind unadulterated pure rock and roll. The pulsating rhythm shook the building. Cowboy hat girl was the consummate entertainer as she roamed the stage displaying a sensual prowess. She continued delivering Truman's lyrics to her captivated audience.

That's right, I say to you………….
Go and do what you wanna do
Ain't nobody gonna live your life for you
Don't be afraid and let it slip away
Life's for living every single day
Step out of the old and into the new
Get out and dance in your brand new shoes
Lace 'em up tight and hit the floor
Dance til you drop, then dance some more
Live your life, yeah, live it up right
Yyou gotta live your life, you gotta do it right
Yeah oh yeah, live your life
Yeah sweet girl, live it up right
Strip off the fear and shed the doubt
Pull yourself in and get yourself out
Cause you're a sunspot baby and you're so cool
You're the queen of the universe
And it's yours to rule
When it strikes thirteen the clock's all done
The clock ran down but you had your fun
Live your life, yeah, live it up right
You gotta live your life, you gotta do it right
Yeah oh yeah, live your life
Yeah pretty lady, live it up right
Knock on the windows, kick in the doors
Keep on kicking til it's lying on the floor
Climb up the mountain where the sleeping Inca lies
At the top of Mandango lies your prize
You're a supernova flare on a dare

You're the one they're pointing at 'looky there'
You're a messy piece of chocolate on a hot hot day
Sweet and melty and ready to play
Live your life, yeah, live it up right
You gotta live your life, you gotta do it right
Yeah oh yeah, live your life
Yeah pretty baby, live it up right

Cowboy hat girl took off her hat and flipped it out into the crowd. "That one's a keeper. The Saturn Starlets would like to thank birthday boy for Live Your Life. Let's keep things rocking. This next one I'm sure you've all heard before—it's titled Begging for Love. Are you ready, girls?"

The silver seven wasted no time as they blasted off into another house rollicking tune. A couple walked over to Truman and congratulated him on his birthday and his well received song.

JP gave Truman a playful nudge. "So tell me, Truman, are you living your life?"

Truman's look said it all. He was having the time of his life. He was locked into sensory overload. It was his 54th birthday, he was spending it on *Saturn*, he was drinking good beer, he was listening to some of his *own* music, he was accompanied by the coolest cat in the entire universe—how could it get any better? He should have known JP wasn't finished yet. He produced the icing on the cake. It came in the form of a sexy native Saturner by the name of Sveto. She tapped him on the back. He turned to see who it was.

"Happy birthday, Truman," she said in a sultry yet unpretentious voice. "I'm Sveto and it's a pleasure to meet you."

Truman looked her over. She appeared to be about forty years old, but Truman instinctively knew she was much older—at least fifty or so. She was a woman who had definitely taken care of herself. She carried herself with an air of confidence and class to go with her amazing beauty.

"It's a pleasure to meet you too. Are you from around…are you from Saturn?"

She laughed. "Yes, I'm from Saturn. I've lived here all my life. I wouldn't think of living anywhere else actually. Hey, I really liked the way my girls performed your song. I hope you did."

"Your girls?" asked Truman. "What do you mean?"

She looked at JP. "Didn't you tell him anything about me? JP! I should have known you'd turn it into a surprise."

JP grinned. "Yeah, I guess I should explain this. Truman—Sveto here is the manager and agent for the Saturn Starlets. It's kind of a long story, so here's the short version. Menza had mentioned to me that you held a fascination with Saturn. Well, I did my homework and talked to somebody who talked to someone else—and arranged this trip. I sent Sveto a couple of your songs and she really liked Live Your Life. She had her girls rehearse it so they could play it tonight. One more thing—did you know you're one of the top ten eligible bachelors on planet Earth?"

"Says who?" laughed Truman. "Not any of my ex-wives I'd bet."

"Says the genomerator," JP replied. "It's a …I guess the closest thing you have to it would be a super computer, but this is more than any computer. It's a piece of crystal about the size of a tennis ball. It can be programmed to collect consciousness and awareness. You can tune it in to a certain planet or space station. Most of the searches are genomel related because, as you know, genomel is the life source of the universe. On your planet people still look at material wealth as important. Advanced societies want the real thing—passion, soul, love and kindness."

Truman was holding it together as best he could. Crystal-line balls that collect consciousness and awareness—okay, he would try to swallow that one and dwell on the details later. This was Saturn after all.

"JP, let me get this straight. Are you trying to tell me that a stone told you that I'm a good candidate for a romantic relationship?"

JP nodded towards Sveto. "It didn't tell me—it told her. She's very impressed by your genomistical data. She's looking for a long term relationship with a good man. The data shows you're a prize catch. It rated you and Sveto at 100 percent compatibility factor. The chemistry chart was the same. It says you're destined to be together. I can tell you that's almost unheard of in the field of genomistics. So now maybe you understand why Sveto just had to meet you."

Sveto smiled at Truman. She didn't seem to be embar-rassed in the least by JP's honest disclosure. She was a woman who knew what she wanted and wasn't afraid to go get it. Saturn culture was beginning to get very interesting.

"So—what did you two think of my girls?" asked Sveto. "Pretty entertaining, don't you think?"

"They're fantastic,' Truman quickly replied. "Their energy is off the charts—unbelievable entertainers."

"Thank you, Truman," said Sveto as she gazed into his eyes.

"Hey, I've got an idea," said JP. "Why don't we let them work their magic at James Café? That's a club I own on my home planet. Can you bring 'em in for a few appearances?"

"I sure can—the girls like to travel as much as I do," said Sveto. "From what you were telling me Novem is quite the planet. I could use a few days relaxing on one of those beautiful beaches you were telling me about."

"We'll book 'em as soon as I get back there," said JP. "The Saturn Starlets will be a smashing success on my planet—I guarantee it!"

"I hope so," said Sveto. "I know they'll pour every ounce of energy into their performance, just like they're doing right now."

JP tapped Truman's foot with his own, but it was no accident. He did that sometimes when he had a surprise up his sleeve. "Sveto, I have an idea. Why don't you go ahead and take that vacation—starting tonight—on Earth!"

"Tonight! That's such short notice. I don't know…how would I get back?"

"I'll bring you back anytime you like. A day, a week, a month—it's totally up to you. Come on, go with us! You wanna lie on a sunny beach? Truman will show you one of North Carolina's finest."

Truman could hardly believe what was taking place. This was truly a birthday to remember, or was it all a dream? He's on Saturn—he meets an incredibly attractive charming lady—a "consciousness" computer determines this sexy Saturner is destined to be his perfect mate—the exotic beauty is actually considering going back with him to Earth—tonight! Did someone slip a hallucinogen in his beer? Was JP playing with his mind? Was this real? The answer came quickly.

"Okay!" snapped Sveto. "I'll go! I'm going to run to my place and pack a few things. I'll meet you back here in an hour. Enjoy watching my girls. See you soon!"

She gave Truman a glance…and more…way more—it was a telepathic message. It was clear and vivid and incredibly sensual in nature. That was it—it was all over. There would be no turning back. Truman would forever be hooked on the smart sexy Saturner that had slipped into his life.

Truman watched as she walked towards the door. She turned back to give him one last telepathic flirt, a little love tap to his consciousness. Truman then turned towards JP. He wanted to ask him how all this had come about, but he couldn't get any words out. JP had been playing the prize-fighter all night and he had just delivered the knockout punch. He was truly speechless.

"Come on, Truman—the night's still young," barked JP. "It's your birthday—let's party!"

And they did.

Chapter 33
STARS ARE FOREVER

M enza was on time—barely. He peeked through the window into the Cow. The others were already there and seated. This was one meeting he did not want to be late for. Operation Hummingbird was now complete and the all important final review was taking place. He saw Tucker look at his watch. The man had always been a stickler for promptness. Menza went inside.

"Menza, you're here," JP said jovially. "I thought maybe you took off on a joy ride in your new biocraft."

"I had some things I was catching up on," said Menza. "That joyride's coming soon though. You can bet on that."

Truman had pushed two tables together to form one longer one. Menza took a seat alongside Marilyn. At the head of the table was Tucker. Sitting beside him was JP and Truman. Accompanying Truman was Sveto, his girlfriend of two weeks. Everyone adored the charming Saturner. It was obvious she and Truman were in love.

Also attending the meeting was President of the World Wright, Chief of Staff Pepper, along with cabinet members Jim and Joan Dixon, Luce, Meier, and Marilyn's mother.

Tucker glanced at a notepad in front of him before speaking. "Thanks to everyone here for attending this meeting. It's as much a celebration as it is a review. Stage three of Operation Hummingbird took a little longer than we expected, but it went very well. Are there any questions before I run through a quick briefing?"

No one spoke. All eyes were focused on Tucker.

"Okay, here's where we stand. Earth and its inhabitants are free. The group that was controlling the planet is on the run. They will undoubtedly try to set up camp somewhere else in the universe. When they do we will find them. We've got informants planted among them who will keep us abreast of their movements. It will take some time, but eventually the universe will be cleansed of their presence.

"Probably the best news I've got has to do with human acceptance. We've placed a priority on making sure the residents of this planet trust us. This has been an emotionally disturbing process for everyone involved. A few short weeks ago most humans thought they were the only life in the universe. Now they see us and our crafts on a daily basis. It has been a crash course in cosmology like the IOS has never seen before. I have to give the humans credit—they've got a lot of spunk. To dig out from the depths of total ignorance is nothing short of amazing. They were entrenched in a fake reality, one designed to give the masters absolute control. The truth was different at every level of awareness, but each truth was a lie. We popped them out of that slavery bubble and they were on their way. It was a massive awakening on their part. Now we are working towards common goals in a trusting relationship. I couldn't be more pleased. The human soul is a powerful entity.

"I'd like to thank all the cabinet members for your hard work. This assignment has been tough on us foreigners, and I know it's been doubly so for you natives. To be thrown into a leadership role under these circumstances must be incredibly difficult. I sometimes try to put myself in your shoes. All you did was innocently befriend someone and that someone ends up being an alien. Before you know it you're being asked to save the planet. That's got to be tough to deal with. I want you all to know how much we appreciate it. Does anyone have any questions or comments?"

Wright eased out of his chair and stood up. "I'd like to take this opportunity to thank you all. It's a real pleasure working with you. Several weeks ago I was sitting in here minding my own business, mulling over my mayoral campaign—and over walks Menza. I'm thinking we're going to talk about the weather, sports or whatever. But it was not to be. Menza casually informs me that he's not from this planet. Well, that's some pretty big news to me, but I try to absorb it. In the next breath he tells me that his extraterrestrial friends will be taking over the planet and that I have been chosen to be President of the World—Me! I will be the one to lead the entire human race into a new era. I accepted his offer, but I've got to be honest with you—I had some serious second thoughts. Did I really want to work for a group who would choose *me*—a beer drinking wannabe mayor—as their leader? Is that the best they can do? What kind of operation were they running?"

Wright took a deep breath. He looked at his friends gathered around the table, making eye contact with each one of them. JP delivered a wink that seemed to put him at ease. He continued.

"Well, I obviously decided to take the job. I've always been told that real courage is doing something you're afraid to do—so I closed my eyes and dove right in. It didn't take me long to realize I made the right decision. I hitched my wagon to a star—literally. I'm blessed to be working with such a fine group of people…Ha!…I guess we're all considered people. Sometimes I forget that we're an intergalactic bunch here. Whatever—all of you are living beings that I *trust*. I'm honored to be working with each and every one of you. Earth is at a crossroads in its history. Together we will make sure the transition is a smooth one. The future belongs to those who believe in the beauty of their dreams. Let's dream together. Thank you all for being my friends."

Joan Dixon softy clapped her hands. The others joined in a brief round of applause. There was no doubt Wright was the right choice for President of the World. Tucker stood up and once again addressed the group.

"Wright, we thank you for that bit of inspiration. You are going to make a fine President of the World. I am certain of it. Does anyone else have any questions or comments?"

No one replied.

"Well, if that's the case, then I guess that's it. But I do want to make an announcement—a big one. As I mentioned earlier, this is a celebration. But we're celebrating more than the completion of Operation Hummingbird. We're also celebrating love—intergalactic love. Menza and Marilyn are going to be getting married—today!"

Everyone stood and began applauding. Menza looked over at his soon-to-be wife. Marilyn had a look on her face that he had never seen before. It was a smile so big, so real, so pure that it could melt the universe. It was raw emotion. It was pure happiness. It was *love*. Menza stood up. He held up his hands to signal for quiet.

"This is the happiest day of my life. I arrived on this planet nearly a year ago. I expected to work for a year and go home. I had no idea that I would fall into *this*. I've got friendships that I know will last a lifetime. I found love that I never knew existed. This Earthling girl charmed the socks off of me from the first time I met her. You all know Marilyn—she's truly special. Someone has blessed me beyond description. I am so happy that I can't even begin to explain it. You guys—and this *very* special girl—have made me the happiest being in the universe. I mean it—*No one* can be any happier than I am at this very moment. I guess we shouldn't waste any time. Let's do it! Truman, I would like to thank you for allowing us to get married right here in your pub. It's practically been my home for the past year."

Tucker stood and smiled. "Menza, there's been a change in plans."

"Oh yeah," said Menza with a puzzled look on his face.

"I'm sorry" replied Tucker, "but the wedding's not going to be held in the pub."

"Why not?" asked Menza. "Is there something wrong?"

"No, nothing's wrong," answered Tucker. "Menza, have you wondered why the pub is completely empty today?"

Menza looked around. Tucker was right. There wasn't one person in the place. The customers who had been there earlier were now gone. Even the employees were nowhere in sight. Smirky smiles were on everyone's face.

"What's going on!" exclaimed Menza. "Something's up, I know it!"

"Menza, you're right," said Tucker. "Something *is* up. You and Marilyn grab your things and come with me. JP's going to drive us somewhere. I'm not allowing you to say another word. Everyone here is going to follow us."

Menza knew better than to question Tucker. He did as he was told and followed the IOS chief out the door. A limousine was waiting outside. JP opened the door for them and they slid inside. The drive to wherever they were going was more of the same—simpering smiles and silence. JP kept his eyes on the road without saying a word. There was definitely something going on if JP was quiet.

Ten minutes into the drive JP turned onto a newly paved road. Menza then realized where he was. He was at the Roy Johnson property. This was the future home of Genomel Brewing Company. The massive brewery was already thirty percent completed. It had been decided that the property would also house the new IOS governmental complex. The huge complex would serve as a major universal hub.

JP stopped the car. They all got out. Tucker pointed towards the brewery that was under construction.

"Menza, Marilyn—follow me. I want to show you the site of the future IOS headquarters. It's going to be built behind Truman's brewery—just beyond this building that houses the fermenting tanks."

Tucker and JP led the way. They all walked around the corner of the building.

"CONGRATULATIONS TO MENZA AND MARI-LYN" The roar was so loud it literally hurt his ears.

Menza could not believe his eyes. At least half of the town had secretly assembled behind the brewery. It was 5,000 people, maybe more. So this is what it was all about—a big party behind the brewery.

"Oh, my God!" shouted Marilyn. "Look at that! Oh God!"

Menza turned to see what had alarmed Marilyn so. His jaw dropped.

Never in his life had he seen anything like it. He had seen a lot of spaceships in his time, but never anything like this. It was several hundred meters in length and half as wide—easily the size of three football fields. A mammoth-sized banner was strung along one side of it.

WISHING YOU ALL THE LOVE AND HAPPINESS IN THE UNIVERSE ON YOUR WEDDING DAY

From the citizens of Ashmont

Tucker gave Menza a playful tap on the shoulder. Then he reached over and hugged a stunned Marilyn.

"Are you guys ready to get married? You've got over 5,000 people waiting to board this spaceship."

"I can't…I can't believe it," stammered Menza. "Where did you get this? It's huge!"

"Let's just say I'm IOS connected. Right now nothing matters but getting you guys properly married. We're going to start boarding everyone. We're all going on a slow scenic tour of your solar system. From Mercury to Mars to Saturn to Pluto and everywhere in between—it's going to be an eight-hour nonstop party. Truman here has dedicated 500 kegs of his fine beverages to the cause. We've got a team of chefs cooking up the best intergalactic fare this side of Hammerhead. JP got ahold of your little black book when you weren't looking and sneaked a peek at some numbers. We've shipped in fifty of your friends and family from Novem. They're waiting for you inside the craft. Oh, and one more thing— Truman and Sveto have set you up with a two-week honeymoon on Saturn. You're leaving in the morning. Sveto will be taking care of everything for you. Before we go inside there is something I want to show you. Follow me."

Menza and Marilyn walked behind another partially constructed building. Tucker stopped at a small structure that was covered with a large tarp.

"This is where the main entrance of the new IOS complex will be built. I had something shipped in from Novem— brought it in especially for you. Maybe you'll remember it."

Tucker removed the tarp. Menza took a deep breath. He leaned in close to the weathered tablet containing the ancient verse. The fading sunlight beamed in on the inscription. This time it made sense.

The stars burn bright,
Over time and space
Shining love and peace,
Upon every race
But fools will be fools,
With their foolish endeavors
The fools can be fooled,
Stars are forever

*Did you enjoy **Planet Folly**? I would love to hear your comments. Please go to Amazon.com and write a brief review.*

Thank you!

Jamie Johnson

Find me on the web at:

JamesCafe.com

Watch for another Jamie Johnson book soon!

www.ingramcontent.com/pod-product-compliance
Lightning Source LLC
Chambersburg PA
CBHW060150260626
47160CB00001B/200